Hornet's Nest

Book Two of *Flight of the Angels*

Allan and Aaron Reini

Cover Design by Michael Vincent

PUBLISHED BY HENDIADYS PRESS

ISBN-10: 0-578-59245-2
ISBN-13: 978-0-578-59245-9

To Ben and Matt:

Friends, Cohorts, and Top-Dog Judgers

Squadron Personnel

Pilots
Captain Dex "Deadeye" D'Felco
Commander Hagen "Sarge" Lebrian
Lt. Commander Lee "Ninja" Onigen
Lieutenant Jani "Rabbit" McLeod
Lieutenant Scot "Flash" Calgaro
Flight Lieutenant Seltrice "Viper" Valani
Flying Officer Adahn "Ghazi" Manasser
Flying Officer Ravi "Sunfire" Voor
Flying Officer Purnima "Moonlight" Voor

Support
Lt. Commander Job Hansen, executive assistant
Flight Sergeant Drager St. James, chief mechanic
Ronnie Wilco, ops tech

Killed in Action (KIA)
Lt. Commander Kevan "Aces" Adlerson
Lt. Commander Fran "Smiley" Simmons
Flight Lieutenant Geffory "Prince" Bennet

Prologue

The smell was overpowering. He tightened the wrap around his nose and mouth and tried to ignore the decomposing, decapitated bodies of his fallen comrades, keeping his eyes fixed instead on the damaged control console. His entire left side felt like it was on fire—a sharp pain radiating from the spot where the stun bolt had hit. Shaking his head against the haze of pain, he fought to maintain consciousness, to focus long enough to complete his mission.

The damnable machine was only moments behind. Capture would mean death—the same horrifying end the others in this room had suffered. Despite his best efforts to concentrate on the task at hand, he became overwhelmed by the sickening, unnatural scene around him—mutilated corpses, some of them close friends, casually strewn about without even the dignity of a proper burial. Even though time was short, he felt compelled to pause long enough to place a small demo charge at the base of a pillar in the center of the room, the only structure holding the crumbling ceiling in place. If he managed to luck his way out of the facility, he could activate the remote and at least give his friends that much of a burial—if not the one they deserved.

Turning his attention back to the comm unit, he shakily retrieved a data chip from his jacket sleeve and slid it into an open port. His efforts were rewarded as the console labored to life—its low, reverberating hum breaking the air of still silence in the room.

It was a wonder that the thing even functioned at all. This room—the entire facility and all the equipment in it—had practically been obliterated in the attack, all of it carried out by a single unstoppable force of hell. And it was still out there, searching relentlessly for its next victim—for him. That's why he'd come alone. Only a handful had managed to escape the first time—the foul odor penetrating his makeshift scarf was a gruesome reminder of the price others had paid to make that escape possible.

He took one final furtive glance around him, his hand hovering over the console. Fully aware that his next actions would alert the machine and once again give away his location, he took a deep breath, working up his courage. It was now or never.

Gritting his teeth, he slammed his hand down, activating the *send* command.

There. It's done.

The display dimmed considerably, evidence of its depleted emergency power. He lingered, knowing that every second he delayed would bring the monster that much closer to him—closer to finishing what it had started. Desperate, he scanned the fading screen, searching for a sign, any indication that his attempt had been successful. It had to be. Everything depended on it.

His eye caught it—a small green icon blinking into view just before the screen went completely dark. He let out a whoop of triumph, cut short by a gasp as the pain in his side reminded him again of the stun wound— and of the imminent danger he was in.

At that instant, he heard an unnatural scream beyond the door. A thin red beam penetrated the metal, slicing through the material with ease. He watched in horror as a large section of the door fell away, revealing the silhouette of his tormentor beyond.

He backed up against the wall. There was nowhere to run. The M-2 glided into the room. It moved purposefully, but not hurriedly, as if sensing that the pursuit had come to an end. Even as the killer lowered its laser cutter, it raised the opposite arm, approaching closer, ever closer.

He knew what was coming next. How many of his friends, his fellow colonists, had he seen this monster torture and murder in the same way? He could already feel the metal rod penetrating his shoulder, could imagine the blue-tinged blade slicing into his neck.

The monster spoke.

You are a Christian.

Despite his fear, the young man found his voice. "No. Not really." He shook his head. Placing his hands carefully in his jacket pockets, he managed a look of practiced indifference. "Just because I'm with these people doesn't mean I think like they do."

A steady drip from an overhead pipe kept time while the thing seemed to process this information.

You associate with the Zealots, and you will be executed.

He tilted his head to one side, a small smile masking the dread he felt inside. "Only if you join me," he said.

In his pocket, he pressed the remote for the demo charge. A blinding flash was followed instantly by a concussive blast, knocking him back against the wall, which crumbled behind him like a wet sand castle. A heartbeat later, the entire weakened ceiling gave way. Tons of processed phirmium rained down, covering both man and machine. For what seemed like an eternity, the rubble kept falling, adding more and more weight to the layers covering him. He was certain that he was dying—or worse, being buried alive.

Then, as quickly as it had begun, the downpour ended. Despite the pain in every part of his body, he was surprised to find that he could still move. He pressed hard against a large piece of debris that was covering him—a section of ceiling, which yielded and fell away to his side. Choking amid the thick cloud of dust, he pushed himself to his knees, then to his feet. Looking up, he realized how fortunate he had been. The horizontal support structure of the wall he had fallen through had remained mostly intact, shielding him from the worst of the rubble. His head was bleeding, and he felt faint, but he could see that the M-2 had taken the brunt of the fallout—though it wouldn't be stopped for long. Already he could hear the monster thrashing from beneath the massive pile, fighting to free itself.

There wasn't much time. Fighting the dizziness and pain, he lurched through what remained of the door, down a short hallway, and into the street beyond. Looking behind him, he watched as more of the building fell, burying the hellish beast inside with yet another layer of wreckage and perhaps buying him just a little more time to escape without being tracked.

A half hour later, he stumbled into the encampment. A stunned middle-aged woman rose to her feet, concern and relief fighting for position in her haggard expression.

"It's done, Mom," he said, falling into her arms. "The message is sent. It's up to Baker now."

Then, blissfully, he lost consciousness.

Chapter 1

The Runaway Tavern in Port Henri, Bellona, sat huddled in the midst of dozens of dives, stim-shacks, and flank houses that infested the land directly adjacent to the Port Authority Terminal, its glaring fluorescent external ad panels promising exquisite pleasures and delights to sate the appetite of any unsuspecting deck hand, who, bored from long weeks bouncing in and out of the ether, was destined to spend or lose his meager pay in one foolish night. Inside, those glowing endorsements faded into the even seamier reality of the rough neighborhood bar that it had become. Long past its glory days, when the entire Grenouille district had enjoyed the prosperity that an active high-traffic port could bring, the Runaway, like all its misbegotten neighbors, had degenerated into a dark foul-smelling hole where hardened men, weary from the drudgery of their lives, crowded around dilapidated tables to drink, gamble, argue, and fight. With only half of the interior lighting panels functioning, the bar was even darker than intended. The sound system, making up in volume what it lacked in quality, blared out decades-old tunes of misery and injustice, contributing to the prevalent atmosphere of drunkenness, long-seething anger, and barely contained violence.

A lone figure in a hooded fleece pullover entered through the front door and cautiously worked through the press of port hands, lading unionists, and teamsters, navigating, as unobtrusively as possible, the jostling mass of heavier-built rowdies.

One half-drunk warehouse stock jockey watched more intently than the others as the figure approached the bar. Trying to look aloof, he strained to overhear the ensuing conversation with the bartender over the cacophony of shouts and curses permeating the room.

"No! Davis Webb!" The voice inside the hood was all but yelling in order to be heard. "I'm trying to locate Davis Webb!"

A sly smile played across the face of the warehouse jock. The clothing had been nondescript, but the voice confirmed what he had suspected. Reaching out, he grabbed the speaker's shoulder and spun her around, just to be sure.

"Well, well, little lady," he slurred. "Look at you, coming in here all alone. It wouldn't be right to have a pretty little miss like you coming into the bar and not be buying her a drink. What will you be having, then?"

"Not interested." She barely acknowledged the drunk before turning back to the bar to resume her conversation. The bartender, however, had backed away and seemed to be deliberately avoiding eye-contact with her.

She was about to demand his attention when the drunk spun her again, more forcefully this time, pinning her back against the bar with two meaty hands clamped down on her shoulders.

"Hey, Phill." He gave a sidelong glance to another, even burlier man next to him. "This one's a little feisty, isn't she?"

Phill lumbered over, his head cocked to one side, eyeing the woman. "I don't know, Vlad. I think she could be downright friendly if she wanted to be." Leaning in, his gray stubble nearly brushed her lips, his breath reeking with what was undoubtedly the cheapest gin that the Runaway Tavern had to offer.

She turned her head to one side, wincing at the foul odor. This, unfortunately, left her looking directly into the face of the first man, Vlad, who still maintained a firm grasp on her shoulders.

"Awww, c'mon, missy." As he moved in closer, she could feel his body pressing against hers, the unyielding bar behind her digging into the small of her back. "Don't be like that. You come in here all alone like this, we know what you're looking for. C'mon, give us a kiss."

She relaxed for just a moment—a move her assaulters took as submission. Phill's face broke into a leer as Vlad closed his eyes and puckered his lips.

What the men hadn't realized was that her momentary yielding was not an invitation but rather had enabled a subtle shift in posture—an inconspicuous means of positioning her body to strike. Her right elbow shot out, catching Phill firmly in his ample gut. As he bent over from the impact, she brought her knee up directly between Vlad's legs before he even had the chance to open his eyes. He dropped to the ground like a stone as the woman towered over him, fists clenched and ready for a fight.

5

"Get up!" she demanded, her eyes flashing inside the hood. Vlad held up a hand, gesturing that, apparently, he had had enough. As he struggled to his feet, he bumped into a high table, causing a few glasses to fall and shatter on the floor.

Phill, his oversized midsection having shielded him from the full force of her blow, used the distraction as opportunity to creep up silently behind her. Pulling a knife from beneath a weathered dock coat, he moved with deceptive speed, pinning one arm behind her back while pressing the blade against the flesh of her neck.

"All right, baby," he hissed. "We tried this the easy way. Now you're coming with us. You're going to learn some manners, and Vlad and I are going to be your teachers, right Vlad?"

Vlad had regained his footing but, to Phill's surprise, was backing slowly away, both hands palms-forward in front of him, blood-shot eyes wide open. Phill's confusion over his partner's sudden retreat was clarified when he felt a muzzle pressed against his temple. He squinted to his right enough to see a solidly built, dark-skinned man holding a Hagg-Sauer BP-105 to his head.

"You *don't* want to do that," the man whispered.

"Take it easy," Phill said, his voice cracking. "We're just messing around."

The pistol dug in more sharply.

"All right, all right!" Phill whined. He lowered his knife and released the woman's arm.

She shot him a poisonous look and shook her head in disgust at Vlad, who was still gingerly backing away into the crowd. Joining her companion, she threw back her shoulders and moved unhurriedly toward the door—the other patrons giving them both a wide berth as they exited the tavern together.

On the streets of Port Henri, a few blocks away, the man took one more look behind them to ensure they had not been followed before strapping down his side arm and turning to face the woman.

"You call *that* keeping a low profile, Lieutenant?"

In response, she reached up to undo her hood. Long auburn hair fell to her shoulders, glowing under the illumination of a single street lighting panel. Jani McLeod returned her commander's level gaze.

"Better?"

He muttered something under his breath as he turned his shoulders to peer down a dark alley.

"I'm sorry, Sarge. I didn't realize this was the night they let the animals out of their cages."

Commander Hagen Lebrian checked his chrono. "Yeah, hard to imagine you'd find trouble wandering alone at night in a seedy bar."

"I know. I need to be more cautious. It's just…"

"We're out of time." He finished her thought with a note of resignation. "We have to go."

"But we can't just leave him."

"We've done all we can. If Dex survived and made his way back here, he would've been dropping his cover name around the bars, lying low, and waiting for extraction—which means we would've had a lead by now."

Jani's eyes dropped for a moment. "Assuming he even knows we're coming. His orders were—"

"Exactly." Hagen stood to his full two-meter height. "His orders were to *not* execute an exfil plan. We're out of line just being here."

"But it's been *three weeks*! We were just sitting there on Pella. We had to do something…"

"I *know*, Rabbit," Hagen said defensively, then moderated his tone. "I know. Who do you think authorized this mission in the first place? But our time's up. Our IDs expire at midnight—either we're on that next transport or we're not leaving at all. And with the way things are going in the colony, I have to get back."

Jani drew herself to attention. "Yes, sir. *You* have to get back."

"No, Lieutenant, don't even think it…"

"Sir, request permission to stay behind and continue the search for the captain."

Hagen regarded the determined lieutenant for a long moment. "I can't leave you here alone. You almost didn't get out of that bar in one piece."

"I'll be careful."

Hagen smiled. "No you won't."

Jani could see that her commander was softening. "Okay, I won't be careful. But Sarge, I have to do this. Dex would never leave one of us. I know you have to go. The colony needs you—the squadron needs you. But I need to be right here, at least until we have an answer—one way or the other."

She took Hagen's silence as a sign to press forward. "I mean, what was the point of all our planning if we're just going to give up after our first recon?"

"Because every contingency, every variation of our plan, *started* with actually locating the captain."

"And that's why I have to stay." Jani drew her hood back up over her head. "We're never going to get him out on a transport—not with the increase in security. By now his biometrics are locked into every port screener. So, we're on to plan Bravo, which means one of us has to stay anyway. Why shouldn't it be me?"

"Because your cover is going to burn at the same time mine does. The difference is, I'd be on a transport out of here, and you'd be stuck on this rock, running naked."

Jani nodded. "I know."

Hagen sighed. "It appears that there's no talking you out of this."

"Nope."

"I could *order* you onto that transport."

"Just like Dex ordered us not to come looking for him?"

Hagen rubbed his forehead above his right eyebrow, shaking his head slowly. Finally, he extended a hand. "All right, Lieutenant, you win. Permission to continue the search granted. But with option one off the table, we're going to have to do this the hard way." He checked his chrono again. "God willing, you'll locate your objective and find him alive. I'll be back in exactly one week with the Raven to pick up you—and Dex—at rendezvous point Charlie."

"All contingencies in place?"

"Roger that, Lieutenant."

"Thank you, Commander." Jani took his outstretched hand. "I'll find him."

"I pray that you will, Lieutenant." Hagen grasped her hand firmly before turning and disappearing in the direction of the Port Terminal.

One hundred meters away, a short, gaunt balding man switched off a scanning device. Using only his right hand, he removed an earpiece and stowed the equipment in a battered carrier bag before ferreting away into the darkness.

Chapter 2

"Think about it, Flash." Flight Lieutenant Seltrice Valani stared across the table. "Back in the Erebus system, when we lost Fran and Kevan, who was out of position?"

Lieutenant Scot Calgaro gazed at the cup in his hand, the liquid inside growing cold, matching the feeling he had in his gut. Against his better judgment, he and Seltrice had wandered together into the squadron's mess to grab a quick coffee, and no sooner had they sat down than she started up on her favorite topic.

"Yeah, I know, I know," he said, doing little to mask his annoyance over being drawn into this particular conversation.

"And Adahn came out of it without a scratch on his Hornet. Doesn't that strike you as odd?"

It was odd. Scot had often wondered why his former wingman hadn't responded more quickly to the attack. Scot's own Hornet had been disabled in the opening seconds of the battle, but where the hell had Adahn been? Yet, despite his personal misgivings, he thought it best to discourage this sort of talk—the situation on Pella was incendiary enough without adding fuel to Seltrice's fire.

"And at Bellona, he was right there next to me. There were Slammers coming in, and what did he do? Nothing!"

Scot held up a hand. "Y'know, Viper, if it's all right with you, I'd just as soon not discuss Bellona—again."

The days following the battle had been wearying. The mission, objectively, had been a resounding success. The Angels had survived an ambush against overwhelming numbers while managing in the process to eliminate a high-priority target, an orbital station that manufactured the dreaded M-2 assassins. However, any hope of remaining in system and finding Dex had been cut short by the arrival of the *Ganymede* and its complement of three full Hornet squadrons—pilots, friends, former allies who the Angels had no desire to fight. Forced to bugout, they had endured the exhausting series of etherspace jumps—necessary to return to their hidden sanctuary on Pella without being tracked—with heavy hearts over the loss of one of their own and the uncertain whereabouts of their captain.

With Geff dead and Dex MIA, there had been no victory celebration upon the Angels' return. And if there had been, two more heroes of Bellona would have been missing as well. The twins, Flying Officers Ravi and Purnima Voor, had somehow lost consciousness during the final approach to Pella, only their Hornets' automated landing sequences preventing them from augering in. Both had been transported directly to sickbay, victims of some mysterious ailment that neither Commander Lebrian nor Lieutenant Commander Onigen seemed anxious to discuss with the rest of the squadron.

To make matters worse, rumors had begun to spread throughout the colony. Despite Lebrian's standing gag order, somehow details of the mission had gotten out. Speculation about murderous M-2s and an alleged security leak had spread like wild fire. Scot now felt distinctly on edge whenever his duties required him to venture down to the colony proper. It felt like everyone he encountered was eyeing him with suspicion, if not outright contempt. At one stop, he had overheard discussion of a meeting—the topic of which appeared to have ranged from removing Pastor Nathan Graham to groups of colonists considering ways to arm themselves. He distinctly heard a reference to "self-policing," followed by derogatory comments about the abilities of the Angels to provide any protection. The speakers had noticed his presence and quickly changed the subject, but the impact of their words hadn't been lost on Scot. The colony was on the verge of boiling over.

Then, in the middle of it all, Commander Lebrian and Jani had just whisked away, leaving their squad mates to deal with the unrest. All this had left Scot in a troubled state that was only compounded by his still-fresh grief over the loss of Geff.

He wanted nothing more, at the moment, than to be alone with his thoughts. But as much as he would have liked Seltrice to just shut up for a change, she was not to be deterred. "Listen, this is important. If Ghazi had assisted, then Geff wouldn't have had to cross the gap like that. Maybe he'd still be—"

"Alive?" Scot had had enough. "Yeah, Adahn's a screw-up. I totally agree with you. Hell, I've been saying that for years. But if you really want to bring up Geff again, there's plenty of blame to go around."

Seltrice gave him a dark look. It was usually a mistake to interrupt the fiery Sicilian. "Okay, Flash. You've been moping around here since we got back, and don't think I haven't noticed you giving me the cold shoulder. You wouldn't even talk to me at Geff's memorial. If you've got something to say to me, why don't you just come right out and say it?"

Scot shook his head. "No. It's not important."

Seltrice was adamant. "It *is* important. We all miss him, you know. Not just you. He was a good guy, a *nice* guy." She looked hard at Scot. "Those are rare."

"All right." Scot said, leaning in. "Here's what I've been wondering. Why did Geff have to help you at all?"

"I just told you. If Ghazi had just—"

"We're not talking about Ghazi, now. I'm asking you. Why couldn't you tally the Slammers?"

Seltrice spoke in clipped, measured tones. "We've been over this. They were coming in on my blindside. I couldn't see them."

"Oh, and was your HUD sour? Seems to me it checked out just fine when we got back."

"What are you saying?"

Scot stood up, his legs bumping the table and nearly spilling his cold coffee on Seltrice's lap. "I'm saying you should have been able to see the Slammers and evade. You panicked—pure and simple."

Seltrice stood as well. "So you're saying it's my fault? Who left Geff to cross the gap by himself, anyway? He was in your flight, Scot. Where were you?"

"Oh. So now this is about me, huh?"

She slammed her cup down, the cold phylline sloshing onto the table. "No! That's what I'm saying—it's not about you, and it's not about me! We've got a security problem in this squadron. I know it. You know it. Hell, the whole colony seems to know it. And only one name keeps coming up again and again every time we lose a pilot. I'm not going to sit on this! We can't trust Adahn to…"

Something in Scot's expression caused her to trail off. She sensed, rather than heard, someone behind her. Turning, she saw Flying Officer Adahn Manasser enter the room. If he had overheard, he gave no indication. He quietly walked to the coffee station, poured himself a cup, and left the room without comment.

Seltrice turned back to Scot, her normally dark complexion flushed with embarrassment.

"This isn't over," she hissed before turning on her heel and striding briskly out the door.

Scot watched her leave, wondering why he felt so angry. Was it over her comment about leaving Geff on his own against the Marauders? Was it her accusation of Adahn? Or was it the way she was blatantly trying to recruit others to her side? He sat down again, sipped his cold coffee, and considered the situation. Maybe, he decided, he was angry because she was right.

*   *   *

The high-pitched whining of servos coming from the hulking trash collector in the alley penetrated through the thin uninsulated wall of the guesthouse. Picking up a battered dumpster, it deposited the foul contents into an open hatch, tossing, more than placing, the dumpster back to its original position. The dumpster clanged against the wall, stirring the occupant of the room. Dex D'Felco opened his eyes. The disorientation, and the sense of amnesia that accompanied it, filtered away a little more readily than it had the last few times he had awakened. This time, at least, he knew where he was. Gingerly propping himself up on his left elbow, he grimaced at the sharp pain in his right shoulder. Even in the discomfort, he noted, with some satisfaction, that he was able to take deeper breaths than he could remember taking the previous day. Slowly and carefully, he brought his right hand around, his fingers feeling the long rough scab along the left side of his neck.

He shuddered. Whether the shocking sensation was physical or some form of post-traumatic stress, Dex couldn't tell. All he knew is that the wound, where that damned machine had nearly taken his head off, was still too fresh, too real—and of his many injuries, it was the one that seemed most reluctant to heal.

Forcing himself into a sitting position on the small bed, he took in the room around him, feeling, in his emerging coherence, like he was seeing it clearly for the first time. The tattered walls held a couple of generic prints, haphazardly attached—a common décor employed by lower-rent guesthouses. A smattering of non-descript stains decorated the floor, and a faded posting on the door displayed the daily rate—confirming Dex's impression of the establishment's price point. Not that the tired furnishings made any difference, considering the rest of the room's disheveled state. There were a handful of battered satchels strewn across the floor, one of them open and on its side, with several instruments Dex could not identify spilling out of the open flap. A footlocker-sized case next to the cot was covered with antiseptic tubes and dermo-patch rolls, one of which had unrolled onto the floor. On a tiny round table near the far wall, opened food packets were piled on and around a portable IR unit that still held partially eaten rations while a nearby chair supported a half-full silver hydration pack—plenty of water, Dex observed, before it would have to be refilled. A thin beam of dusty light from the room's only exterior window fell to one corner, shining directly on the crumpled mess that were his pants and bloodstained undershirt, still lying where they had been tossed the night his rescuer had dragged him, unconscious and near death, into this room.

Dex couldn't remember if he had even spoken to his benefactor and roommate. He could recall being in and out of consciousness dozens of times in the past few weeks and at least rising to use the room's lav on occasion, but in none of his ambulatory moments had he been lucid enough to begin a conversation. He knew nothing about the man other than what the current state of the room told him about his suspect housekeeping habits. Of Dex's personal items, only the micropulse vest had been treated with any care. It hung neatly on a hook, a jagged hole visible in the right shoulder where the M-2's metal rod had impaled him.

The sight of the vest brought back the memory, and with it the pain in his shoulder. Gritting his teeth, Dex stretched his right arm as far as he could, pulling at the scarred tissue, willing it to respond. Stretching his neck to the left, then the right, he gathered his strength and stood up. He had been down long enough.

Ignoring his screaming muscles, he padded unsteadily across the room. He would start with that pile of clothes. Bending over, he stopped short. Something under the pile was moving. Dex stared at the shifting heap while reaching down to his right to grasp a metal slat that had broken off the underside of the bed. He pointed the slat at the pile and was preparing to prod whatever it was out of hiding when he heard the sound of the door sliding open behind him. He pulled himself back upright.

Dealing with the unknown pest would have to wait. Dex's "nurse" had returned.

"Hey, what are you doing up?" The little man in the doorway tossed a battered carrier bag on the floor and quickly scurried over to Dex. Grabbing him by the arm, he began to tug him awkwardly back toward his bed. "You shouldn't be trying to walk when I'm not around."

Dex resisted the pull. "No. I'm all right. I need to start getting back on my feet."

"Well, at least sit down for a minute. You're pale as a ghost."

Dex hadn't realized until that moment just how dizzy he was becoming. Without further protest, he moved the hydropack off the chair and slumped into its place, what little energy he awoke with already depleted. The thin, balding man cleared a space for himself on the footlocker. Watching from his chair, Dex was struck by a peculiarity in the way the man went about the task. He was picking up each item one-by-one and setting them on the floor, all with just his right hand. It was only when he sat and turned back to face Dex that the reason became clear. His left hand was missing.

The man followed Dex's gaze down to his left arm, shifted uncomfortably, and moved the stump into his jacket pocket. Embarrassed for staring, Dex quickly looked up and met his eyes.

"How long have I been here?"

"A few weeks," the man said. "You were pretty out of it most of the time. I'm surprised you even recognized me when I walked in."

"I know you've been taking care of me. Thank you, by the way—in case I haven't said it."

"You've said it. Several times. You've said a *lot* of things."

Dex suddenly felt at a distinct disadvantage. The past weeks had been a nightmarish haze. He had vague recollections of the little man cleaning him up, redressing the bandages, feeding him. He knew he owed his life to the guy, but what information had Dex blurted out in his delirium? What had he overheard?

He decided to start with the basics. "I'm Davis. Davis Webb," he said, using his cover name as a precaution. He extended his right hand.

"Davis..." The man repeated the name aloud as he shook his hand. "I'm Nikky. Nikky Weis."

"And how did you find me, Nikky?"

14

"It wasn't hard. I knew you were in the testing facility. Then I heard your pilots discussing whether or not to come down and evac you."

Dex held up a hand. His head hurt. "Wait a minute. You *heard* my pilots discussing it?"

"Yes I did, *Deadeye*. Over the comm."

Dex shook his head—a mistake that he immediately paid for with a fresh wave of pain in his right temple. "How could you hear them? They would have been on an encrypted, military-grade channel."

Nikky looked at him as though he were a child. "Like I said, it wasn't hard. Once your squadron jumped out, I figured it was pretty much up to me to find you. That micropulse pad you were wearing made it a little tougher, but if you're careful, you can still spot a heartbeat with a focused scan. The problem was, you didn't have a lot of heartbeat left by the time I found you. Another couple of hours and I don't think you would have made it."

Dex couldn't tell if Nikky was fishing for another thank you or if he was just practically relating the facts.

"So how did we end up here? And exactly where *is* 'here,' anyway?"

"We're in Port Henri, a couple kilometers from the port terminal. As far as how we got here, that part wasn't so easy. For the first few days, you were impossible to move, so we just camped out where I found you. Once I thought you were ready, I managed to get you into the shuttle I'd rented and bring you back here. You are not a nice passenger when you're delirious, by the way."

Dex had a sudden twinge of concern. "I'd also picked up a rental—an airbike. Do you know what happened to it?" He couldn't be sure how thorough Nikky would have been in "sanitizing" their makeshift campsite—if he covered their tracks at all—and was worried about the long-overdue bike leading back to them.

Nikky held up his only hand. "Relax. I found it and removed the tracker before we left. I reported it stolen right after we got back here and tossed the tracker in the river. I'm sure by now that the rental place has traced its signal and written it off. I'm not stupid, you know."

Dex could see that he wasn't. Looking around at the scattered phytochems and bandages, he was reminded again of what Nikky had done for him. "Well, I'm just grateful for all your help—I wouldn't have made it without you."

Nikky shrugged. "I just patched you up with what I had available. I couldn't very well take you to a med facility, could I?" He rose from his chair. "After all, you *are* Dex D'Felco."

Knowing that Nikky had listened in on the battle, tracked him down in the bush, saved his life, and spent the past weeks nursing him back to health, it shouldn't have come as a shock for Dex to hear him using his real name, but it did. His head pounding along with his rising heartbeat, he was about to ask a follow-up question when his attention was drawn again by movement from the floor. A small greenish-brown head poked slowly out from under the pile of clothing.

"Wait, is that…a *turtle*?"

Nikky reached down with his right hand and scooped up the small creature. "Oh. Yeah." He quickly deposited the turtle in a case beside the footlocker. "That's Louise."

Dex closed his eyes. One bizarre mystery at a time, he decided.

"Okay, Nikky. You've told me how you found me and how you got me back here. What you haven't told me is why."

"I have my reasons," Nikky said as he walked over to the IR unit. He grabbed an open package of food sticks and dropped one into Louise's case. "But now that you're actually up and coherent, the first thing we should do is make plans to get you back to Pella."

Seeing Dex's expression, Nikky continued. "Like I said, you talk *a lot* in your sleep. Oh, and that reminds me—something I planned to ask you if you ever woke up. Who is Jani?"

Chapter 3

The sign, hung from a rusted pole, swayed back and forth in the wind, its dilapidated internal wiring arcing portions of the display on and off with each rotation, alternately telling Jani that the establishment rented "Shuttles and Airbikes" on the forward swing, or just "Shut les Airbik" as it blew back.

Putting on her nicest smile, Jani entered the small office. She could have saved the smile—the office appeared to be deserted. Greasy spare parts were piled on every flat surface in the room. The worn brown walls were dotted with posters of airbike models, already outdated when Jani was a young girl. A panel advertising a favorite local tranquility beverage seemed to be suffering from the same malady as the outdoor sign. Sniffing the air, Jani's pressed-on smile faded into a wrinkle of disgust. She detected a distinct foul odor mixing with the more pleasant smell of fuel and industrial lubricants. Somewhere, very near this office, a lav was backing up.

"Can I help you, miss?"

The voice startled Jani. Looking in the direction of the worn and heavily stained front counter, she realized that the office hadn't been deserted after all. The older man behind the counter was so filthy, his disheveled clothing so closely blending in with the rest of his surroundings, that in the dim lighting, Jani hadn't noticed him at all.

She composed herself, remembering once again to smile.

"Yes, uh…hi!" she said. "I hope you can help me. I'm trying to meet up with my brother. He moved here a few weeks ago, and he probably rented transport when he first got here."

Through the grime, Jani could just make out a name printed on the left shoulder of the man's work shirt. *Galen* it said—at least that was her best guess.

Galen scratched the gray scruff of his chin. "Doesn't your brother have a handpod?"

"Oh, you know how it is. First time on a new planet, sometimes the pod has trouble updating. Besides," she said, adopting a conspiratorial tone, "he doesn't know I'm coming to visit. It's his birthday, and I want it to be a surprise."

"Well, all right." Galen activated his workstation. "I guess I can check to see if he's been in here. What did you say his name was?"

Jani hadn't, but this wasn't the time to point that out.

"Webb. Davis Webb," she said.

Galen scowled. "Davis Webb? I don't even need to look that one up. Your brother rented an airbike weeks ago, and I never saw him, or the airbike, again."

"Oh no!" Jani never considered herself much of an actress, but she felt she was doing a passable job of hiding her excitement at finding the first tangible lead to Dex's whereabouts while, instead, conveying concern for her "brother." "Do you think something happened to him?"

"How would I know?" Galen's mood had soured considerably at the memory of the lost airbike. "A week after he rented it, I get a comm from the locals that it's been reported as stolen. Nobody checks in here, mind you. I just get a burst from Port Henri Enforcement, and the bike's on the list. Not that I relish the thought of those guys poking around my shop anyway—I really don't need their hassle. So, anyway, I fire up the thing's homer, and it shows that the bike's sitting at the bottom of the Tenebres River. Even if I could afford to get it out of there, the dang thing's probably beyond repair by now anyway. You want to know what I think happened to your brother?"

By now, Jani *was* concerned. "Yes, I do."

"I think he got drunk, put *my* bike in the river, and didn't have the guts to come back here and own up to it. That's what I think."

"Oh no, Davis would never do anything like that. He doesn't even drink. There's got to be another answer." Jani's mind raced. With time running out, she didn't need another dead end. "You say the bike had a homing tracker. Will it show you where else it might have gone?"

"Who cares where it went? I know where it is, right now, and that ain't helping me much."

Jani reached out and grasped Galen's arm. "Please. *Please*. I've got to find him. If anything's happened to him, I don't know what I'll do. Can't you help me? Please?"

That did the trick. Galen softened. "All right, young lady, all right. We'll try. What did you say your name was?"

Again, Jani hadn't. "Bethinee," she said. "Bethinee Webb."

"Okay, Bethinee, come on around here, and we'll take a look."

Jani had to watch her step navigating her way behind the counter. Stepping over a pile of broken fuel pumps, she pulled up a stool next to Galen and focused her attention on the workstation screen.

"Okay, here you go." Galen called up the airbike's tracking history. "After he rented it, it looks like your brother headed out to the twenty-first district. Don't know why he'd do that—there's nothing interesting out there. Was your brother an outdoorsman?"

"Is. *Is* an outdoorsman. Yes, he is."

Galen advanced the screen. "It looks like he was out there about a week, and then"—Galen paused to stroke his beard—"that's strange."

"What? What's strange?"

"From the homer data, it looks like he came back into town and actually brought the bike back here for a few minutes. That's impossible."

"Are you sure? Could you have missed him?"

Galen pointed at the screen. "I'm sure. Look at the time stamp. It says the bike was here for about a half an hour, and I was here that whole day. Trust me, I would have seen him."

A thought occurred to Jani. "Were there any other shuttles or bikes rented or returned at the same time?"

Galen flipped the screen again. "Yeah, I had rented a small Cygnus shuttle to a guy. It looks like he brought it back right around that same time. See, that's why I couldn't have missed the bike coming around. I was in the same garage checking the shuttle back in."

"Can we take a look at the shuttle? Please?"

Galen shrugged. "I don't see why not. Come with me."

The rental garage showed no more evidence of upkeep and basic sanitation than the main office or its proprietor. Galen led Jani between rows of rusting heaps, many of which looked as though they hadn't moved in years. Jani smiled to herself, imagining how the squadron's flight sergeant would react to the disarray. She could picture Drager stamping around the room in a fit, head swiveling back and forth, hands flailing wildly toward each infraction.

Galen stopped before a yellow Cygnus-model shuttle. "There it is, Beth. Not much to look at, but it's reliable. One of my last still going, to be honest."

Jani bent over and gazed inside the covered cockpit. "Has anyone else taken this shuttle out since it was returned?"

"Nope. Nobody. Don't know if you noticed, but it's not exactly boomtown around here right now. Why?"

Jani pointed at the passenger seat. "Take a look."

"What? Is that blood? I didn't see that before."

Considering the state of the rest of the shop, Jani wasn't surprised. Galen did not strike her as being particularly fastidious when it came to inspections. She straightened up and shook her head sadly. "I think there's been some foul play here, Galen. I think we'd better contact Port Enforcement."

That got a reaction. "Port Enforcement? Aw, come on. For a little blood?"

Jani sighed. "Yeah, I think we have to..."

She could see Galen considering the new course the conversation had taken, undoubtedly counting the cost of dealing with a possible impound and investigation.

"Can't we just keep them out of this?" He didn't sound desperate, just resigned.

Jani appeared to think it over. "Well, I know it's an unusual request, but do you think it's possible for me to get the entire route for the airbike and the shuttle?"

To copy the file over to her would be an obvious violation of Coalition data-privacy statutes, but Jani was counting on the dread of local enforcement crawling all over his shop to be of greater concern to Galen. She was correct.

"Sure. Yeah, sure. We can do that. Is *your* handpod working? We can go back up front, and I'll send it to you right now."

Leaving the office with her first solid lead, Jani turned to face the grimy shop owner. "I don't know how to thank you," she said sincerely.

"You can thank me by keeping this between the two of us. But you're welcome, Beth. I hope you find your brother."

"So do I, Galen. So do I."

*   *   *

Job Hansen guided the transport dolly to a smooth stop in front of the colony's agricenter. For the hundredth time, he wished that the squadron had a fully staffed mess crew to handle these matters. As the squadron's executive assistant, he would have loved to delegate all procurement, cooking, cleaning, and similar tasks to a qualified and dedicated team. Instead, it mostly fell to him and Flight Sergeant Drager St. James to pull delivery duty. And it wasn't like the stocky chief mechanic didn't have other work to do as well. As the one responsible for keeping the Hornets functional and flying, Drager was the busiest person on Pella. Helping Job with the stock order was simply an extra favor, a tacit acknowledgement that for the colony to survive, everyone needed to pitch-in beyond their assigned duties.

Sometimes a pilot or two would assist them on particularly large deliveries, but this month, with the ranks already diminished, including the Voor twins still mysteriously laid up in sickbay, it just didn't seem like the right time to press anyone into extra service. He and Drager would handle this one on their own. Neither man minded that much. The pilots were pretty self-sufficient when it came to preparing their own meals. The least that he and Drager could do, Job reasoned, was to keep the galley well-stocked for them—as well-stocked as the colony's fluctuating supplies would allow.

Walking through the front entrance, the two men were instantly greeted with the sweet aroma of ripening vegetation. Bins of tomatoes, green leafy lettuce, red and green peppers, and other vegetables indigenous to Pella sat next to pallets piled chest-high with 25-kilo sacks of dark wheat flour. Throughout the large phirmium warehouse, there were dozens of additional bins, all providing ample evidence that, despite the colony's other concerns, it had been a good growing season. Starvation was not going to be a problem—at least not this year.

"Hey guys!" A colonist greeted them from behind an overturned bin serving as a front counter. "We have your order all ready for you." The young man's rough appearance—dirt and grime from 16-hour days of processing the recent harvest covering his face and overalls—was offset by his soft voice and friendly demeanor. "Is it just the two of you today? I can give you a hand getting it out to the dolly."

21

"Thanks, Colby," Job said. "Yes, we're a little short today, so that would be nice."

Colby's expression dropped. "Oh, yeah. Listen, I'm sorry. I didn't mean that like it sounded. We all heard about Lieutenant Bennet. We're very sorry for your loss."

Drager stepped up. "We know what you meant. Thanks for the help."

Colby reached behind the counter for a large box of orange beans. Job and Drager each followed suit with similar cases. They progressed through several trips to the waiting cart in silence before Colby spoke again.

"Guys, can I ask you a question?" The agricenter clerk shuffled his feet on the sidewalk.

Job wrestled a crate of yellow-green tomatoes into place. "Sure," he said, knowing that he and Drager likely wouldn't be able to provide a satisfactory response. The colonists had no shortage of questions about the Angels—and most of them went unanswered due to security concerns.

"Well, you know that all of us down here in the colony, well, we think the world of you guys up there on the base…" Colby hesitated.

"But?"

"Well, you also gotta know that I work with a lot of guys—guys who like to talk, probably too much…"

Job put a hand on his shoulder. "Colby, you still haven't asked us a question."

Colby cleared his throat. "Well, guys, there's talk—a lot of talk—that things have been going wrong out there." He tilted his head upward toward the afternoon sun. Job shot Drager a glance, but both men remained silent, letting Colby's thoughts run their course.

"Guys are saying," he continued, "that there's some kind of traitor running around and that nothing is being done about it."

"A traitor?" Job cocked his head. "Who's saying that?"

Colby was clearly ill at ease. "You know, people. Almost everyone's saying it. And there's a bunch of rumors flying around about who it might be. There's some talk about that Jordanian pilot, Officer Manaseer. They're saying he might not be a Christian—that he's holding some sort of grudge, that he's going to get us all killed. There's others that are even wondering about Pastor Graham, what with him being so close to Captain D'Felco and all. Like he's in a position to know a lot about your missions, maybe too much, you know? Folks are really scared, guys, and there's some people who are saying that if the squadron won't police itself, they might have to."

Drager stopped him. "Now hold on—you're getting into some wild speculation here."

Colby held up his hands. "This isn't *me* talking, guys. You gotta know that! I'm just saying that's what I'm hearing." He looked down at his worn shoes, toeing a small lima bean that had fallen to the sidewalk. "I probably shouldn't even have brought it up."

Job softened. "No, it's okay. We appreciate the information. I'll tell you what. Do you really want to help us out?"

Colby looked up, meeting the exec's eyes. "Yes. Of course I do."

"Can we ask you to keep your ears open for us? If people are that concerned, we need to know about it, and we need to know who has been saying these things. Commander Lebrian is due back any day now, and he might want to ask you a few questions, if that's all right."

Colby looked uncomfortable but nodded. "Sure. Yeah, I can do that." The three men continued loading the dolly until the last case was secure. With Drager in the passenger seat, Job was preparing to pull away when Colby appeared in the doorway with a small box.

"Guys! Guys! I almost forgot!" His positive expression returned with the package he was delivering. "It's that ration of kale you asked for. We didn't have much of a crop, but I managed to set this aside for you." Colby placed the package on top of the rest, securing it in place.

"Thanks, Colby," Job said. "Lieutenant Valani will be happy to see that. It's one of her favorites."

At the mention of Seltrice's name, Colby's expression darkened. "Oh, I didn't know it was for her."

Job raised an eyebrow. "Something wrong?"

Colby shifted his weight from one foot to the other. "Well, it's just that, I probably shouldn't say this, but…"

"Come on!" Drager had reached the end of his patience. "Out with it!"

"It's just that I've seen Lieutenant Valani around the colony. I've overheard her talking. She's the one that's been saying it."

"Saying what?"

Colby looked Job squarely in the eyes. "She's been saying that Officer Manasser is the traitor."

Chapter 4

Dex woke from a fitful sleep. Something wasn't right. His unusually sharp eyesight adjusted quickly to the room's darkness, evidence that his body was continuing to heal. He could just make out his benefactor, Nikky Weis, crouching by the door.

"Nikky, what—" he began.

"Shhh!" Nikky hissed. "Stay there. There's someone coming."

Not a chance. Dex was not about to just lie there if they were in danger. He tried to get up, moved too quickly, and collapsed on the cot again, fighting a new assault of pain.

"I said, *stay there.*" Nikky whispered harshly. There was a soft scraping sound of someone on the other side jimmying the door's locking mechanism. Nikky reached into his pocket, pulled out a tiny stun pistol, dropped it, and picked it up again. "Don't worry," he said. "I've got this."

"Who's worried?" Dex muttered through gritted teeth.

The door flew open, and Nikky stood to his full height—not that impressive.

"Hold it right there. I have a stun—Hey! Ow! Stop that!"

The figure in the doorway took only an instant to knock the stunner away from Nikky, whirl him around, and place him in a chokehold from behind. Together, they moved into the room, the door sliding shut behind them. The assailant used a free hand to activate the room's lighting panels.

"Okay," Nikky rasped through the chokehold. "Now I'll take a little help, if you're up to it."

"Uh, Nikky?" Dex shielded his eyes from the glare of the lighting panel and saw the pair more clearly—one feebly struggling, the other in complete control. "You know when you asked me earlier who Jani was?"

Nikky continued to thrash in the strong grasp of his captor. "Yeah. So?"

Dex pushed himself upright on the bed, smiling, in spite of the pain, for the first time in weeks. "Allow me to introduce you."

Dex wanted to jump up, run to Jani, embrace her, and maybe never let go. Two details, however, prevented this. First, there was the debilitating pain screaming at him from every part of his body. Second, he remembered, again, that he was first and foremost her commanding officer. He remained, instead, on the cot and nodded curtly, a wry expression on his face.

"Lieutenant."

"Captain."

"I distinctly remember giving an order that there was to be no evac mission."

Jani shrugged while continuing to secure her chokehold on Nikky.

"Yeah, well, that was before Sarge was in command, and he saw things a little differently. I have to say, I've grown rather fond of the new regime."

"Hagen? He's involved in this, too?"

At the mention of Hagen's name, she gave him a quick sharp look and glanced toward Nikky before continuing casually. "Well, temporarily. He had to head back to the colony. Command stuff—you know how that goes."

"Reasonable. At least someone has some sense."

"Uh, guys?" Nikky continued to struggle against Jani's arm. "If it's not too much trouble?" The little man was beginning to turn blue.

Jani shot Dex a questioning glance. He nodded, and she released Nikky. He turned to face her, rubbing his neck ruefully. "Thank you for not choking me to death."

"Don't mention it." Jani picked up Nikky's stunner and tossed it to him. "Next time you try to stun someone, remember to remove the safety first."

Nikky examined the stunner. "There's a safety?" he said as he slumped into the room's only chair. For the moment, Jani continued to stand.

"Relax, Jani. Have a seat." Dex motioned to the footlocker.

Jani looked again at Nikky and raised a thin auburn eyebrow.

"Oh, I wouldn't worry," Dex assured her. "He already knows our names. I don't think there's a lot he doesn't know." Still looking somewhat wary, Jani sat down while Dex made introductions.

"Nikky Weis, Lieutenant Jani McLeod. Jani, meet Nikky, the man who—" Dex was caught by a sudden memory. "*One* of the men who saved my life."

*　　*　　*

Darik Mason stretched his arms over his head, luxuriating in the feel of the Argenian silk sheets and ruffed grouse-down pillows. It was, without a doubt, the best sleep he had experienced in months. Pulling his arms back down, he brushed against the sleeping form next to him—the other reason he felt all was right in the world. Liana Reyes sighed softly and rolled over on her side, prolonging the restful slumber as long as she could.

Keeping as quiet as possible, Darik slipped out of bed, grabbed a robe, and headed for the kitchen. Catching a glimpse of himself in the hall mirror, he marveled at what a difference a few weeks could make. The haggard, over-worked stress magnet that used to stare blankly back at him was gone. Instead, he now saw a confident JenKore vice president—the bright rising star entrusted with the entire M-2/A initiative.

Any anxiety Darik had once felt—concern that his rash decision on Bellona to save the terrorist, Dex D'Felco, would be discovered—had vanished once he had returned to Earth and gotten back to work. To his relief, no one had said a thing. After his initial explanation of his whereabouts to Kristof Haman, the subject had not been broached again.

Darik remembered that night on Bellona. Already regretting his decision to save the former UCN captain, he had sprinted back to the test facility's relay building where he found two inert forms prostrate on the grassy field near the entrance—a couple of stunned guards, undoubtedly taken out by D'Felco himself on his way to disabling the launcher communication.

Then, his handpod had vibrated.

"Mason, where the devil are you?" With the pod set to ambient, Darik had heard Haman's nasally voice screaming within his ear. "We just lost the M-2 that was tracking D'Felco!"

In his apartment, Darik absently waved his hand past the phylline brewer, activating its morning sequence early. He waited for the steaming russet beverage to dispense, his mind still focused on the events of that night—how he had, in what only could have been a moment of temporary insanity, disabled the M-2 with a borrowed laser cutter. Then, unable to explain his actions even to himself, let alone that maniac, Haman, he had been forced to construct a hasty, if not imaginative, alibi.

Darik had thought furiously. "Yeah, uh, copy that," he'd said, looking down at the two stunned guards. "I figured something was going on. A couple of the guards here commandeered my laser cutter—said it was an emergency. They headed into the complex pretty fast."

Haman had sounded quite agitated. "Yes, something is certainly *going on*. They used that laser cutter to decapitate my machine!"

"Hold on, I can see them." Darik nudged the inert form of one of the guards with his foot. "They're on their way back."

"Take care of them," Haman said. "And hurry—with the station gone, we are most assuredly the next target."

Darik became annoyed once again at the memory of Haman's sudden concern for the facility. He had raised the same possibility hours earlier, only to be laughed aside.

"I want them alive." Haman had continued. "Do you have a stunner?"

Darik reached down to retrieve a pistol from one of the guards. He allowed himself a thin smile. "Yeah, I do."

"There will be a reckoning for this night," Haman said, more to himself it seemed. "Be quick about it."

Darik considered his situation. Yeah, he could blame the entire thing on these two hapless guards, but what would happen when they woke up with a different story? He felt a not-so-unfamiliar sensation radiating from the knife he had picked up. An idea formed in his head.

Muting his handpod, Darik promptly fired a stun bolt into each unconscious man's temple.

At the memory of pulling the trigger, the phylline dispenser chimed, startling him. His hands slightly trembling, Darik grasped the mug, bringing the hot liquid to his lips. The infused drink had its usual soothing effect on him. Taking in the pleasant aroma, he deliberately chose not to dwell on the images of the stun bolts burning into each man's temple, their heads recoiling sharply from the shots. He focused, instead, on the moment he'd keyed the pod channel open, desperately hoping that the point-blank stun bolts to the head would have their usual effect on short-term memory. "I'll take care of it," he had told Haman, secreting the glowing knife under his tunic. "Send your men."

Darik took another long draw of phylline. He still couldn't quite believe that he had gotten away with it. The two guards had, indeed, lost their memory of that night. After delivering the "guilty" men over to Haman and making sure that Liana had arrived safely down to the facility, he'd had to sit through an interminable debrief with some UCN admiral who had parked his carrier in system right at the end of the battle—too late to save the station. Released from that meeting with a promise that he would be contacted back in Compton if they had further need of his cooperation, Darik had caught back up with Liana, and together they had taken the *Golden Crow* back to Earth. As for Nikky, Liana had told him that he'd wandered off shortly after the *Crow* had touched down on Bellona—and that had been just fine with Darik. On the voyage home, Nikky's absence had allowed Liana and him to become more acquainted— much more acquainted.

"So, are you going to make breakfast, or what?" Shaken from his reverie, Darik turned to see Liana standing in the doorway, wearing a dress shirt she had borrowed from his wardrobe—and looking much better in it than he ever had.

"I don't know," Darik replied casually. "I was just taking inventory. We've got Hyperion ostrich eggs, some faux-bacon, the bread doesn't look too bad—we could probably toast it. And there's always coffee. What are you in the mood for?"

"Oh, I think you know the answer to that." Liana shot him a suggestive glance and turned back toward the bedroom.

Darik smiled, but his mind turned, unbidden, from thoughts about Liana to the knife he had picked up on Bellona—a knife now hidden right here in his apartment. The sensation was not violent in nature but intensely pleasurable—the memory of the object radiating through his being.

Doing his best to set aside the distraction, Darik followed Liana. For the first time in his life, he felt absolutely invincible.

On the kitchen counter, his handpod blinked to life. It displayed a simple message: *Meeting with Mr. Jenkins. 7:00am. Urgent.*

*   *   *

The LT-11 Raven touched down lightly, its dorsal thrusters kicking up a small cloud on the landing pad. No matter how diligently Flight Sergeant St. James and his crew worked at site maintenance, the severe winds on

Pella left a persistent fine layer of dust on most surfaces. Lieutenant Commander Lee Onigen held a short scarf in front of his mouth and nose as he waited for Hagen to descend the ramp.

"Commander, welcome back." Onigen peered over Hagen's shoulder further up the ramp into the light transport's interior. When no one else appeared, he looked back at Hagen—his expression a mix of resignation and concern. "I take it you are alone?"

"That's correct." Hagen waited while a burst of compressed air escaped from the settling landing gear. "The mission was a flop—not a single lead on the captain's location."

Onigen continued to gaze up the ramp as if, by hoping, he could change the reality of the news he was receiving.

"And Lieutenant McLeod?" he asked.

"Lieutenant McLeod"—Hagen cleared his throat of some of the settling dust—"Jani stayed behind. She, uh, volunteered to remain and continue the search. And I granted her permission."

Onigen raised an eyebrow. "Granted permission?"

Hagen snorted. "Yeah. It sounds better than admitting that a junior officer pretty much gave me a direct order."

"Better you than me. How long did you give her?"

"We'll go get her in a week. But this time, we use your plan—all the way in and out with the Raven. The lockdowns on public transport have tightened up a hundredfold since our operation. I was lucky to get out."

Onigen paused to consider this. "Any trouble with the destroyers?"

"No, thank God. As you suspected, there are so many Bellona-to-Occator cargo runs that clearance was a formality. Let's hope it stays that way."

"Speaking of which," Onigen said, "was our cache in the freight yard still secure?"

Hagen motioned toward the Raven's small cargo hold. "Yeah, I grabbed the rest of it. Slammers and Leeches, one crate each." In response, two ground crew approached the Raven's dorsal hatch to receive the payload.

Onigen studied the cargo from a distance. "A pity both crates weren't Slammers—even then, it wouldn't have come close to covering what we've expended on the last couple of missions." He lowered his voice. "Commander, we are getting very low on munitions—vulnerably low."

"I'm aware of that, Lee." Hagen squared his shoulders. "Walk with me. You can fill me in on the situation here."

With a nod to Drager and the ground crew, the two men turned and headed toward the hanger.

"We have a supply problem," Onigen said, continuing his thought. "With Dex gone…" he quickly corrected himself in response to Hagen's sharp look. "With Dex missing in action, we may never hear from his supplier again. He was the only one with the contact information."

Hagen agreed. "Yeah. *When* we get the captain back here, that's something that needs to change—it's going to have to."

"At least the harvest started coming in, and it's better than expected—all the vegetables you could possibly want, Sarge."

"I'm elated," Hagen said, angling his large frame through the hangar's man door. "Any other news?" From his tone, Onigen surmised that Hagen was looking for an update on one matter in particular.

"There have been the same rumors, the same grumbling—but it's grown worse. I'm not as concerned about the squadron—they seem to be abiding by the gag order. It's the rest of the colony that worries me. Fear is contagious."

Hagen looked around the empty hangar before turning toward Onigen. "Just how bad is it?"

"You can feel it everywhere you go, a nervous energy in the air. People are ready to panic—or revolt."

Hagen smiled without humor as they resumed their pace. "I don't suppose we can order the entire colony to just shut the hell up?"

"Not likely."

"Has it gotten any better for Nathan Graham?"

Onigen's dismissive shake of his head answered Hagen's question. "Everyone knows how close he is to the captain. There's been more talk about him since you left—questions about how much Pastor Graham has known about our missions and whether he can be trusted. The latest word is that groups are starting to call for his removal."

They exchanged a look as they turned into a corridor. There was an obvious conclusion to their conversation that was left unspoken—neither of them, the two officers who were now responsible for leading the squadron, and the colony, had any good solutions to this mess. They needed Dex back.

Onigen broke the brief silence. "I do have some good news, however."

"Great I could use some."

Their path had taken them past the squadron infirmary. Onigen stopped in front of the door.

"The Voor twins are awake."

*   *   *

At ease, Officers. No, don't get up." Hagen held out a hand, stopping Ravi and Purnima from scrambling out of their cots. The dark-haired twins settled back, but with eyes alert and at attention.

"We apologize, Commander," Ravi said. "We should have been up by now and back on duty."

"Belay that." Hagen's firm tone was betrayed by the smile on his lips. "Lieutenant Commander Onigen informs me that you've only just awakened. I don't want either of you out of those bunks until we have a better idea just what in blazes happened to you in the first place."

Ravi and Purnima exchanged glances.

"I believe we can answer that, sir." Purnima said softly.

"You can?" With no doctor in the squadron, or in the entire colony for that matter, medical diagnoses were the product of database searches and good old-fashioned guessing, neither of which had proven to be much help when the Voors were dragged from their cockpits, unconscious, following the return from Bellona. And so, any information the enigmatic twins themselves could provide would be beneficial.

"Yes, sir," Ravi continued. "As you are aware, Purnima and I possess certain…abilities when we are allowed to operate in cooperation with each other."

That was an understatement. While notably unremarkable as individual pilots, the two, together, had eliminated three full squadrons of Marauders over Bellona. Hagen had never seen anything like it. He remained silent, allowing the twins to continue.

Purnima took up the thread. "When we operate in that capacity, it exacts a physical toll on us. Usually, we can recover with a short period of rest, but this time…"

"This time it was different," Hagen concluded.

Ravi answered. "Yes, sir. While we had operated in tandem before, like we did in training and on the Milk Run, this mission—what we did—it was much longer…and much more intense."

"And the strain on your systems was much greater."

"Yes, sir," Purnima said. "We knew we were experiencing difficulty after the mission. We both managed to maintain consciousness long enough to initiate re-entry over Pella."

"That's when we blacked out," Ravi added.

"All right," Hagen said, processing the information. "You both knew you were in distress, but you didn't feel the need to report that?" There had been no communication on the multiple jumps home from either of the twins. Hagen would have asked how each managed to know the other was in trouble but decided that was a foolish question.

"Our apologies, sir," Ravi answered. "There wasn't anything anyone could have done to help us, and it took all our combined concentration just to stay conscious and pilot our Hornets home. As far as reporting the problem, as we said, *we* knew."

Hagen grunted. "In the future, Officers, you will report all pertinent medical status assessments to your flight commander. Is that understood?"

"Yes, sir," both answered in unison, coming to attention, of sorts, in their cots.

"And am I to understand," Hagen continued, "that your condition is currently improving?"

"Yes, sir."

"And you are expected to make a complete recovery?"

"Yes, sir."

Hagen smiled. "Then get your rest. God knows, you've earned it. Make a full recovery and then report back for duty." His smile faded, just a little. "Something tells me we're going to be needing you." He saluted, turned, and left the infirmary.

As the door slid silently shut, Ravi turned to his sister.

"Perhaps we should have told him."

"No! We can't say anything! Not yet." The forcefulness in Purnima's voice caused a sudden coughing fit. She held the bed sheet to cover her mouth, waiting for the spasms to subside.

Ravi sighed heavily, settling back on his cot, a renewed weariness invading his body. "You may be correct, Nima. But we can't keep this up forever. Eventually, our friends are going to need to know the truth."

Purnima pulled the sheet away from her mouth and turned to face her brother. Her eyes revealed a mixture of fear and determination as dark flecks of fresh blue blood splattered the sheet in her hands.

Chapter 5

Darik burst into the outer office at a dead run. Out of breath, he stole a quick peek at his chrono as he rushed toward Jenkins's door. He was over an hour late.

"And just where do you think you're going?" Clara Kinsey's acidic voice turned his blood to gelatin.

Darik pushed on toward the door without even a glance at Jenkins's personal secretary. If anything, he increased his pace. This turned out to be a miscalculation as the normally automatic door ignored his proximity, remaining steadfastly closed at his approach. Unable to check his momentum, he ran directly into it, painfully smacking his right knee in the process.

Wincing, he turned to acknowledge a face that had occupied far too many of his nightmares.

"You are not only late, Mr. Mason," Clara said, removing a bony finger from the locking icon on her workstation, "you have missed your appointment entirely. I sincerely hope that whatever unseemly distractions you use to occupy your morning hours, rather than responding to your messages, are worth jeopardizing your position in this company."

Darik met her steely gaze. While he doubted her "sincerity," he couldn't argue with her logic. A JenKore vice president was expected to be accessible to Kirrone Jenkins at all hours of the day at a moment's notice. How could he have been so careless, disabling the ambient notifications on his handpod? He knew exactly what he'd been thinking—that Liana, for once, deserved his complete and undivided attention, that one morning away from the constant demands of his handpod wouldn't kill him. No, it wouldn't kill him, but it might just cost him his job.

"Did he say anything?" Darik sighed.

"Nothing that I can repeat. Will you be needing assistance cleaning out your office? I can call maintenance for you."

Darik ignored her jab and instead forced his best smile. "Come on, Clara." He leaned toward her desk, remembered her fastidiousness about fingerprints, and lurched backwards mid-lean, his hands raised apologetically. "He must have said *something*. Did he mention rescheduling?"

Clara stared at him.

"Anything?" Darik asked weakly.

"As I said," Clara hissed through clenched teeth, "he didn't say anything that I could repeat. I *am* a lady after all."

Debatable, Darik thought. He turned back toward the outer door, resigned in the knowledge that his only option was to go about his regular work day and await Jenkins's wrath.

"Of course"—Clara's voice stopped him in the doorway—"I do have his schedule. I *could* let you know where he was heading next if you wanted to risk interrupting him."

Darik turned around. "What do you want?" There was resignation in his voice.

"Want?" Clara spat out the word. "I don't *want* anything. I'm merely trying to help you keep your job—something I seem to care about far more than you do."

"Okay, okay. I'm sorry." Darik knew this was going to cost him, something, at some point, and it was going to be unpleasant—but at the moment, he knew he had no choice. "Where was Mr. Jenkins heading?"

"Helios." Clara consulted her planner. "He's going to be there for another hour. He had mentioned for you to join him if you ever showed up."

"Thanks, Clara." Darik turned back toward the doorway. "I won't forget this."

"No, you won't." Her voice carried no hint of a threat. She was merely stating a fact. "And Mr. Mason."

"Yes?"

"You might want to pick up some workout clothes. You wouldn't want to spoil that nice suit."

*   *   *

"It's not going to be easy, Captain." Jani took a bite from the warmed-up carrageenan bar Nikky had handed her, scowled, and thought about spitting it back out. Setting the rest of the bar on the table, she forcibly swallowed the portion in her mouth before continuing. "Carrier Group Five has been patrolling the system since the battle. The *Ganymede* left after a couple days, but there are still a pair of destroyers parked over the jump lanes—with no sign of leaving."

Nikky looked at the bar Jani had rejected, shrugged, and retrieved his own from the IR unit. "Hanging around for weeks, huh?" he mused. "Who knew the UCN took terrorist attacks so seriously?"

Jani dismissed his comment. "Hagen was still able to get on a commercial transport, but he doesn't feel we can risk it on cover IDs again. The port terminal is crawling with spooks—if anything, they've stepped up the security in the past week."

Nikky had the bar's wrapper in his teeth and was struggling to rip it open with his one hand. Not bothering to pull it away, he spoke from the other side of his mouth. "Well I hope no one followed you here. You *were* careful, right?"

Dex closed his eyes and shook his head. Nikky didn't know who he was dealing with.

"Was I careful? Yeah, I was careful." Jani's voice had a distinct edge. "A lot more careful than *you* were."

Nikky set the still-wrapped morsel on the table beside Jani's. "What are you talking about?"

"Haven't you wondered how I was able to find you?"

Nikky stammered. "Well, I...I thought he had a tracker or something. I mean, I scanned him for one—twice—and didn't find anything. But when you showed up, I thought he must've had some high-end, military-grade tech. Like, I read an article the other day about an experimental procedure where nano-trackers are diffused into the bloodstream and—"

Jani interrupted him, putting a hand delicately on his shoulder. "Oh wow—you really know a lot about trackers, don't you?"

Nikky's cheeks flushed. "Yeah, you could say I know a thing or two."

Dex was tempted to intervene but decided against it. He owed a lot to Nikky and had come to trust him. If they were going get off Bellona, Dex knew they would all have to work together. Better to let them size each other up, right here and now, so they could move on to more important matters.

Jani leaned in. "So, naturally, you knew that you had to get rid of the tracker from the rented airbike."

Nikky looked offended. "Of course. I pulled it from the bike and dumped it back here in the river."

"Interesting," Jani said, slowly nodding. "Was that before or after you brought Dex here? Before or after you returned the shuttle you rented?"

"Well, after. I couldn't very well...oh, wait..." Nikky trailed off. "Oh, boy."

Jani turned back to Dex. "He had the tracker with him the entire time. All I had to do was pull the data log. He stopped here, probably to get you settled, then returned the shuttle." She glared at Nikky. "Then, *finally*, you had the sense to swing by the river and get rid of the tracker—*after* it logged every place you'd been!"

Nikky opened his mouth to say something, paused, then began again.

"Oops" was all he managed.

"*Oops*? That's all you've got? *Oops*? Dex, are you sure we can trust this guy?"

Dex held up a hand. "All right, Jani, that's enough." He stood, still feeling the effects of his wounds but a sense of urgency now spurring him on. "Yes, we can trust Nikky. More importantly, we need to plan—and move."

Jani began to gather up supplies, including the opened carrageenan bar, which she re-wrapped and shoved in her pocket. Nikky, too, started to stuff items into his battered carrier bag, his expression conveying the realization of just how critical his mistake might have been.

*   *   *

Three kilometers away, a tall figure exited the rental garage's office. Pulling off a pair of blood-stained gloves, he casually tossed them behind a pile of rusting shuttle parts. With pale, ashen eyes, he regarded the data on his handpod before switching it off and walking unhurriedly into the night. Behind him, the swaying sign blinked out one final time.

Chapter 6

"At ease, Lieutenant." Hagen Lebrian motioned toward a chair across the table. "Take a seat."

Seltrice Valani broke from attention and slid into place opposite her commander, her casual tone failing to mask the apprehension every other aspect of her body language was indicating. "What's this all about, Sarge?"

"You tell me." Hagen distractedly tapped a duty roster display on the table top. "It is my understanding that you've been rather talkative of late." Earlier in the day, Hagen had run into Job Hansen, and it hadn't been difficult to notice that something was on his mind. Job had been hesitant to spill any details, but Hagen eventually dragged the information out of the reticent exec. He didn't like having to put Job in an awkward position, but maintaining calm and order in the increasingly volatile colony was priority number one.

Seltrice shifted in her seat. "I'm not sure what you mean, Commander."

Hagen squared his broad shoulders. Even while he was sitting, the posture added a couple more centimeters to his impressive height. "You're not sure. Are you sure you know what a gag order means, Lieutenant?"

Seltrice sighed, somewhat loudly. The sound of her breath gave Hagen the impression of irritability more than resignation.

"I assume you're talking about Ghazi."

Hagen nodded. "Adahn. Officer Manasser. A member of this squadron." He leaned forward. "Yes. I'm talking about him. But more importantly, *you've* been talking about him."

Seltrice looked to her left, past Hagen's stare. Her voice was low. "Well, somebody has to."

Hagen slammed his open palm on the duty roster. The sharp sound brought Seltrice's eyes back to front, her own posture instinctively snapping back to attention.

"Not with unauthorized civilians, we don't." Hagen rarely shouted—his imposing frame had always rendered a raised voice unnecessary. Backing off a few decibels, his tone still remained clipped and firm. "If you have something to share, Lieutenant, if you have grounds for any suspicion, you express those concerns here, and nowhere else. Is that understood?"

Seltrice looked down at the table. "Even when no one wants to hear them."

"What was that, mister?"

Seltrice looked up, meeting Hagen's even gaze. "Yes. I understand, sir!"

Hagen regarded her for a time, the moment stretching to the point of awkwardness. Finally, he raised an eyebrow. "Well?"

"Sir?"

Hagen leaned back in his chair. "What have you got, Lieutenant? What is the nature of your suspicion of Officer Manasser? What is so pressing that you have felt the need to defy orders, spread innuendo throughout the civilian community, and put everyone in this squadron on edge?"

"You really want to know?"

"Now, Lieutenant!"

"Well," Seltrice stammered, "it's just that…it's, uh, impressions mostly. I go back to the Erebus mission when we lost Smiley and Aces—it was Ghazi who was out of position, right?"

Hagen's eyes narrowed. "You're bringing up a two-year-old incident? A mission that was reviewed—in detail—in which all pilots, including Adahn, were cleared? You're starting with that?"

Seltrice shot back. "Yes, I'm starting with that. I never agreed with the findings, and neither did Scot—and several other pilots, too. And since then, it's been more of the same."

"Like what, specifically?"

"It's like I said, it's been impressions mostly. The way he acts, the way he sneaks around here. We…I…just don't trust him, Sarge."

Hagen stayed silent.

"And then, over Bellona," Seltrice hesitated. "When we lost Geff, while I was getting pressed, it was the same thing all over. Where was Ghazi? It was all too familiar."

Hagen placed his hands together, two thick index fingers creating a steeple in front of his chin. "You want to talk about the Bellona mission, again, fine. Let's discuss Bellona. Who was in your flight, Lieutenant?"

"Sir?"

"Answer the question, Viper. Over Bellona, we were in two flights, executing a defensive Thach Weave. Who were the pilots comprising your flight?"

Seltrice eyed him warily. "Well, there was you, Sunfire and Moonlight, Ghazi, and me."

"And when you came under fire—when the Slammers locked on to you—what was your position in the flight?"

"We were in tight formation—a star pattern. My Hornet was at the bottom of the flight, Ghazi on my wing, the Voors were aft, and you on lead."

Hagen placed his hands on the table. "And the Slammers were approaching from beneath you. In your blind spot."

Seltrice nodded once. "Yes."

"You couldn't see them."

"Of course not!" Seltrice fumed. "How could I? No one could!"

Hagen settled back into his seat. "Exactly, Lieutenant. No one could. Prince picked them up from across the gap, but our entire flight was blind to them. Do you blame Sunfire and Moonlight for that? Do you blame me?"

Seltrice looked down. "But Ghazi was on my wing. It was his job."

"Seltrice," Hagen's voice softened. "The Slammers were locked onto you. They should have been visible on your HUD." He waited, letting the impact sink in. "You're blaming the wrong person, Lieutenant."

She considered his words while avoiding his eyes. "It's not just Bellona, sir. It's so much more than that. I've been watching him. The way he acts, the way he keeps to himself." She paused. "Like I said, it's mostly…"

"Impressions," Hagen said.

"Yeah," Seltrice brightened. "Impressions."

Hagen shook his head. "In other words, you've got nothing."

"Not nothing, Commander. I'm certain of this! Even if I'm the only one—"

Hagen stood. "You are certain of nothing. Hear this, Lieutenant Valani, and hear it well. You will cease from speculation and idle chatter concerning Officer Manasser or any other member of this squadron whom you happen to feel a little suspicious about. If you have something concrete, something other than impressions, you can bring it to me, but in the meantime, I suggest you spend less time spreading flack about your fellow pilots and more time scrutinizing your OODA process, starting with your own performance over Bellona. Is that understood?"

Seltrice's cheeks flashed crimson as she stood to attention. "Yes, sir!"

"You are dismissed, Lieutenant."

Seltrice wasted no time exiting the room. She strode down the hall, turning a tight corner without looking and nearly bowling over Adahn Manasser in the process.

"Great," she hissed, pulling an entangled arm from his side with more force than necessary. "It figures."

Adahn absently straightened his uniform tunic. "Lieutenant?"

"Forget it." Seltrice turned to leave, then stopped abruptly. She spun back to face Adahn. "Say, where are you heading, anyway?" She indicated a direction with a shake of her head. "It's almost mid-watch. Quarters are that way."

Adahn faltered. "I…uh, I know. I'm on watch tonight."

"No," she said. "You're not."

He raised an eyebrow. "Now you're studying my schedule?"

"*Ma'am*. 'You're studying my schedule, *ma'am*.' I know the duty roster. What are you doing out here?"

"Well, perhaps I…" Adahn stopped. "You know what? I don't report to you, so it's really none of your business."

Seltrice moved in close. "Watch your tone, *Flying Officer*. You might think you have everyone fooled, but you're wrong." She turned, her shoulder bumping into his as she marched pointedly in the direction of her quarters.

Adahn watched her until she disappeared around the far corner, his jaw set in a half-frown. Once she was out of sight, he turned back toward his original direction and hastily exited the barracks.

Chapter 7

Helios Athletic Club, reserved for the exclusive use of the highest executives in JenKore, was located in a smaller high-rise, two blocks east of the Unity Tower. Darik used to wonder why Jenkins and his inner circle hadn't simply dedicated a floor or two of their own headquarters to this function but eventually came to realize the CEO guarded his workout time zealously. The off-site location helped prevent needless interruption—the very type of intrusion Darik was about to make.

All the same, Darik was feeling decidedly better as he keyed the access code to the facility. As a newly promoted vice president, he had full privileges to the private club but hadn't, as yet, taken the opportunity to use them. While not as fanatical a fitness freak as Jenkins, Darik tried to maintain a reasonable workout regime at the small gym back in his own building. It was high time, he reasoned, to start enjoying the extra luxuries of his position and the inherent networking possibilities that came with them. Despite his initial nervousness as to why Jenkins had demanded a meeting in the first place, he was actually looking forward to joining this higher level, more elite group at what was sure to be a far superior facility to the one he used back home. And after all, he thought, late for the original meeting or not, hadn't Jenkins himself invited him?

The club's interior exceeded his expectations. Even in the spacious locker room, he could see that no expense had been spared in furnishings or in comfort. The darkly paneled walls framed recessed holos of various extreme activities from tether-free rock climbing on Hermes's famous *Milla Alta* cliffs to lava surfing on Vesta. Lush plants from several worlds filled the open spaces, creating a sweet rainforest aroma that effectively eliminated the stark sanitary smell so typical of the locker rooms Darik normally frequented.

He found a seat on a thick real-oak bench in front of an unoccupied locker. Reaching down into the gym bag he had procured at the pro-shop on his way in, he pulled out a workout tunic, shorts, and a pair of designer court shoes. He had been lucky. The shop had had a good inventory of sharp, high quality gear in his size readily available. Sure, the price had been exorbitant, but, as Darik had to continually remind himself, he could afford it now, and at this level it was critical to look the part—to fit in.

Fitting in during a workout, he decided, was not going to be a problem. Glancing around the room, he noted small knots of other execs, lounging around in various stages of undress. He noted, with some satisfaction, the physical condition, or lack thereof, in his new peer group—a bit of paunch here and a certain flabbiness of the arms there. A rugby player from his university days, Darik was glad that he had never let himself go entirely. In fact, as he activated the court shoes, completing his own preparations, he realized that there was a good possibility that he would be second only to Jenkins himself in overall fitness when he entered the gym. With a curt nod to a half-naked division head that he recognized, Darik squared his shoulders and strode purposefully through the doorway leading to the main fitness center.

His first perusal of the room revealed no indication that Jenkins was even there. A quick wave of nervousness ran up Darik's spine. Had Clara sent him on another wild goose chase? When was he going to wise up and stop listening to that withered old crow?

"Mr. Mason." Jenkins's voice caused Darik to jump. "I've been expecting you. Do you play checkball?"

Darik turned abruptly to find Jenkins standing directly behind him. The tall silver-haired CEO had obviously been working out for the better part of the hour. A fine sheen of perspiration was apparent on his forehead and chest. He was not, however, even remotely out of breath.

"I'm sorry," Darik stammered, hurriedly trying to recover his composure. "What?"

"Do you play checkball?" Jenkins repeated. "I have a session already loaded for us."

Even though Darik knew his boss's loathing to repeat himself, Jenkins's tone was cordial enough, even a trace of a smile in his expression. Perhaps he wasn't in trouble after all. Darik relaxed visibly.

Darik nodded. "Yes. Yes, I can play." A version of full-contact squash, the game had always fit well in his off-season activities at university. In fact, Darik considered himself to be quite adept, having won a few tournaments in his younger days. This was going to be all right, he decided. He would have to be sure not to show off too much in a one-on-one match with his employer, of course.

"Step this way." Jenkins moved through the sliding doorway to the checkball court. "We have much to discuss."

Strapping a micro-controller to his wrist, Darik took his place at the ready line and waited for Jenkins to begin the match. A beat passed, then another.

After several uncomfortable seconds, Jenkins spared Darik a sideways glance.

"Your privilege," he said, one eyebrow raised with a look of amusement.

Of course. Jenkins had set up the session. As such, Darik was the designated visitor and by tradition held first serve.

Taking a breath, he activated the micro-controller and swept his hand in a downward, cross-body motion. The glowing checkball shot from an open panel near the upper left ceiling, bouncing sharply in Jenkins's service zone.

The athletic CEO responded quickly, striking the ball with his open ungloved hand, sending it rocketing back off the far wall—which immediately glowed bright blue, indicating that the ball was now in Darik's zone.

Darik prepared to return the ground stroke. Positioning his feet front to back, he pulled back his left hand and tracked the ball into his zone. Just before he could swing, a vicious body check to his back sent him sprawling to the floor. The ball bounced harmlessly past, coming to rest in the back corner of the court. A floor panel opened, dropping the ball out of sight as the scoreboard holo indicated a point for Jenkins.

Darik picked himself up and concentrated on not rubbing a newly scraped elbow.

So that's how it's going to be.

The check had been borderline legal. Darik's first impulse had been to call a "hinder," but then he realized that Jenkins had contacted just enough of Darik's side—a legal check—to make Darik's claim questionable. Besides, what was he going to do? Call his boss for an illegal hit on the first rally? Instead, Darik granted himself the freedom to take his game up a notch. This was going to be fun.

"So tell me," Jenkins said, activating his own server, "what progress has been made investigating the destruction of the M-2/A on Bellona?"

Darik had been anticipating this question all morning and felt ready for it.

"Well, I thought the investigation was pretty conclusive. Two Zealot sympathizers, posing as guards, took out the M-2 with a laser cutter just as it was about to execute D'Felco."

"Yes, the laser cutter." Jenkins readied himself to serve. "I keep hearing about laser cutters." He brought his hand down in an inside-out sweep. The ball shot from a panel midway down the right corner of the room.

Darik had seen this technique before—clever, and well executed, but hardly beyond his skill level. He picked up the blue-red glowing rotation of the ball as it streaked toward his zone. It bounced to his left but quickly changed direction, careening toward his right.

Darik was ready. Striking the ball with his right hand, he sent a perfect shot off the wall and back toward Jenkins. As the room glowed red from the changing hue of the service wall, Darik quickly noted that Jenkins would have to return the ball with his left hand, leaving himself open to a legal front-check from Darik.

Darik crouched, ready to spring forward and block Jenkins for an easy point, but suddenly hesitated.

Laser cutters? What else was he hearing about laser cutters?

Darik moved forward for his check, but it was a half-hearted, half-speed effort.

Jenkins easily side-stepped the assault, slapped the ball to the service wall, and watched it bounce, once again, through Darik's zone for another point. His pale blue eyes sparkled.

"Mr. Mason, you could not possibly be sandbagging, could you? Such a move would bring your integrity into serious doubt."

Darik straightened up and met his employer face to face. A familiar sensation—dread, accompanied by an almost exhilarating anger—began to fill his gut. His confidence returned in abundance.

"No. No sandbagging." He met Jenkins's amused gaze with a cool stare of his own. "Your serve."

"Very well." Jenkins readied his controller. "The two Zealot spies have been dealt with. If you are satisfied with the outcome of the investigation, that is sufficient for me." He brought his hand down sharply, initiating a straightforward high-velocity serve. "It is, after all, your division."

You got that right, Darik thought. He returned the ball with equal force, sending it low, the shot skittering just under Jenkins's right hand for his first point of the match. It disappeared into the floor, resetting for the next serve.

"An excellent shot. You are quite adept when you are not distracted."

The game progressed, point for point, serve for serve. With the pressure of the nagging M-2 question behind him, and his boss apparently placated, Darik found himself relaxing, enjoying the game and immersing himself in the flow of the competition. He also began to realize that his earlier assessment was correct—he *was* considerably more skilled than the CEO and would have to hold back a little in order to not flaunt his superiority. He was still checking hard, continually knocking his opponent off balance, but never to the floor. With each succeeding service, Darik felt more in control and confident that, while he would definitely win, he could subtly keep the score close enough to not embarrass his superior.

With the score tied at fifteen-all, Jenkins held up a hand, calling for time. Darik was pleased to see that Jenkins was actually breathing heavily, something he had never known the man to do. Jenkins motioned to the doorway, which slid aside to admit an M-2 service model carrying a pair of hydration units.

"A short break if you don't mind." Jenkins received one of the offered units, activated the electrolyte infuser, and proceeded to drink it down, leaning somewhat tiredly against the side wall.

While not as worn out as his boss, Darik still gratefully accepted the refreshment, choosing instead to stand in the middle of the floor as he drank, a subtle message to his opponent that he didn't need to recline. He was exhilarated. Here he was, Darik Mason, just a working-class kid from the Midwest, enjoying a checkball match with Kirrone Jenkins himself. His anxiety over the last-minute meeting notification, the report on the M-2 debacle, and all his other recent concerns had vanished, replaced by the thrill of competition—and the accompanying sense of equality, of belonging.

"You never told me you were such a skilled checkball player, Darik." Jenkins seemed to have recovered much of his energy. "We will have to do this more often."

"I'd like that," Darik said. "Of course, it's always a challenge to find the time."

Jenkins handed the expended hydration unit back to the M-2. "Speaking of that, do you think you could set aside the next few days for a special project?"

Darik adopted his most serious—executive-level, he liked to think—expression. "Of course. What do I need to do?"

"Oh, I think you will find it quite engaging. I have a business associate—someone heavily tied into our supply chain—who has invited me on an expedition, a hunting trip, as it were, to Silvanus. This man's connections could prove vital to our procurement needs for the next phase of M-2 development. With that in mind, I would like to invite you along. A connection with this man, at this point in time, could prove very beneficial to your growth at this company."

It was all Darik could do to keep from breaking out in a stupid grin. This day kept getting better. He wasn't going to let the fact that he didn't know the first thing about hunting temper his enthusiasm—that was beside the point. His participation in this sort of high-level networking opportunity would have been unthinkable just a few weeks ago. All the work, the sleepless nights, were finally paying off.

He composed himself. "Absolutely. I would enjoy that."

"In addition," Jenkins continued, "I have another opportunity to discuss with you—an assignment that I'm afraid I must ask you to add to your already full plate."

The last thing Darik needed was more work piled on his schedule, but Jenkins's tone indicated that his enlisting of Darik's help was meant to be a compliment—a far cry from the usual chastisement and recriminations that had punctuated his career to date.

"Sure," he said. "What is it?"

Jenkins shook his head. "It's not something we can discuss freely here. Suffice it to say that we have a situation developing that, if left unaddressed, could make the Bellona failure look like a hiccup by comparison. I would like to take the Silvanus trip as an opportunity to fill you in completely."

Finally, Darik thought, *a "situation" that doesn't start out as my fault.*

"I'll be happy to help," he said. "And I look forward to our conversation."

"Very well." Jenkins appeared satisfied. "Shall we resume?"

It was Darik's serve. Riding a wave of newfound professional confidence, he relaxed even more. He scored quickly, going up sixteen-fifteen. Serving again, he was mindful, as he had been all along, to keep the match close. Jostling for position, throwing elbows and body checks, returning strong forehand shots back and forth, the two men traded point for point, bringing the score to twenty-all. Checkball rules did not include a win-by-two requirement. The next point would determine the match.

Now a little winded himself, Darik readied himself to serve. The feeling of confident power he had been experiencing throughout the match now surged even stronger. This had been fun, but he was clearly in a higher skill class than his boss. *No sandbagging*, Jenkins had said. Okay, he had kept the game close enough, and he had held his own during their conversation. Now it was time to put him away, to earn his respect and walk off the court as less a subordinate and more an equal.

Darik activated the controller and brought his arm around in a sweeping haymaker swing, twisting his wrist over the top—his best serve and one he had saved the entire match for this moment. The ball shot from the panel, low and fast. He knew that it would skid past Jenkins before the CEO would even have a chance to react.

Jenkins barely moved. With a subtle flick of his left wrist, he struck the ball so casually, so easily, that at first, Darik didn't think he had hit it at all.

The ball rocketed back toward the wall, striking it low and then, inexplicably, falling dead in the corner—a perfectly executed drop shot. There was no ricochet, no chance at all for Darik to return the volley. All four walls, floor, and ceiling glowed red, indicating that the match was over.

"The ship leaves tomorrow for Silvanus at 8:00 a.m. This time, Mr. Mason, do not be late."

Jenkins turned toward the door, retrieved a towel from the waiting M-2, and exited, leaving Darik to stare helplessly at the dimming checkball in the corner, struck by the realization that he could never make a shot like that, even if he worked at it for the rest of his life.

Chapter 8

Pella's sun was just breaking over the horizon, casting long shadows off the modular phirmium buildings of the colony. Any hope that Hagen Lebrian had harbored that the early hour would allow for a more inconspicuous visit vanished as he saw the large group of colonists milling about the street. He wondered what on earth a group that size was doing gathering so early.

Slipping through that crowd unnoticed was unlikely. As second-in-command of the Angels, he was too well known—and it didn't help that at two meters in height, he stood a full head taller than most of the colonists.

He briefly considered turning around and plotting a more circuitous route to Pastor Nathan Graham's office but then thought better of it. He'd already been spotted—the only option now was to head directly into the fray.

"Hey, Commander Lebrian!" A thin older man with shocks of wispy graying hair stopped him with a shout. "Some of these folks here have a question for you. Is it true what we've been hearing?"

Hagen faced him. "That depends on what you've heard."

The man's sunken eyes showed concern—and accusation. "We heard that Captain D'Felco isn't coming back. We heard that he's dead."

"We don't know that," Hagen said. He attempted to keep moving forward, but two more colonists, a heavyset woman and a taller square-jawed man, joined Wispy-hair in front of him.

"With the captain dead, who's going to protect us?" the woman asked.

"We heard," the taller man injected, "that there were machines."

"Monsters." Another man joined the huddle.

"They'll find us!" The woman's voice increased by several decibels, a fleck of saliva landing on Hagen's cheek. "They'll find us and kill us all!"

The crowd was growing and pressing in too closely for Hagen's liking. He held up his hands, both to calm the crowd and create some space.

"Now hold on, people. Nobody said the captain is dead. And whatever threats might be out there, that's why the Angels are here—to protect you."

"Fat chance!" someone shouted from the back of the crowd.

"Yeah, you can't even watch over yourselves."

"It's no secret you've got a traitor on your hands."

"What about that Arabic kid? I keep hearing that he's—"

Hagen raised his voice. "Now that's enough! Look at you people. I can't believe you're acting like this." He turned, taking in the entire crowd. "What are you all doing out here anyway? It's six in the morning for crying out loud."

Wispy-hair stepped forward. "Ah, I understand, Commander." He shook his head sadly. "That's how it's going to be now, I guess. Now we don't have the right to assemble? Do we answer to you now?"

Murmurs of agreement chimed in behind Wispy-hair as the crowd pressed in further.

"We might ask you the same question." Wispy moved in very close. Hagen considered forcefully reasserting his personal space but refrained. "What are you doing down here so early, Commander, right in the middle of our meeting?"

"Meeting? Is that what you call this?" Hagen stopped himself. "No, I don't have time for this right now. If you will excuse me, I have to get going."

He moved to one side to push ahead, but Wispy moved to block him. His sunken eyes squinted.

"Where?"

"Excuse me?" Hagen couldn't believe it.

"*Where* are you going this early, Commander? Down here in our colony?"

"The man has an appointment, Jaq," a voice from the edge of the crowd said. "Why don't we all just let him get to it?"

Hagen looked in the direction of the voice. A rotund balding man burrowed his way through the crowd in Hagen's direction.

"C'mon, Commander." He took Hagen by the arm and, without hesitation, pulled him in the direction of a side street. "Why don't I make sure you make it there on time."

Looking back over his shoulder, the man called back, "Okay, Jaq, we're out of your way now. You can get on with your *meeting*."

He kept Hagen moving down the side street. "This way, Commander. Your appointment is with Pastor Graham, right?"

"Uh, yeah." Hagen took a final look back. Through the narrow opening, he could see the crowd still gathered on the main street. They now appeared to be huddled in a large circle. Jaq, their apparent leader, stood in the middle.

"Thanks, uh…"

"Granderson," the man replied. "Milo Granderson."

"Well thanks, Mr. Granderson."

"Milo is fine."

"Okay, then thanks, Milo. I didn't want it to get out of hand back there." Hagen ran a hand over his head. "What in the world was that all about?"

"Oh, them?" Granderson indicated the group with a backwards wave of his thumb. "That's Jaq's bunch. Whatever he's thinking or saying, the rest of 'em will be thinking it and saying it, too."

Hagen scratched his right temple. "Does Pastor Graham know that they're behaving like that? It doesn't seem right."

"Oh, he knows. This way." Granderson guided Hagen down another walkway to the right. "Yeah, he knows, but I don't think his approval or disapproval will mean much to them."

"What do you mean?"

Granderson stopped. "Jaq and his group are the ones pushing for Pastor Graham's removal."

Hagen opened his mouth, but no words came. The whole thing was just too ridiculous.

Granderson continued. "They get together like that every day—a prayer meeting they call it. But what it really turns into is a bunch of pious nonsense about how God needs to *heal* our wayward pastor."

Hagen frowned. "Heal him?"

"Oh, it's all couched in the most flowery language, of course. But the longer they go, the more it comes out. *The pastor needs to be turned from the path he's on. He's being deceived. He's too close to those prideful pilots*…oh, I'm sorry, Commander. That's not what I think."

"Don't worry about it." Hagen smiled tightly.

"My wife says I never know when to shut up."

"No, it's okay," Hagen demurred. "How many of them are there?"

Granderson considered the question. "Enough to be a concern, and their numbers are growing. Jaq keeps everything he's saying just spiritual enough to sound like he's really taking these concerns to God, but if you want my opinion, he's just gathering votes."

Hagen grunted. "That doesn't sound good."

"You don't know the half of it."

"What do you mean?"

Granderson drew a deep breath, small beads of perspiration appearing on his balding forehead. Despite the cool of the early morning, the walk seemed to have taken a toll on his respiratory system.

"I mean that little group back there is the least of your worries. This colony has factions that are far more dangerous than them. But I'm not the man to discuss that with."

They arrived at Pastor Nathan Graham's office. Granderson keyed the chime, and moments later, Graham opened the door. Tall and lanky with dark hair and soft features, his appearance defied the pressure the young man must have been under. He smiled broadly.

"Commander Lebrian, come on in." He stepped to one side. "And Milo! It's good to see you."

"It would appear that I needed an escort this morning," Hagen said.

In response to Graham's raised eyebrow, Granderson piped in. "Commander Lebrian ran into one of Jaq's prayer meetings. I just steered him through it."

Graham's eyes showed concern, despite his smile. "Thanks, Milo. I appreciate it."

"No problem, Pastor. That's what I'm here for." Granderson smiled. "I'll leave you two to your meeting. Don't forget, Jineen and I want to treat you to dinner this week."

"I'm looking forward to it."

"Just let me know when!" Granderson gave him an enthusiastic thumbs-up, turned, and ambled up the walkway.

Hagen watched him go. "Seems like a good man, Pastor."

"He is." Graham smiled. "And you can call me Nate by the way. Dex always does."

Hagen hesitated. "If it's all the same, I think I'm more comfortable with 'Pastor.'"

Graham laughed. "Fair enough. C'mon, let's have a seat."

Hagen took in the room around him for the first time. A battered desk in the corner was loaded with data chips, empty coffee cups, and piles of notes. It looked like the actual desk surface had not been seen in some time. Closer to him, a worn easy chair sat across from a small but comfortable looking sofa with a short table in between. Graham directed Hagen to the sofa and settled himself into the easy chair.

"Coffee?" Graham grabbed a thermal unit on the table and poured into two glazed cups. Hagen gratefully accepted one of them.

"Speaking of Dex…" Graham's question lingered in his eyes over the top of his mug. Hagen shook his head.

"Nothing, at least not when I was there," Hagen replied. "Jani stayed on Bellona to continue the search. I couldn't have dragged her away if I'd wanted to. We're going back for her soon." He caught a quick glimpse of his chrono. "Thanks, by the way, for moving this meeting up."

Graham acknowledged him with a smile. "Not a problem. I appreciate you responding to my request, and I don't want to take any more of your time than I need to." He took a sip of his coffee. "So," he said quietly, "do you think she'll find him?"

"If anyone will, it's Jani. There's no way she's leaving without him. And I know how she feels—I would have liked to have stayed and continued the search myself." He looked the young pastor directly in the eyes. "But I knew that I had to get back."

Graham set his cup down. "Because of all the turmoil."

Hagen glanced at the exterior door leading to the street where the crowd was likely still gathered just a few blocks away.

"Yeah. I mean, I knew things were bad, Pastor, but I didn't know how bad. If that group back there is any indication…"

"Jaq?" Graham smiled sardonically. "Oh, I can handle him and his bunch." His smile faded. "No, he's not the reason I asked you down here."

Hagen stopped drinking his coffee in mid-sip. "Milo mentioned that his gang was the least of our worries."

Graham settled back in his chair again. "And Milo would be right. People are scared, Commander. And fear makes people do foolish things."

Hagen leaned forward. "Like what things?"

"You name it," Graham said. "It starts with people closing themselves off. Differences of opinion, that used to be discussed rationally and with humility, lead instead to further division. People stop listening to one another, factions form, and tempers erupt—sometimes violently."

Hagen frowned. "What, specifically, are we talking about here?"

"I'm sorry." Graham smiled again. "I'm not being clear. Let me put it this way. That group you met, the prayer meeting. Jaq has never been a big supporter of mine, even back on Aphea, but it was always civil, a 'one man sharpens another' kind of situation. We could have our discussions, ourselves, man to man. Now, mostly because of fear, I think, he's taking it right out in the public square"—he glanced up—"trying to call down fire from heaven to consume me, I don't doubt."

"But you said you could handle that. That there are other concerns."

Graham nodded. "Yes. That's just an example. Now imagine all the different factions you normally get in a body of believers, only with fear adding fuel to their ideas. Some speak out their personal anxieties as if they were divine prophecy, others see the apocalypse in every eclipse or supernova…"

Hagen cocked his head slightly to one side. "I'm still not sure where I come into this."

"There's more, Commander. I mentioned that people are scared. Well, fear also sends people looking for answers."

"Isn't that what you're here for?"

Graham took a long sip of his coffee. "It would be nice if that were true, wouldn't it?" He stopped. "I'm sorry, you're right, of course. But we both know that I don't have all the answers. I just have to do my best, with God's help, to remind people that their hope isn't in me, the Angels, or anything else, but in Christ." He caught Hagen's eye. "There is always, *always* hope when our trust is in him."

Hagen couldn't help thinking of Dex, and, internalizing Graham's words, he pushed aside the ever-creeping worry and allowed himself to wholeheartedly hope and believe for the safe return of his captain.

"That's true," Hagen said quietly. "But in the meantime, there are quite a few who aren't listening anymore."

"No, they're not. Like I said, fear leads people to do foolish things."

"Stupid things."

"That, too. Some have turned to tranqs. How they're synthesizing them is beyond me—but when you start mixing mind-altering substances into the situation, when tensions are as high as they are, it can get ugly pretty fast."

"Any violence?"

Graham's expression was calm, but the stress lines near his eyes became pronounced. "At least a dozen incidents. And it's been getting worse." He leaned forward. "This colony is starting to unravel, Hagen."

Hagen's coffee continued to cool on the table top. "What you're describing. It just doesn't sound…Christian."

Graham laughed again, without much humor. "As if that's ever stopped anyone before. This is far from the first time violence has been done in the name of Christ. As long as a group believes they are in the right—that God is on their side—they can justify just about anything."

"Is that the worst of it?"

Graham shook his head. "I assume you're familiar with those in our colony who aren't exactly pleased with your presence."

Hagen leaned back, picking up his mug again. "You mean the pacifists?" Hagen sipped the coffee, found it cold, and set the mug down again.

"You can call them that. They're not bad people. They simply don't believe in violence of any kind. To them, there is no military action that is justified—no such thing as a 'just war.' They'd prefer it if the Hornets were grounded and scrapped."

Hagen's patience was running thin. "Not my problem."

"Probably not," Graham agreed. "But fear makes strange bedfellows."

"What do you mean?"

"I mean that there's another group, larger than the pacifists. Call them the militants. These are the folks who don't trust that they're actually being protected. The rumors about a traitor up there"—his eyes moved briefly in the direction of the squadron base—"aren't helping much."

"Rumors never do," Hagen replied. "Trust me—we're handling that."

"But all the same," Graham continued, "it's bizarre. The pacifists and militants would ordinarily have very little in common, but now they seem to be in agreement on one thing—the Angels are not good for the colony. Now, the pacifists just wish you weren't here. The militants, on the other hand, are convinced that you're ineffective or, worse, an outright threat. Blame the rumors if you will, but their argument is that if there is a traitor, nothing is being done about it. They feel that that Angels are compromised, and that the only way to truly ensure their own safety is to take matters into their own hands."

"I don't like the sound of that. Do you know of any specific plans?"

Graham considered. "Nothing really organized, yet. So far, it's a lot of talk, but the talk is getting louder. And like I said, we've had some incidents. Milo had to break up a fight the other night, if you can imagine that."

"I'm trying to. What happened?"

Graham swirled the dark liquid around in his mug. "He came across a knot of guys, about a half-dozen or so. Half of them were militants. The others, I guess you could say they were squadron supporters. Well, Milo says they were arguing pretty loudly—he figures some of them had been drinking."

"I'm not surprised." While the squadron base was dry, it was no secret that there were a handful of private stills, wine kits, and other homemade setups scattered throughout the colony. "So Milo broke up the argument."

"Yeah," Graham said, "but not until some shoving started and a couple punches were thrown. To hear him tell it, he didn't even think at that point. He just waded right in the middle of them and gave them a 'piece of his mind,' as he put it. He told them all to settle down, grow up, and get back to bed to sober up."

Hagen laughed softly. "Yeah, a good man, that Milo. Sounds like he diffused the situation the best he could."

Graham didn't laugh in return. "Yes, he did. But he was concerned with a parting comment one of the militants made."

"And what was that?"

"Well, according to Milo, there were a few more over-the-shoulder remarks tossed back and forth. One of the militants shouted back that if they were armed, like the squadron, they wouldn't have anything to worry about."

Hagen sat forward on the sofa. "So you're saying that the militants want to arm themselves?"

Graham shrugged. "Maybe, if they could. Or it was just more frustration coming out. I don't know. How secure is your armory?"

"Secure enough."

"I would make sure," Graham insisted.

"You're not suggesting that someone would consider taking a run at the base?"

"Probably not." Graham's tone was uncertain. "But I thought you should know. Like you said, scared people do *stupid* things."

"I wouldn't worry about it, Pastor," Hagen said, "but we can step up our watches, just in case." He paused, looking past Graham's shoulder at nothing in particular. "To tell you the truth, I wish we had enough arms for the entire colony. If we ever were attacked, these people have a right to defend themselves."

Graham looked down. "Ordinarily, I would agree with you. But right now, with the state of mind people are in, we're just one bad decision away from panic, chaos."

Hagen shifted in his seat, his internal clock telling him that it was about time to leave. "So, besides making sure the base is secure, what else would you like me to do? We're a little light on personnel at the moment— we can't exactly post an armed officer on every street corner."

"I suppose not. And I don't think that would have quite the calming effect we're looking for, anyway."

Hagen allowed himself a sly smile. "I could send Seltrice down to patrol the streets—let her administer a little law and order. She'd straighten out our friend Jaq real fast."

Graham smiled back sadly. "Or maybe she'd end up agreeing with him."

Hagen felt a ring of truth in his words but let the comment pass.

"No," Graham continued, "I mostly just wanted to brief you on the situation. With Dex, uh, temporarily out of the picture, you need to have a handle on what's going on down here." He met Hagen's eyes. "God has prepared you for this position, Hagen. He will give you the wisdom to lead the squadron, to lead us, through this mess."

"And, hopefully, give us the ability to get Dex back," Hagen said softly.

Nathan settled back once more in his chair. "And speaking of Dex, that's one more reason I called you down here. He and I had a custom, especially before big missions or decisions. And I'd like to continue that custom with you, Commander—now and, if you'd like, even after Dex returns."

"And that is?"

"I'd like to pray with you."

Hagen affirmed the request and gratefully bowed his head, the problems of the day, which moments ago had felt so overwhelming, slowly losing their grip as the two of them quietly spoke and waited and listened.

Chapter 9

Duncann Obervell didn't really like his job, but it paid the bills—barely. The desk clerk at the Happy Guesthouse wasn't at all interested in the comings and goings of its inhabitants. As long as they paid their rent, even sporadically, and didn't cause him any trouble, he was content to collect his pay, spend it all on sims and enough meager rations to stave off starvation, and other than that, mind his own business. The best days and nights behind the desk were the quiet ones—no screaming from the rooms, no disgusting messes to swab in the hallways, and above all, no bothersome interruptions from Port Henri Enforcement or anyone else holding an undue curiosity about one of the residents.

Looking up from behind the front desk, he could see that it wasn't going to be one of those good days. The man walking through the door clearly wasn't interested in a room. He was well dressed and carried himself with an air of authority that informed Duncann he was there on business—official or not—that involved one of the guests.

"Pardon my interruption, young man, but perhaps you can help me."

Something about the visitor, whether it was the tone of his voice, his appearance—tall, completely bald, nearly colorless eyes—or the fact that his polite tone nevertheless carried the weight of a command, set Duncann on the defensive.

"Uh...I don't know," he stammered. "I'm just a...I mean, I don't really...That is, what do you need?"

The man chuckled softly, conveying no warmth. "I'm looking for some friends of mine—three of them, traveling together. I have reason to believe that they might be staying here."

One of the primary rules of the Happy Guesthouse—pretty much the only one Duncann's employer cared about—was that guest data was to be safeguarded zealously. Unless there was a warrant involved, Duncann's orders were clear—do not divulge information about anyone, for any reason. He attempted to make that point.

"Well, sir, do you have documentation, forms, anything like that?"

The man smiled. "Oh, come now"—he glanced down at the worn metal ID plate resting on the desk—"Duncann, is it? I don't think that will be necessary." He looked up again, raising the bald ridge of his forehead, widening his eyes and looking directly into Duncann's. "As I said, they are old friends."

An uncomfortable sensation began to build in Duncann. He was not accustomed to feeling any kind of dread—he usually did not care enough, about anything, to feel fear. But now, at the casual mention of his name and the sight of those ashen eyes staring into his, he felt off balance—a churning beginning in his gut and radiating out, causing his knees to feel wobbly.

He considered demanding to see a badge or asking the gentleman to leave but instead found himself blurting out, "Okay, uh…so what are their names?"

The man tapped the desktop with meticulously groomed fingernails. "Webb. Bethinee and Davis Webb."

When Duncann heard the names, his stomach constricted. He didn't recognize either of them. Despite the Guesthouse's rules, all he wanted to do now was tell this stranger whatever he wanted to know, find the guests he was looking for, and just get him out of there. But he couldn't. He had to tell him the truth.

"I…I'm sorry. I've never heard of them."

"A pity," the man sighed. "But they would have been traveling with another friend, and they may have registered under his name." He paused, apparently searching his memory. It seemed to Duncann that if he knew him so well, the name would have come much more easily, but he was far past daring to point that out.

"Xander Glavos?" the man continued.

Duncann's fear accelerated into panic. Why couldn't this guy give him a name, *any* name, that he recognized? He could say *sure*, point him to the correct room, and be done with it.

"No. Sorry." He checked his guest display just to be sure. "No one by that name either."

The man appeared to consider. "Well, he *is* a performer, so he goes by many stage names. Nikky Weis, perhaps?" He leaned in, causing Duncann to shudder involuntarily.

"No." The thermo-pocket Duncann had wolfed down at lunch began to turn flips in his bowels. "No one by that name either. You've got to believe me!"

"Calm yourself, Duncann. Calm yourself." The stranger's tone was soothing, but his expression was not. "I believe you. He may have used another of his pseudonyms. Perhaps if I were to describe him to you."

Duncann clung to the idea like a life buoy. "Yeah, yeah. That might help."

"He is very easy to spot. A short man, middle aged. Thin, balding, and oh…" He locked eyes with Duncann again. "He is missing his left hand."

Duncann had to steady himself against the desk to keep from falling over from the sense of sudden relief. "Oh! *That* guy! Yes! He checked in about two weeks ago under the name of…Sanders, I think it was."

"Yes." The man brightened. "Sanders. That's one of his monikers. Tell me, which room is he in?"

Duncann let out a deep breath. "Let me check for you." He consulted his display, suddenly sucking the breath back in. There was Sanders's name, plain enough, alongside all the other guests. But the room numbers were all changing right before his eyes.

"I—I don't believe it. This can't be happening."

For the first time, there was a distinct edge to the stranger's voice. "What is it?"

"The room numbers. They're all messed up! It's some kind of glitch." Sweat that had been beading on his forehead now ran together, forming tiny rivulets that ran into his eyes, stinging them and making the display that much harder to read. "I'm sorry! I've never seen this happen before." He managed to swipe the display to back view, allowing his visitor to see it for himself. "See! You've got to believe me! Please?"

Duncann felt like the thermo-pocket was about to erupt completely out of his abdomen and into his trousers. The man stared at the screen, scowling for a moment, then his expression turned. He nodded, with what Duncann thought was almost a grudging respect.

"Fear not, Duncann. These little glitches happen. Tell me, do you have a security system?"

*   *   *

"I'm keeping it light. We might have to move pretty fast." Jani stuffed another dermo-patch into a satchel. She had already gathered up the most essential supplies out of the mess strewn about the room. A hydration pack was still sitting, half-full, on a chair in the corner—important, but cumbersome to lug around. In the other corner, hunched over a small display and feverishly inputting commands, was Nikky Weis—not nearly as important, to Jani's thinking, as the hydro-pack, and much more cumbersome, but she imagined that they would have to drag him along as well.

"Move pretty fast?" Dex closed up his own bag. "Have you taken a good look at me?"

She had. From the long red scar on his neck to the slow, deliberate movements he was making just to pack a simple rucksack, it was clear that something had messed him up severely.

"You'll be fine," she said, not entirely believing it.

Dex shook his head slowly. "You shouldn't have come back for me. You're in danger now—you and anyone else involved in this."

She checked her chrono. "Speaking of which, we have a rendezvous to keep, so a little more hustle here, please?"

"You're not hearing me, Lieutenant."

She turned to face him. "I am hearing you. I'm just not listening. I came back for you, all right? I *had* to come back." She fussed with the buckle on her bag, tugging at it with more force than required. "You know I had to come back. Tell me you wouldn't have done the same."

He locked eyes with her. "I just wish..." he faltered. "I mean, if anything were to happen to you...because of me."

"Nothing's going to happen. We've got this." She moved toward the door. "We do have a plan, you know."

"About that." Dex followed her. "You've been pretty stingy with the details. So far, I've got Hagen picking us up at point Charlie. Then what?"

"Then, we will see." The door slid open, just a crack, allowing Jani to peer out. "I can tell you more on the way, but right now, we have to move."

"She's right."

They both turned as Nikky closed down the display he had been working on. His face had paled considerably.

"We should go."

61

"Why?" Jani asked warily. "What's going on?"

Nikky rubbed the stub of his left wrist. "I…I'm not sure…"

"Not helpful. Are we in danger? Do you know something you're not telling us?"

Nikky struggled to come up with a response.

"Hey!" Jani demanded. "Talk to us!"

"It's okay, Lieutenant," Dex said, studying Nikky's troubled expression. "You said yourself we're on a deadline. Let's get going."

Jani seemed unsatisfied but opened the door regardless. The trio made their way into the hall and began moving toward the front office. They made it only a few meters, however, when Nikky stopped, beads of sweat visible on his forehead.

Jani gave him a nudge. "Come on. Let's move."

Nikky just stood there, his eyes wide and his mouth moving without saying anything.

"What's the matter with you?" she hissed. "Move!"

"Not…not that way," Nikky stammered. "We can't go that way."

Jani was about to object, but Dex stopped her with a shake of his head. He reached up, absently feeling the scar on his neck. "He's right. We should find another way out of here." Jani gave him an odd look, and he tried to pass off his own irrational sense of foreboding as ordinary caution. "The main entrance is too exposed—too many eyes. Nikky, is there a back exit?"

He didn't respond.

"Hey, zombie—wake up!" Jani whispered harshly. "He asked you a question."

Nikky twitched, perspiration flinging off his forehead, a bit of it landing on Dex's cheek.

"Uh, yeah," he said. "Behind us, down the hall to the right. There should be a back door that leads to the alley."

"Is it locked?"

Nikky shook his head. "I don't think so." His voice gained confidence. "But it likely has integrated panic hardware installed. I can get us around that."

Dex frowned, peering down the hallway in the direction they had been heading, one turn from the Guesthouse's front desk. "Yeah," he said. "Let's try that."

They crept back along the hall, past the room they had just vacated. As they approached the intersection of hallways, they were startled by the sudden blaring of the building's fire alarm, the antiquated system still employing an eardrum-piercing klaxon.

All around them, doors started to open as various residents stumbled out of their rooms, some still shaking off the aftereffects of the previous night's ingestions, others just trying to recover some sleep after a long shift in the warehouse or loading bay.

Nikky was about to follow a handful of guests shuffling toward the rear exit when Dex and Jani stopped him, the two of them exchanging a look.

"I'll check it out," she said, struggling to be heard over the noise of the alarm. She fell in line behind a young stimmed-out couple, then slowed, sliding up cautiously to the intersection. She peered around the corner and quickly pulled back, cursing softly to herself.

"What is it?" Dex asked when she returned.

"Scanner. Over the back door."

"Options?" Dex asked, looking back down the hall at the last bunch of stragglers exiting toward the main entrance. While they had no concrete evidence of a pursuer, he couldn't shake Nikky's haunted expression from moments ago—or the feeling in his own gut. He kept expecting to see an M-2 suddenly appear at the end of the hallway.

"I can take care of the scanner," Nikky said. "I'll just use my emulator to splice in a false image." Seeing Jani's dubious look, he added. "I've done this sort of thing once or twice before."

"No good," Dex decided. "If someone's trying to flush us out, they'll be waiting at the back door anyway. You know this building better than we do. Is there anywhere else we can go?"

Nikky considered. "Yeah, there is. But you're not going to like it." He pulled them down the hallway back toward the main entrance. "C'mon, this way."

They stopped at a grimy-looking door with a peeling decal.

"Basement," Nikky said, working the access code on the door's locking mechanism. "And a utility access to the building across the street—it might get a little tight though."

"How could you possibly know that?" Jani asked incredulously.

"Municipal plans. You don't study the blueprints when you stay somewhere? That's pretty irresponsible of you."

"Listen, you little—"

"Concentrate, people," Dex scolded. The building had emptied out. If the alarm had been an attempt to flush them out, whoever or whatever had triggered it would now be changing plans.

With a satisfied click of his tongue, Nikky entered a final sequence, and the door slid open. They were immediately met with a dank, stale odor wafting up from the stairs beyond. It was apparent that no one at the Happy Guesthouse had ventured downstairs for quite some time.

The door shut, dampening to a degree the noise from the fire alarm but also closing them off in a foul darkness, the illumination panels in the tunnel access apparently not functioning.

"I'm on it." Nikky set down his carrier bag and began rummaging through it. "Hold this a moment," he said, handing something to Jani.

"Ugh, what is it?" Jani said. The object didn't feel like a typical piece of equipment.

"Just be careful," Nikky insisted. He dug around some more and pulled out a small handheld beacon, illuminating the space around them.

"Auuugh!" Jani jumped back, her hands separating, letting the roundish green object drop between them. Dex barely had time to reach down and catch the small turtle.

"Hey! I said be careful!" Nikky handed the beacon to Dex and cradled his pet in return.

Jani narrowed her eyes. "Why. Did you bring. A turtle?"

"It's Louise," Nikky stated as though that were an explanation. "Now hold on." He gently tucked the turtle back into his carrier bag and then entered a code on the inside panel of the door. "There." He clicked his tongue again, a trait that Dex had unfortunately come to anticipate. "They won't be following us anytime soon."

"Uh, guys?" Jani sounded uncharacteristically nervous. "Is it just me or is something moving around down there."

Dex adjusted the setting on his beacon, illuminating a two-meter space at the base of the stairs. A scurrying mass of grayish black shapes confirmed his suspicion.

"Rats," he said, leaning against the stairwell. "Looks like there were a few more guests in the Guesthouse."

"Don't worry," Nikky said, sliding the carrier bag over his shoulder. "They won't hurt us." He trotted down the stairs into the midst of the horde—the rats giving him a wide berth.

Jani watched him descend. "Kindred spirits."

"Lieutenant…"

The utility passage, full of conduits, lav pipes, and fibroc cables, had not been designed for human traffic. The route proved to be excruciating for Dex, with several pinch points necessitating a full belly crawl, forcing him to stretch painfully forward to grasp a clamp or crack in the floor and pull himself under the latest obstruction. If not for his compromised physical condition, he felt he could have managed with little difficulty— Nikky and Jani seemed to be having far less trouble. But as it was, his body was screaming at him. By the time they cleared the passage, he felt like he needed to take an extended break—though he wouldn't have dreamed of actually asking for one.

At least the furry residents of the sub-levels had left them alone. Once or twice, they had spotted movement on the outskirts of their beacon's illumination and heard the click of claws scrambling over the damp floor, but other than one confused rodent running directly across Jani's legs, the animals had made themselves scarce.

Nikky rose to his feet and jimmied the hatch that, presumably, led into the basement of the building across the street from the Guesthouse. Jani brushed a glop of yellowish slime from the shoulder of her tunic and stepped through the hatch first.

"Clear," she called back.

Dex and Nikky followed her through the hatch and up a small flight of stairs that led to a door very similar in appearance to the one in the Guesthouse. "Ready?" she asked.

With Dex's nod, Jani pushed the door open a crack, peered out, and pulled quietly back.

"Out of the frying pan," she said. "Have a look."

Any hope Dex had held that they would come out in an abandoned warehouse or other deserted building was dashed as he looked through the crack, taking in the busy slop house kitchen on the other side. Battered prep tables, covered with ingredients and half-prepared entrees, lined both sides of the narrow walkway beyond the door, leading to a row of glowing IR ovens and range tops. More importantly, it seemed that every inch of workspace was occupied by a worker—sweating, cursing, smoking cooks and scullery hands, all bustling around, trying to keep up, slinging the local version of hash for the Grenouille district's motley dinner crowd.

"So much for a quiet exit," Dex murmured. Straightening his shoulders, he forced his aching back upright, standing to his full height and pushing the door open. "Follow my lead."

They had jostled their way halfway down the narrow aisle when a voice shouted.

"Hey! Hey, you three! What were you doing down there?"

The man bustled up to them, wiping one of his hands on a stained apron. The menacing expression on his face was aided all the more by the sharp meat cleaver in his other hand.

Dex reached into his tunic and pulled out an ID chip. "Decker. Port Authority Health Enforcement." His voice did not carry nearly the strength that he had intended. He pulled the chip back and tucked it away before the man could as much as peek at it. "Where is the owner?"

The man scowled. "I *am* the owner. The name's Wojcik. What did you say your name was?"

"Decker," Dex repeated, still trying to catch his breath. "Environmental Health."

"Uh huh." Wojcik's meaty fingers clenched and unclenched on the cleaver handle. "And what happened to Jojo?"

"Vacation," Jani said. "Decker here is taking over this week." She stepped forward. "And I'm training him," she added.

Dex stiffened ever-so-slightly, almost certain he could see a trace of a smile on her lips.

"Is that right?" Wojcik did not seem to be impressed. "Well, down here, Jojo and me have an understanding. And part of that understanding is that he doesn't go poking around here uninvited, you know?"

Jani tilted her head back. "Did you know that you have rats down there, mister?"

"Big rats," Dex agreed.

"Thousands of them," Nikky chirped.

"Callahan," Jani ordered. "You got your pad with you?"

"Right here, boss." Nikky patted his satchel.

"Good. You're going to need it. Now, Mr. Buoystick, is it?"

"Wojcik."

"Yeah, we're going to have a long list here, Buoystick." Jani abruptly strode away toward the front of the kitchen. "Take over, Decker. This is your bust."

Finally finding his breath, Dex nudged Nikky, who began to rummage around in his bag.

"Let's see," Dex said. "We have rodent control, that's a 502-1. No hair restraints, especially in the shoulders"—he pointed at a particularly shaggy tank-topped cook—"that's a 627-b, and oh—" Dex nudged a trash can to the side with the toe of his boot, sending a flurry of roaches flitting under the table. "Pestilence, that's a tier-three violation."

Wojcik set the cleaver on the table. "Now hold on just a minute. Didn't I say that Jojo and I had an *understanding*? Now, really, there's no reason we can't figure out something as well, right?"

Dex cocked his head to one side. "You're not saying what I think you're saying, are you?"

Nikky looked up from his bag. "Sounds to me like he's trying to offer some excuses—or offer something anyway."

"No, no excuses..." The man was beginning to stammer. "When...when did you say Jojo is coming back?"

"Decker!" Jani had returned from a small round window opening to the main dining area. "How many times do I have to tell you? We don't have time for this! This man has *customers* coming in right now that need attention." She gave a quick nod toward the dining room door. Dex understood.

"Yeah, yeah. You need to listen to your boss. I got customers. We can always talk about this later, right? Same as Jojo?" He looked pleadingly at Jani. "You know, same deal for everybody."

"All right," Jani said. "We're going to let you off this time with a warning." She gave him a knowing smile. "Just like Jojo."

Dex stepped in. "I don't suppose you really want us parading through your front room with a pad full of citations in hand, do you? You got a back door out of this place?"

"Yeah. It's right back here. Leads to the alley. You can slip out that way, real quiet like." Wojcik led them toward the back of the kitchen and pointed to a rusted door on the far side of the stock room. "It's not locked. No one will see you." He breathed a sigh. "Let me tell you folks, I appreciate this."

"Don't mention it," Jani said. "And Wojcik"—she waved a thumb in the direction of the hairy-shouldered cook—"get a shirt on that guy."

*   *   *

"That will be enough." Graves waved his hand at the desk clerk, never taking his eyes off the security display. Behind him, Duncann silenced the fire alarm.

"Anything?" Duncann asked hopefully.

Graves straightened up, stretching out his back. "Nothing, I'm afraid. Are you certain the back door is the only other way out of this building?"

"Yes, sir. All the windows are fixed in place." He tapped the office's outside window. "It's a security thing."

Graves gazed through the grimy acrylic. "Indeed." He cocked his head minutely to one side. "And no other accesses? Are you sure you are being completely honest with me?"

"Yes, absolutely!" Duncann insisted. "I wouldn't lie to you!"

Graves continued to stare out the window, fixated on the restaurant building across the street.

"No, Duncann, I do not believe you would," he said finally. "At least, not intentionally." He turned toward the entrance. "Thank you for your time."

He walked unhurriedly out of the Guesthouse and toward the restaurant. The moment the door closed, Duncann rushed into the lav, clutching his stomach and shaking uncontrollably.

Chapter 10

Darik felt the JenKore luxury transport *Vahati* touch down gently on the surface of Silvanus. Flicking off his workstation, he made a quick survey of the gear he had hastily gathered prior to the journey.

The pile of assorted hunting equipment and clothing looked ridiculously new, some of the pieces still bearing the NFC inserts identifying the shop where Darik had purchased them—an outfitter he had visited on the advice of his friend Eliot Liddle.

"Rik's, on Hastings," Eliot had assured him. "They've got everything you need. But don't pay full retail—it's robbery. No, make sure you talk to Rik directly. And tell that leathery old bastard I'm the one who sent you—he owes me one." Eliot had leaned back, clearly impressed by the quality of his recommendation.

Darik hadn't been convinced. "So, you're telling me that a store-front business actually sells hunting gear? How can they get away with that?"

Eliot took another bite of his steak. Darik's half-eaten faux-chicken sandwich continued to cool on his plate. "They never say the stuff is for actual hunting. It's all marketed toward the virtual gaming crowd. They get all dressed up and play deerstalker and whatnot. No real animals, no live shooting, nothing gets hurt—therefore, legal. I hear the duck hunt sim is a blast—we should try it sometime."

"Sure. But I need real gear for my trip."

"That's the thing—Rik's stuff is real, and it's all top-end. He sells it for virtual purposes, but if someone ends up using it otherwise, that's not his concern, the way he sees it."

Darik picked at a piece of lettuce on the side of his plate. "I don't know. Are you sure about this?"

Eliot feigned offense, his hands palms-up in front of him. "C'mon, have I ever let you down before?"

"Too many times to count."

"What? Name one."

"Well, there was—"

"Doesn't matter. Trust me on this one. I know what I'm talking about. Listen—marketing is everything, and right now, you need to be marketing yourself. You're heading out on some high-level, testosterone-filled, off-world excursion with Jenkins and his wealthy friends, right?"

"Pretty much," Darik said, feeling both excited and anxious as he considered the prospect.

"Then go and see Rik." Eliot finished his last bite and reached for Darik's sandwich. "If you're going to go play with the big boys, you have to look the part. You don't want to show up looking like an idiot."

Now, slipping on the fire-red hunting vest, complete with an absurd number of utility pockets and dangling attachments whose function he couldn't even begin to ascertain, Darik felt exactly like an idiot. The neon cap, emblazoned with a bullseye in front, completed the effect. Grabbing a canvas bag, filled with more crap that Rik had assured him he needed, Darik left his cabin. He was thankful that the invitation hadn't required him to purchase a firearm. Kirrone Jenkins had been infuriatingly light on the details of this trip but had at least bothered to let him know that all weaponry and ammunition would be provided on-site. Darik would have liked to have asked Jenkins for more information about the trip, to prepare for his meet-and-greet with the important business associate who had invited them, but during their only meeting en route to Silvanus, the CEO had other priorities to discuss.

"Bellona, as disastrous as it was, cannot be compared to this newest threat," Jenkins had said. "I have reason to believe that the M-2/A initiative has been infiltrated. Internal forensics are pointing to a covert gathering of information, the imprint signature of which has all the earmarks of a Coalition agent."

Darik tried to piece it together. "And you think this agent tipped the UCN about the Bellona station?"

Jenkins sighed, his impatience evident in his tone. "You are not thinking, Mr. Mason. It seems highly unlikely that the Coalition government would utilize their most wanted fugitives for a sensitive military action. No, I'm afraid that your associate, Mr. Weis, was behind the Bellona leak. Your *friend* tipped the Zealots off directly. But rest assured, Mr. Weis will be of no further concern to us."

70

Darik fought to keep his face expressionless. A memory rushed unbidden into his mind—standing in the chilly cargo bay of the *Golden Crow*, Nikky holding up a bloodied, bandaged stump where his left hand should have been. Hadn't he been punished enough already? Now Jenkins was implying that he'd had Nikky killed. Darik felt a rush of guilt—they would've never known about Nikky's involvement if he hadn't let his name slip in front of Jenkins. He could only hope that Nikky's death had been quick and painless—but he highly doubted it, especially if Graves was once again involved.

Keeping his eyes fixed straight ahead, Darik nodded impassively. In delivering the troubling news, Jenkins's word choice had been deliberate, referring to Nikky as his "associate" and "friend." As ever, Jenkins was trying to throw him off balance—for what purpose, Darik couldn't guess. Maybe he didn't need a reason. Regardless, Darik was determined to remain strictly professional, to not give Jenkins the satisfaction of knowing he was getting under his skin.

Jenkins turned and looked out at the ether through the cabin's viewport. "But with that leak sealed, a newer, potentially more dangerous situation has surfaced. We've discovered that data—critical data concerning our M-2/A operations—has been incrementally extracted over the last several weeks. Fortunately, all evidence indicates that this agent is still in the fact-gathering phase. Given our security protocols, tech screens, body scans—I don't need to list them all for you—it will be difficult and time consuming for him to permanently steal and deliver any solid evidence as to our activities."

Setting aside his thoughts about Nikky, Darik tried to do his job, to focus on the question before him.

"Difficult," he said, "but not impossible."

"Of course it's not impossible," Jenkins said. "Your Mr. Weis was able to do it right under your nose, wasn't he?"

Again with "my" Mr. Weis. Whoever this Coalition agent was, Darik was confident of one thing—he was no Nikky Weis.

Jenkins continued. "This is your division, Mr. Mason. My patience for failure has worn thin. I have forwarded the information we have on the infiltration to your workstation in Compton. When we return, you are to investigate, locate the spy, and eliminate the threat."

Darik balked at the implication. "Eliminate? Eliminate a Coalition agent?"

"Do I need to educate you as to the exact implications of the Coalition government discovering the full measure of our M-2/A initiative? We have sympathizers, friends in positions of power who are not unfriendly to our objectives—but not enough, not yet. If exposed at this time, this information would be devastating—to *everyone* involved."

The point was clear to Darik. Any delusions he once held about the legality of his actions had disappeared while watching the M-2 perform its gruesome work on Bellona. No, he was just as culpable as Jenkins, Graves, Haman, or anyone else. And the current penalty for their actions under Coalition law was not open to interpretation. Then he remembered the Zealot captain, Dex D'Felco, and his own momentary weakness in saving his life. When he considered everything D'Felco—the Christian, the terrorist—stood for, he realized that he could not make that mistake again. Blatantly illegal or not, Darik was on the right side. Religious fanatics had proven time and again to be too volatile, too dangerous—their ignorance and blind devotion invariably led to oppression and violence, threatening the universal peace that the Coalition had worked so hard to maintain. Jenkins was right—the agent would have to be found. Found, and dealt with.

He pictured the M-2/A's blade—yes, the methods were brutal, but they were necessary. As he curled his fingers around his seat's armrest, he imagined himself gripping the Travarian knife—the artifact secreted away back at his flat in Compton, an instrument, he had come to learn, of justice. "I'll take care of it," he said.

"See to it that you do," Jenkins had replied. Shortly after, without another word regarding the details of their current trip, the CEO had disappeared into his suite, and Darik had not seen him since.

Until now. With the *Vahati* safely settled on the surface of Silvanus, Darik made his way toward the front of the ship, stopping once to disentangle himself as one of the bothersome utility straps protruding from his bright red vest snagged on a wall-mounted bio-sensor. Jenkins was waiting for him near the exit ramp, and Darik immediately had the sinking realization that, as he should have suspected, his choice of attire was entirely inappropriate. There Jenkins stood, thin and tall, in full camouflage. The twig and leaf motif of his tailored pants and jacket were of a somewhat different hue than what might be typical on Earth, corresponding, no doubt, to Silvanian flora. Jenkins looked Darik up and down, taking in his appearance with what seemed like a mixture of amusement and scorn.

"Mr. Mason, I assume you are prepared for our activity today?"

Why the hell didn't he tell me? I'm really getting sick of these head games.

"Yes, sir," Darik said. He straightened his shoulders and walked down the ramp. A tall heavily built but muscular middle-aged man waited at the bottom. He was wearing camo nearly identical to Jenkins's, with the exception that it appeared slightly more field-worn. He greeted Darik with a nod.

"Young man, the first thing you're going to want to do is lose that vest and cap."

Darik's face burned with embarrassment. He considered turning around and heading right back up the ramp and back to his quarters to try to locate something less garish to wear, but Jenkins followed so closely behind him that Darik was forced to continue forward—ridiculous attire and all. Jenkins was suddenly all smiles. "Benjamin Whitaker, I'd like to introduce you to Darik Mason, vice president in charge of the special M-2/A division. Darik, this is Benjamin Whitaker, CEO of Whitaker Industrial."

Darik shook Whitaker's proffered hand. The grip was warm and firm. He had, of course, heard of Benjamin Whitaker. While not as massive as JenKore, Whitaker Industrial was a big player in both military and civilian manufacturing and supply. Their clients included the Aurora Company, Prackard Gunn, and the United Coalition government. Darik recalled their involvement in JenKore products as well, mostly in targeting and sensor components for the GN-55 and SoC processors for their signature Echo Monitoring System. As far as he knew, Whitaker Industrial provided only a small number of component parts used in M-2 production, but clearly Jenkins was hoping to change that arrangement. He wished, for the hundredth time, that Jenkins would have bothered to fill him in on the details of this meeting, but his boss could be maddeningly tight-lipped to the point of absurdity.

"It's a pleasure to meet you, Mr. Whitaker. Thank you for inviting me to attend." Darik glanced down self-consciously at his fire-red vest. "Uh, I'm sorry about the bright colors."

Jenkins chuckled. "I'm afraid our Mr. Mason is unaccustomed to actual hunting. He seems to have gained most of his experience from play facilities."

Darik's face reddened further, but Whitaker brushed the comment aside. "Don't worry. I have extra gear in my shuttle. You can change on the way. I take it you haven't hunted before?"

Darik shook his head. "No, sir. Never had the opportunity, I guess."

"Well, I'm not surprised. With the morons running Terran eco-enforcement these days, you can't even order a real ham sandwich at a deli. There's no way you'd ever be allowed to shoot something. *Cruel and unusual*, they say." Whitaker snorted. "To me, it's cruel and unusual to deprive us of our right to a great meal."

Whitaker indicated the surrounding countryside with a sweep of his large hand. "That's why I bought this preserve. No enforcement twerps out here—just unspoiled country and all the indigenous wildlife you need for a good expedition. What do you think?"

For the first time, Darik surveyed the vista around him. The *Vahati* had landed on a high plateau. In every direction, lush valleys were filled with verdigris-hued vegetation, the large grassy expanses giving way to thick, gnarled forests that stretched up mountainsides in the distance. Dominating the far horizon, the mountains displayed bluish-yellow tinged snow caps, due, no doubt, to the unique but breathable oxygen and phosphorus atmosphere.

Darik whistled appreciatively. "Yes, sir. It's breathtaking."

Whitaker snorted and spat on the ground. "And it was almost wasted, at that. A few years back, right before I bought it, one of those damn church groups had their eye on it—wanted to colonize the whole thing. Can you imagine that?"

Darik raised his eyebrows. "What happened?"

"Well, I pulled a few strings in the Coalition Council, called in a couple favors," Whitaker said. "In the end, I just outbid them. They ended up choosing some slimy mud hole instead—good enough for them."

Darik stifled back a laugh. "It certainly is beautiful."

"Well, you haven't seen anything yet. Hop aboard, and we'll head into the field."

"Yes, lead on, Benjamin," Jenkins said. Whitaker boarded his shuttle, with Darik following eagerly. Jenkins trailed a few paces behind them, his face returning to a mask of impassivity.

The trip to the hunting field was a short one. Darik had little time to gaze out at the deep river-bottomed chasms or to take in the curious plant and animal life as the shuttle descended into the western valley. Once on board, he had gratefully accepted Whitaker's offer of a change in clothes. Somewhat uncomfortable with the close quarters in the passenger compartment, he disrobed and slipped into the appropriate camo as quickly as he could, barely sparing a glance out the starboard window despite the wonders that flew by just outside. On one of his few looks, he did catch a glimpse of a fleet, six-legged, orange-pelted creature scurrying into the woods to the right of the rough path.

"An orgullam." Jenkins noted Darik's look of curiosity. "We won't be hunting them today. Perhaps that is for the best, given your lack of experience. You might find them a tad too *aggressive* for your taste." With his trousers half pulled on, Darik turned his attention back to a particularly stubborn buckle that was preventing him from pulling them the remainder of the way up. "In fact," Jenkins continued, "you may want to stay close to me when we begin—for your own safety."

Darik wanted to fire back that he could take care of himself, but he realized that at the moment, he couldn't even take care of his own pants. With a final tug, the buckle loosened. Pushing himself a few centimeters off the short bench, he pulled the camo bottoms all the way up and slipped into a matching jacket just as the shuttle came to a halt.

"Here we are, men." Whitaker stood, ducking in the low-ceilinged cabin. "Welcome to Wheelridge Valley, home of the best fazant hunting anywhere." Whitaker hit a command, opening the rear hatch. A welcome aroma of fresh vibrant plant life rushed in, filling Darik's nostrils and chasing away the tight, claustrophobic atmosphere of the shuttle. Whitaker moved to the side and opened a storage compartment.

"Here are your firearms," he said, removing a trio of meter-long, rifle-shaped weapons. "Kirrone, I know that you are familiar with these."

"Indeed." Jenkins hefted the gun in his hands. "It feels good to hold one again." He popped the weapon up to his shoulder, sighting down the long barrel with practiced efficiency.

Whitaker handed an identical piece to Darik. "Now, I don't suppose you've ever handled a model like this before, am I right?"

Darik studied the item in his hands. The long metallic barrel was almost two centimeters in diameter and hollow all the way back to the enclosed firing mechanism and trigger assembly. Behind that, the dull gray metal gave way to a dark wooden stock. A shoulder pad at the end of the stock indicated that the weapon delivered a considerable amount of recoil. Beneath the firing chamber was an elongated spring-loaded opening, undoubtedly for loading cartridges, stun or kill, Darik imagined. What he couldn't discern was where the energy source was located. It was unlike any firearm he had ever seen. Darik turned the gun one more rotation, gave up, and looked back at Whitaker.

"No, I haven't. To be honest, I couldn't even tell you how it fires."

Whitaker smiled. "It's called a shotgun, son. Twelve-gauge, to be precise. All the power is in the cartridges." He handed Darik a small satchel. Inside jostled about two dozen finger-length cylinders. The red plastic tubes were capped at one end with a copper metal casing.

"Gunpowder," Whitaker continued, tapping one of the cartridges on the metal end. "It's all packed in there, and ignited, it can pack quite a wallop."

Darik felt the heft of the gun in his hands with a new appreciation.

"An enlightening history lesson," Jenkins said, his eyebrows arched, "but perhaps it's time to proceed with the hunt?"

"Absolutely, Kirrone, by all means." Whitaker led the way down the ramp. Intending to follow, Darik was arrested by Jenkins's cold hand on his shoulder.

"Remember," he hissed into Darik's ear, "you are not here on a sightseeing tour. That man has access to technology and equipment that could greatly enhance our, *your*, efforts in the next phase of M-2 deployment—deployment, I might add, that has been greatly hindered by your utter failure on Bellona. I know that Whitaker is sympathetic to our mission—he has no more love for the Christian Zealots than you or I."

At the word *Christian*, rasped so forcefully in his ear, Darik felt a tangible wave of anger flow through his body—a sensation he hadn't experienced so strongly since that night in Jenkins's office, the night of his promotion. Long-buried memories and emotions welled up within him. Repressed feelings of betrayal, loss, and abandonment jostled for position in his psyche. A younger version of himself cried out from a decade ago, screaming for justice—and vengeance. He grasped the door frame with his left hand, suddenly feeling dizzy and unsure of his balance.

Jenkins either didn't notice Darik's discomfort or didn't care. He continued. "I also know that Whitaker is quite anxious to expand his involvement with us. What he does not know, cannot know, is how much you need what he has to offer. Nor can he become aware of the recent security breach—the one you will soon be rectifying." Jenkins pulled Darik even closer. "Do you think you can manage to keep that in mind today?"

The feeling of Jenkins's heated breath on his face made Darik recoil. Irritation and rage boiled in his gut, finally finding a target in the man standing so oppressively close. His equilibrium returning, he steadied himself and turned to face his boss. Enough was enough.

"That would have been easier," he said, his tone precisely measured, "if you had briefed me on the particulars before we got here."

Jenkins's eyes grew cold. "Are you questioning my judgment?"

Darik felt a tightening in his chest. A cold shiver radiated the length of his spine, any resolve he had felt quickly dissipating in the process.

"No. No, of course not."

Jenkins's hand was still gripping his shoulder. With a purposeful thrust, he guided Darik down the ramp. "Then let us proceed," he said, then raising his voice so Whitaker could hear, added, "and pay attention to what you are doing. I don't think Benjamin or I want to be caught in your line of fire."

*   *   *

"There." Whitaker pointed into the brush between two large trees. He spoke softly out of the side of his mouth, a dark brown whistle protruding from the other side. "Just above the second branch. Do you see it?"

Darik didn't. Three hours into the hunt, and he was feeling worse than ever. Part of his discomfort arose from the fact that he had been chosen to carry the morning's kill. Five fazants, blue-plumaged game birds roughly twice the size of a Terran wild turkey, had been ceremoniously stuffed into the pouch in the back of his hunting jacket. As the greenhorn, he had been informed by Whitaker, it was his responsibility to shoulder the burden, and his back was beginning to ache from the cumbersome load. The rest of his unease was due to the embarrassment that none of the fazants he was carrying were his. Whitaker had bagged three of the elusive fowl; Jenkins had two. Darik had to admit to himself that he stunk at this—an assessment, he realized, that was more than apparent to his companions.

He looked harder. A subtle movement caught his eye. Darik raised the shotgun stock to his shoulder, closing one eye and sighting down the long barrel. He could just make out a small head with an unblinking black eye. He released a breath and tried to keep his hands from shaking.

"Ready," he whispered.

Whitaker sounded the whistle—a high-pitched trill squealing from the narrow tube. Immediately, the fazant took to the air, its ruffed wings creating a rapid staccato as it rose swiftly above the brush line.

Darik raised his barrel, lining up the small sighting bead with the flying bird. He pulled the trigger. His shotgun fired, kicking hard against his shoulder. The fazant continued flying, unhindered. A miss.

Dammit.

An instant later, a second blast roared, right next to his ear. The fazant nearly disintegrated in a ball of flying blue feathers before plummeting to the ground.

Darik turned to see Jenkins ejecting an emptied shell from his own gun. Through the ringing in his ears, he could still easily detect his employer's condescending tone.

"We couldn't very well let another one escape, could we? Now be a good lad and retrieve it." Without another word to Darik, Jenkins turned back to Whitaker. "Now, where were we? I believe we were discussing the component depot system you employ."

Whitaker placed the whistle back in his pocket, retrieving in its place a large half-smoked cigar. "Yes," he said, striking a flint to light it. "Your need for replacement parts is substantial, but we have the network and the infrastructure to get anything you need, anywhere you want, right out to the border of the Frontier Systems, if necessary."

Feeling completely ignored, again, Darik set his jaw and traipsed into the thick brush to search out the dropped fazant. A few yards in, at least partially concealed from his hunting partners, he took a moment to pull down his collar, exposing his right shoulder.

The twelve-gauge had certainly taken its toll. Ugly dark purple bruises revealed where the stock had slammed against his shoulder with each shot. A half-dozen shots with nothing to show for them, other than an increasing ache that he was sure to feel for days. He was well past ready to go home.

Behind him, he could hear Jenkins and Whitaker continuing their conversation. Jenkins had spent the morning outlining the various component needs for the M-2, with Whitaker explaining how and when he could meet those needs, virtually guaranteeing an uninterrupted supply. At one point, early in the hunt, Darik had attempted to join in, clarifying a question about specifications for the M-2's omnisensor. Jenkins had summarily brushed him off and sent him back to the shuttle for hydration units.

Darik had begun to wonder why he was even on this trip. A shifting of the fazants weighing down his jacket pouch reminded him of his primary function.

Just an errand boy. Again.

It seemed that the volume of the conversation behind him was increasing; at least, Whitaker's voice was raised. Although he was unable to make out the words through the heavy brush, it was apparent that the two men had touched on a subject that elicited some passion in the older man. Darik tried to focus on the task he was assigned. Why should he start to get involved now?

He nearly stepped on the downed bird before he saw it. It lay in a crumpled heap, draped over an exposed root, its head and neck lying at an impossible angle in relation to the rest of its body.

They were beautiful birds, the fazants. Up close, Darik could see that the bright blue feathers were, in fact, an astonishing mixture of violet, aquamarine, and sapphire, all blending together in a pleasing array of radiant color. In flight—something Darik had seen for only precious seconds at a time—the fazant was a majestic creature. Now, lying at his feet, the matted plumage caked with blood oozing from dozens of tiny puncture wounds, it was only another object—a prize to be picked up and carried back to his superior.

Ignoring the sharp pain in his back, Darik stooped down and retrieved the fallen bird. Reaching behind himself, he felt around for the opening in his jacket and stuffed the fazant in with its five companions. He could feel the extra weight already pulling at his over-burdened lat muscles as he turned and trudged up the short incline where the conversation had escalated in his absence.

"*Christians?*" Whitaker had his cigar out of his mouth and was waving it emphatically, the hot ash nearly sprinkling Jenkins as it scattered from the end. "*Terrorists* is the more accurate term if you ask me. After what they did in London, Buenos Aries, you name it, well, the hell with all of them."

"So, you can see," Jenkins said, his steely voice sending a chill through Darik, "why it is so critical that we continue our work, our mission, uninterrupted. Surely you understand this."

Darik stumbled unsteadily into the clearing, not sure whether his lack of balance was due to the uneven load of fazants or the nauseous exhaustion he was suddenly feeling. Jenkins noted his return.

"Ah, Darik," Jenkins said. "As I told you, Benjamin, Darik here understands the danger these criminals present better than anyone." Jenkins's pale blue eyes bore into Darik. "His history, his understanding of the atrocities that these Christians commit, is quite *personal*."

Darik's eyes widened. He and Jenkins had never discussed his past—what had happened to his parents. Yet somehow, Jenkins knew. Even in the shock of the moment, Darik realized that he shouldn't have been surprised. Of course Jenkins knew. He knew everything.

Darik looked Whitaker in the eye, a cold hatred replacing any discomfort, any embarrassment, he had felt up to now on this trip.

"Yes," he said. "I understand. I understand that I'm just one small example among far, far too many. They're a threat to everyone in the Coalition. The difference is, JenKore is doing something about it."

Jenkins looked over at him. His reaction to Darik's addition to the conversation, if not outright approving, indicated that he was not entirely displeased.

Whitaker placed a strong hand on Darik's shoulder. "I get it, son. The Christian bastards are dangerous—they're deadly. You've been hurt by them—hell, most of us have been, one way or the other."

He turned to Jenkins. "Kirrone, I've known you for a long time. I invited you on this trip, hoping we could increase our business together. Now that I see more closely what you're trying to accomplish, and what you're up against, I'm absolutely sure that I can help you. We'll work out the details, but Whitaker Industrial is at your disposal."

Jenkins gave his most practiced, professional smile. "Then I believe our business here is concluded." Turning to Darik, he added, "It would seem that we have found an ally in our cause. I will expect you to coordinate all procurement needs for your M-2/A division with Mr. Whitaker. With his assistance, I am confident that your initiative will get back on schedule."

Darik felt cold—cold and exhilarated.

"Yes, I'm sure it will."

"We can start discussing details on the shuttle," Whitaker said. "It's time we headed back. I watch the fazant population in this valley pretty closely, and a half-dozen birds is a pretty healthy bag limit for one day.

We don't kill too many, and we can keep coming out for more." His expression softened. "I'm sorry about your parents, Darik. We'll get the bastards. We'll get them all. We'll make them pay for—"

A sudden staccato drumming erupted from the bush directly in front of them. Darik's gun was up in an instant, its report pounding the ears of his two partners.

Darik walked over, picked up the fallen fazant, and handed it to Whitaker. His voice was flat, emotionless.

"One more dead bird isn't going to make that much difference, is it?"

Chapter 11

The night air had picked up a sharp autumn chill since Dex's last venture out into the Bellona countryside, burning his lungs with each labored breath. While he had endured his share of aches and pains over the last few weeks, he had not fully appreciated the physical toll that ill-fated night had taken on his body until this moment as he struggled to keep pace with Jani on what should have been, for him, a simple cross-country hike. The fact that Nikky was similarly straggling behind, panting and wheezing the entire time, did nothing to soothe Dex's wounded pride.

The landing zone was a hilltop a little over five kilometers from the outskirts of Port Henri. As they'd planned their exfiltration, Dex had vetoed renting a shuttle—one, because a lone vehicle racing across the countryside might attract unwanted attention and two, Dex, despite his injuries, had been confident in his ability to traverse the relatively short distance.

Now, he wished that he had reconsidered. The terrain, rocky and uneven, was much more challenging than he had envisioned, and though the near-full moons of Bellona cast a pale light on the landscape, the shadows of the pre-midnight hour made it difficult to find sure footing. Nikky, absent a hand and not in peak physical condition to begin with, was clearly having problems. And for his part, Dex, with every uncertain step and intermittent pause to catch his breath, was becoming increasingly self-conscious about just how much he was slowing them down.

Jani never outright asked Dex if he needed help, but she was quick to reach back and assist him with any particularly tricky passages of terrain. It was evident from the way she kept glancing at her chrono that she was anxious about arriving on time. The fear wasn't, of course, that Hagen would impatiently wait only a minute or two before ditching them. Rather, the plan was for Hagen, aided by a ghillie generator, to pass off the Raven as a light shipping transport, and the longer he was forced to wait for them, the more likely it was that the ruse would be discovered. Ideally, Hagen would be able to land and dustoff within a thirty-second window. But for that to happen, Dex knew he had to drastically pick up the pace.

"That's it," Jani said, pointing to a hillcrest about 150 meters ahead. The twin moons of Bellona hovered just above, acting almost as a pair of beacons illuminating the extraction point. Dex glanced up higher into the night sky, wondering if he could see the Raven descending, though he knew it was unlikely. Hagen would certainly have the running lights switched off, meaning they would hear the Raven coming well before they would see it.

With the destination in sight, Dex steeled his resolve and willed himself forward, determined to catch up to Jani who had subtly picked up her pace as well. The steep hillside—the sort of incline that earlier in the night would have slowed them to a near halt—did little to impede their progress, the three of them climbing gamely to the crest, trying to recover a few precious seconds after falling so far behind.

Jani was first to reach the top. Even though Dex, with the recent surge of adrenaline, felt capable of hoisting himself over the last little ridge, he found it odd that Jani did not turn around to lend a hand or at least see how he and Nikky were faring. Instead, she was standing eerily still, staring out across the hilltop.

Pulling himself up to his feet next to Jani, Dex was startled to see a figure standing about thirty meters away, his features veiled in shadow, silhouetted under the twin moons.

"Hagen?" Jani whispered to Dex. She sounded as doubtful as he felt.

The figure, though, certainly had a similar build as Hagen, tall and broad around the shoulders. Dex stared intently, trying to make out any distinguishing characteristics. He became distracted, however, by a sudden sharp pain in his right shoulder. Nothing had physically struck him, and yet the sensation was powerful, as though the machine were once again standing in front of him, driving its impaling rod through his flesh.

Nikky shuffled up beside him, clutching his truncated left arm.

"That's…that's not your man," he said, his voice trembling.

Dex's heart was racing. The new yet distressingly familiar pain in his shoulder led him to consider the worst possible scenario—that an M-2 was standing before them. If that were the case, they were already dead. They had only one weapon among the three of them, Jani's sidearm, which Dex knew from firsthand experience would do absolutely nothing to slow down the machine. And even if each of them had been fully armed, Dex still wouldn't have liked their chances. The machine was too fast and strongly shielded. It had taken nothing short of a miracle for Dex to have survived his first face-to-face encounter with an M-2.

The only thing preventing Dex from giving up hope was that the profile didn't quite match. Though he still couldn't see the figure in any sort of detail, everything about the frame was a little off—the waist was thicker, the arms weren't the right shape. Whoever was standing in their way was definitely man, not machine.

The realization only slightly eased Dex's fears. If this person proved to be hostile, Dex knew that they were woefully unprepared. Nicky was useless in a fight, and Dex, in his current condition, was probably worth even less. Jani was more than capable of handling herself, but armed with only a pistol and having to defend both him and Nikky was not an advantageous position for her, especially if they ended up being outgunned. After all, though they saw only one person, who knew how many more might be lurking in the shadows?

He caught Jani's eye. She was tense but ready, her body positioned to spring into action at a moment's notice. Dex noticed, though, that she hadn't yet pulled her sidearm. It was a wise decision—no sense provoking a fight if they could at all avoid it.

He gave Jani a wary look and stepped forward.

"Ninety-one," he called out to the figure. As far as he knew, Jani and Hagen hadn't pre-arranged a special countersign for this mission, so Dex used the squadron's standard challenge. The correct reply was "eleven"—a reference to Psalms 91:11, a verse with special significance for the Angels—though Dex, in this case, had little hope of hearing the correct response.

"Ninety-one…" the figure repeated back, slowly stepping forward.

Jani placed her hand on her sidearm.

"Ninety-one…" he said again, this time with amusement in his voice. "A challenge, I presume, to determine if I am friend or foe. What might the correct response be? Perhaps it's the answer to a question: How many fugitives remain alive in your illegitimate colony? Is that it? Have times really been that tough, Captain D'Felco?"

Dex knew that he should be putting a stop to this immediately. The man clearly had ill intentions, and Dex certainly didn't like being toyed

84

with. He should have interrupted the man's monologue, but his mind and body wouldn't cooperate. The pain in his shoulder had intensified the moment the man had started speaking, and it was as though a thick haze had settled over his mind, making it difficult to concentrate.

The man continued. "More likely the number is some reference to sacred scripture. In that case, I fear you've gotten the better of me. My apologies, Ms. McLeod, but it's been so long since I've last read the good book."

Jani likewise didn't respond to the direct address. Dex wasn't certain if she didn't want to dignify the comments with a response or if she too was suffering the same sense of disorientation.

"Or it could be something far simpler. Maybe I just need to add or subtract the digits—though it seems I've already subtracted some digits, haven't I, Nikky."

Nikky retreated a step to the edge of the hilltop, mouthing one word in a barely audible whisper. "Graves."

The name didn't register with Dex, and he was more than a little surprised to hear Nikky, of all people, recognize their antagonist.

"It's good to see you again." Graves came to a standstill about ten meters away. "How's Louise?"

Nikky didn't respond.

"You know," Graves continued, "the offer still stands. Help me now, and I can see to it that you're made whole."

"That's enough!" Dex barked, fighting through the mental haze. "What do you want?"

"I'm here to offer each of you safe passage off Bellona."

"That's very generous, but we'll manage on our own."

"Every security system in every port on this planet is searching for you—your face, your voice, your heartbeat. And if you try to bypass the shipping lanes, there are a pair of UCN destroyers in orbit ready and eager to administer swift justice."

"We'll take our chances."

"I'm afraid I must insist." There was a new layer of threat in his tone as he took another step forward.

Jani drew her pistol quickly and cleanly, holding her aim steady on Graves's chest. He didn't flinch.

"Maybe you haven't noticed," Dex said, mustering as much confidence as he could, "but you're outnumbered."

Graves smiled thinly. His eyes, just now visible, were cold and pale, and when he spoke, the timber of his voice fell sharply, reminding him of the M-2's chilling intonations.

"I can assure you I'm not alone."

The air around them instantly dimmed as if a cloud had passed over and obscured the moons above. The night sky, however, remained clear. He could still see the moons, but everything looked as though he were viewing it through a dark filter—a dense fog he couldn't quite see but could most certainly feel.

The left side of his neck throbbed in pain as he felt the blade of an M-2 cutting into him. Moments from death, he came to the sinking realization that Graves had been distracting them the whole time while his machines had waited in ambush. Dex, though, couldn't see the blade in his periphery vision nor any physical sign of an M-2. Placing his hand on his neck, he didn't feel any blood, only the scar from weeks ago, though the pain felt as intense as when he'd first received the wound.

Graves had not yet advanced. It may have been a trick of the fog, but his eyes now appeared black. In his hand was a knife—a knife that looked very much like the one Dex had once possessed.

A shrill cry behind him pierced the night air.

"I can't see! I can't see!" Nikky repeated in a panic.

Dex turned to help but was struck with a violent nausea. The ground around him started spinning, and it became a struggle just to keep his balance and remain on his feet.

Out of the corner of his eye, he saw Graves approach, knife securely in hand. Dex was wondering why Jani hadn't yet fired until he saw, to his dismay, that she was facing the wrong direction, bent over, eyes shut, both hands pressed against her ears, her mouth open in a noiseless scream.

Dex tried to move toward her, but even the slightest motion made him sick to his stomach. The ground tremored beneath his feet, underscored by a guttural roar that grew louder and louder. As Graves closed to a few paces away, a violent rush of wind picked up, pelting his face with sand and gravel. It was difficult to see anything with clarity in the swirling cloud, but Dex thought he saw a new group of figures surrounding them, shadows spinning in the dark, dust passing through their amorphous shapes.

The swirling cloud had completely obscured the others—Nikky, Jani, Graves. It was all storm and dust and the dancing shadows and the dark fog and the trembling earth and the deafening roar. Dizzy and disoriented, Dex stumbled to the ground, full of despair. They were about to be executed—or, worse, captured and tortured for information—and he was powerless to do a single thing about it.

And then there she was, Jani, just ahead of him, bathed in a brilliant white light from above. Her hands were still over her ears, but her gaze was now skyward, looking up at the new light source—searchlights on a rapidly descending LT-11 light transport, its engines roaring in descent. Hagen had arrived.

The Raven's lights had illuminated Jani but not the others. As invigorated as he was by Hagen's arrival, they were still far from making it safely off Bellona, with their most immediate threat still out there somewhere in the swirling dust and shadows. The Raven's ventral landing thrusters engaged, firing off at full power in a deafening staccato. There was nothing subtle about Hagen's descent. The Raven hurtled to the ground as rapidly as possible, making less a landing than a controlled crash.

Seconds after impact, the portside personnel hatch opened, and Hagen emerged, his sidearm drawn and ready.

"Tangos, Sarge!" Dex hollered above the engine noise, warning Hagen that there were multiple threats in the vicinity. Though Graves was the only hostile he had definitely seen, the image of the shadow figures still lingered in his mind.

Hagen acknowledged him, sweeping his eyes across the hilltop. Dex turned to find Jani, but she was no longer in the searchlight, veiled once again by the haze.

"Nikky, Rabbit—let's go!" he shouted.

"I can't—" Nikky cried out from somewhere off to his left.

"I've got you," he heard Jani say. She sounded hoarse. "Move!"

They emerged from the cloud of dust, Jani firmly guiding Nikky toward the Raven. It looked as though she had recovered, at least partially, from whatever had been tormenting her. Dex realized that he, too, didn't feel nearly as nauseous as he had moments ago, though the fogginess in his head remained.

He fell in behind Jani and Nikky, watching their backs for any sign of Graves. That they were now so close to the Raven did little to lessen Dex's sense of vulnerability. He kept waiting for a burst of red bolts to come screaming out of the darkness or to feel one of those accursed blades thrust suddenly into his neck. He could feel Graves's eyes on them, observing their every move from some unseen location—what he was waiting for, Dex couldn't fathom.

They reached Hagen, who had stepped a few paces out from the Raven to help cover their evac. Dex nodded to his second-in-command as he shuffled past, and Hagen nodded in return without averting his eyes from the hilltop beyond.

Dex assisted Jani in helping Nikky into the Raven, and then she waved him in next. He knew it was pointless to waste time arguing with her. With Hagen to his left and Jani to his right, he ducked in through the side hatch, allowing himself to believe, for the first time since Graves had appeared, that they might just make it. Even so, he half expected a bolt to strike him in the back as he entered. But there was no shot, no attack of any sort. Hagen closed the hatch and stepped into the cockpit while Jani helped strap Nikky into one of the netted troop seats lined along both sidewalls.

Dex instinctively turned and entered the cockpit but saw both seats occupied—Hagen in the pilot's seat with Ronnie Wilco sitting as navigator.

The young ops tech turned and smiled broadly upon seeing Dex.

"Welcome aboard, Captain. Let's get you home!"

Dex backtracked and strapped himself into the troop seat closest to the cockpit while Jani took the seat directly across from him, both wanting to be as close as possible to the action, though they would be, in actuality, little more than spectators. As much as they respected and trusted their squad mates, it was a position neither Dex nor Jani was entirely comfortable with.

He felt the Raven lift off the ground, and an instant later the right side of his body was slammed into the restraining straps as Hagen wasted no time blasting skyward on an aggressive pitch. Most spacecraft had gyroscopic devices in the seating to minimize the discomfort of extreme trajectories, but the LT-11s were designed to be cheap and efficient personnel transports with no such luxuries. As one particular strap dug sharply into his ribcage, Dex was once again acutely reminded of how broken his body was.

With no portholes in the cabin, Dex leaned as far forward as possible, craning to see through the thin forward viewport in the cockpit. Nothing but the night sky was visible as the Raven continued its steep ascent. He could only guess what had become of Graves. Jani caught his eye, and they shared a knowing look—whatever *that* had been down on the hilltop, they were relieved to be distancing themselves from it as fast as possible.

"The ghillie set?" Hagen asked Ronnie.

"Yessir. I cycled it the moment we touched down."

"Good. Keep a close eye on it."

Hagen and Ronnie had already successfully disguised the Raven as one of Baker's light shipping transports, using a ghillie generator to mask its sensor signature. Now, for their departure, they would be attempting to pass themselves off as a different transport. Since the ghillie had worked once, there was no reason it shouldn't work again. There were, however, two main dangers with this plan. One, if the ghillie generator wasn't carefully calibrated, the ship would give off a sporadic sensor reading, arousing suspicion. That's why it was a risk to cycle it mid-mission. Great care went in to carefully calibrating a ghillie prior to takeoff. To fine-tune it on the fly required a great amount of skill and precision. Fortunately, he knew that Ronnie was up to the task.

The other danger was the possibility of someone performing a close visual inspection of the ship. Even the most meticulously calibrated ghillie generator couldn't physically change the appearance of the Raven, and if some sharp-eyed officer spotted a light military transport in a commercial shipping lane, their escape would be short-lived.

Dex didn't have to look at the instruments to know the moment they escaped Bellona's atmosphere. The sensation of exiting the upper atmosphere of a planet always felt like exhaling after holding a deep breath. The tension he'd been involuntarily carrying in his stomach released, and the artificial gravity, functioning at a few points less than standard on the light transport, was a pleasant reprieve after the extreme g-forces of takeoff. He deliberately took in and exhaled a deep, full breath despite his injured lungs, relieved to finally be free of the planet that had caused him such misery.

Having cleared the atmosphere, Hagen eased into a new course, guiding the Raven to the commercial departure lanes. Two rows of ships drifted into view, one lane for automated freighters, the other for manned ships. Normally, the clearance to jump would've been handled remotely from the surface of Bellona. But given the recent commotion in the system, all departures were now required to pass through a naval checkpoint. On the sensor map, Dex could see two UCN destroyers on opposite sides of Bellona. The *Agenor* was keeping watch over the departure lanes while the *Ajax* patrolled the far side of the planet, ready to pounce on any ships that attempted to bypass the checkpoint.

The presence of the destroyers, while expected, was unsettling. If the Raven's true identity were discovered, the warships would make quick work of them. UCN destroyers were designed to hunt down and kill ships much more fearsome and elusive than an unarmed personnel carrier.

Hagen fell in behind an old D-Line freighter at the back end of the manned shipping lane. The automated freighters next to them were jumping into the ether at a steady rate while the queue for the manned ships was at a near standstill with only brief, intermittent forward progress. Dex imagined the freighter captains had uttered a few choice words about the new checkpoints.

"They're jamming the lane," Ronnie reported.

This was typical naval checkpoint procedure—a short-range jamming beam which disabled the ethernav capabilities of each ship until it received clearance to jump. Ahead, they could just make out a gray speck in the distance even as smaller freighters toward the front of the line faded from view—the *Agenor* holding position over the departure beacon.

A prompt appeared on the HUD, indicating that it was their turn to transmit a departure request. Hagen activated the comm.

"Bellona Departures, Starlight one-zero-two-one Juliet requesting jump clearance."

The interval before the *Agenor* replied felt several seconds longer than customary.

"Stand by, Starlight."

Hagen and Ronnie exchanged a look. There was no way of knowing for sure whether the extended pause was typical for this checkpoint or if the hesitation was a sign of suspicion. The next couple of minutes passed in tense silence, the Raven continuing its slow crawl forward while they anxiously waited for clearance from the *Agenor*.

Ronnie broke the silence. "The ghillie's holding form," he said, mostly, it sounded, to reassure himself.

Another couple of long minutes passed, the Raven little by little creeping closer to the departure beacon—and the *Agenor*. Ahead, the D-Line freighter rapidly accelerated and disappeared, jumping into the ether, leaving nothing between them and the destroyer, a giant dagger suspended directly over them.

And still they had received no word from the *Agenor*, one way or the other. The wait had become unbearable. The departures ahead of them had been slow but steady, with a deliberate yet identifiable pace. It was clear by now that they were purposefully being delayed. Hagen, to his credit, showed no visible signs of worry—even though, if they didn't receive clearance, there was certainly plenty to be worried about.

After so many minutes spent in uneasy silence, the hiss of the comm crackling to life was startling.

"Starlight one-zero-two-one Juliet, reroute to the holding beacon, power down your engines, and await further instructions."

After a beat, Hagen activated the comm. "Roger, will comply."

Switching off the comm, he turned to Ronnie. "It looks like it's plan Bravo. What's the ETA?"

"Three minutes."

Hagen grunted. "I guess I'll have to milk it a little more."

Continuing to remain remarkably calm, he maneuvered the Raven in a slow arcing turn toward a beacon about a kilometer from the *Agenor*—far enough from the departure lanes so as not to disrupt the flow of traffic but still right under the nose of the destroyer.

Dex hadn't been made aware of any alternate plan—he'd barely been informed about the first one. He assumed that the ETA referred to the Angels arriving—though he wasn't sure how the Hornets would help much in this situation. If the *Agenor* was determined to detain, or destroy, the Raven, there wasn't much a few fighters would be able to do to stop it, particularly since the squadron's rules of engagement would prevent the Angels from attacking the destroyer. In fact, the arrival of the Hornets would likely just further provoke the *Agenor*.

Hagen, Jani, and the rest of the Angels had more than earned his confidence—he would have to do his best to trust them now. Still, he would have felt considerably better if he had known a little more about the plan they were attempting to execute.

Arriving at the holding beacon, Hagen slowed the Raven to a stop, its nose no longer following the departure lane but rather pointed back toward Bellona. With the system's distant red star nearly directly behind them, the ochre-yellow planet and its twin moons were close to fully illuminated. Under ordinary circumstances, the view would have been breathtaking, but Dex was dismayed to see just how large Bellona loomed in the viewport. Only minutes into his escape, here he was, pointed back toward it, as though the planet were pulling him back in.

A stern command was issued through the comm. "Starlight one-zero-two-one Juliet, power down your engines immediately."

While Hagen had brought the Raven to a stop, Dex realized that he hadn't yet fully powered down the ship.

"ETA?" Hagen asked Ronnie again.

"Two minutes."

"Close enough."

The commander punched the throttle forward, rocketing the Raven toward Bellona. The momentary elation of taking some action—any action—was tempered in Dex's mind by the fact that they had essentially trapped themselves. With the planet in front and the destroyer behind, they weren't anywhere close to having the time and open space necessary to find the groove for an ether jump.

"Starlight, you have been positively IDed as a stolen UCN LT-11 transport. Power down immediately or you will be destroyed."

The command was a formality—they all knew that there was no chance the Raven would comply. Hagen had successfully put some distance between them and the destroyer, but they were still well within its range, something that was soon made abundantly clear by a violent series of blasts that shook the transport. The space in front of them was lit up with bright golden bursts as the *Agenor*'s flak guns hammered them on all sides. Hagen was getting the absolute most out of the Raven, throwing it into a wild series of evasive maneuvers, but the LT-11 was no Hornet, and despite the commander's best efforts, the transport was easy target practice for the *Agenor*'s gunners.

All through the evasive maneuvers, Dex noticed that Hagen had kept a course toward Bellona—and, it seemed, the twin moons in particular. He had no idea why. If the goal was to jump into the ether, they wouldn't be able to get in the groove until they were past the moons, and the *Agenor* would easily destroy them before that point.

"Aft shields at twenty percent." Ronnie sounded nervous. Whatever the plan was, it didn't seem to be going the way he'd hoped.

"Transfer pow—" A burst exploded directly in front of the viewport, momentarily blinding everyone within and shaking the ship so severely that Dex thought it was going to tear in two. As his senses gradually recovered, he saw Hagen hunched over, his left hand on his head, covered in blood.

Jani unstrapped herself and raced to Hagen with Dex following a split second behind. Blood was streaming down Hagen's face. Glancing up, Dex noticed that a compartment above the pilot's seat had opened from the blast, hurtling its contents around the cockpit. Jani helped Hagen out of the pilot's seat while Dex found the offending object, a med kit lying on the cockpit floor, blood splattered across one corner. With Jani's assistance, Hagen stumbled forward into Dex's arms. When it became clear that Dex had a good hold on him, Jani wasted no time sliding into the pilot's seat. Dex wasn't about to object. At this point, Jani was far more physically fit to fly than he was.

Hagen was able to shuffle along a little on his own power, but most of his substantial weight was resting on Dex, whose body strained under the exertion. Dex succeeded in dropping Hagen, somewhat gracefully, into the seat he'd been occupying. After strapping Hagen in, he stepped back into the cockpit, grabbed the med kit, and began cleaning Hagen's wound.

As he worked on applying a dermo-patch, he looked over to see if Nikky was okay. Having grown accustomed to Nikky's fidgety demeanor, it was odd to see him sitting so still. He was staring straight ahead, his hand clenched in his lap, feet firmly planted on the cabin floor. It was unclear whether he'd recovered from his blindness on the hilltop.

"We've cleared the jamming beam," Ronnie said, informing his new pilot.

That was one bit of good news, at least. The Raven also seemed to have edged out of flak range as the intensity of the bursts lessened and then ceased altogether. On the sensor map, Dex could see the *Agenor* turning in pursuit. It likely wouldn't be able to once again close within flak range of the speedier Raven.

While a reprieve from the steady pounding of the *Agenor*'s short range guns was welcome, Dex knew that they were in an all-too-brief calm before the storm—when the *Agenor* stopped batting around its prey and lunged for the kill.

An ominous rhythmic tone echoed through the cockpit, replaced, moments later, by a more urgent alarm.

"Archer archer," Ronnie called out. "Two Slammers on our six—twenty seconds to impact."

Twenty seconds was not enough time for the Raven to execute a jump, especially not since they were still inexplicably flying toward Bellona's moons. Their shields were nearly drained, and even at full strength, they couldn't prevent even a single Slammer from shredding the transport. And with no cannons to shoot down the Slammers, the less-than-agile Raven was going to need to evade not one but two missiles.

Dex used the sensor map in the cockpit to monitor the steady advance of the Slammers. Jani had kept a straight course for the moment—evading early would only give the missiles more time to adjust course. The most effective tactic for evading tracking missiles was to take a sharp evasive maneuver at the last possible moment—the best tactic in a fighter, at least. As confident as Dex was in Jani's abilities as a pilot, he wasn't certain the ship itself possessed the necessary agility.

"Three seconds."

"Bugs away," Jani said evenly before slamming the flight yoke forward. The Raven dove, releasing an emergency reserve of micro-jammers in its wake. The cockpit immediately went dark as the micro-jammers knocked out everything but the mechanical instruments. The cloud of jammers had a similar effect on the missiles, disabling their tracking systems and causing the Slammers to go ballistic. Without the sensor map, it was impossible to see where the missiles were. Dex instinctively braced for impact, but after a few seconds passed, it was clear that the missiles had been successfully trashed.

The cockpit screens soon came back to life as the Raven passed out of the limited range of the micro-jammers. Unfortunately, the sensor map now had a lot more activity on it than before.

"More Slammers incoming—two groups of twelve," Ronnie said.

Launching three waves of missiles was a standard Navy tactic—the first wave to deplete countermeasures, the second wave to force evasive maneuvers, and the third wave, close behind, to course correct and eliminate the target. Typically, each wave consisted of two missiles each. That there were now a full twenty-four Slammers on their tail felt like a personal message from the *Agenor*—*here's what we think of thieves and traitors*.

"We're winchester bugs," Jani informed Ronnie.

It had been something of a miracle that the Raven, with its one-time reserve of micro-jammers, had evaded the first pair of missiles. Now that they were out of countermeasures and still nowhere close to being able to attempt an ether jump, Dex couldn't visualize a scenario that resulted in their survival. Not wanting to bother Jani, he looked over at Hagen to ask if there was any more to their plan, but his friend still looked dazed.

"Next wave, thirty seconds to impact."

"Angels ETA?" Jani asked.

Ronnie looked up. Bellona was drifting past below while the smaller of the twin moons was rapidly filling the viewport.

"Now."

Dex followed Ronnie's gaze. He could see no discernable difference, no new movement, no new objects visible in the starscape. But after a heartbeat or two, there was a new sound—the Angels' private comm channel crackling to life with Lieutenant Commander Onigen's voice.

"Sarge, Ninja. Status?"

Dex felt a chill run up his neck. While his mind still doubted that the Hornets, in this situation, would make much of a difference, his heart swelled with hope, however irrational, at the arrival of the Angels.

"Rabbit here. Sarge is injured but stable. Proceed as planned."

"Roger."

The sensor map showed two S/A-81 Hornets ahead of them— identified as Lee Onigen and Scot Calgaro—just beyond the far side of Bellona's smaller moon. He felt Hagen stir beside him, and it looked as if he was starting to come to. After a glance into the cockpit, he leaned back and caught Dex's eye with what looked to be a glimmer of a smile. Dex could only shake his head and smile as well. Here they were, the two elder statesmen of the squadron, achy and sore, sitting this one out as a couple of mere passengers, their fates in the hands of their junior squad mates.

His smile soon disappeared after taking another look at the sensor map. The Slammers were now twenty seconds out, and as encouraging as it was having Onigen and Scot supporting them, they had arrived too far out of position. It was impossible for two Hornets to gun down twenty-four missiles in such a short amount of time, and they weren't close enough to effectively deploy their micro-jammers.

"Hogs away," Onigen reported.

Bewildered, Dex looked over at Hagen to try to get some answers, but the commander's eyes were focused intently on the viewport. Whatever guesses Dex might've had about the Angels' plan, he couldn't have imagined that Heavy Ion Bombs would be involved. The slow but incredibly potent ordnance had very particular uses—most of which involved obliterating large stationary targets. The HIBs wouldn't be of any use against the incoming Slammers, and if they had been launched at the *Agenor*—which would have been a gross violation of the squadron's rules of engagement—the destroyer would easily gun them down long before impact.

Watching the sensor map, Dex saw that the two HIBs, indeed, were headed neither toward the missiles nor the destroyer but rather were rocketing toward Bellona's smaller moon. Dex had to double-check to be sure. Two dozen lethal missiles were closing rapidly on the Raven's tail, and the grand plan seemed to be to ignore them and instead give one of Bellona's moons a couple of new craters.

Jani flew directly toward the small moon as well, as though she were racing the HIBs to it. The moon now completely filled the forward viewport, and Dex saw it had a reddish hue that hadn't been visible from afar. The tiny moon had also taken a beating, its surface marked by hundreds of deep craters. It struck Dex as a little odd—a few craters were to be expected, but he'd never seen anything quite like this. Bellona's larger twin moon should have protected it, pulling the majority of meteors into its greater gravity well.

Through the forward viewport, Dex spotted the pair of HIBs in the distance diving toward the moon's surface. Watching the bombs near impact, he grew concerned, wondering if, even at a distance, the Raven's weakened shields could withstand the raw force of the detonation. Reaching the surface, however, the HIBs did not detonate but continued falling, descending further down through one of the craters into the depths of the moon.

"Slammers, ten seconds."

"Hold on!" Jani hollered back into the cabin.

The Raven was now skimming the surface of the moon, racing toward the same crater that the HIBs had just disappeared into. Next to him, Hagen took a deep breath and gripped the harness over his chest.

The crater erupted, a wall of red and brown blasting up into space. Rather than turning to avoid the debris, Jani pulled up slightly, flying the Raven toward the sudden obstruction. Hundreds of rocks had already escaped the moon's atmosphere, launched into space, destined soon to create a spectacular meteor shower over Bellona. Below them, clouds of gray dust billowed steadily out of the mouth of the crater, but they were heading toward the middle, toward a dense group of red rocks shooting up even as the Raven screamed toward them.

On the sensor map, Dex saw that the Slammers were only a few seconds from impact. Though he couldn't physically see them, he could feel them closing. Looking forward, however, Dex wasn't sure whether the greater danger was behind or in front. Jani plunged the Raven into the debris cloud, juking hard upon entry to avoid a particularly nasty looking rock that flashed across the viewport. The Raven then climbed sharply as Jani attempted to match the upward trajectory of the eruption.

Dex thought he understood the plan now—create a bunch of new obstacles and hope the Slammers struck the rocks instead of the ship. But something still wasn't adding up. With twenty-four missiles tracking them, the odds were high that more than a few of them would slip through the screen.

The hull directly behind his head shuddered from a violent impact, and for a moment, Dex thought that was it—a Slammer had caught them. He'd seen the missiles do their work often enough to know that the transformation upon impact was sudden and final—in one moment, a ship, an object of design and purpose, the next, nothing but light and fire and scattered fragments. He'd often wondered what it felt like—if the pilot, the crew, the passengers were aware of the moments from impact to light to fragments. When his missile had slammed into the fighter at Artemis, had the pilot felt the heat of the explosion, were his final thoughts filled with pain and terror, or had it all happened too fast to consciously experience?

The ship was struck several more times by similar sounding impacts, and Dex realized that they were being peppered by rocks. Normally, the shields would protect a ship from small debris, but this wasn't a single stray rock or two. They were, rather, in a dense meteor shower of their own making—and the shields had already been on the verge of collapse before they'd entered.

Dex kept waiting for the big impact when one of the missiles finally caught them—or detonated on one of the nearby rocks, which would be nearly as devastating. But the blast didn't come. He looked at the sensor map to see the status of the Slammers, but the map was dark along with the rest of the cockpit—just as it had been when Jani had released the micro-jammers. She had said, though, that their countermeasures were depleted, and the Hornets were still too far away to have used theirs.

"Taconic," Hagen muttered, noticing Dex's bafflement. "The mineral used in jammers. It's buried under the surface. Ninja's idea."

And now the Angels' plan was starting to make some semblance of sense. It was convoluted, dangerous, and dependent on more than a little luck—all necessary ingredients, it seemed, to have any hope of escaping a fully armed UCN destroyer. That this had been Onigen's idea came as little surprise to Dex—the taciturn, reserved lieutenant commander had developed a reputation for coming up with the squadron's most outlandish yet brilliant plans. If Onigen was behind it, Dex knew that, however insane it might appear, the plan had been thoroughly researched and meticulously thought-out.

It now become clear why the moon was so full of craters. The deep holes weren't the result of natural meteor strikes but rather manmade blasts. A troubling thought crossed Dex's mind.

"Any active mining on the moon?" he asked Hagen.

"Shut down by the eco-enforcers."

Seeing the current state of the moon, Dex could understand why. And now the Angels had contributed their own act of eco-terrorism against the sad hunk of rock. The eco-enforcers would now most certainly number themselves among the many enemies the Angels had managed to accumulate.

Looking through the forward viewport, Dex saw that Jani had succeeded in flying perfectly in line with the rising rocks. The cockpit was still dark, meaning the trace amounts of taconic in the surrounding rocks would be having the same effects on the guidance systems of the Slammers, causing them to go ballistic.

Another blast shook the Raven, but Dex was familiar enough with the sensation to know that this hadn't been one of the moon rocks. A Slammer had detonated, not on the Raven itself or they'd already be dead, but rather on a rock in their vicinity. A small hole, about the size of his fist, had appeared on the tail hatch. Thankfully, the Raven's automated force fields had properly initiated, protecting them from being gruesomely sucked out into space. It was also fortunate that the damage had been relatively small—anything much larger and the light transport wouldn't have had enough power to generate a strong enough force field.

A quick check around the cabin revealed a piece of the hull sticking out of the sidewall just a couple inches from Nikky's head. Despite the close call, he continued to sit motionless. It wasn't clear if he'd even noticed the explosion or the shrapnel.

Pulling back on the flight yoke, Jani pitched the Raven back out of the rock cloud in order to avoid any more stray explosions from the Slammers. The *Agenor* came briefly back into view in front of them before Jani banked the Raven hard left, looping around the cloud of debris. A few seconds later, the instruments flickered back to life as they put some distance between them and the taconic rocks. The destroyer, while still aggressively pursuing, hadn't yet launched another wave of missiles, deterred, no doubt, by the newly created jamming cloud.

Ronnie quickly cycled his screens to a readout of damaged systems, the details of which Dex couldn't quite make out from his seat. He could only hope that the essential systems were still operational, most notably the ether drive.

"Shields are down. Critical hull damage in the aft section—force field is engaged and holding. Port ventral thrusters and landing gear are damaged." Ronnie exhaled. "That was close."

"E-drive?" Jani asked.

The ops tech switched to another screen.

"The chamber's compromised. We're leaking antiparticles. There might be just enough juice for one jump."

"Then one jump will have to do. Get to work on those shields."

It was standard procedure for the Angels to execute a series of jumps on the way back to base in order to lose anyone trying to track them. This time, they would have to risk jumping straight to Pella—a rather long jump that was going to strain their already damaged E-drive.

Onigen spoke through the comm. "Rabbit, be advised. All Slammers are trashed. You're clear to find the groove. We'll cover your jump."

"Roger." She glanced back at Hagen. "Sarge, I'm going to need Pella's coordinates."

Hagen gave Dex a quick look for confirmation. Dex nodded.

"Encryption November one-zero Juliet," he rasped. "Enter six-seven-five, mark one-one-three. The system will load the jump. Then transmit to Hornets one and two, same encryption, theta-band."

"Got it." Jani's hands flew over the Raven's console. "And when we get back, we are going to have a word about these security measures."

Jani worked the ethernav screen while Ronnie scrambled to restore even a little shield power, some extra insurance for the ether jump. The ship, technically, didn't need shields to make a successful jump, but considering that they were going to be screaming in and out of star systems at incomprehensible speeds, everyone on board would feel more comfortable with the added protection.

On the sensor map, Dex saw that the two Hornets had now saddled with them. Having received Jani's transmission, they were positioned and ready to escort the Raven through the jump.

"Any time now, Ronnie."

"I've got us back up to ten percent."

"Good enough." Jani activated the comm. "Finding the groove," she reported as she engaged the autopilot, holding the Raven on the perfectly straight course required for an ether jump. Dex saw a countdown appear on the HUD—if they could avoid any unexpected disasters for the next thirty seconds, they were somehow going to make it through this mess alive.

"Excuse me. I don't...I don't think we should jump," Nikky said, appearing at the edge of the cockpit, his eyesight apparently recovered.

Jani looked back in surprise and frustration at their formerly unobtrusive passenger. Ronnie gave a dubious look to Jani, but she now seemed hesitant as she continued to stare at Nikky. At every step, their escape had looked improbable, but somehow, here they were, seconds away from jumping safely back home—and yet, there was something in Nikky's voice that had given her pause.

She flipped a switch and activated the comm. The countdown on the HUD vanished.

"Ninja, Rabbit. We're aborting the jump. Stand by." She whirled around, looking impatiently at Nikky. "Well?"

His voice wavered as he felt the eyes of everyone around him, well aware that he was holding them all up.

"Well, I was thinking about how we were identified."

"And?" Jani demanded, taking note of the sensor map. Though the *Agenor* still hadn't launched another wave of missiles, it continued at full speed on an intercept course.

"And...and why didn't the ghillie generator work?"

"It was working just fine," Ronnie jumped in defensively. "We were visually IDed."

"It's possible," Nikky said, his tone uncertain. "But they seemed suspicious when we were still beyond visual range."

Jani glanced at Dex. He couldn't recall the timing precisely, but it had seemed as though the *Agenor* had been a good distance away when Hagen first requested jump clearance.

"The delay could have just been normal procedure for this checkpoint," Ronnie replied.

"Are you willing to bet our lives on that?" Nikky responded, this time with a touch of assertiveness. "The ghillie is calibrated to match the shape of the ship, correct?"

"Yes," Ronnie said. "And I was carefully monitoring it the whole time."

"I'm sure you were. But what if something had changed the shape of the ship?"

"Like what?" Jani asked, starting to sound convinced.

"I don't know, but if it were me, I wouldn't jump without checking first."

Taking another concerned look at the sensor map, Jani activated the comm.

"Ninja, requesting visual inspection of the Raven prior to jump."

"Roger."

On the sensor map, Scot's Hornet reduced speed to check the aft of the ship while Onigen banked right in order to perform wide sweeping turns around the transport.

For the first time, they heard Scot's voice through the comm. "Well, for one, your port side's shot to hell."

They were all well aware of how badly the Raven had been battered around—Hagen had the bandage on his head to prove it. But, to Nikky's point, the shape-altering damage to the ship had all occurred after they'd been identified.

"Ventral thrusters are likely bent," Scot continued. "That'll make for a fun landing. Hold on—you're not carrying any external cargo, are you?"

While her voice remained steady, Dex noticed a slight slump in Jani's shoulders. "Negative."

"Well, you've definitely picked up a parasite, behind the portside landing gear compartment."

"Confirmed," Onigen added. "Scanning now."

Their time was running out. The *Agenor* had nearly reached the small moon, and once it passed the taconic cloud, they'd have fresh waves of missiles incoming—and this time, they'd be all out of tricks.

"The device is unregistered," Onigen reported. "It's transmitting encrypted data—a microburst every ten seconds."

"Tracking device?" Jani asked.

"I believe so."

Dex recalled their encounter with Graves on the hilltop. He had seemed intent on taking them prisoner until the Raven arrived, at which point he'd disappeared into the dust storm. He must have altered his plan, slipping a tracking device onto the Raven in the brief window between landing and dustoff. In any case, it explained how they'd made it off the surface alive—he'd let them go.

"Suggestions?" Jani asked the question into the comm but was looking at everyone in the Raven. With their escape, looking so promising just moments ago, now dead in the water, she was open to ideas from anyone.

Before there was a chance to speak up, however, an all-too-familiar rhythmic tone sounded in the cockpit, warning that a ship was achieving missile lock. The sensor map showed the *Agenor* just now clearing the cloud.

"New contact," Ronnie said nervously, "heading zero-one-seven, high. It's the *Ajax*. Twenty seconds to missile range."

Even as the *Agenor* continued to chase them from behind, its counterpart had swung around Bellona, boxing them in from the front— both destroyers now in missile range. Jani turned hard left, trying to hold off the *Ajax* for even a few extra seconds.

"Dex?" She was looking directly at him, her eyes searching his for any sign of an answer.

He so desperately wanted to come through for her, for all of them, to think of a brilliant way out. But no matter how hard he scrambled to think of a solution, he kept coming up blank. With the E-drive having only enough power, maybe, for one hop through the ether, they couldn't jump straight to Pella with a tracking device attached to them. And if they jumped to another system, they'd be stranded—with Graves and company tracking them and likely arriving close behind. The cockpit alarms and Ronnie's calls of "archer" only further clouded Dex's mind. The best he could come up with was ordering Onigen and Scot to bugout—to make sure at least two of them made it back safely to the colony so that the mission wouldn't be a total loss.

When Scot, then, came up with the most obvious solution, Dex was relieved, naturally, but also more than a little ashamed that his mind had frozen when his friends had needed him the most.

"Rabbit, I'll splash the tracker. Drop your shields on my mark."

Ronnie looked over at Jani, who nodded her approval.

"Roger, Flash. On your mark," she said.

"Intercepting the Slammers," Onigen reported, maneuvering his Hornet toward the missiles to take out as many as he could before they reached the transport. "I've picked up four. Flash?"

"Two on me. I'm fine," Scot said. "Hold still, Rabbit, will you?"

Dex could imagine the strain Scot was under. Before he could worry about the pair of missiles headed his way, he first had to splash the tracking device, and to do so, he had to match the Raven's flightpath perfectly. It wasn't enough for him to simply shoot the tracker—he had to fire at just the right angle so his cannon bolt wouldn't puncture the exposed belly of the ship after tearing through its intended target.

Jani had continued turning the Raven, but she was going to have to find a way to compose herself and hold a completely straight course. With waves of missiles incoming, it would go against her every instinct.

"Trashed my Slammers," Onigen said. "Winchester bugs. Eight inbound to the Raven." The lieutenant commander had used his micro-jammers to evade the missiles tracking him, but there were still plenty more Slammers inbound, most of which were screaming toward the transport.

"Twenty seconds to impact," Ronnie called out.

"Flash?" Jani asked.

"Yeah, that's better. Just about there." Through the viewport, Dex saw that Jani had stopped turning and was maintaining a level course.

"Fifteen seconds."

"Splashed four. You're clear, Flash. Six incoming, Raven. Beyond my gun range." Onigen had done everything he possibly could to stop the missiles, taking out the pair headed for Scot in the process, but the half dozen continuing to close were still far too many for the Raven to handle.

"Mark."

On Scot's command, Ronnie lowered the shields, leaving them all once again completely exposed to the incoming missiles and, of greater concern at the moment, Scot's cannons.

While it was too late now to do anything about it, Dex suddenly had the disconcerting thought that none of them had considered whether the attached object was actually an explosive device. To punctuate the point, he felt a loud bang directly beneath his feet that rattled the cabin. There was, however, no hull breach, no new holes in the cabin floor. Scot had hit the device cleanly.

"Tracker's splashed."

"Seven seconds."

"Shields, Ronnie."

Destroying the tracking device, at this point, had been little more than a moral victory. While disposing of the tracker had freed them up to make the ether jump, there simply wasn't enough time for Jani to find the groove before the missiles struck.

A familiar green indicator on the HUD, however, caught Dex's eye. He shook his head in admiration, impressed as ever by the brilliance of his longtime wingman. Moments ago, Scot had been annoyed that it had taken Jani so long to hold a straight course, and Dex himself had thought that maybe she'd lacked the nerve. But Jani hadn't been turning because she'd been concerned about the missiles—rather, she had been maneuvering the Raven into the groove so that by the time Scot shot the tracking device, they would already be positioned for the ether jump.

"I'm in the groove," she confirmed through the comm. "See you boys back home."

On the sensor map, the missiles closed to four seconds, three seconds, two seconds—then one hundred, then one thousand, then numbers too large to comprehend as the Slammers, the destroyers, Bellona and its moons, Graves and the shadows were left far behind, and Dex could only hope left behind for good.

Chapter 12

Ravi and Purnima Voor leaned on each other for support as they made their way down the hall. The infirmary, and the respite it promised, lay just around the next corner. Only twenty minutes had passed since the pair had struggled from their berths, determined to begin their rehab in earnest, but it felt like it had been hours. Ravi kept one hand against the wall, steadying himself, while his other arm wrapped around Purnima's waist, holding her up, urging her along the narrow corridor.

"Come on, Nima, just a few more feet. Then we can rest." Ravi's encouragement was as much for himself as for his twin sister.

"I know, I know." Purnima resolutely kept her feet moving. "It's never taken this long before."

"We've never been that close to the edge before—never had to exert ourselves like that. Not even when Pickett had us in the worst—"

"Stop!" Purnima gritted her teeth. "This is hard enough. I don't want to think about that."

"Okay, okay. It's all right. Those days are over. It's different now."

Purnima stumbled, barely catching her balance in time to avoid collapsing to the floor. "And yet," she breathed, "it still feels the same."

"Physically, yes." Ravi helped her straighten up. "But there is a difference. Commodore Pickett isn't here—"

"If he were here, I'd kill him!" Purnima snapped.

Purnima's demeanor had changed so suddenly, Ravi was taken aback. He had seen this transition before.

"Nima…"

"No, I'm serious, Ravi." Purnima paused to regain her breath. "What he did to us—I'd make sure that monster never had the chance to do it again, to anyone else, ever."

Ravi pursed his lips. "I'm not sure he could. We don't even know if there are any others like us left."

"But what if there are? You just said that you don't know. I don't know, either. How could we? What if he finds others and takes them, too? No! I'd kill him. I'd slit his throat if I had the knife. No one should have to go through…to do the things he made us do…" Purnima's voice faltered. She swallowed hard, a hint of blue-tinged blood forming at the corner of her mouth. She leaned against the wall, her remaining strength sapped.

Her brother faced her, placing both hands on her shoulders, both to steady her and to ensure that she focused on his words. "Listen to me. You have to understand. When you talk like that—when I see that look in your eyes—it worries me. It's like you're giving in. And we can't do that, not here, not ever. I understand your motives—I agree with them. But if we let our past, our nature, rule, we won't be any better than Pickett. We'll be worse, in fact. It's got to be different this time."

Purnima's voice was barely a whisper. "I don't see how it can be."

"It already *is* different. Pickett isn't here. No one is forcing us to do anything." Ravi looked into Purnima's eyes. "We're among *friends*."

She avoided his gaze. "For now," she said. "But what will happen when they learn the truth?"

"Do you really think it will matter? After all we've been through with them?"

Purnima abruptly turned to face him, fighting through the ensuing dizziness. "Of course it will matter! Even back on Earth, when we had to explain ourselves to Captain D'Felco, do you think he would have kept us around if we had told him *everything*?"

Ravi shook his head. "I don't think you're giving the captain or the others enough credit. They would understand."

Purnima pushed herself away from the wall and began taking unsteady steps in the direction of the infirmary. "How can you say that? I'm not even sure I really understand."

Ravi kept pace, continuing to support her with his arm. "Neither do I. But someday we will. And then, when the time is right, we'll tell the captain everything."

"And in the meantime?"

"In the meantime, we have to concentrate on getting stronger. The Angels are going to need us again."

Purnima stared straight ahead. The infirmary door was only a few meters away.

"Yes," she said. "I'm sure they will."

*   *   *

If Dex, earlier, had been frustrated by his limited view from the Raven's aft section, he was now thankful for it. A quick look forward into the cockpit, where Jani mechanically monitored the instruments from the pilot's seat, gave him the smallest glimpse outside the forward viewport—into the ether. Despite being a seasoned pilot, he still found the sheer emptiness of etherspace unsettling. There was simply nothing there. No doppler-affected streaks of light, no stars, not even the normal blackness of space—nothing. The view left him nauseous—a condition, Dex ruefully acknowledged, that was not appropriate for a veteran squadron captain.

He leaned back again into the troop seat, his shoulder and neck aching with a dull pain that permeated his entire body. The adrenaline surge from the escape having dissipated, his body was reminding him of his current pathetic condition. His mind, meanwhile, kept returning to that disturbing encounter with Graves on the surface of Bellona. What the hell had happened down there? The memory of the eerie shapes in the dust cloud haunted him, calling to the deepest parts of his psyche, upsetting his equilibrium as he swayed in the reinforced netting of the seat. He had tried to explain away the moment, reasoning that that the figures in the dark had only been a trick of the swirling dust and low light, but he had done a poor job convincing himself. Whatever the explanation, he couldn't escape the tangible, sickening feeling the experience had left in his gut.

With a concerted effort, Dex pushed himself past his disquieting introspection, forcing his attention back to his conversation with Hagen.

"So that's it, Captain." The burly commander adjusted the newly applied dermo-patch on his forehead, its blood-soaked predecessor already used up and discarded. "Don't ask me how it could get so bad in the short time you've been gone. All I can say is, I'm glad you're back."

"Don't sell yourself short, Sarge." Dex said, closing the med kit. "Something tells me it was only a matter of time, no matter whose watch it was."

"Either way, boss, we have to get this under control."

Dex sighed. "I agree. This ends, and it ends right now. Pastor Nathan can handle the colony. We'll handle Viper." He peered forward again, knowing that, despite the visual evidence to the contrary, Scot was out there in the ether, meters off their port wing. "And anyone else who gets out of line."

"Approaching Pella." Jani's voice sounded wooden. "Dropping in…ninety seconds." Dex wondered just how much she had been affected by the events on the surface as well. A couple seats back, Nikky Weis sat alone, having withdrawn into his own thoughts shortly after the jump. Ronnie had tried to engage him, trying to clarify how he had known about the tracking device, but Nikky had been uncooperative, his responses uncharacteristically terse. Finally, Ronnie had given up and returned to the cockpit, where he'd spent the majority of the jump with his eyes closed, absorbed in his own thoughts.

"Sarge, can you do me a favor?" Dex gestured toward the cockpit. "Are you up to taking over for Rabbit? I have a couple questions before we land."

"No problem," Hagen grunted, getting up. Even if he were missing a leg, Dex thought, Hagen would never admit to being unfit for any duty.

"That was some gutsy flying," Dex said as Jani dropped into the netting beside him. "Diving right into that taconic blast."

"Yeah." Jani's eyes were unfocused. "Ninja's idea." Dex could see that she, too, had come down from the combat rush. If she was feeling any aftereffects of the events on the ground, he decided it was not the time to start a discussion about her hesitation or his complete lack of leadership—neither of them had responded according to their training, not by a long shot. He opted instead for another question—one that had been bothering him since the escape.

"Yeah, about that." He stared straight ahead, matching Jani's unfocused study of the bulkhead across from them. "Is there any reason why you chose to keep that part of the plan from your captain?"

Jani turned to him, a glimmer of confidence returning to her eyes.

"You're kidding, right?"

"No. I'm not, Lieutenant. As the ranking officer, I expect to be briefed on all mission parameters and contingencies—ideally before said contingencies are actually engaged."

Jani let out an exasperated sigh. "Exfil protocols," she said flatly, before turning back to stare into the space in front of her.

"What?"

"Standard Operating Procedure, Captain." Ronnie chimed in from the cockpit. His voice became even, reciting a regulation of which Dex was already aware. "No personnel, having been detained or unaccounted for in hostile territory, shall, upon their evacuation, be given any sensitive strategic information until the possibility of their being compromised can be effectively ascertained and evaluated."

Dex took a breath, started to say something, looked from Ronnie to Jani and back again, and bit his tongue.

"In short, Captain," Ronnie said, "you were on a need-to-know basis."

"And this time around, Deadeye," Hagen added, keeping his attention focused forward as the Raven dropped from the ether, the brightness of Pella's yellow dwarf sun causing the viewport to darken in response, "you didn't need to know."

Out of the ether, the external view was much more inviting. As Pella filled the viewport, Dex could just make out the gray ice-covered mountains and turquois sea, the colony and the Angels' base nestled in the plains between. He tried to clear his head of the recent tumultuous events and enjoy the ride back—back to a home he never thought he would see again.

"Hang on," Hagen said, a layer of strain evident in his voice. "This is going to be rough."

Dex reached down and tightened the belt strap in his harness as Jani did the same. Ronnie was secure in the cockpit, and looking back, Dex saw that Nikky had seemed to come out of his haze long enough to tighten his restraint as well. The Raven continued to descend, a little too rapidly for Dex's liking, as Hagen's hands flew furiously over the controls, attempting to compensate for the damaged ventral thrusters.

"Brace for impact," Hagen shouted. "In three, two...*one!*"

Dex felt the impact of the Raven striking the landing pad from the bottom of his boots all the way up his back and neck. He could hear the landing gear groan on the hydraulics, the ship listing slightly to port before righting itself and settling back into position, the high-pitched whining of the overworked thrusters winding down to a low hum.

"Sorry about that," Hagen mumbled.

"Belay that." Dex unstrapped his restraint and flexed his back, trying consciously not to display too much discomfort. "We're here, and we're safe. Well done, Sarge."

"Any landing we can walk away from," Jani added.

Powering down the engines, Hagen hit the controls to open the portside hatch. The swirl of dust kicking up all around outside told Dex that Scot and Lee had also just touched down alongside them.

The five occupants of the Raven made their way through the hatch. With the exception of Ronnie, each one was hobbled by the rescue, physically, mentally, emotionally, or a combination or all three. Dex emerged last, more out of command habit than any conscious decision. He wasn't sure what kind of reception the rescue party was going to receive. Hagen had emphasized that operational gag orders were still in place, but Dex knew that those orders had been ignored all too often.

As relieved as he was to avoid the discomfort of a raucous landing pad welcome, he was also struck by the small size of the group. Job Hansen was there as usual, and Flight Sergeant Drager St. James had arrived with a pair of ground personnel—and that was it. Seltrice and Adahn weren't present, not that Dex had expected them—they were simply obeying orders.

No, it was the absence of three other pilots that hit Dex the hardest. Hagen had already filled him in on the Voor twins, laid up in sickbay, mysteriously rendered infirm in the aftermath of the battle. But it was the news that Flight Lieutenant Geffory "Prince" Bennet had died in the attack, his Hornet vaporized by a trio of Slammers as he protected Seltrice Valani's blindside, that forced home the reality of just how costly the Bellona offensive had been—and how much worse it could have gone. He knew it had to be done. The station modifying the M-2s into assassins had to be destroyed. But Geff had given his life in exchange for that objective, a sacrifice that must be remembered.

Dex turned to Hagen, but his attention was drawn past him. Flight Sergeant Drager St. James had been forlornly inspecting the damage to the Raven, clucking his tongue in disapproval at every scratch, every ding, of which there were many. He was in the middle of caressing the misshapen ventral thrusters when his face broke into an expression of disbelief, not at the extensive damage, but at Nikky Weis. Without warning, the stocky mechanic rushed at Nikky, enveloping the gaunt little man in a massive bear hug—something Dex had never seen Drager do. Nikky stiffened at first but then pulled back to look his embracer in the face. A sudden recognition crossed his features, and he raised his arms, returning the hug, albeit more lightly.

"Hagen, what?" Dex was dumbfounded.

"Beats me, boss." Hagen glanced at Lee Onigen. "You know anything?"

Onigen just shook his head.

"Captain!" Drager broke the hug long enough to face Dex. "How? I mean, where did you find him?"

"I didn't," Dex said. "It was more like he found me."

"I take it you two know each other?" Hagen asked.

"Yes, uh, sorry, sirs." Drager, remembering protocol, drew himself to attention. "Allow me to introduce Nikky Weis." He threw an arm around Nikky's shoulder. "My brother."

"Your brother?" Hagen sounded incredulous.

"Yes, sir."

"Huh."

Dex looked at Drager and Nikky. He considered the time he spent on Bellona—Nikky finding him, caring for him, refusing to leave his side. He had asked Nikky repeatedly why he had rescued him, and the little man had simply replied that he had his own reasons. It all started to make sense. Dex was beginning to see a pattern of being out of the loop. It was a feeling he didn't enjoy.

"So, Mr. Weis, this was the reason you helped us? Why didn't you just come out and tell me?"

Nikky shrugged. "I didn't know you that well."

"So, you think I might have refused to take you along if you had told me that Drager was your brother?"

"Well," Nikky demurred, "your base is *supposed* to be a secret."

"And yet, I brought you along, without you telling me anything, anything at all." Dex turned to Hagen. "Sarge, Ninja, be honest with me. Am I losing my touch?" Lee raised his eyebrows. Hagen just frowned.

"Besides," Nikky said softly, almost under his breath, "you needed my help."

"Sir," Drager said quickly. "You'll have to forgive Nikky. He's always been pretty cautious." He looked at his long-lost half brother fondly. "He has, how should I put this…some trust issues."

"You think?" Dex had to suppress a smile. The entire situation was just so unexpected, so absurd. He kept a straight face. "In the future, Mr. Weis, in your dealings with me, or my officers, you will endeavor to be more forthcoming with relevant information. Is that clear?"

Nikky straightened to a reasonable facsimile of attention. "Yes, Captain. I understand."

"Sir," Drager stepped in again. "Permission to be dismissed? We have a lot to catch up on."

"Granted," Dex said. "Get Mr. Weis settled. Sergeant St. James and Mr. Wilco, you'll be expected later when the rest of the squadron is assembled. And Mr. Weis, welcome to Pella."

"Thank you, Captain." It might have been the first time Dex saw Nikky smile.

"So, Nikky, you've met Ronnie, then?" Drager indicated the ops tech.

"Yeah, we got acquainted on the transport."

"You're going to like him." Drager guided both of them toward the hangar. "He's almost as smart as you."

"Almost?" Ronnie huffed.

"Don't get too excited," Drager added. "I've got you both beat by a longshot."

"Poor Drager," Nikky said, leaning toward Ronnie. "I see he's still as delusional as ever. I thought that might pass with age."

The three trundled off, still chatting as they departed the landing pad. Suddenly, a few meters away, Nikky stopped. Dex saw him reach into his pocket and pull out a small wriggling object.

The turtle, Dex thought. *Louise.* He was surprised with everything else that was going on that he actually remembered its name. He watched Nikky gently hand the animal to a visibly moved Drager, who held it up to his face, nuzzling it to his cheek.

"Son of a gun," Hagen whistled.

"Full of surprises," Onigen said.

"Well, that little reunion helped us dodge one other bullet, anyway." Hagen continued to gaze after them. "I kept waiting for Drager to ask about Dex's Hornet. Not really like him to miss a detail that big."

"Yeah, I was about to ask that very question," Onigen said. "Where is it?"

"Still parked safely on an asteroid in the Purborus system, right where he left it." Hagen looked at Dex, but the captain's attention seemed to be focused elsewhere. "Deadeye's plan was to pick it up on the way back, but we only had fuel for one jump. We'll go after it as soon as the dust settles around here."

Dex only half-heard Hagen and Onigen's conversation. He was preoccupied, watching another development. Scot had been waiting beneath the port wing of his Hornet as Jani walked past. Scot turned to her, extending a gloved hand, but she brushed past him without a word. Across the landing pad, Scot glanced at Dex with a puzzled expression, but Dex just shook his head. However the business on Bellona had affected her, she was choosing to deal with it on her own. Scot jogged after her, saying something out of Dex's earshot. He watched Scot continue to follow her, but Jani just kept walking.

He tried to focus his attention back to the business at hand but suddenly felt very weary. The aftereffects of the confrontation on Bellona still lingered, weighing on him. "Sarge, Ninja. We'll let everybody catch their breath. Then, we're going to assemble the squadron and all senior personnel. There are some things I have to say."

Dex turned and left the pad, being mindful to hide his limp as much as possible. He needed a coffee and an ion shower. And then he needed to send a message—one tightly encrypted burst off-planet, a signal to an old friend.

Chapter 13

"Trust me, you're going to love this place." Darik tried his best to sound reassuring.

Liana bunched her overcoat tightly around her neck, gazing suspiciously at the row of boarded-up businesses lining the trash-strewn street.

"Sure. *Let's go out to eat tonight*, you said. *We'll have a good time*, you said." She caught her step in mid-stride, the right heel of her black pumps barely missing a small pile of rotting matter on the sidewalk—whether it was discarded food or something far more disgusting, she couldn't tell. "Did your plans for the evening include getting mugged?"

Darik stole a glance between two buildings to their right. He wasn't quite sure, but he thought he could just make out a couple of human forms moving about in the darkness. One of them seemed to note his presence, nudging the other before both retreated into the shadows. With his eyes adjusting to the dimmer light, Darik could see that the two had been huddled over a small crumpled heap. Squinting harder, he could see now that it was some sort of dying animal—a dog, cat, or something entirely different. He had no idea what the dark forms had been doing to the helpless creature, nor did he want to know. Suppressing a shudder, Darik consciously picked up the pace.

"No, really." He forced himself to keep his tone light. "Don't let the neighborhood fool you. That's one of the reasons I like this place. It's off the beaten path."

"Really? I couldn't tell."

"C'mon, don't worry. It's just ahead around the corner." Darik put his arm around Liana's shoulder. He noticed that she was shivering. "It'll be worth it."

Liana pulled her coat even tighter and trudged forward. "You keep saying that. This had better be the best meal of my life."

The couple turned the corner onto another street, more dingy and foreboding than the previous one. Sparse street light panels flickered on and off, revealing glimpses of dilapidated siding, peeling paint, and barred windows.

Darik stopped, his tone brightening significantly. "See? Here we are!"

Liana stiffened. "Here we are? Where? Here?" Next to a battered red door, above a window box full of decaying plants, a small sign glowed at half-intensity—*Welcome to Bistro Riservata.*

"Yes." Darik opened the door with a flourish. "Here."

Whatever darkness and despair existed outside the restaurant instantly disappeared as Darik and Liana stepped inside. Soft white incandescent light replaced the nearly non-existent panel lighting of the street. Where they had been hearing distant sirens, whining dogs, and the occasional moan of a gutter prehab, they now could hear soft tones of Sicilian melodies playing through old-fashioned metallic coiled acoustic speakers. The general smell of rotting garbage and human waste outside gave way to a delightful scent of baking bread, good wine, and fresh vegetables.

Darik allowed himself a smile. "There. Did I tell you?"

"All right." Liana visibly relaxed. "I see what you mean. But I'm warning you, Mason, this had better be the—"

"Darik! My little *ragazzo!*" Liana was interrupted by a large dark-haired woman bursting into the small entryway. She swept Darik into a huge bear hug, nearly lifting his feet off the ground. Turning to Liana, she took both her shoulders in a pair of strong hands, appraising her with a smile.

"And this must be Liana! At last, we get to meet you!"

Liana smiled back. "Yeah." She gave Darik a quick sideways glance. "At last."

Darik stepped in. "Yes, Liana, I want you to meet Josephine Brobergo, one of the owners. Josephine, as you've already guessed, this is Liana."

"Such a beauty for my Darik to bring to dinner. I didn't think he would ever be finding such a one as you." She wrinkled her nose. "Lately, all he has been doing is showing up with that little *criceto* and his plain spaghetti." Josephine nearly spat the last words out.

Darik felt a sharp pang of regret at her mention of Nikky. It had been right here, a few months ago, that he had recruited the diminutive systems analyst to help him look into the mystery of the M-2 disappearances. That meeting had eventually led to Nikky losing his hand and most likely his life. He found himself wishing that Nikky was with him right now—absorbing Josephine's disdain, fidgeting around with the silverware, dismissively explaining his latest tech wizardry. With Jenkins saddling him with this new assignment, Darik certainly could have used the little guy's unique abilities again—and despite his annoying quirks, he'd realized that he'd missed his company.

Darik shook himself back to reality. Who was he kidding? Nikky wouldn't have been any help whatsoever. He had made it abundantly clear, on the way to Bellona, just how he had felt about Darik and the M-2/A initiative. Darik had chosen his side, and Nikky his. And now he was gone.

Besides, Darik reasoned as Josephine helped Liana remove her coat, who would he rather be dining with tonight? A mousey former co-worker with a tendency to speak with flecks of salad greens stuck in his teeth or the vision of perfection standing next to him right now?

Liana looked stunning. She had chosen a metallic blue shimmering evening gown, perfectly fitted and covering just enough places to be respectable dining attire yet revealing enough to tempt Darik into skipping dinner completely. He was about to voice his admiration when Alphonse—Josephine's husband, co-owner, and chef of Bistro Riservata—greeted them from the dining room.

"Mister Darik!" he shouted. "Josie! What are you holding them up for? Come in! Come in!"

Darik offered Liana his arm and escorted her into a small but comfortably decorated dining room where Alphonse was waiting for them. An awareness of his stained apron and Liana's elegant dress prevented him from matching Josephine's hug, but he managed to make up in exuberance what his greeting lacked in physical expression.

"Ah, but what a special night this is, eh?" Alphonse beamed at the pair. Darik couldn't tell if Liana was enjoying all the attention or not. "The first time we get to meet the lovely Liana. I'll tell you what. Forget the *Penne Rustica* tonight. I have been preparing a special dish just for you. Tonight"—Alphonse waved his meaty hand in the air—"Tonight you will be having my very own *Quattro al Forno*."

Josephine smacked her husband with a menu. "Not if you don't get back into that kitchen, they won't. What are you doing out here, anyway? Off with you! *Rapidamente!*"

With a wave of his hand to deflect Josephine's assault, Alphonse smiled warmly and ambled back toward the kitchen. Josephine placed an arm around both of her charges and guided them through a small door near the back.

"You two get comfortable. I'll be back with some bread and wine."

"Oh my," Liana breathed, and Darik smiled broadly. The private dining room was breathtaking. Hidden lighting accented the coved ceiling but did not overwhelm the flicker of soft candlelight throughout the room. Glass votive holders and hurricane lamps all held authentic wax candles. At the center of the room's lone table, a single taper burned in a round-bottomed wine bottle, illuminating the multi-colored wax accumulating down its sides. The effect, in contrast with the artificial illumination so common in most establishments, was intoxicating. The décor had been completely redone since Darik's last visit, possibly just in time for tonight. Taking in the soft wood trim, the fresh floor covering, the elegant tablecloth and place settings, Darik recalled how he had casually mentioned to Josephine that he wanted to bring Liana someplace special. She and Alphonse had obviously taken that innocuous comment as yet another opportunity to practice their unparalleled hospitality.

Only one element in the renovation caused Darik to pause. As he held out a chair for Liana, his eyes came to rest on a framed holo recessed in the far wall. The image within was unmistakably that of Stephen XII, the exiled Bishop of Rome. Darik frowned. While not explicitly illegal, displaying a holo of the Pope was a risky choice. He had never considered the Brobergos to be particularly religious. Why they would decide, now of all times, to present such a blatant reminder of their Catholic heritage was beyond him. Stephen XII had been on Callixtus since the early days of Prop 413, along with at least a half-million of his followers. Racking his brain, Darik couldn't recall any info-feed reports about a thawing of relations between the Coalition Council and the outspoken Christian leader. He wondered what it might mean for Alphonse and Josephine, as close to family as anyone Darik had in this world, to be aligning themselves with such a radical. A fleeting vision ran through his mind—a dark alleyway behind the bistro, the fearful couple cowering behind a dumpster. Out of the darkness, a silent apparition sliding into the dim light, approaching, a blue blade extending from its arm—.

"Hey, are you in there?" Liana's voice shook Darik out of his reverie.

117

"Yeah, yes." Darik worked his way around the table and slumped into his own seat. "I was just, uh, looking at the décor."

"I could see that." Liana gazed in the direction Darik had been staring. He sincerely hoped that she wouldn't ask him any follow up questions.

Thankfully, she didn't get the chance. Josephine burst back into the room, pushing a cart laden with a wicker basket of dark crusted bread and a large green bottle.

"Sangiovese for you both then?" she asked. Without waiting for an answer, she tipped the bottle, pouring the rich red contents into two sizable goblets. Alphonse was planning a special dish for them, and Darik knew better than to question their pairings.

While Josephine cut into the crispy oval loaf of bread, Darik sampled the wine. He saw Liana doing the same, her distorted image through the wine glass breaking into a smile. Lowering his glass and looking back at her, he smiled as well. Any concern about the Brobergos, that holo of the Pope, or any of the other countless Zealots still out there faded from his mind. Here he was, about to enjoy a private dinner in his favorite restaurant in the company of an incredibly captivating woman. He accepted a slice from the rosemary basil loaf, feeling the distinct crinkle of the dark brown crust between his fingertips. Josephine busied herself pouring a generous pool of olive oil onto a saucer.

"So tell me, my *principessa*," she said, winking at Liana while grinding fresh pepper into the olive oil, "how is it that our Darik managed to coax you out here with him?"

Liana dipped a portion of bread in the oil mixture, stirring it thoughtfully. "Oh, I don't know," she answered. "He can be kind of persuasive when he needs to be."

"Ah, he coerced you, did he?"

Liana took a small bite of the bread. "Begged, is more like it."

"*L'oh mio!*" Josephine laughed, lifting her eyes to the ceiling and placing a hand over her breast. She reached out and gave Liana's cheek the gentlest of pinches. "Oh, this one is one in a million, Darik." She turned and retreated toward the kitchen, glancing back over her shoulder. "You treat her right, eh?" Josephine continued to chuckle as she left the room. "*Begged* her, he did. *Bella fanciulla*. Alphonse! The prosciutto! What is taking the prosciutto?"

Liana turned her attention back to Darik. "I like her."

Darik narrowed his eyes, but his smile betrayed his tone. "I *begged* you, huh?"

"Well, you were pretty pathetic all those months. Fumbling all over yourself, finding excuses to talk to me."

"Finding excuses!" Darik took a sip from his glass, allowing his mock annoyance to play out. "You were my secretary. It was my job to talk to you."

"Of course. All those after-hours conversations were strictly a professional obligation. I get it."

Darik decided to change the subject. "So what do you think of the place?"

"It's lovely. You were right—I never would have expected it. If the food is half as good as you say, I may have a new favorite."

"Oh, don't worry." Darik took another sip. "It's better than I said."

On cue, Josie trundled back in, this time balancing a large salad bowl in one arm and a platter in the other. As she placed them on the table, Darik could sense the slightly pungent yet pleasant aroma of prosciutto, garlic, spinach, and ricotta cheese wafting up from the plate. The dried ham had been shaped into cups, filled with all manner of delightful ingredients and baked into bite-sized morsels. Humming softly, Josie served up a healthy portion of salad to each of them, leaving the platter of appetizers near the center of the table. "Here you are, my friends," she said. "The *Quattro al Forno* will be a while yet so you have plenty of time to enjoy each other's company. I will leave you to that, but if you need anything, you holler, all right?"

That was a trait Darik deeply appreciated in Alphonse and Josephine. The two most hospitable people he knew also had an innate sense for when to allow their guests privacy.

Liana watched Josie disappear once more into the main dining room. She reached for one of the prosciutto cups. "So tell me, Mr. Mason. Why *did* you insist that we come out here tonight? I mean, we could have easily IRed something back at your—Oh my. Wow. These are amazing!"

Darik helped himself to one of the cups. "Well, that's part of the reason. I wanted you to experience Alphonse's food for yourself. The other reason"—he paused to swallow a tantalizing morsel of the prosciutto and cheese and take another sip of wine—"the other reason is that I wanted to make it up to you for how I've been behaving lately."

"Well, you have been pretty distracted since your little hunting trip. What in the world happened out there, anyway?"

"Nothing much. We shot a few birds, hung out with a business contact, pretty basic stuff."

Liana set down her glass. "Then why the big change after you got back? Something must have happened."

Darik suddenly felt uncomfortable discussing the hunting trip. Liana didn't need to know the details. Wasn't it enough that he was here, now, treating her to the finest Italian cuisine in Compton? He shook his head.

"It's no big deal. Really. Just business. Standard business."

Liana leaned across the table—normally a sight Darik would have enjoyed. But not this time.

"Listen—just what have we been playing at these last few weeks? Am I a part of your life or not? You can't shut me out, not if this is going to work. Now what exactly is going on with you?"

"I told you it's nothing."

"Nothing?"

"Nothing."

Liana crossed her arms and leaned back in her chair.

"Bullshit," she said.

"Oh come on! What do you want me to say?"

Liana had never looked so determined. "I want you to level with me. If something is going on, if you're having trouble, I can help! Forget that I'm your girlfriend, your lover, your whatever—I'm not really sure what I am. I'm also your secretary—your assistant—and a damn good one, I might add. Whatever is going on, we can work on it—together. But you have to keep me in the loop. I'm no good to you otherwise. So I'm going to ask you one more time, Darik. What is going on?"

Darik's mouth had gone dry. The Sangiovese wasn't helping. He looked around for his water glass, reached for it, but neglected to open his fingers. He bumped the glass, sloshing water onto the prosciutto platter. He looked down at his lap.

"All right. The trip, it wasn't just about the new business contact. Jenkins had"—he swallowed, which did little to sooth his dry throat— "other concerns."

"What other concerns?"

Darik bit his lip. How much should he tell Liana? It wasn't that he didn't trust her—he trusted her with his life. But every detail he shared would only draw her further in, implicating her in any future actions. He thought again about Nikky and the fate of his one-time co-conspirator.

Before he could answer, Josie reentered the room, this time balancing a large oval tray with two plates holding the main course. Grateful for the time to think, he greeted her enthusiastically.

"Josie, that smells incredible! What did you say it was?"

Josie beamed. "Oh, it's something very special that Alphonse has been working on. *Quattro al Forno*. It's got cheese manicotti, chicken cannelloni, cheese ravioli, and some very special stuffed shells." She smiled at Liana. "You're going to love it."

Liana stared directly at Darik. "I'm sure I will."

"Oh, my *principessa*, is there something wrong?"

Liana turned to face Josephine. "No, I'm sorry. That was rude of me. I'm sure it will be wonderful." She paused. "Josephine, may I ask you a question?"

Josephine cocked her head to one side. Liana had her complete attention. "Of course, darling. You can ask me anything."

"You've known this guy a while, right?" She indicated Darik with a wave of her hand.

"Several years, yes. Not only is he one of our best customers, but Alphonse and I like to think of Darik as one of our friends."

"And he is generally a warm, honest, and outgoing person?"

Josie pulled over a chair, dropping her ample frame into it. "Oh, sweetheart, whatever gave you *that* idea?"

Liana laughed, and Josie did, too. Darik sat in his place and stewed. So far, the evening was not exactly going the way he had planned.

Josie leaned toward Liana, her voice taking on a conspiratorial tone. "Listen to me, Liana. Our Darik, he's a good man. We like him. I think you like him too, eh?"

Darik had not often seen Liana blush, maybe never, in fact. But in the candlelight, he thought he detected a slight rosy hue to her cheeks as Josie continued.

"I'm sure he would be good to you, *principessa*, but if it is an open, honest man you are looking for, well…" She shot a hard look at Darik, then shook her head sadly. "If that is what you want, you may have to look somewhere else. This one"—she pointed a thumb in Darik's direction—"he plays it pretty close to the vest, I think."

Darik couldn't tell if the two were playing him or not. Liana and Josie had just met. How was it they were teaming up on him so effortlessly?

Liana nodded thoughtfully. "Yes, Josie, I do believe you are right about that."

"The question is, my little one, can you handle this one? Make him see the error of his ways?"

Liana arched an eyebrow. "What do *you* think?"

There was a moment of silence before both women broke into laughter.

Darik had had quite enough. "All right. I think it's time for us to eat, Josie. We wouldn't want Alphonse's newest creation to get cold."

Josie stood. "Oh, you're right, *ragazzo*, you're right. I'll be on my way. But Darik," she said, placing a hand on the back of his neck and pulling his face close to hers, "you pay attention to what this one says." She tapped him lightly on the cheek with her open palm. "She's good for you, my young friend. Don't mess it up!"

As Josephine disappeared once more, Liana pondered a piece of ravioli impaled on her fork. "She's right, you know."

"About messing it up?"

"No, she's right about openness and transparency being conspicuously absent from your list of character traits."

Darik definitely did not like the way the evening was shaping up. His plan had been simple—take Liana out for a wonderful dinner, have a little wine, get his courage up, and share with her what was burning up inside him, put into words the feelings for her that he'd realized he had been burying for months. That was what he wanted to do, but now it seemed all she wanted to do was press him about work.

He stirred at the wondrous food cooling on his plate, pushing around a stuffed manicotti like a squeegee. "I'm not really sure what you're talking about."

"Would you like an example?"

"It would help."

Liana put down her fork. "Okay, remember when you took your little side trip to Cacarus?"

"Yes, and as I recall, you covered for me."

"I *lied* for you."

"And I said I'd make that up to you."

Liana shook her head. "That's not the point. You didn't level with me, at least not until later when we were on our way to Bellona. And even then, you weren't completely honest—just like Josie said."

Darik made a mental note to avoid letting Liana and Josie get too near each other in the future. "I still don't understand what you think I'm hiding from you."

"Remember, back on the *Crow*, you were going to tell me what was really happening to your M-2s. Then you changed the subject, and you never did come back to it."

"As I recall, we both had a lot to drink that night, and then Nikky—"

"That's another thing. One minute, Nikky's your guest or something on the ship—it seems like you two are friends at least—then the next moment, we're heading off without him. You didn't explain where he went, what happened, nothing."

"I keep trying to tell you it's really not that big of a deal."

"But it is a big deal. I can tell this whole thing is bothering you. You haven't been sleeping at all since your hunting trip."

"That never seemed to bother you before." Darik smiled, a poor attempt to lighten the mood.

Liana ignored his comment. "You're up at night, moving around the flat like a wraith, and when you do nod off, you're tossing about, muttering things in your sleep that I can't even understand. This whole thing is hurting you. I can see it in your eyes, the way you sleep, and the way you stiffened up tonight when Josie mentioned Nikky."

Darik's look of surprise prompted Liana to go further. "That *was* Nikky she was talking about, wasn't it? The two of you used to come here."

"A couple times, yeah."

"So what is it? Do you miss him that much?"

Darik sighed. "Let's just say I could have really used his help with the latest project Jenkins has me on."

Liana picked up her fork again, speared a stuffed shell, and smiled. "Okay, now we're getting somewhere. You were about to tell me earlier that Mr. Jenkins has, as you put it, *other concerns*."

"Yeah, you could say that."

"And you need Nikky's help to deal with them?"

"He could've helped, yes."

Liana washed down a bite with another sip of wine. "Well, Nikky's not here, so I'll make a deal with you, Mr. Vice President. We'll enjoy this, *wow*"—she stopped short, experiencing the full impact of flavors in Alphonse's dish—"this *fantastic* meal, you can tell me about these concerns, and then you and I will figure out how to handle them, together."

*　　*　　*

By the time Josephine arrived with a cheesecake and coffee tray, Darik was in a much better mood. The final cheesy remnants of the *Quattro al Forno* stuck to the sides of his plate; their second bottle of Sangiovese was empty.

"So, okay." Liana's voice sounded melodic through the pleasant haze of rich food and wine. "We do some research, put all the data together, track down this mole, agent, whatever, find out who it is, and turn the whole thing over to Jenkins to deal with. Simple, right?"

Darik smiled. No, it wasn't that simple. Jenkins would not be getting his hands dirty. He would expect his newest vice president to see the investigation all the way through to its inevitable conclusion. But Liana was so confident, so supportive, so *beautiful*, that he wasn't about to bother her with details like that.

Josie set the tray on the table. "So, my darlings, the new dish. Was it to your liking then?"

Darik was about to say so when Liana spoke instead. "Oh, Josie, it was absolutely incredible! The entire meal, I mean. I've never had anything like it."

Darik chimed in. "You'll have to let Alphonse know. If the *Quattro* isn't on the main menu yet, he should seriously consider adding it."

Josie poured the coffee. "He'll be glad to hear it. Maybe you can still tell him yourselves a little later. I'll drag him back out before you leave. So, you are enjoying your time together as well?"

Liana grinned. "Yes, we certainly are. Thank you, Josie."

Josie set the coffee decanter on the tray and gave both of them a gentle pinch on the cheek. "Anything for our Darik and his beautiful, sweet companion. *Dolce mangiare*, you two!" And with that, she was gone.

Liana inhaled the brisk coffee aroma before sipping it. "I think she's rooting for me."

"*Rooting* for you?" Darik laughed. "She *loves* you! And so do—"

A larger piece of crumbly cheesecake crust caught in Darik's throat. Coughing, he reached for the coffee, burned his tongue, and grabbed a glass of water instead.

"You okay there, ace?" Liana looked amused.

Darik held up a hand and waited for the coughing fit to subside.

Liana held her coffee cup with both hands. "You were saying?"

"Uh, I was saying that Josie loves you. I've known her a long time. She's nice to everyone, but she took a special shine to you."

"And?"

"And I think Alphonse likes you as well."

"Right. Anything else?"

Still red from his coughing fit, Darik wanted to say more but felt the moment passing. "No, uh, I don't think so."

"Well, I'm sure it will come to you," Liana said. "Let me know when it does. How's your cheesecake?"

"Exceptional, but I'm so full, I don't think I can finish it."

Liana pushed her dessert plate gently toward the middle of the table. "I know, neither can I. That was amazing—everything you said it would be."

Something in her expression told Darik that, light as her tone was, she was just, perhaps, a little disappointed. He wondered if he should have said more, but when he opened his mouth, all he heard was his own voice saying, "So, ready to call it a night?"

"Yeah, I think so. Does Josie bring the check?"

Darik stood and walked over to pull out Liana's chair. "They have my credits on file. She'll just put it on account."

"You really are a regular here, aren't you?"

"Kind of, yeah. I'm a loyal customer at the very least." Darik took one more glance at the holo of Stephen XII and wondered just how far his loyalty to the Brobergos would stretch if it were actually tested. Dismissing the thought, he escorted Liana back into the main dining room where Josie was waiting.

"Ah, here they come. Alphonse! Get yourself out here! Our guests are leaving."

Alphonse rambled out of the kitchen, wiping his hands on a stained apron. "Well, my friends! Did you enjoy your dinner?"

"Completely." Liana squeezed both of Josie's outstretched hands. "It was, by far, the best dinner I've ever had."

Darik agreed. "You've really outdone yourself this time, Alphonse. I don't know how you will ever top it."

"Ah, but we will try, eh?" Alphonse grinned broadly. "But in the meantime, you two, I feel something special between you two." Still smiling, he shook a meaty finger at them. "Now don't you argue with me. I have a sense about these things!"

"Sure you do, sure you do." Josie was already herding her husband back toward his kitchen. "Enough already! That kitchen is not going to clean itself. Back to work!"

Alphonse hesitated, his expression suddenly more serious. "In a moment, Josie, in a moment."

Without warning, he stepped forward and enveloped both Darik and Liana in a firm embrace, stained apron and all.

"You listen to Alphonse." His whisper had a husky rasp. "You keep your eyes straight ahead—no matter what happens. God Almighty, our Father in heaven, has something for you. I don't know what, but a time is coming children. Watch, and be alert, okay?"

Darik shuddered. *No, Alphonse, don't ruin it. Don't destroy an otherwise lovely evening.* As Alphonse stepped back, Darik could see his eyes were beginning to brim with tears. Josephine dabbed her own with a soft lace handkerchief.

"He's right, children." Josephine helped Liana with her overcoat. "Now go, enjoy the rest of your evening. And God be with you!"

Back on the street, Liana pulled the collar of her coat more tightly around her neck. "What was *that* all about?"

"I don't know." Darik was aware of a rhythmic pounding in his chest.

"Well, they did serve us a wonderful meal," she said. "And as for that weirdness at the end, I'm sure they meant well. They seem harmless enough."

"Yeah, they are, I'm sure." Darik's tone betrayed that his mind was somewhere else. "Al and Josie are two of the—"

He stopped short. In the dim light of the street, he could see a tall figure approaching. Even observing from a distance, Darik was struck by a sense of recognition. The broad shoulders under a sleek gray overcoat, the smooth but purposeful gait, it looked all too familiar. His twinge of suspicion was confirmed as the man drew closer, the lighting panels reflecting off a perfectly bald head and revealing colorless, ashen eyes.

No! It can't be. What is he *doing here? Now?*

"Good evening, Mr. Mason."

"Graves." Darik tried to sound calm, certain that the quaver in his voice told otherwise.

"Are you going to introduce me to your companion?"

Like you don't know who she is.

"This is Liana, my, uh, personal assistant. Liana, this is Mr. Graves. He's a—"

"I'm an acquaintance." Graves grasped Liana's hand. Darik sensed Liana's slight shudder as he did so. "I take it you and Darik are out sampling the cuisine in this unique establishment?"

Liana brightened. "Yes. We just finished. Are you familiar with it?"

Graves smiled. "Oh, yes. I make a point to keep track of emerging trends, especially in my areas of interest. The owners of Bistro Riservata have attracted my attention of late."

No! Not Al and Josie.

Darik felt sick. He looked at Graves, his eyes wide in horror.

Reading Darik's unspoken plea in his expression, Graves shook his head imperceptibly.

"So I look forward to this visit." His smile didn't change. "I'm interested in some of the bold new choices the owners are making, but I'm not prepared to make any final judgments." He looked directly at Darik. "Not yet."

With a polite bow, Graves released Liana's hand. She rubbed it absently, as if it had suddenly grown cold. Finally, she shoved both hands into the pockets of her overcoat. "Well, I'm sure you'll find your evening every bit as satisfying as we did."

"I'm certain that I will. Good evening to you both."

Graves stepped into the bistro, the door clicking shut behind him.

Chapter 14

Scot Calgaro occupied his customary place in the squadron ready room—a swivel chair positioned near the back wall. For this meeting, however, he chose to forego his usual habit of resting his feet on another chair in front of him. From the terse announcement calling all pilots and senior ground personnel to assemble, he sensed that someone was about to get his or her rear end chewed, or several someones for that matter. Scot did not want to be in that particular group—again.

Glancing to his right, he saw Jani McLeod enter through the rear door. News of her heroics had spread quickly throughout the base. When the team had returned with Captain Dex D'Felco alive and in relatively one piece, there had been plenty of credit to go around, but everyone knew that none of it could have happened without Jani's single-minded obsession.

But for someone who had spearheaded a successful mission, Jani's demeanor since returning had been downright sour. He had wanted to congratulate her on the landing pad, maybe even give her some good-natured ribbing, but she wasn't having any of it. It wasn't like she was just brushing off a compliment—Jani was as self-assured as any of the Angels and not exactly known for false humility. No, this was different. She had shut down, and Scot couldn't figure it. Something down on that planet had shaken her—he could see it in her eyes. And, as much as he was reluctant to admit it, seeing Jani rattled shook him, too.

He hadn't spoken with her since. Rising from his seat, he sidled up to her for another try.

"Well, what can I say, Rabbit? You were right."

Jani kept her eyes straight ahead. "Yeah, it looks that way."

Scot spread his hands out, palms up. "That's it? You're not going to rub it in my face? All the things I said before you left about it being a fool's errand, how you were just going to get yourself killed on a wild goose chase—aren't you at least going to say I told you so?"

Jani barely moved her head. "No. It's over. That's enough, all right?"

"No," Scot said. "It's not enough, and it's not all right. Because you're not all right. What happened down there, Jani?"

She stayed silent.

"C'mon, it's me. With everything we've been through, together, you can't even tell me?"

He waited. Still no response.

Scot shrugged. "Okay, have it your way. I just wish I had been down there with you. I could have had your back, you know. Watched out for you." He turned away from her. "Somebody has to."

She turned and grabbed his shoulder, hard, spinning him back in her direction. "I don't need you looking out for me, Flash. I'm not your little sister, I'm not your…anything. Got that?"

Scot refused to look away. He met her gaze, eye to eye. "Fine, yeah, I got it." Uncomfortable, he couldn't resist a smirk. "Are you sure *you* do?"

She released her grip. "Oh, believe me, I am crystal clear on where we stand—which is nowhere. And as for the mission, it doesn't matter what happened. We pulled it off. Like you said, I was right. Now do me a favor and drop it."

The finality in her tone told Scot that it would be pointless to press the matter any further. Instead, he turned his head, looking around the room. Commander Lebrian and Lieutenant Commander Onigen had entered through the front door and were huddled in conversation near the first row of seats. Hagen still had a dermo-patch covering a large part of his forehead but other than that wasn't looking too worse for the wear. Lebrian's wingman, Flight Lieutenant Seltrice Valani, occupied a seat just to his right. Not part of the command conversation, she sat quietly, like most of the room's inhabitants, waiting for the meeting to begin. Exec Job Hansen, Flight Sergeant Drager St. James, and civilian Ops Tech Ronnie Wilco were also present, seated off to the left, about halfway back.

All pilots and senior ground personnel, the order had said. There were only a handful of personnel still missing, Scot mused, a couple of them with good reason, as he knew the Voor twins were still laid up in sickbay, the other uncharacteristically—and suspiciously—late.

"So, tell me, since you're right all the time and all"—he tried to keep his sarcasm at a properly low level—"is this meeting just a nice official *welcome home* for Deadeye?"

Jani shook her head. "I doubt it. That's not really the captain's style. No, I have a feeling some people are about to get chewed out."

"Some people?" Scot smiled to himself—at least she was talking now. He remembered Dex's order that there was to be no rescue or attempt to evac him after the Bellona mission and how Jani had somehow cajoled Hagen into letting them try. "Like you, for instance?"

"Maybe. I don't know. We really didn't discuss it much." She frowned. "No. I think this one is bigger than that. I overheard a little of him and Sarge recapping on the flight back. I think they've both had it with all the crap that's been going on since Bellona."

"Ah," Scot's eyes tracked toward the front of the room. "I take it you're referring to our good friend Lieutenant Valani."

"Among others. I thought you were going to keep an eye on things around here while I was gone."

"Hey," Scot said, "you knew how volatile everything was when you left." Given Jani's behavior on the landing pad, and her silence since then, he was determined to keep engaging her, even if it meant being on the defensive. "All I agreed to do was try and keep a reasonable lid on things. And I did! Right until we loaded up to come after you. I did my best to keep the fire under control."

"Or throw some fuel on it. I know how you are, Flash. You can't help yourself. You see Seltrice getting all bent out of shape and spouting off half-baked conspiracy theories, and you just can't resist egging her on."

Scot leaned back against the wall. "I really don't know what you're talking about."

Jani snorted. "Don't give me that. I've seen the way you are with her— you listen and you nod and you throw in subtle comments instead of just setting her straight. I don't think you even care about how much trouble she's causing—just as long as you get to have your fun."

Scot's face flushed. "Really. You think I just sat idly by when she and the others started talking about Pastor Nathan? *He's always there*, they've been saying. *They bring him in for prayer. He knows about every mission. Who else has that kind of access?* C'mon, we both know how stupid that sounds. And I would say so, every time I heard it. What else would you have me do?"

"I'm not talking about the accusations against Pastor Nathan. Most of the pressure against him is coming from inside the colony, and he can handle it. Some of the people in this room"—she glanced toward Seltrice—"have another target."

"Yeah," Scot agreed. "And that one I'm not sure is all that misguided."

At that moment, Adahn Manasser entered the room, squeezing past Scot on his way to a seat in the back row.

"Speak of the devil," Scot said under his breath.

"You don't know that," Jani hissed. "And Seltrice doesn't know that. You don't know anything."

"Exactly," Scot whispered. "We *don't* know anything. Don't be so naïve, Rabbit. Maybe Seltrice is on the right track. Maybe she's the only one getting us close to the truth."

"By spreading rumors without any proof? By hanging one of our own out to dry without any due process? Where is that going to take us?" Jani turned and headed for her own seat. "You're the one who's being naïve, Calgaro."

Scot considered going after her but was brought short by a brisk "Ten-Hut!" from Commander Lebrian. Captain Dex D'Felco had entered the ready room, and he did not look happy.

Casting his gaze over the assembled pilots, Dex made a conscious effort to avoid limping as he took his place behind the podium. Despite taking, at Hagen's insistence, some extra time before calling this meeting, he still did not feel completely up to the task.

"At ease. You may be seated." Dex placed both hands on the podium edges, grateful for the added support they provided. He allowed his eyes to rest on each person in the room before continuing. "I will be brief. During my absence, it is my understanding that Commander Lebrian and Lieutenant Commander Onigen have had this squadron under a strict gag order concerning the events over Bellona as well as any and all speculation regarding the security of this squadron, its mission data, and the overall security of this colony. Is that correct?'

The room remained silent, not one pilot or attendee particularly anxious to speak up first.

"I asked a question, Angels. Is that correct?"

"Yes, sir." The answer came from Ops Tech Ronnie Wilco.

Dex acknowledged him. "Thank you, Mr. Wilco. Interesting that the response would come from the only civilian in the room. Am I also to understand, therefore, that Mr. Wilco is the only person present who understands what a gag order means?"

Murmurs of "no, sir" floated about the room. Dex watched his pilots and friends fidgeting in their seats. This wasn't his preferred approach, but based on what Hagen had reported to him, the colony was on the verge of disintegration through in-fighting, mistrust, and fear. Any doubt, any rumors, even a single false report about their security, could be the catalyst to outright panic. The Angels needed to stand strong—and united. If there was a traitor among them, that person would be found out and dealt with, but he would not allow vigilante justice—not in the colony and definitely not in his squadron. His eyes fell on Scot Calgaro.

"Perhaps Lieutenant Calgaro would like to explain the meaning of a gag order. Lieutenant?"

Scot stood. "Yes, sir. A gag order restricts any and all conversation or correspondence regarding the subject matter included in said order among squadron personnel or with civilians, sir."

"And Lieutenant Valani, do you agree with that definition?"

Seltrice stood. "But Captain, on certain unforeseen occasions—" A sharp look from Dex cut her off. "Yes, sir," she said before returning to her seat.

"Lieutenant McLeod?"

"Yes, sir!"

"Officer Manasser?"

Adahn nodded, standing briefly. "Yes, sir."

"Mr. Hansen?"

Job answered quickly. "Yes, sir!"

"Flight Sergeant St. James?"

"Yes, sir."

"Commander Onigen?"

"Yes, sir."

Dex looked to Hagen. "Sarge, did I miss anyone?"

"Only us, Captain."

Dex started, and all eyes turned to the back of the room. Ravi and Purnima Voor stood side by side in the doorway, supporting each other's weight, Purnima leaning on Ravi's arm, with Ravi leaning against the door jamb. All hands, despite the tension of the moment, broke into spontaneous and heartfelt applause. The Voor twins looked momentarily stunned, then simply smiled, acknowledging the unexpected outpouring of affection.

"Sunfire, Moonlight, at ease. Please, take a seat." Dex smiled in spite of himself. "It is my understanding that you have been incapacitated following your performance over Bellona. As such, you were not aware of, or in any position to violate, the gag order in question."

"All the same, Captain," Purnima said, "we wish to stand accountable with our fellow squadron mates."

"Very well. Officer Voor and Officer Voor, do you understand, and agree with, the definition of a gag order?"

"Yes, sir," they both said in unison.

"So," Dex continued, "it would appear that we are all in agreement. He leaned forward, allowing his expression to harden again. "Then tell me. Why the hell has that order been repeatedly violated in such a haphazard, reckless, and indiscriminate manner?"

The room was silent. Dex waited. It was an uncomfortable process, but he knew that the stability of the colony, and the Angels' ability to continue to protect it, hinged on the next few moments.

"I will take your silence as acknowledgement that there are no acceptable excuses for the recent behavior of this squadron." His voice was low but firm. "So hear this. We will tolerate no further unauthorized discussion or speculation regarding the operations or security of this squadron or colony."

Dex surveyed the room again. He had everyone's attention. "Now, it is evidently the worst-kept intel on this planet that our mission details have been at risk for some time. It has been speculated, by many in this room, that said leaks may have come from a mole, a traitor, who may sit among us right at this very moment."

He paused, understanding that the Angels had just heard, for the first time, official acknowledgment from their commander regarding the possibility of an internal spy. It was impossible to know for certain whether keeping silent for so long had been a mistake or whether discussing it now would only make matters worse. Regardless, he had to trust his instincts, which told him that now was the time to get it all in the open.

"If that is the case, the perpetrator will be discovered. No one can hide in the shadows forever, and that person's deeds and identity will come to light. But also know this—individual speculation and rumor will only hurt any investigation, harboring the guilty under a cloak of innuendo rather than evidence. If any of you have credible information, you will bring it to Lieutenant Commander Onigen, Commander Lebrian, or myself. I want to be clear. If your information concerns one of them, you will bring it to me. If it concerns me, then you will bring it to one of them."

The looks of disbelief on the pilots' faces told Dex they had gotten the message—no one was getting a free pass. He continued. "Therefore, in the interest of security, as well as ensuring the ongoing gag order will not be violated—something this squadron has not yet shown itself capable of accomplishing—the lockdown that Commander Lebrian ordered will remain in place until further notice. Curfew will be enforced. Afterhours movement will be confined to standard watches only. All other personnel will be restricted to quarters. Is that understood?"

No one spoke.

"And finally, understand this." He forced himself to avoid looking directly at Seltrice. "The behavior of one individual affects this entire squadron. Not one of us has the right, or authority, to act without concern for the whole."

He waited, taking in the entire room again. "I believe that this needs to be said. We are all aware that, while we continue to follow a military structure in this squadron, the reality is that when we left Earth, we severed our ties with the UCN. Because of that, this squadron no longer falls under any official governing authority. In essence, each of you continues to serve at your own free will."

His eyes fell on some of the room's empty seats, three of them standing out, highlighted in his mind like ghosts from the all-too-recent past. "And you have done so with distinction," he rasped. "Some of your companions, Lieutenant Commanders Simmons and Alderson and, now, Lieutenant Geffory Bennet, have honored that commitment with their very lives."

Dex found strength in his voice again, steeling himself for what he had to do. "You have all made that same commitment. Yes, you serve at your own free will, but you also serve at our good judgement. If anyone here, anyone, has a problem with these current orders—if you decide to disregard these orders, if you feel the need to take the operation and security of this squadron into your own hands rather than working under the accepted parameters of the team, then you are free to resign. Your

Hornet codes will be canceled, and you can take your personal belongings and relocate to the colony proper because, frankly, we don't need you."

Dex regarded the silent room, seeing the looks of shock on various faces. In the two years that the Angels and the colony had been linked together, he had never needed to deliver such a message.

He allowed his voice to soften. "We have been given an assignment, Angels—whether that task is by divine appointment or just good moral sense is for each of you to work out in your own faith and conscience. But know that as long as I am alive and in command, we will stay true to that assignment. We will protect this colony, and others like it, from those who would seek to do them harm—to oppress them, persecute them, and even torture and kill them. We will respond to any and all threats against this colony with force—with the tools and gifts we have been allotted for that purpose. We will take up the offensive whenever and wherever we find locations and operations that would seek to deal destruction on those we have sworn to protect. That is our task, Angels. That is the mission we accepted two years ago. It is my intention to continue that mission. I cannot speak for anyone else—"

The sound of Hagen's and Lee's chairs scraping against the floor interrupted him. Both men faced him, standing at attention. Dex dipped his head in acknowledgment. One by one, each member of the squadron stood, quietly but firmly renewing their vow to serve and protect.

"All right." Dex's voice was hoarse. Feeling physically and emotionally drained, he was once again grateful for the solid support of the podium. His body wanted to collapse, but he held himself upright, gripping the platform even more securely, knowing he owed one more public acknowledgement to the squadron.

"I have only one more item to speak about. Unfortunately, this also has to do with an egregious violation of orders, insubordination of the highest level."

He looked first at Hagen, then at Jani.

"Mr. Lebrian, Ms. McLeod."

Everyone else regained their seats. Jani and Hagen stood alone.

"Did I, or did I not, leave specific orders regarding my possible evac from Bellona?"

"Yes, sir." Both kept their eyes straight ahead.

"And was I not clear that there was to be no rescue? That no one was authorized to take such a foolhardy risk?"

"Yes, sir."

"And yet the two of you deliberately chose to violate those orders and managed to involve Lieutenant Commander Onigen, Lieutenant Calgaro, and Ops Tech Wilco in your scheme as well?"

Jani and Hagen said nothing. Scot shifted uncomfortably in his chair.

"I really don't know what to say to you," Dex said, shaking his head. "Other than," he smiled, "thank you."

The entire room erupted in applause. After a few moments, Dex silenced them with a hand.

"And to the rest of you who supported their misguided mission to find me and who performed so admirably in the days leading up to and including our victory over Bellona, I also want to say thank you, job well done, and"—he paused before continuing, allowing himself to once again meet the eyes of every person in the room—"it's good to be home."

*　　　*　　　*

The Laurentian wine sparkled brilliantly in Kirrone Jenkins's glass, the rising bubbles reflecting a thousand tiny times the pale eyes of the man seated across from him.

"To that which was," he said, tilting his glass toward his companion's.

"And will be restored." Graves returned the salute before settling back into the comfort of Jenkins's lounge chair. A cool breeze played across the open terrace, causing a slight creasing of the skin on the top of his head, but Graves didn't appear to mind. In all the years he had known the man, Jenkins realized, he had never seen Graves adorn any kind of head covering, no matter how harsh the climate or conditions. He followed Graves's gaze out over the night skyline. The transparent deck and railing of the cantilevered balcony atop the Unity Tower provided one of the most spectacular views in the entire Coalition. The illusion of floating, without support, over a two-thousand-meter drop was entirely intentional. Most guests would have found the sensation to be nausea-inducing, but Jenkins rarely, if ever, entertained those of such weak constitution in his private penthouse residence.

In order to maintain the effect of furnishings and occupants floating in mid-air, Jenkins insisted that the maintenance crew keep the deck and rail meticulously polished and without defect—no easy task considering the dozens of birds that smudged the surfaces daily, impacting a barrier they could not see, paying the ultimate price for the view the two men were now enjoying. Through the crystal floor, the city of Compton fell away below them in all directions, the steady, gradual decline in building height giving silent testament to the power emanating from the single imposing edifice at the center—the Tower where the two men sat on its uppermost level, commemorating an overdue reunion, celebrating an old friendship with an even older bottle.

Jenkins eased back into his own chair, the soft leather yielding to his frame. He said nothing for a time, contemplating his friend over the lavish amber beverage he held. Finally, he took a sip, setting the crystal flute on the table beside him.

"It's good to see you again."

Graves smiled. "And you as well, my friend." He gestured with a sweep of his glass, the small arc tracing Jenkins from head to toe. "You're looking fit, as usual. I imagine that the difficulties of the past months haven't taken too physical a toll."

The left edge of Jenkins's thin lips curved upward, just the trace of a wry smile. "It hasn't been easy, but I've managed to maintain my regimen, in spite of everything." His expression softened. "After all, I shouldn't forget my training."

"You never would," Grave said.

"Since you brought up *difficulties*," Jenkins's continued, "it would seem, then, that Bellona was a total disaster."

Graves took a sip, rolling the priceless nectar around his tongue before answering.

"You could say that. Yes, the station was destroyed—completely unsalvageable. We can thank our mutual friend, Haman, for that. And the Zealots eliminated four squadrons of Marauders even though we had vastly superior numbers. I'm comfortable placing blame for that on the M-2 pilots if you are."

Jenkins grunted. "They never were my favorite modification. Complete mismatch of intended use and capabilities if you ask me."

Graves chuckled softly. "We're not being asked, but for what it's worth, I agree with you. As I recall, you were hesitant about using the M-2s as pilots since the beginning."

Jenkins swirled the Laurentian in his glass, casting multi-hued refractions as the spinning liquid clung to the sides, stopping just short of spilling over the rim. "We needed to establish orbital superiority to contain any Zealot colonists who would attempt to escape the ground assaults. M-2-piloted Marauders might have seemed like a solution at the time, but they've been an abysmal failure, and their manufacture and replacement have only slowed down our primary emphasis."

"Your project. The M-2/As." Graves had a sly smile on his face.

"Yes. Of course." Jenkins regarded him quizzically. "What are you getting at?"

Graves's smile broadened. "Well, if we're keeping score..."

"I wasn't aware that we were."

"Well, if we *were*," Graves continued, "that would be one failure on Haman, one on the M-2 pilots themselves, since neither one of us will take responsibility for them..."

"And?"

"And I'm afraid, my friend, that by your own logic, the failure of the M-2/A assigned to purge D'Felco on Bellona ultimately belongs to you."

Jenkins's felt a flash of anger, but only for a moment. Graves sat across the table from him, a look of good-natured self-satisfaction on his pale face. Jenkins had seen that look before—far too many times since he was a young teen, sitting under the smug tutelage of his mentor. He realized that no matter how much time had passed, no matter how much he had grown, Graves still knew how to bait him, how to set him up, as if this were still some sort of lesson.

But those days were long over. Now, he could address his former teacher as an equal, as his superior, in fact. If this was to be one of their thrust and parry exercises, Jenkins was more than up for the challenge.

He allowed himself a smile. "All right. Yes, the ultimate blame for the M-2 failure falls on me. And you know that I accept that responsibility."

Graves's expression turned more serious. He leaned forward, fully engaged in the contest. "You could have prevented it, you know. You could have kept that subordinate of yours on a tighter leash."

"I could have. But I didn't." Jenkins's eyes narrowed, but his smile remained. "I actually do have a plan, you know."

Graves sighed. "Ah, Kirrone, why you insist on playing this macabre little game of cat and mouse with that underling is beyond me."

"You mean like the one we're playing right now?"

"No. It's not analogous, and you know it. He can never achieve what you have—he'll never become what you are. Why do you waste your time on someone so lacking in heritage?"

Jenkins studied the glass in his hand, the bubbles bursting on the surface of the wine—each one carrying, and then releasing into the thin air, the minutest hint of unique flavor and aroma. "I don't expect you to understand. Just know that he is my responsibility, and he still serves my purposes. I will deal with him, appropriately and decisively, when the time is correct."

"Well, it doesn't really matter. As I said, the M-2/A failure is ultimately on you."

Jenkins leaned forward in his chair, his eyes reflecting the nighttime illumination of the city below.

"As the ultimate escape of D'Felco from Bellona is on you, my friend."

Graves laughed. "I'm impressed. Your level of intel has improved. You've clearly gathered additional resources that I wasn't aware of."

"So, you admit responsibility for his escape? And the loss of the tracker? That the failure was yours?"

"I will admit that I took on the responsibility of locating him and completing the task that seemed to so easily confound you and Haman, yes. So, in that light, what you are saying is true—D'Felco and Weis managed to evade me."

Jenkins offered Graves a dry look. "That's something that doesn't happen very often."

"Ever," Graves said.

"Until now." Jenkins walked to the railing and leaned over it, his back to Graves. A story below and several meters away, a flock of black swallows dipped and soared in formation, feasting on an invisible swarm of insects filling the cool night air. While the exercise of wits with his former teacher had felt pleasingly nostalgic, there was no further point, Jenkins decided, in the two of them bantering their way around so critical a subject. When he spoke, his voice was quiet.

"There will be a reckoning, I imagine, for both of us."

Graves sipped his wine again. "Oh, don't take it so hard. This was just a minor skirmish. I'm already exploring alternative paths to accomplish my objectives. Blackfriar is in place, and it's only a matter of time before he's able to reveal the location of D'Felco's colony, and by then, I'm sure you will have remedied whatever problems are causing your M-2s to fail in the field."

Jenkins whirled around. "I shouldn't *have* to remedy anything! A single M-2 could lay waste to an entire colony in minutes! The only reason there's even a chance of failure is because of the damn..."

He stopped, glancing around the empty terrace as though suddenly fearful of being overheard.

"It's all right. It's just me. You can say it."

"No. It's nothing."

Graves stood. He placed a hand on Jenkins's shoulder. "Kirrone. How long have we known each other?"

Jenkins raised his eyebrows. "A lot longer than most would believe was possible."

"Exactly," Graves affirmed, "and the history we share *wouldn't* be possible without the kind of relationship, the understanding—the *trust*—that we've always maintained. Something is on your mind, my old friend, and you know me well enough to know that I'm not going to allow you to carry it yourself."

Jenkins hesitated.

"He's not listening. If He were, I would know it. *You* would know it."

Jenkins's shoulder slumped. He looked into the pallid eyes of his mentor and closest friend.

"It's the restrictions. Our task is to seek out the Zealots, every colony, every man, woman, and child."

"Yes." Graves let his hand slip from Jenkins's shoulder, stepping back and allowing him to continue.

"And purge them," Jenkins finished.

Graves eyes widened, the hairless brow rising in question.

"Yes, yes, I know." Jenkins allowed the exasperation he was feeling to creep into his voice. "We only purge them *after* the interrogation. And that is precisely the problem." Conviction returning, he began to pace. "The M-2s are ready. One could easily take out a colony of a thousand, two...ten thousand! If we could just let them do what they are designed to do, there would be no stopping them."

"But instead?" Graves prompted.

"Instead, they have to stop at each Zealot, interrogate them, and give them an opportunity to renounce their faith."

Graves had taken his seat again. "And you disagree with that?"

Jenkins turned back toward him. "No. Of course not. You know yourself, nothing is more satisfying, more fulfilling, than watching one of them die moments after denying their god."

Graves pursed his lips. "Or, barring that, seeing them perish while still under the delusion of their lie."

"Yes," Jenkins said. "I'm not disputing that."

"But?"

"But it's just so damn inefficient. Each time an M-2 slows its assault to focus on a single captive, the chance of others escaping increases exponentially."

Graves tilted his head to one side. "Have any gotten away?"

Jenkins swallowed, looking over his shoulder at nothing. "Yes. A few. The individual interrogations are simply too slow, too time consuming. In one isolated instance, an M-2 failed to process an entire colony. Several of the Zealots escaped."

Graves sighed. "I see. And now, D'Felco has escaped as well, with intimate knowledge of the M-2 and its operation."

"But that's just it. It shouldn't matter." Jenkins ran a hand through his closely cropped silver hair. "Yes, there are problems with the laser cutters. But it's only when we stop their assaults long enough to perform the interrogations that the weakness can be exploited."

"You understand, of course, that the interrogations are compulsory."

Jenkins's impatience strained his voice. "Yes. I know that. But the M-2s are still vulnerable."

Graves took another sip of the Laurentian, realized that the effervescence had subsided, and placed the glass pointedly back on the table.

"So, fix it," he said.

"What?"

Graves's expression was impassive. "You heard me. You have a weakness in the M-2s. Fix it."

"Who are you to—" Jenkins stopped himself. "You don't understand." He shook his head. "You've never really understood."

Graves watched the flock of swallows, just off the balcony, soaring, weaving in and out with complex patterns, missing each other by mere centimeters, the combined beating of their wings underscoring their conversation with a pervasive low-frequency hum.

"I fail to see what there is to understand. You've been given an assignment. The M-2s are expected to be ready. Make sure that they are."

Jenkins strode over to face Graves, leaning over his former teacher, his jaw set. He spoke through gritted teeth, emphasizing each word slowly and distinctly.

"I don't have the time."

Graves picked up the wine glass he had rejected. He waved it in the direction of Jenkins's empty chair. "Sit down. Calm yourself."

Jenkins straightened, slowly unclenching the fists he had been making, his manicured fingernails pulling away from the scarred palms they had penetrated many times before. Turning, he retreated to his seat, leaning forward and rubbing his temple.

"There just isn't any more time," Jenkins muttered. "He said to release them all. He wants the job completed. And I could do that, right now, the way the M-2s are. Stun bolts, concussion grenades, the laser cutters—even in their intermittent state—they can do the job without a problem. But if you add the interrogation, the interminable pauses, and those damn Angels running around with their intel—" He caught Graves's eye. "And with Weis escaping, we also lost our only living link to Baker and the source of that intel, you know."

For the first time, Graves seemed genuinely perturbed. "Yes. I know."

Jenkins continued. "Considering all of that, it's only a matter of time before someone seizes upon our weaknesses and the entire initiative fails."

"All the same," Graves said, "that is the way He wants it accomplished. And neither you nor I are in a position to argue, are we?"

Jenkins shook his head. "No. But He won't allow another failure, either."

"One way or another, you are going to have to come to grips with this *conflict* of yours. The assignment must be completed, as required."

Their chairs faced each other, a meter apart, the crystal railing providing an invisible but secure barrier next to them. Jenkins looked up at his mentor, his teacher, his friend, searching for a sign, a glimmer of an alternative in those colorless eyes.

"It's not just my conflict, you know." Jenkins's voice was flat. "Kristof. Kristof Haman. He created the M-2s. He knows exactly what they are capable of. And he agrees with me."

A sudden dull thud made Jenkins, his nerves already on edge, start in his chair. One of the swallows, off-course from his companions, had struck the railing directly between them. It peeled away, leaving a bloody smudge on the spotless surface. Jenkins watched it fall, collapsed and lifeless, until it disappeared from view, tumbling toward the ground far below.

Graves drained the rest of the Laurentian in one gulp, his expression barely betraying the distaste he had for the stale drink.

"Yes," he said. "I'm sure that he does."

Chapter 15

There was a stark—and, Darik thought, perhaps deliberate—contrast between JenKore's and Whitaker Industrial's corporate headquarters. Merely stepping foot inside the Unity Tower—the tallest building ever constructed, located in the heart of Compton, the Coalition's most important city—filled one with an immediate sense of significance, a feeling that only inflated the higher one traveled up the tower. Earlier that week, from his newly appointed JenKore vice-presidential suite on the penultimate tier of the tower, Darik had been treated to a particularly intoxicating view—a thick layer of clouds having settled that morning in around the tower just a tier below while the sun, unobscured, shimmered over the soft blanket of white, creating the impression that Darik was like a god gazing down from his heavenly paradise. In the Tower, power was palpable.

Whitaker Industrial's headquarters, on the other hand, was made up of an unassuming series of one- and two-story buildings—a rural campus on the outskirts of Arlenn, a small southern community notable only for the seemingly out-of-place presence of Whitaker's company. The office spaces were simple, well-maintained, and above all functional, lacking the extravagant and often obscenely expensive design flourishes of so many of the corporate offices in downtown Compton. If JenKore's headquarters kept one's head in the clouds, Whitaker Industrial's was very much grounded.

Actually underground, in this instance, Darik mused, glancing around the subterranean R&D facility. In what had become an unfortunate habit of his, he began considering the life-choices that had led him to this moment, staring at a screen for the last two hours in some basement hundreds of kilometers from any civilization worth mentioning.

"Relax, son, we'll get it figured out," Benjamin Whitaker said, observing Darik's agitation while, it seemed, not correctly identifying the cause of it. To emphasize his point, Whitaker tapped the display screen with the end of his cigar, the hot ash poking directly through the holographic image. Whitaker Industrial apparently didn't have the same prohibitions against smoking as the corporate offices in Compton—that, or Whitaker felt comfortable bending the rules in his own building.

Darik was tempted to push the cigar to one side but didn't yet feel comfortable enough with the man to do so. He reminded himself that Whitaker, despite the rustic setting and folksy affectations, was one of the most powerful men in the Coalition. Instead, he shifted his weight to the left in order to view the laser cutter schematic from another angle.

"Whatever the defect is, it's hidden pretty deep," Darik said wearily. "It fails intermittently but catastrophically—the cutter just fizzles out, with no warning and for no apparent reason."

He looked up from the display, regarding the CEO. *It would seem we have found an ally in our cause,* Jenkins had said. *I will expect you to coordinate all procurement needs for your M-2/A division with Mr. Whitaker.*

In other words, trust him.

Darik set his jaw and continued. "The laser cutter failure is one of the main reasons D'Felco was able to evade the M-2 on Bellona."

At the mention of D'Felco's escape, Darik noted a slight twitch in the corner of Whitaker's eye. Had he already said too much? How much did Whitaker already know? Did Jenkins, or anyone else, still hold suspicions about Darik's own behavior on Bellona? His fears seemed to be confirmed with Whitaker's sharp gaze.

"I'm not sure I take your meaning there, kid. As I recall, Kirrone said that a couple of renegade guards took out the M-2 just before it finished up on Captain D'Felco—took it out with a spare laser cutter, no less."

"Yes," Darik insisted. "But if the M-2's own cutter hadn't failed earlier, it would have had D'Felco in the bunker, before those two had a chance to rescue him."

"And he'd be dead, just like the rest." Whitaker took a puff on the stogie. "Didn't those two guards get that cutter from you?"

Darik did not like the way Whitaker was eyeing him. He felt a clammy sweat forming just under the neckline of his tunic.

"Yeah, they, uh, confiscated it. That would be a more accurate way of putting it. Said I wasn't *authorized* to be carrying it around. I would have argued with them, but I wasn't really in the mood to be stunned."

"Uh huh." Whitaker chewed on the end of the cigar. "Well, it sounds to me like the fool thing worked just fine when they were taking that M-2's head off."

"But that's just it." Darik was anxious to get back to the main subject. "Like I said, it's an intermittent problem. It'll be operating just fine, cutting through phirmium, even duranium, you name it, and then suddenly it will just cut out. I've been through the specs a thousand times already." He waved his hand through the display in frustration. "It has to be a compatibility problem with the M-2 itself—a conflict between a couple of modules—but without being able to isolate it right at the point of failure, I'm stuck."

"And when the cutter fails, the thing is left without one of its primary weapons."

"And that's not the worst of it," Darik said. "Until I can find out what's causing the compatibility glitch, we have no way of knowing what other systems might start to fail because of it."

Whitaker frowned. "Now you're just starting to sound paranoid. Has anything else gone wrong with those units out there?"

"Not directly." Darik pointed to a feed in the lower right corner of the display. "But look at those readings—how close they are to the tolerances. They've never been that out of whack before. Whatever is causing that cutter malfunction"—he swallowed, shaking his head—"it could be cascading."

Whitaker's expression did not look like he was convinced. "So what do you think you should do?"

Darik motioned toward another icon, in the opposite corner. "I already did it. I've placed a temporary maintenance lockdown on all M-2/As currently in modification. I can't do anything about the ones that are already out there, but the ones in the facilities—the ones in production—they're going to stay there until I can figure this out."

The trail of smoke from Whitaker's cigar swirled around the telltale icon, circling Darik's handiwork, highlighting his responsibility in shutting down virtually all growth in the M-2 initiative. "Kirrone is not going to like that."

"What choice do I have?" Darik was exasperated. "Yeah, if I shut down production, even just a temporary hold, then I'm in hot water. But if I let us keep producing these units like they are, and then the failures start to multiply out there—failures that could leave witnesses coming right back at all of us…"

Whitaker patted his shoulder. "All right, son, all right. It's your call. Like I told you before, you just need to relax a bit. Look at this situation calmly. I'll tell you what. My company supplies at least a dozen components for those cutters, and I know their specs like the back of my hand. Why don't we start with those?"

Darik allowed his shoulder muscles to unclench and took a deep breath. "That would be very helpful." He glanced back at Whitaker, sincerely hoping he had actually found an ally, then back at the lockdown order prominently flashing on the screen. "Jenkins is going to be on my ass to get this solved, now more than ever."

Whitaker grunted. "Yeah, he's going to want his little monsters out there in the field working again, I suppose."

"As soon as possible, if I know what's good for me." Darik sighed. "You're right, he's not going to like this hold, but I don't have a choice. I have to get this figured out, and I can't have any more units failing out there while I'm working on it." He hesitated, trying to decide if opening up so much to Whitaker was safe or foolhardy. "It's just that I've never seen him so adamant. He's always been driven, but now, it almost seems like—"

"Like someone else is driving him?"

Darik narrowed his eyes. What Whitaker was saying sounded right, but who could possibly drive *Kirrone Jenkins*?

"I don't know. Possibly." Darik considered the point. "At any rate, I can't say I blame him. The sooner we have the M-2s back out there doing their job, the better."

"Their job?"

"You know. Finding the Zealots. Taking care of the problem."

"And avenging your parents?"

That stung, but as Darik shot a look at Whitaker, he didn't see a challenge, only a soft, empathetic expression.

"I understand. I really do. You're still hurting over what happened, and I suppose it's natural to want to get even."

Darik kept his expression hard despite Whitaker's understanding words. "And can you think of a better way?"

"Maybe." Whitaker put the cigar back in his mouth and took a deep draw. "For now, I guess you dance with the girl you brung. But you might want to watch yourself along the way."

"What do you mean?"

Whitaker exhaled slowly, the thick aromatic smoke all but obscuring his face. "I don't have to tell you what kind of man my friend Kirrone is. Or what he and his associates are capable of—what they do to people who cross them." Through the gray wisps, Darik could just make out Whitaker's unblinking dark-blue eyes. "I just think you should be careful."

At the mention of his safety, Darik became again acutely aware of his surroundings, two floors underground in a desert in the middle of nowhere. His muscles had involuntarily tensed once again.

"I'm *being* careful. Why do you think I took the time to fly all the way out here? I have to get these cutters fixed! I don't want to be on the wrong side of Jenkins."

Whitaker narrowed his eyes. "Or worse—end up just like him."

Darik considered Whitaker, trying to read his expression. Had Jenkins put him up to this? Was Whitaker intentionally trying to get him to trip himself up, to make a mistake and say something he shouldn't? He finally concluded that it didn't matter. If Jenkins knew about Bellona, he could deal with Darik any time he wanted. If this was some sort of test—another one of Jenkins's mind games—well, that was fine, too. Darik had already survived more than enough of them. Right now, all he wanted to do was solve the riddle of the laser cutters so he could move on to yet another one of the impossible tasks Jenkins had assigned to him, not the least of which was finding the security leak in the M-2/A project itself.

Suddenly feeling quite annoyed at Whitaker's close, personal line of questioning, he turned back to the cutter schematic.

"So, are we going to check those components or not?"

"Sure, kid," he said, smothering the remains of his cigar on the worktable. "Back to work."

*   *   *

Their first outing, a simple twenty-minute walk, had ended with Ravi and Purnima Voor staggering back to the infirmary and collapsing into their berths, unable to move for another two days. Their second journey, surprising Dex and the rest of the squadron during the briefing, had taken a similar toll, though their recovery time had been quicker. The twins were slowly getting stronger. They could feel it.

"I'd like"—Purnima strained to put together the words between forcefully drawn breaths—"to stop at our quarters since we're so close."

She pulled on Ravi's arm, simultaneously relying on it for support while urging him further down the dimly illuminated hall. "I want to pick up something new to read."

Ravi allowed his sister to lead on. He knew she had exhausted every option on her handpod and was looking for something to ease the boredom that would soon follow, as this 0300 rehab walk would almost certainly tax them back to a bed-ridden state for another day or two. Still, the pilot quarters were the farthest they had managed to travel from the infirmary—a clear sign of progress—so why not take advantage of the situation and restock their libraries?

He was about to key the access code to their shared quarters when the sound of soft footsteps just around the corner made him pause. Ravi turned and leaned back against the door, preparing his explanation as to what he and Purnima were doing out and about so many hours after lockdown. The night watch, whoever it was, would have to understand that when the ability to move about returned, the twins had to take advantage of it, no matter what time of day or night it might happen to be.

Adahn Manasser seemed to be as surprised to see the Voors as they were to see him. He hesitated only a moment before his face brightened with a soft smile.

"Sunfire, Moonlight. It's good to see you on your feet again."

Purnima smiled back cautiously. "I imagine you are wondering what we are doing out so late?"

Adahn dismissed the question, one shoulder moving noncommittedly. "Not really. Why would I?"

Ravi frowned. "Aren't you the night watch?"

Adahn laughed. "No. Not tonight. For some reason, I keep getting skipped over for that duty. No, I'm just on my way back from the lav."

Ravi and Purnima both grew suddenly faint. If they hadn't been leaning against the door, they might have fallen. An overload of new sensory information flooded their minds, shocking their nervous system and threatening to overwhelm them. Ravi put a hand to his temple.

"Are you all right?" Adahn took a step forward.

Purnima stepped between them. "Yes, we're fine," she said quickly, then slowed, allowing her voice to calm. "We're just—worn out. And a long way from the infirmary."

"And we'd better be heading back," Ravi added.

Adahn's expression showed concern. "Would you like me to accompany you? Make sure you're all right?"

"No, we'll be okay," Purnima said. "We just overdid it a little."

Adahn started to turn away, then stopped. "Are you sure?" he asked.

Ravi took Purnima's arm, heading back in the direction they had come. "Yes, we are certain. Good night, Officer Manasser."

"If you say so." Adahn did not look convinced. "Good night." He moved down two doors, keyed in his sequence, and stepped into his quarters.

"What was that?" Purnima breathed.

"Keep walking." Ravi pulled on her arm.

"But you felt it too, right?"

Ravi nodded weakly. "Let's just get some distance right now, okay?"

It took several minutes at their restricted pace to make their way down two more corridors, the siblings finally stopping, on the verge of exhaustion, near the squadron mess.

Ravi looked around. The hall was understandably deserted. "Okay, yes. I felt it, too."

"But what *was* it?"

Ravi drew a deep breath. "I honestly don't know. I was just overwhelmed with the feeling that Officer Manasser was lying. No," he corrected himself, "it wasn't just a feeling. I *know* he was lying. It was almost like I could see it. I was looking directly at him, but my mind was seeing something else."

Purnima's eyes widened. "He wasn't retuning from the lav. He wasn't even on the base."

"No," Ravi agreed. "He wasn't. He was coming back from the colony."

Purnima looked back in the direction of the pilot quarters. "But how did we both know that? Nothing like that has ever happened before."

Ravi shook his head. "I don't know. Maybe it's a latent ability."

Purnima pursed her lips. "It could have been triggered by the strain on our systems. Every time we were pushed in the past—" She stopped, a memory forming while tears brimmed in the corner of her eyes. "No. Not again."

Ravi put his hands on her shoulders. "It doesn't have to be like that. It *won't* be like that."

She shook him off. "No! Every new ability, every slight anomaly we showed, the intrusion, the pain. I can't Ravi! I just can't!"

Ravi grabbed her shoulders again, keeping a firmer grip this time. "Stop it! Listen to me. He's *not here*. Pickett is not here. Nothing like that is going to happen."

They stood face to face, Purnima hyperventilating, her eyes wild with fear. Ravi held his grasp, looking into her eyes, waiting, holding her until the panic attack subsided.

"Nima, no one here is going to hurt you," he said with as much authority as he could muster.

Finally, she looked down. "You're right," she panted. "I'm sorry. But until we figure this out—what happened, what it meant, if any of it was real in the first place—we can't tell anyone."

"Nima…"

She met her brother's gaze. "No. I'm serious. This is new for us, and new always means danger."

"But if Officer Manasser is lying, we have a responsibility to the squadron."

Purnima stood up straight. "And just what are we supposed to say? *Captain D'Felco, we don't know what happened, we don't really know anything, but we* have a feeling *Officer Manasser just lied to us about going to the lav?* Isn't that exactly the kind of speculation the captain warned us against?"

Ravi sighed. "You have a point. But this is different, isn't it?"

"Yes." Purnima set her jaw firmly. "It is different. It's different because *we* are different. But nobody knows, or can know, just how different we are. And right now, with this new, whatever it is, even we don't know how different we are." Her eyes softened. "Don't you understand? We can't risk that right now."

Ravi looked away. "But we have to do something."

Purnima nudged her brother's shoulder. "We will. We'll stay alert. We'll keep getting stronger." She took a deep breath, shuddering as she exhaled. "And we will find out, together, what this new ability means."

Ravi acquiesced. Experience told him that prolonging the debate would be pointless—she had always been the more stubborn of the two. Besides, there was a good possibility that she was, in fact, right about this.

They turned in the direction of the infirmary, taking only two steps before Purnima stopped them again.

"Wait. We're already near our quarters. Why go back to the infirmary at all? We can rest, here, just as well, perhaps better. And it will be easier."

"Easier?" Ravi asked.

Then, comprehension dawning, he answered his own question.

"To keep our eyes on Officer Manasser."

Chapter 16

"There it is again!" Liana pointed at the screen. In her excitement, she overshot the mark, her neatly manicured bright red fingernail poking completely through the suspended array of intersecting platonic solids floating in the upper left corner of the display. She pulled her hand back, allowing Darik a better view of what she had seen.

Darik leaned in, his brow furrowed. "Yeah, I see it. But tell me again, what does it mean?"

"It means, my darling, that we are that much closer to a well-earned vacation—a proper one this time."

Darik continued to stare at the gyrating mess of symbols. "What? You didn't enjoy our trip to Bellona?"

"The fireworks were impressive, I'll admit, but I didn't exactly care for all the waiting around beforehand. See, I think Josephine had you dead to rights—your idea of a romantic getaway is to drag me along on some *business* trip."

Liana's mention of Josie brought a flood of memories to Darik. He had been more than relieved, following the encounter with Graves outside Bistro Riservata, to hear her joyful voice on his handpod the next day. Josie had expressed again how much she absolutely loved Liana and how diligent Darik had better be not to lose her, if he knew what was good for him. When Darik had casually inquired about their last customer of the evening, Josie had simply stated that the delightful Mr. Graves had enjoyed a wonderful meal, been very complimentary, and left. Darik had come away from the conversation more confused than ever. Just what was Graves up to?

Setting aside for the moment his concerns about the Brobergos, he glanced over at Liana, studying her expression to see if there was any underlying sign of genuine resentment about Bellona. They had both, in

153

the following weeks, made light of the ordeal—the absurdity of "vacationing" to that hellhole of a planet only to suddenly find themselves caught in the middle of a warzone. But as much as they had tried to brush it aside, there was no escaping the fact that it had been a harrowing experience—for both of them. "You're right," he said. "At least Bellona set the bar low. I promise our next destination will be far more romantic. They say the dust storms on Cacarus aren't so turbulent this time of year." He turned his attention back to the screen. "So you're saying that those symbols there—they will lead us to the leak?"

Liana zoomed in until the rotating solids occupied the entire center of the screen. "No, they won't lead us to the leak. Those symbols *are* the leak, or more accurately, they are the leak's signature."

The enlarged display was almost dizzying. Bluish lines intersected with amber and red, pulsating whenever their vectors crossed. Their motion was entrancing but, for Darik, utterly inscrutable. For the hundredth time, he wished Nikky was there. Sure, Liana was much better company, and she certainly smelled better, but when it came to explaining the nuances of their now-shared investigation, she could be even more enigmatic than the bald little tech.

The pulsing display was hurting his eyes. He blinked and turned again to Liana. "I still don't get it."

She sighed, not an altogether unpleasant sound. "See, what we're looking at here is the residue left over from an unauthorized intrusion. Every cyber-dink would like to be in and out without a trace, but to my knowledge, it can't be done. There's always a trace, a signature, if you will, that's left behind—if you know where to look."

Darik stared at the display. "And how do you know where to look?"

Liana laughed as she continued to manipulate the screen, displaying the signature from several angles at once. "What? Do you think my first job was as your secretary?"

"Administrative assistant," Darik reminded her.

"Whatever. I took a few courses at university and found a job at JenKore was down in the bit bucket. It was really entry-level, but I saw low-end versions of this stuff all the time. Nothing like this, though." She brushed his arm, the soft touch of her fingers sending a slight shiver all the way up to his neck. "Working for you was a step up."

She turned her attention back to the screen. "What I can't believe is how you *don't* know all about this. How did you get promoted so high up in mining security without that kind of training? And how did you expect to cover your tracks when you started digging around?"

Darik shrugged, embarrassed by this apparent glaring omission in his professional skillset. "I guess I must've been lucky."

"Lucky is right, Mason—lucky you had me watching your back. I mean, can you imagine what would have happened if—Wait, there we go!"

"What?"

"I've got it! This same signature pops up on twelve different time stamps, each one indicating a breach."

Darik was impressed. "You have *got* to show me how you do that."

"It's not difficult, with the right tools." Liana indicated her handpod. "I've got the subroutine that isolates them right here."

Darik grabbed his own handpod. "I want to try. Can you shoot that program to me?"

Liana regarded him skeptically. "Are you sure? Isn't it more fun having minions like me to do your bidding?"

"I'm serious. You said yourself that you were surprised I got this far without this kind of knowledge. Call it professional development."

Liana laughed and wiped the screen clear.

"Hey!" Darik stared at the blank space over the desk. "What did you do that for?"

"Relax." Liana waved her handpod near Darik's. "Those signatures aren't going anywhere. I figure if you want to learn this, we need to do it right. Now open up the pack I just sent you."

Feeling very much like the newest of trainees, Darik looked down at his handpod. A new icon, a pair of bright red lips, floated just above its surface. He wiped his thumb through the image, which promptly disappeared.

Liana noticed his concern. "Don't worry. That's it. It's running. It's the kind of pack you want to keep in the background. But as long as you are near the workstation, you can use it to filter out the trace signatures." She brought the standard display back up over the desk. "Now watch the screen."

"What am I looking for?"

"Anything even slightly unusual. When you see it, tap your pod. It will isolate the anomaly and bring it up for you."

Darik's hands were shaking. He stared at the screen, feeling a little foolish. "I don't even know where to—"

"There. You missed it." Liana swiped the display backwards. "Now try again." She squeezed his free hand. "And *no talking*."

This time he saw it. A sudden, minute flash in the upper right corner of the screen. It was the kind of glitch he had probably ignored his entire career as just so much static. He reflexively brought his right index finger down, tapping his handpod. He was rewarded with the same list, the same twelve time stamps that Liana had uncovered earlier.

He whistled softly. "That's—that's pretty cool."

"It's all in the timing. Well, that and an above-average hacking packet. Take a look."

Darik followed her eyes down to his own handpod. A smaller version of the hacker's signature gyrated above it.

Liana frowned just a little. "So there you go. You have the signature locked in, and you know how to isolate it to individual time stamps. Congratulations. You are now Nikky 2.0." She feigned getting up from her chair. "So if you will not be needing me for anything else, Mr. Mason—"

"Very funny." Darik placed a hand on her shoulder, gently guiding her back into her seat. "Yeah, I have an idea how to spot an anomaly. I even have a cute new tool to isolate it. But I still don't know what to make of any of it."

Liana smiled again. "Sure you do. Come on, think it through."

Darik still felt self-conscious about his lack of expertise, but he decided to take a shot. "So, each breach is a part of a package the leak was after, right?"

"Exactly," Liana said. "He couldn't risk going after it in one big chunk. It doesn't even look like he could. The data is spread all over the system. Compiling it would have been too noticeable—he had to piecemeal it."

"So, we have the signature, and we have the time stamps—"

"So that's *when* he was hacking," Liana said, prompting him to go on.

"So how do we find out *who* it was?"

"That's the question, isn't it. All right. Here we go." Liana wiped the screen to one side, a new display resolving in its place. "The hack had to come from within the Unity Tower. The JenKore system is just too tight for an outside intrusion. Here's a list of everyone who could possibly have been in the system during any of these breaches. Now we narrow it down by cross-checking the names to match *all* of the time stamps and *viola*. Uh-oh."

"What?"

Liana pointed at the screen. "Just how many employees does this company have?"

Darik was deflated. The screen scrolled through a seemingly endless list of names, every one of them apparently in the building each time the system was compromised.

"That's a lot of people," he said.

"Damn it," Liana said quietly, resting her hands on the desktop.

Darik stared at the list. "And there's no way to narrow it down further?"

"Not without potentially losing our suspect. I mean, we could pare it down by job class or access level, but it could be anyone. There's just no way…" She suddenly sat up straight. "Unless."

"Unless, what?"

"Unless we set a trap. You said yourself that Jenkins told you the leak is still digging—apparently still working here, right?"

"Yeah. He figures the mole doesn't have everything he needs—yet."

Liana raised an eyebrow. "So, if we could figure out what data he's going to go after next, we could catch him in the act. Slap a trace-agent on the signature and we'd have him."

Darik frowned. "Right—but how do we determine that?"

"Well, we can at least get a general sense of direction from his old tracks. The problem is, we don't know what *specific* data he's been targeting." Liana swiped the original screen back to center.

"You can't tell?"

"No," Liana said, motioning toward a garbled mess of text beneath the hack signature. "Every byte he's gone after has been hyper-encrypted. There's no way I can break it. I don't know anyone who could."

"I can think of one person," Darik said, "but we left him on Bellona."

"You're right," she said, resting her chin in her hands. "I'm sorry, but this was the best I could do." Her shoulders sagged. "Unless we want to personally investigate about twenty thousand individual people, I think we're at a dead end."

Darik gazed down at her. As confident as she had been moments ago, she looked equally as defeated now. He could help her, he realized, and in doing so help himself. Yeah, he knew damn well what information the leak was going after—the M-2/A project archives. And if Liana could identify that data, perhaps she could get one step ahead of the hacker, catch him in the act, and they could be done with all this. In fact, she wouldn't even have to decrypt the JenKore system. Everything Liana needed was on a simple data chip he had given to Eliot before his trip to Bellona. Upon his safe return, he had sought out his friend, retrieved the chip, and stowed it safely in a lockbox in his apartment right alongside D'Felco's knife.

The memory sent a new chill through Darik. Why not give Liana the information? He pictured the two of them on a beach on Virgilia, celebrating their accomplishment. The hacker would be caught and dealt with, the information would be safe, and the work of the M-2/As would continue.

No. He realized that he had taken too much of a risk getting Liana involved at all. The data the hacker was after—the same information that was on the chip in his apartment—if it were leaked to the Coalition government, it was enough to get Kirrone Jenkins, that weasel Kristof Haman, himself, and anyone else who had incriminating knowledge of the project arrested and convicted on a fourth-degree offense. Capital punishment in the Coalition was rare, but a distinct exception was made for violation of the Asimov Accords. The potential for unwittingly creating an existential threat to humanity was too great to be taken lightly. Darik knew the machines—their programming, their limitations. He knew that they were nothing close to resembling the abominations humanity had fought in the old wars. But he also knew that Coalition authorities would not be sympathetic to nuanced arguments on the matter.

He looked at Liana, her eyes still staring wistfully at the screen, as if willing another elusive key to the puzzle to reveal itself. No, it was better this way. She shouldn't—she couldn't—know the details.

She noticed his attention, her eyes narrowing. "Hey, sport. Is there something else you want to tell me?"

Darik picked up his handpod, the hacker signature retreating as he saved it. He shook his head. "No. Nothing. Like you said, it's a dead end."

*   *   *

The relief in Baker's voice was obvious, despite the ever-present comm encryption.

"Dex, my boy! I can't tell you how good it is to see you alive and kicking."

The two men had navigated the customary security questions and protocols. Both were reasonably certain the comm was secure and that they were, indeed, who they claimed to be. This seemed especially important to Baker, who gave the impression he was talking to a ghost.

"We thought you were a goner for sure. The last thing my sources were able to tell me was that you got yourself all jammed up planet-side disarming those launchers."

Jammed up was an understatement. Dex unconsciously rubbed his right shoulder. "Yeah, it got a little messy. I ended up face to face with an M-2."

"You don't say." With the image and voice distortion, it was difficult for Dex to detect nuances in Baker's expressions, but he certainly didn't sound as surprised as Dex might've expected. Baker, as usual, likely knew more than he was letting on. "And how'd you manage to survive that?"

"Mason, the M-2 project lead, saved me—took the thing's head off with a laser cutter."

"Mason...now that's interesting. A secret believer?"

Dex remembered the look in Mason's eyes—the anger, the loathing. For a moment, Dex had wondered if Mason was going to execute him himself.

"I don't think so. I'm not sure why he did it..." Dex recalled Mason picking up the knife and disappearing into the dark. Since that night, he had thought about that odd encounter dozens of times, but he still wasn't quite sure what to make of Mason or his motivations. "So, yes, the mission was a little rough. But we both know what I signed up for."

Baker's obscured facial expression was obvious enough this time—he did not look pleased. "Yeah, kid, and as I recall, we also disagreed about it. I never bought in to your fool idea that you'd order your squadron to jump out without you. That was stupid, and we almost lost you because of it."

Dex felt weary. "We don't need to have this conversation again, you know. It just wasn't worth it—it wasn't *tactically sound*—for anyone to risk capture in an evac attempt, not to mention the danger to the colony that any delay would have—"

"No, you're right. We *don't* need to have this conversation again, ever." Baker didn't often sound angry, but he certainly did now. "You're their leader, Dex. Those pilots, that colony, they still need you. I don't know what kind of crazy you had messing up your mind, hotshot, but your endgame on Bellona sounded more like a death wish than a strategy. You don't have time for that kind of self-pity."

Dex sighed. He wondered if, perhaps, Baker was right. Had that knife—the artifact that had mysteriously appeared in one of Baker's shipments—messed him up even more than he realized? Yes, the mission to Bellona had been critical. The modification of the M-2s had to stop. But what about his personal mission—the cowboy tactic of going it alone on the surface, hoping for the off-chance that he might run into Darik Mason and have an opportunity to take vengeance on the man he felt was most responsible for Bulldog's death? That element of the plan had been ill-conceived from the outset. Now, he was grateful that he hadn't managed to track down Mason earlier that evening—if he had, they would both undoubtedly be dead.

He shuddered to think of how much more his lapse in judgment might have cost. Geff Bennet was gone—how many more might have died just to satisfy his misguided desire for revenge? But no, Dex reminded himself. The station had to be destroyed, and the Angels had needed every hand at the stick out there. His plan, despite his questionable personal motivations, had been the only way. He smiled grimly at Baker's distorted image. "I don't have to tell you how this works. You give us the intel. You set up the drops, the targets, the locations. But the squadron tactics and mission parameters—those are my decisions to make."

"Including ordering your pilots, your friends, to leave you behind?"

"Exactly."

Baker's image leaned forward. "And how did that work out for you?" Dex could detect a trace of a smile on the pixelated face.

"I think you can guess. Jani, *Lieutenant McLeod*, defied orders and came back to get me—with some help from her friends."

Baker chuckled, the sound coming through as a tight staccato. "I'm not surprised. That's another hug you give that gal for me, all right? Assuming you didn't get all law and order and lock her in the brig when you got back."

"If that were the case, she'd be cellmates with half the squadron. No, I'm going to overlook this one, given the circumstances"—he moved his shoulder to a more comfortable position—"and the outcome."

Baker seemed satisfied. "Good. It sounds like you're coming to your senses after all." His voice grew more serious. "It really is good to see you," he said, "especially now."

That got Dex's attention. "Now? What's going on?"

"You're sure you're okay? Are you functional?"

"Yes, I'm fine," Dex lied. "What's this about?"

"Well, I hate to put this on you and your people, especially considering what you just went through. I wouldn't ask, but this situation is critical, and time is short. I've got some intel. And now that you're back..." He shook his head. "No, I can't ask this. You folks are in no shape for another mission."

Dex felt an electric chill shoot up his spine. The dread and uneasiness he had felt in the weeks leading up to Bellona were gone. He recalled the sense of purpose and peace he had felt gazing up at the stars that night after he had faced the M-2—the sense that he and the Angels had accomplished something meaningful, something beyond themselves. He brought himself to a posture of attention in his chair.

"Baker, what have you got?"

"Are you sure?"

Patience was a virtue Dex was still working on. "Yes. I'm sure. C'mon, you said it was critical. What have you got?"

Baker reached for a data chip. "I've received a transmission. Now, we know that Aphea wasn't the last colony that was attacked. I'm glad you and your team were able to make a difference in that instance, but there have been others. We've been receiving reports—it's not pretty. You all destroying that station slowed them down, but who knows how many of those damn machines were already out there?"

Dex felt a pang in his stomach. The thought of an attack on a defenseless group of colonists was horrifying. He had seen firsthand what a single M-2 could do. "So another attack is imminent? Where?"

"No, not imminent, at least not any that I know about." Baker's distorted image pixelated further, giving Dex the impression that he was fidgeting in his seat. "I've been working on that, trying to get a better handle on our intel and maybe slowing them down in the process if I can. Maybe it's working, maybe not, I don't know." His image paused, looking directly at Dex, the lack of motion bringing the encrypted feed to almost full clarity. "This isn't about an upcoming offensive. The attack I'm talking about has already happened."

Dex had a vision of carnage, hundreds of slaughtered colonists, the aftermath of a massacre.

"Already happened? I'm not sure I understand. You said time was short. If the attack has already happened, what could—"

"That's just it. This time, there are *survivors*."

Dex's eyes widened. "Survivors? Someone actually survived one of those things?"

"Yeah. No small feat, as you know. Not only did a few of them survive, but they managed to get out a distress call. I have it here if you want to see it."

Baker moved to slide the data chip into a port, then hesitated.

"There's one more thing you need to know. We've had some time to analyze the original data feed I showed you—the one that showed your friend dying. My guys aren't one hundred percent certain, but they think they've got its origin coordinates isolated. And there seems to be a match between the two signals."

The twisting in Dex's gut doubled over itself in a knot. His mind raced back to that feed—his friend, Bulldog, interrogated and brutally executed by the loathsome M-2. Now, Baker was saying that there were possibly survivors from that same attack. Baker's next words echoed Dex's own thoughts.

"So I'm thinking there's a possibility you might already know some of the people in this feed. Are you ready, Dex?"

Dex nodded mutely, and Baker slid the chip into the port. A few beats later, the feed appeared on Dex's screen. His breath caught in his throat.

A thin, haggard woman appeared, her brown hair matted and stringy while smudges and bruising obscured her elegant features. Next to her stood a young man, probably in his late teens, his clothing torn and bloodstained. Both were looking down, appearing to adjust the recording equipment. Behind them, slightly out of focus, he could make out several others, some standing, others laid out in makeshift cots. All of them looked like they had passed through hell.

As the woman and young man looked up, their faces fully visible to the feed, Dex gasped. Full recognition and an overwhelming sense of déjà vu overrode his other senses. He had experienced this same feeling, this shock of recognition, when Baker had played the last transmission for him, the day he had learned that Jonathan "Bulldog" Buhl had been captured and executed by an M-2.

162

The figures in the recording told their story. They, along with nine others, were all that was left of a colony, over five hundred souls attacked and slaughtered by a lone M-2. They had been powerless against the machine, unable to stop its relentless attack. Dex's mind was reeling, unable to adequately process the torrent of new information and raw emotions. Sorrow, despair, anger, determination—all were vying to influence his next thought, his next decision.

With effort, he concentrated on the facts. The surviving colonists had managed, through a combination of ingenuity, sacrifice, and outright miraculous deliverance, to escape, at least temporarily, the onslaught of the machine. Hidden in a cave, kilometers from their destroyed base, they had prepared the recording, a distress call, and undertaken the bold plan to find the way back to their main communications array, transmitting their location to the only man they felt they could trust—a man who had quietly supplied their colony throughout the duration of Prop 413. Now they were turning to him in their most desperate need. Through his shock, Dex realized that Pella was not the only colony under Baker's benevolence and protection.

The two figures froze in the hastily ended transmission. Text beneath their images revealed encrypted coordinates and a time stamp. The recording was already two weeks old.

"Baker, why didn't we get this sooner? That M-2 might already have those people."

"Now hold on. It took that long to get to me. The equipment they used must have been all but trashed. The data was so messed up, it took my guys all this time just to decrypt it. And even if I had gotten it earlier, my only contact with the Angels—that's you, son—was missing, presumed dead."

Dex understood. "Okay, but I'm here now. We have to rescue those people."

"I thought you'd feel that way. But are you sure you and your team are up to this? After Bellona, and what you went through—"

"We're soldiers. Pilots." Dex's jaw was set. "That is why we're here. You said yourself that you had nowhere else to turn. If we don't help them, no one will. Besides," he said quietly, "I owe it. I owe it to Bulldog."

Baker cocked his head. "Bulldog? Your friend? So we were right— it's the same colony."

Dex's eyes burned. "Yeah, you were right. The two people in the transmission, their names are Janet and Jason. That's Bulldog's wife"— he continued to stare at the two static images on the screen before him— "and one of his sons."

Chapter 17

Kirrone Jenkins staggered, his shoulder brushing against a shelf, knocking a pair of ornate Travarian urns to the floor. He brought his hands to his ears, not in response to shattering crystal, but in a vain attempt to shut out the sonorous voice reverberating through his mind.

Failure, the voice intoned, over and over. *You have failed.*

"No." Jenkins's breath came in ragged sobs. "We are making progress."

There were to be no more delays. You were to unleash them all.

Jenkins doubled over, gasping. "They…they aren't ready."

The voice raged, driving Jenkins to his knees.

Your excuses stink of cowardice. Every moment the Zealots survive is an affront to the Natural Order. You have failed.

"No!" Jenkins craned his face up toward the darkened ceiling. "Please! I just need a little more time."

You will choose a colony and proceed—tonight.

"What you are asking, under the conditions you impose…if we experience another failure like D'Felco—"

A burning blue haze encapsulated Jenkins's eyes, obscuring his vision, its tendrils winding around the neurons in his brain, shooting excruciating pain throughout his body and driving away any semblance of independent thought.

Do not think to oppose me. Your failure to locate the militant colony and your reluctance to act against the others will no longer be tolerated. You will obey, and you will succeed—or you will be replaced.

Jenkins, fully prostrate on the thick Argenian carpet, could only nod his head weakly in compliance.

"Yes," he muttered, his hoarse voice barely a whisper.

Slowly, the haze dissipated, draining the pain that accompanied it. Jenkins stirred, testing the strength of his arms beneath his weight and then pushing himself to a standing position. He staggered unsteadily to the lav where he crouched over and vomited into the bowl. Finishing, he straightened and activated a warm water stream over the sink. As he washed himself, he glanced up and was disgusted by the tear-streaked face staring back at him. Rather than looking away, he increased the magnification on the reflecting display and began to attend to his appearance. He dabbed at his face with a warm towel and worked meticulously with a comb until every short-cropped silver hair was neatly in place. Concluding his regimen, he grabbed a container and closed his eyes, rubbing a cream over his eyelids and cheeks. When he opened, his pale blue eyes were once again bright and clear.

He strode back into the room, located his handpod on the floor where he had dropped it hours earlier, and keyed in a call sequence. A connection chime was followed by a fatigued voice acknowledging the call, the receiver undoubtedly having been roused from a deep sleep.

"Mr. Mason. Our timetable has been accelerated. I will see you in my office in twenty minutes. I have an updated assignment for you."

*   *   *

"Captain, may we speak with you for a moment?"

Dex and Hagen looked up from the conference table to see three figures silhouetted in the doorway. The two in front—one stocky, the other rail thin—bore a striking resemblance to each other, despite the noticeable difference in kilos. In his brief time interacting with the reunited half brothers, Dex had observed that they shared a number of mannerisms, from an irregular tapping of their fingers while they were speaking to their distinctive gait when they were in a rush—a flurry of short choppy steps. Drager St. James and Nikky Weis had certainly been cut from the same cloth. Behind them hovered the ever-present Ronnie Wilco. The three had been nearly inseparable since Nikky's arrival.

Dex paused the playback he and Hagen had been viewing. An image of a dark green planet froze over the table, tiny lines of static playing across its southern hemisphere as the rendering awaited the command to resume.

"What can we do for you, gentlemen?"

The three men squeezed through the doorway into the small conference room. Standing between Nikky and Ronnie, Drager took the lead. "It's about the *Forerunner*, sir. We've been looking at it—"

"—recovering system files—" Nikky added.

"—and doing structural integrity tests," Ronnie continued.

Hagen raised his eyebrows. "And?"

Drager straightened his shoulders, coming to a posture of attention. "We think we might be able to get her to fly again."

Hagen shook his head and looked back down at the paused display. Dex tilted his head to one side and regarded the odd trio. The *Forerunner*, the ship that had brought the colonists to Pella, had been critically damaged in the escape from Aphea. With the entire bridge crew killed in the first wave of the attack, Ronnie himself had ended up at the helm and had guided the battered cruiser to a crash landing on the spot where she now lay. The fact that all remaining on board had survived was nothing short of a miracle and a testament to Ronnie's engineering skills. His jury rigging of a polarity-lifter's magnetic pulses through the cruiser's duranium skeleton had kept the *Forerunner* intact enough to protect its inhabitants through the crash, but the ship itself had suffered irreparable damage.

"Fly?" Dex asked. "You mean atmospheric flight?"

"All of it, Captain." Ronnie placed a data chip on the conference table. "If this works, we can get her space-worthy again." He caught Dex's eye. "Jump-worthy."

It was hard not to get excited by the thought. To get the *Forerunner* off the ground, providing the colony with a much-needed cruiser capable of ether travel, would be miraculous—which, in Dex's mind, was about the likelihood of it actually happening. He smiled to himself. "As I recall, Ronnie, you didn't leave her in very good shape."

Ronnie didn't bite at the good-natured jab. Everyone knew that Dex held a deep respect for Ronnie's remarkable rescue of the colonists during his one and only time at the controls.

Nikky piped in. "That's just it, De...uh, Captain. I've looked at the data from Ronnie's original landing. The magnetic integrity subroutine he ran was quite impressive. It worked before, and if we can reconfigure it, boosting the field intensity—"

"—and there are a number of key structural points that we can repair," Drager added. "We've accumulated some extra materials over the last two years, and I think they can be adapted—"

"—and I've been reviewing life support, shields, navigation—critical systems only, of course. It won't be pretty—" Ronnie continued.

"—but it will work," Nikky concluded.

Ronnie indicated the chip he had placed on the table. "It's all there, Captain. All we need is the go-ahead. We know it's a long shot, but—"

Dex held up a hand. "A long shot that could get a functional evac vehicle back in service? You sold me. See Commander Lebrian for whatever supplies you need. Enlist manpower from the squadron. Any civilian recruitment that you need goes through Lieutenant Commander Onigen for security clearances. Understood?"

All three men snapped to attention, Nikky trailing a second behind the others.

"Yes, sir." Drager saluted.

"You three are getting to be quite a team," Dex said. "Do you really think you can get this done?"

"Yes, sir," Nikky said. "Integrity subroutines—"

"—structural repairs—" Drager added.

"—critical systems—" Ronnie chipped in.

"—she'll fly," they all concluded.

"Then go to it, gentlemen," Dex said. "You're dismissed."

As the door slid shut behind the departing team, Hagen turned to Dex.

"You've seen the *Forerunner*. You know what kind of condition she's in. We've given it countless tries already. Heck, Drager himself declared it a total loss two years ago. You don't seriously think they can get it off the ground again, do you?"

"I don't know," Dex said. "I kind of doubt it. But I am going to let them try."

"But why?" Hagen asked. "Critical resources, manpower—all on a hopeless cause?"

Dex resumed the playback. More of Baker's data feed streamed across the space above the table, superimposed over the dark green planet. "You may be right. It may really be a lost cause, but there's a couple things I've learned. The first is this—with everything going on in the squadron and all the discord in the colony, it's important to keep people busy. We have to give them something to hope for, even if it's an irrational hope."

"And what's the other thing?"

Dex gazed thoughtfully at the closed door where the trio had departed, his left hand absently rubbing the scar on his neck.

"Nothing's impossible, Sarge."

Chapter 18

Darik, having been roused from a fitful sleep by Jenkins's call, was grateful for at least one aspect of being summoned at this ridiculously late hour—he would not have to put up with his boss's acerbic secretary. Clara's customary place behind her desk was empty.

The doorway to Jenkins's office was open. Seeing no reason to wait, Darik adjusted his collar and walked inside, pausing only to knock on the threshold to alert Jenkins that he had arrived.

"Come in." Jenkins looked through a display hovering over the ivory desk. With a flick of his hand, the information vanished, and the door behind Darik slid silently shut. He indicated the plush chair opposite him. "I require a status report. Brief me on your progress regarding the laser cutter malfunctions."

Darik swallowed hard. "Well, sir," he began. "We still haven't been able to isolate the fault. It's been frustrating how evasive and intermittent it is. I've been working directly with Benjamin Whitaker, and even he's been baffled by it."

Darik knew that bringing Whitaker into the conversation was a deflection. Counting on Jenkins's friendship with Whitaker to spread the blame and, perhaps, soften the blow was a cheap maneuver, and Darik knew it. Worse yet, even as it came out of his mouth, he was aware that Jenkins knew it as well. The responsibility for correcting the M-2s' vulnerabilities was his, and he had failed. Having braced himself for the inevitable onslaught of abuse and criticism that he knew he deserved, Darik was rather surprised by, and somewhat wary of, Jenkins's even-tempered response.

"It is unfortunate. I would have preferred to have the units at peak efficiency. As I stated in my communication, our timetable has been accelerated."

Jenkins stared past Darik, seemingly at nothing in particular. Darik resisted the urge to turn his head and follow his boss's gaze. It was disconcerting. He had almost grown accustomed to feeling ill at ease in the stifling environment of his boss's office, the uncomfortable atmosphere created by the Travarian artifacts, an air of power and oppression subtly but consistently pressing against him. There was, however, none of that this time. Instead, Jenkins himself seemed to be the one out of sorts. Unaccustomed to this new dynamic, Darik wasn't sure that he liked it any better than his typical encounters with the CEO. If anything, he found it more off-putting.

Finally, Jenkins broke the silence. "The laser malfunction notwithstanding, what is the operational status of the M-2/As?"

Darik considered. "On the surface, they appear ready to go. But we have to understand—the laser still represents a critical fault. And we don't know if it lies within the cutter or the programming of the M-2 itself. That's why I had to put them into maintenance lockdown. If the breakdown *is* in the M-2, it could spread beyond the cutter interface and into other critical operating systems."

Jenkins tapped his fingernails on the ivory desktop. "So what are you suggesting, Mr. Mason?"

Darik drew a deep breath. "We still need to find and eliminate the fault, sir. I'm certain that we are getting closer. I just need a little more time."

It was a shameless lie. He was no closer to solving the mystery than when he had first laid eyes on that damn laser cutter. But he had to tell his boss something.

Jenkins stopped tapping, his fingers coming to rest on the desktop. "Time...Time is exactly what we do not have. You were given time in abundance, and now that time has run out."

Now this was the Jenkins Darik was used to. He could see his boss's confidence returning with each word. Jenkins's stare returned to Darik, his eyes sharp, his expression set. "You will remove the maintenance lock you've placed on the M-2s."

Darik chose his words carefully, responding as calmly and deliberately as he could. "Sir, I'm not sure that's a good idea. I truly believe that until we figure this out, the M-2s could be vulnerable. We need to do more research." He paused, fully aware that Jenkins was not one to appreciate opposing viewpoints. His customary response to such disagreements would usually range from a terse reiteration of his commands to a sudden burst of rage. Jenkins, though, said nothing, an impassive expression on his face.

Darik was surprised. Was Jenkins actually considering his advice? When Jenkins spoke, his tone was softer, resigned.

"Very well. But you don't need them all locked down, do you? To continue your research?"

Darik shifted uncomfortably in his chair. He wished that Jenkins would choose a mood and stay with it. "Well, no. But all the same..."

Jenkins didn't wait for Darik to finish. He recalled the display over his desktop. Hundreds of bright star icons appeared in a sphere hovering over his desk. Several dozen of them were highlighted with a solid red border. Darik's stellography was a little rusty, but he thought he recognized the pattern. He was looking at a chart of the Anibus sector—still in Coalition space but very near the border of the Frontier Systems.

Jenkins breathed, his voice taking on a soft rasp. "These systems"—he made his way around the desk, placing a cold hand on Darik's shoulder, his other hand indicating several of the red-highlighted stars—"each contain a known infestation of Zealot colonists."

Darik felt a familiar tugging inside. His breath caught, a sense of partial asphyxiation suddenly constricting his chest. He coughed, trying to shake off the feeling. Jenkins appeared not to notice.

"And you are to choose one of them."

"What?" Darik found his voice through the tight muscles of his throat.

"You heard me, Mr. Mason. Each one of these colonies represents our mutual enemy—an enemy that you have pledged to destroy. And now I want you to choose one of them."

Darik shuddered. He could feel a cold sensation emanating from the hand on his shoulder. His difficulty breathing worsened to the point that he felt he might pass out. What was he doing? He had pledged his life to defeating those people. Why was he faltering now?

Even as the question flitted through his thoughts, another impression, softer than Jenkins's irascible presence, but no less forceful, whispered in his conscience. He found his mind racing back to Bellona, remembering the choice he had made, when he had input the command to release the M-2—a killing machine that had hunted down and executed three people. One, a man he had briefly met before, a mechanic who had seemed to want nothing more than to do his job and mind his own business. The other two, an elderly couple—frail and old, no harm to anyone.

No! Not just a mechanic. Not just a helpless old couple. Thought-terrorists, like all the others—propagating hate and oppression. He squeezed his eyes shut, reassuring himself with all the usual arguments while trying to block out the conflicting voices in his head.

"Darik." Jenkins's voice had grown soft, kind. "Every colony we cleanse takes us one step closer to discovering the Zealots who caused you so much pain. One step closer to justice. You merely need to choose one of them."

One of the icons seemed to glow more brightly than those surrounding it. Darik slowly reached out, his hand trembling. Steadying himself, he touched the icon, turning it from red to a bright purple.

"Ah, yes," Jenkins smiled. "The Vidarr system. You've chosen well." He waved through the display, highlighting a pulsing green icon three stars away. "A detachment of M-2s could be there in a matter of hours." He waited, his finger lingering over the green icon, his other icy hand still gripping Darik's shoulder. "Now you will remove the maintenance lock on this M-2 facility."

Darik shook himself. "But the M-2s, the cutters…" He floundered, finally daring to look Jenkins in the eyes. "They're still not ready."

Jenkins finally removed his hand. "You will rectify the problem soon—I am certain of that. In the meantime, you've chosen the target, and the honor is yours to remove the lock on the closest facility. We simply want the M-2s to be available as soon as we determine that they are fully operational."

A weight that Darik had not known he was carrying lifted from the back of his neck. He couldn't explain, even to himself, why he didn't want the M-2s deployed immediately. Was it a genuine concern for their functionality or was it more? All the same, Jenkins had just effectively agreed that they wouldn't be released just yet. He reached out toward the highlighted facility. Poised to enter an access sequence, he hesitated.

"And we're not sending them in until they are ready, right?"

"Until they are ready."

Darik keyed the access code. A small line of text scrolled beneath the facility's icon, indicating that the maintenance lockdown had been lifted.

Jenkins smiled broadly. "Well done, Mr. Mason." He glanced at a chrono in the desktop. "Now, the hour is late. You should be returning to your rest."

"Thank you, sir." Darik rose from the chair and exited the office, already replaying in his head the details of the unusual meeting.

Time, he kept thinking. He had just bought a little more time—the commodity that Jenkins had become so preoccupied with.

But what to do with that time? He had two pressing tasks as he understood them—to solve two mysteries. He had to isolate the cause of the laser cutter malfunction, and he still needed, with Liana's help, to discover the identity of the mole within JenKore. While separate, both tasks, he knew, would serve to bring him that much closer to his ultimate objective—discovering and bringing to justice the terrorists who murdered his parents. More than his career, more than the material success he was enjoying, even more than his relationship with Liana, the thought of completing that quest filled him with a sense of purpose.

Yet, walking down the darkened hall in the direction of the main lift, he couldn't shake a competing impression. There was another reason he required more time. It was a feeling he'd had before, and it had manifested again, moments earlier, just before selecting the Vidarr colony. It had congealed with the memory of watching the M-2 on Bellona coldly slicing through the necks of its captives, how repulsed he had been, and his subsequent rash decision to grab the laser cutter and rush out to D'Felco's rescue.

Darik wasn't sure why he was feeling this conflict within him. He firmly believed in the guilt of every Christian terrorist out there—D'Felco included. So why had he rescued him? Why couldn't he leave him to the same fate as all the others—interrogation, admission of guilt, and execution at the hands of Haman's machines? Two voices, he realized, were reaching out for his allegiance, one screaming for justice, the other whispering of mercy. One voice seemed stronger, the other more persistent. Darik didn't know which to listen to. He only knew he needed more time—time he had just bought with his uncharacteristic negotiation with Jenkins.

The lift doors opened in front of him, and Darik—having grown acclimated to the dark and lifeless state of the uppermost tier of the Tower at that late hour of the night—was startled to see that the car wasn't empty.

And the identity of the inhabitant did little to put him at ease. He stepped back, giving room for Graves to pass through.

"Mr. Mason, it's very late for you to be here, is it not?"

Darik set his jaw. "I was called here by Mr. Jenkins."

"Important business, I would imagine."

"Yes," Darik said curtly. "And now that business is finished, so I'll be on my way."

The lift, however, had already closed its doors and begun its swift descent to ground level without him. Darik would have to retrieve it. Before he could wave the call command, Graves moved between him and the sensor.

"Business with the imminent escalation of M-2 deployment?"

For a brief moment, standing there face to face with Graves, any sense of confusion, of conflict, vanished. The still soft voice within Darik rose to the surface.

"There's nothing imminent about it," Darik said smugly. If Graves wanted one outcome from the night's work, suddenly Darik found himself much preferring the opposite. "Nothing is going to happen until the M-2s are ready."

"Ready?" There was an ominous tone in Graves's voice.

"That's what I said." Darik brushed past Graves's shoulder and waved for the lift. "Nothing happens until I say so."

Graves was unruffled. He stepped to the side, allowing Darik to pass. "But you've chosen a target?"

Darik turned back toward him. "Yes. Of course."

"And the temporary lockdown has been lifted?"

A sinking feeling began to creep into Darik's gut.

"Yes..." He found his voice weakening.

Graves tilted his head, his ashen eyes boring into Darik.

"Then what gave you the idea we were not proceeding?"

*   *   *

The M-2 glided silently forward, its legs powering through heaps of human flesh as it moved forward on blood-soaked feelers, methodically seeking another victim. Its two companions followed behind on either side, their omnisensors searching for any movement, any heartbeat, any solitary sign of life. Over seven hundred distinct life signatures had existed only minutes earlier. The machines had been thorough—stunning, slicing, and disintegrating bodies with ruthless efficiency.

The carnage had begun without warning—interrupting a prayer service. With so many gathered so closely, many on their knees, there had been no chance of escape. The few who did try to flee were brought down by a flurry of concussion grenades while searing thin red lasers cut through the huddled congregation, their cries of horror cut short in gurgles of agony.

The M-2 on the right paused, swiveling silently to one side. Even without advanced sensors, it could have easily detected the sound—a small voice, crying, the sound coming from under the torso of a human adult.

Moving toward it, the M-2 effortlessly flicked the body aside, revealing a child, covered in blood, terrified, but somehow physically unharmed. It hovered over her, a blue blade sliding into place in its right appendage.

She looked up as the horrible creature towered over her. Her sobbing ceased, catching in her throat as her eyes widened in terror.

Her mouth moved. The last living colonist on Vidarr spoke quietly, her small voice rasping out a final prayer.

"Jesus, help me," she whispered.

Chapter 19

Graves peered through the transparent barrier separating the checkball court from the elevated observation area. Meters below, his protégée and friend, Kirrone Jenkins, was completely manhandling an opponent half his age. Graves smiled thinly as he watched Jenkins knock his adversary off balance with a subtle hip check while simultaneously delivering an unreturnable drop shot to the left corner of the court. The four walls, floor, and ceiling instantly glowed red. He watched Jenkins turn without a second glance at the loser, retrieve a towel from an attending M-2, and head for the court door.

Graves leaned forward, tapping a pale finger on the barrier. Jenkins stopped, looked up, and acknowledged him with a nod. A subtle side shake of his head indicated that the two could meet in a less populated area of the club.

Fifteen minutes later, Jenkins emerged from the locker room, freshly showered and dressed in a perfectly tailored suit.

"An enjoyable match?" Graves's expression held the hint of a smile.

Jenkins grunted. "Hardly. It's so difficult to find a worthy opponent." He waved his hand in the direction of the club lounge. "I find myself sincerely wishing that you would take up the game."

"Ah, Kirrone." Graves matched his gait. "You know better than that."

"Yes, I know, while I find the distraction recreational..."

"I've determined that recreation is a distraction," Graves finished. "A distraction that I can't particularly indulge at this time."

"Or ever, as I recall." Jenkins waved open the lounge doorway. "There is a table near the back. We can talk there."

Sliding into the faux-leather chair, Jenkins took a sparkling mineral water from the full serving tray of a waiting M-2. As a member and regular patron of Helios, a variety of his post-match preferences were preprogrammed into the club's service units. He shot a questioning glance at his table mate.

"The same," Graves said. Jenkins handed another sparkling water to his friend and tilted his crystal glass in his direction.

"To continued successes," Jenkins smiled.

"Indeed." Graves returned the salute. "Well, I must say, you are certainly in good spirits."

"And why shouldn't I be? As you know, I purged a hive of Zealots last night."

"Of course."

"I'm only sorry that you weren't able to stay and observe the outcome. The feed was exquisite."

Graves sighed, but not without humor. "Yes, it is unfortunate. I would have preferred to witness the results with you, but as you know, I had pressing matters elsewhere."

A pair of mid-level JenKore executives made their way toward a table near the two men, but a stern look from Graves stopped them in their tracks. They stumbled into an awkward turn and proceeded hastily to a friendlier area of the lounge.

Graves leaned across the table, the dim light emanating from its translucent surface, highlighting his pale features.

"So, it was your puppet who chose the colony on Vidarr?"

The corners of Jenkins's mouth turned up a degree. "Yes, I made sure that Darik chose the colony. Of course, I also made certain that he selected the one I wanted him to." He paused, his smile broadening. "I also had him lift the maintenance lock on the M-2/A facility in that sector."

Graves shook his head. "You didn't need him to do that."

"Of course. I had that trio of M-2s activated and already in position over Vidarr long before Darik made his 'decision.' But it was still important to his development that *he* do it."

Graves stared at his friend, a look of mild curiosity on his face.

Jenkins took another sip of mineral water before continuing. "I feel that it is time for Darik to become more personally involved in the actual execution of our quest. His growth requires a more active role."

Graves placed his steepled fingers against a pair of pursed lips. "I still fail to understand your interest in this unaccomplished, uninitiated young man. How did he respond? Was he resistant to the added responsibility?"

Jenkins smirked. "I sensed a small amount of pushback from him, traces of a misguided sense of morality."

"And yet, you still managed to persuade him to choose a target and personally lift the maintenance lock."

Jenkins chuckled. "As I said, this was an important *step* in his development. This first time required some persuasion. The next will proceed more organically."

Graves lowered his hands back to the table, the edges of his fingers glowing brightly from the contact. "And what did you say to persuade him?"

Jenkins smiled over the water crystal. "I assured him that it was an intermediate step. I told him that we wouldn't deploy until the M-2s were ready."

Graves cocked his head. "But you did deploy. I was there when you sent the command."

"Yes. I simply determined they were ready, immediately."

"I see." Graves said, a smile forming. "Clever. And you preferred this tactic over lying to the boy? Or forcing the issue?"

Jenkins finished his water and motioned to the attending M-2 to bring another. "Of course. It's important that Darik trusts me, so it's advantageous to have some semblance of truth in my dealings with him."

Graves laughed. "You really are an interesting study, my old friend."

Jenkins considered the mineral water on the M-2's tray, reconsidered, and chose a stronger alternative from the assembled drinks—a corn and barley spirit, aged in pure Riksenian wood barrels. He tipped a glass in Graves's direction, the dark liquid righting itself and leaving light droplets along the sides of the goblet. "I am only what you have taught me to be." He smiled again, indicating the tray with a sideways nod.

Graves selected the bourbon as well. "In that case, lords help us—what madness have I unleashed upon the galaxy?"

Both men laughed. With the conversation having reached a concluding lull, the two friends settled back, the soft chairs adding to the relaxing effects of their drinks. For a long while, neither spoke, both seeming to enjoy an uncharacteristic pause in their lives' hectic pace. Jenkins finished his drink and called for another while Graves nursed the first one in his hand. Finally, his crystal half drained, Graves broke the silence.

"There is one detail that I still need to understand. You were so concerned about the potential effects of the laser malfunction and the admittedly time-consuming interrogations. You were afraid that the combination of those two factors could lead to another mission failure—a failure that you could not afford, as you know. How did you manage to overcome your fears?"

Jenkins answered casually, the strong drinks impacting his system more than he would have cared to admit. "It was simple, really. I decided that I needed to be certain that the potential fault would not lead to any escapees."

When Graves spoke next, there was a note of concern in his tone that belied his otherwise relaxed countenance. "And how did you do that?"

"I made sure that they acted quickly." Jenkins casually took another sip.

"Speak plainly, Kirrone."

Jenkins placed his crystal on the table top. He leaned forward, his eyes unblinking. "I removed the interrogation protocol for the mission."

Graves's eyes widened. "You what?"

"I removed the interrogation protocol. There was nothing this time to delay the M-2s." His secret now revealed, Jenkins began to speak with increasing enthusiasm. "You should have seen it! There was nothing— nothing—to impede them! Concussion grenades, stun bolts, even the laser cutters—*especially* the cutters! They worked so quickly, so efficiently, that there wasn't even the possibility of failure."

Jenkins had never in his life seen Graves look worried. Had he not been completely enraptured by his recollection of the unequivocal triumph on Vidarr, he might have noticed it now. Instead, he went on.

"I tell you, it was breathtaking!" He drained the last drop of liquid from the crystal. "My only regret is that it was all finished too soon."

"Quite possibly." Graves began lightly coughing. He pulled a folded cloth from his coat, raised it momentarily to his mouth, and returned it to his pocket, flecks of blue now dotting the white fabric. Pushing his half-full crystal glass to the side, Graves spoke again, his voice quiet. "I'm not sure what to make of this, Kirrone. This is a big step, and most certainly a reckless one. Are you sure you know what you're doing?"

"Yes, I do." Jenkins continued to smile, a mixture of intoxication and zeal. "Don't you see? This is the only way! He wanted the M-2s released. He was extremely clear on that point. There was only one way to do that and still prove how effective they can be. This success, the extermination on Vidarr, shows what they can accomplish once the shackles are off.

You'll see, my friend—He will see! This is the strategy going forward. This is what gets results. Every Zealot, on every colony, will be eliminated." He picked up Graves's half-full crystal, draining it himself with a flourish.

"And I feel better than I have in years."

Chapter 20

Darik Mason woke with a start. Trembling and disoriented, he stared wide-eyed into the darkness above him, overwhelmed by a nauseous dread.

He felt a presence nearby. Someone, something, was there. His instincts were urging him to get up, to flee, but he was held down by a paralyzing fear. Unable to move, he searched the room with his eyes, looking intently from shadow to shadow, but couldn't make out anything of substance. His other senses, heightened by adrenaline, became acutely aware of every sensation—the uncommonly still, cold air, the sound of his anxious breathing, the pounding in his chest, the damp sheets clinging to his body from sweat.

His sheets. His bed. That's right. He was in his bed, his room. As reason slowly returned to him, the fear of an intruder evaporated. Of course there was nothing there. He'd had a bad dream, that was all. As usual, he had difficulty recalling any of the details—other than that he had woken up screaming.

Embarrassed, he turned toward Liana to apologize for disturbing her sleep only to find her side of the bed empty. He remembered, then, that Liana was out late with friends. That, at least, was a relief. The last thing he wanted was to once again wake her in the middle of the night with one of his nightmares. The first time it had happened, he had leaped out of bed and run to the door, yelling gibberish. She'd been frightened in the moment, but they had been able to laugh it off the next morning. As his night terrors, however, had begun to occur with more frequency, she had recommended sleep medication, a suggestion that Darik had dismissed. The most troubling aspect to him was that the last couple of episodes had passed without comment from her. They'd both grown accustomed to it. Still, he felt deeply foolish, and apologetic, each time.

A dryness in his throat caused a short coughing spasm. Throwing aside the clammy sheets, he rose and made his way toward the lav. Halfway there, he paused in front of a hallway closet. Something familiar gnawed at the edge of his consciousness, a vague recollection of an impression, buried within the haze of the dream he had just fled.

He slid the closet door aside, stepping into the cramped interior. There it was, nestled safely behind a short stack of poly-storage containers. Darik reached back and retrieved the small security box, his heart beating faster at its touch.

He adjusted a lighting panel to his left while setting the security box on the stack of containers. It took only a moment to enter the proper code, disengaging the locking mechanism while simultaneously deactivating the onboard tamper protocol—a simple subroutine that would have sent an automatic alarm to his handpod if anyone else were to try to open it.

His pulse pounding in the sides of his neck, Darik grasped both sides of the lid, prying it upwards with his thumbs. A blue light escaped through the small crack, growing brighter and wider as he pushed the lid completely open.

His breath caught in his throat. It was striking in its simple beauty— the ancient knife that D'Felco had desperately thrown at the M-2 that night on Bellona.

At the time, Darik hadn't had a particular reason for picking up the knife. Afterwards, he had concluded that, having made the inexplicable and regrettable decision to spare the terrorist, he hadn't wanted to turn his back on D'Felco while leaving him a weapon. But perhaps, he now reasoned as the bluish metal blade vibrated in synch with his own pounding heart, perhaps he had simply wanted the knife for himself.

His mind wandered to an old memory—a young man at university receiving the news of his parents' brutal death, victims of the widespread Christian rioting he had been impassively following on the past week's info-feeds. Until that moment, the news hadn't made much of an impact on him—sure, the Christians were acting like idiots, but that was to be expected. Then, in an instant—in a frantic handpod message from his sobbing younger brother—it all came crashing home. The weeks and months that followed had been a maddening and fruitless wait for answers. Were his parents' murderers among the hundreds of Zealots that were arrested, and would their crimes be accounted for? The investigations had plodded along for months, but no hard evidence could connect a single rioter to the fatal attack on his mother and father. The uprising had been chaos, feed relays had been destroyed, and any visual data that had survived was inconclusive in connecting any individuals with the rampant violent acts that had occurred. In the end, the entire cadre of Zealots had received nominal prison sentences with re-education orders. For all Darik knew, his parents' murderers had finished their term and were now healthy and happy and living out their lives. He had no way to know.

After a listless semester in which his grades had suffered from his lack of focus, Darik realized he had a decision to make—was he going to continue to be consumed by a mystery that could never be solved, looking for justice that would never truly come, or would he grieve and move on, living a full, successful life, a life his parents had sacrificed so much for in the first place? He had decided on the latter—but he had never forgotten.

The vibrant color of the blade gradually faded as Darik shook himself from his reverie and turned his attention to the only other item in the security box. The data chip, containing all of Nikky's data on JenKore's M-2/A project, was still there. He picked it up, turning it between his finger and thumb as he recalled the exchange at the Black Swan a few weeks ago.

Eliot had wasted no time inviting Darik to lunch the moment he'd returned from Bellona, and his reason was made clear in how anxious he was to rid himself of the data chip.

"Here take it," he'd said, sliding it across the table. "I don't ever want to see that thing again."

Darik had quickly covered the blue chip with a napkin and stuffed it in his breast pocket.

"You didn't try to look at it, did you?"

Eliot's expression had lacked any of his usual guile. "No," he'd said. "Of course not. I don't think I *want* to know what's on it, do I?"

"No," Darik had said flatly. "You don't." He looked down at his menu. "We should order something soon—I've got a busy afternoon."

They'd finished their lunch in silence.

Later, Darik had returned to his apartment and had secreted the chip away, setting it next to the knife, securing the box with the security code. The two articles—modern and ancient, unimaginably complex and brutally simple—had rested there, undisturbed, until this moment. Now, turning the chip over and over in his hand, Darik wondered why he hadn't just destroyed it himself. He had given it to Eliot before the Bellona mission as insurance—just in case something happened to him. Now, having returned and having immersed himself so deeply and inextricably into the M-2 initiative, he wondered if the data chip could ever be of positive use to him. It could, perhaps, prove useful in anticipating the JenKore hacker's next move, but far more likely, the evidence contained on it would serve another purpose—if made public, it would bring down JenKore and destroy Darik in the process. And that made it far too dangerous for Darik to be keeping—in a closet in his own apartment, no less. He squeezed the polynitride-encased chip between his thumb and fingertips, knowing full well that he didn't have the strength to snap it in half.

Snap. If only it were that easy. Standing there in the dead of night, red-eyed and exhausted, he wished he could just snap his fingers and make his problems go away. Jenkins was being as duplicitous and unreasonable as ever, and now these recurring nightmares were straining him further. He didn't recall having this many restless nights prior to his promotion, but he wasn't convinced that the added pressure of his new position was the sole reason—he suspected, rather, that it was the nature of the work that was troubling him. While he could never remember his nightmares in detail, he knew from the impressions, from the images that lingered in his mind, that he was being subjected to scenes of horrifying violence—screaming and terror and unseen pursuers and slicing blades. He would be a fool not to think that the M-2 project was affecting him on some level. While he could rationally justify JenKore's secret initiative, the vicious reality of the work was gnawing at his subconscious.

Was it worth it, he wondered. He believed in the M-2s' mission, but the work would proceed without his involvement—probably more effectively in Jenkins's estimation. Why did he stay? Why did he keep suffering the daily exhaustion, the sleepless nights, Jenkins's constant abuse? If it was vengeance for his parents that he wanted, this wasn't the way to find closure. When the M-2s entered a colony, they had one purpose—which did not include investigating a ten-year-old incident. Overseeing the M-2 initiative enabled him to seek justice against Christians in general, but it was never going to lead to personal answers.

So why not leave? He'd be giving up a lot of money, that was certain. But had he ever been truly happy even once over the last several years, living alone in his high-rise, working virtually non-stop to try to meet Jenkins's impossible demands? No, he realized, he hadn't felt happy in a long time—not until Liana. There had been a brief window of time—a couple of weeks, perhaps, after he and Liana had begun their relationship—when he had felt genuinely at ease. Was it so crazy to consider leaving JenKore and starting a new life with her? Surely, having been a vice president at JenKore, he could find a good job elsewhere, a company, ideally, with a less maniacal CEO. While he enjoyed the prestige of living in Compton and working in the Tower, he would be open to relocating to a different city, maybe even off-world. Liana, he was sure, had no particular love of JenKore, and she struck him as the adventurous sort. If he could somehow convince her to go, what was stopping him?

Jenkins. With everything Darik knew about the M-2 project, there was no way Jenkins would allow him to leave that easily. But maybe, he thought as he gazed again at the data chip in his fingers, he could think of a way out.

"Isn't it kind of late to be doing housework?" Liana's voice startled him. He jumped, dropping the chip back into the security box and turning around in one motion.

"What?" Darik's voice was shaking.

Liana was smiling. "Or did you lose something?"

"Yeah," Darik said as passively as he could. "Kind of." He turned back around and quietly closed the box, making sure to reset the security protocol before sliding it back behind the stack of containers. "I didn't hear you come in," he said over his shoulder. "How was your night?"

"It was good. Fun. Sorry for startling you. I didn't expect you to be up at this hour." She moved in closer. "Is everything all right?"

Darik shut the closet door and faced Liana. "Yeah," he said. "I was just doing some thinking."

Liana remain silent, her expression inviting him to continue.

"I don't know," he said, "considering my options. Our options," he added, catching her eye.

"Options." Liana frowned. "Are you looking for a change? Because I have to say, I've been pretty happy with how things are going."

"Me too." Darik jumped in quickly. "It has nothing to do with us. It's work." He looked to the side, aware that he was suddenly in danger of tearing up in front of her. "I've been pretty miserable."

Liana regarded him—sagging shoulders, bloodshot eyes, strands of sandy hair darkened and plastered to his forehead from sweat—her expression conveying both sympathy and concern.

"It's okay," she said, grasping his hand. "It's natural to feel stressed about a new position. You'll get the hang of it. You've always done a great job."

Darik shook his head, a slight smile on his face.

"You have to say that."

"Hey, come on—you know I tell it to you straight." She leaned over into his eyeline. "But are you being completely straight with me? Is it really just the pressure of the new role that's been bothering you, or is there something else?"

Darik felt a tightness in his chest. He had already decided that there was no way he could share about the M-2 project with Liana. The thought of her getting entangled in this mess made him sick. No, he was going to have to carry this one on his own.

"I think I'm just ready for something new, that's all."

"I get it," she said gently. "It's been tough. But I also know how much you've wanted this—how hard you've worked to get here. I would hate to see you throw it all away." She began leading him toward the bedroom. "Now's not the time to decide anything. Let's get some rest. We can talk more tomorrow."

Following her down the hallway, Darik knew she was right. Things always felt bleakest in the dead of night. He needed to sleep—he just wasn't sure, once he closed his eyes, that he would find any rest.

*   *   *

"Okay, we're all set," Nikky said, his hand subconsciously moving toward the seat restraint.

"All right—hit it!" Ronnie Wilco yelled into the comm.

Far below and aft in the engine room, Drager forced a cadmium switch closed, completing a circuit through a tangled mess of spliced fibroc cables, jumpered ignition modules, and bypassed safety breakers. His efforts were instantly rewarded, but not with the result he was looking for.

"No! No! Shut her down—now!" he yelled back while simultaneously pulling several sparking cables free from their sockets.

On the bridge, Nikky watched as Ronnie frantically shut down the master control bus before it, too, could begin to smoke—again.

"Not supposed to do that, huh?" Nikky said, a note of apology in his tone.

"No. It's not." Ronnie wasn't amused. Hours into their attempt to coax new life into the *Forerunner*'s primary lifters, it was beginning to look like Commander Lebrian was right—the old cruiser would never get off the ground. He slumped back in his seat. "Well, there's another cross-off."

"But the maneuvering thrusters are the only propulsion system that's still intact," Nikky said. "Re-routing lifter power through the thruster controls is our only option."

"And it makes sense—in theory." Ronnie pointed to a flickering reading on the console. "But what I've been trying to tell you is that the thruster infusers are preset at a lower-grade mix than the lifters. They can't possibly handle both functions at the same time."

"So what are you saying?" Nikky asked.

"I'm saying that your concept is promising—it's the application that's the problem." The two sat in silence for a moment. A flock of gulls outside caught Ronnie's attention. He watched through the viewport as they took turns diving toward the turbulent coastal sea. Next to him, Nikky was staring at the floor, brow furrowed, his fingers absently tapping an irregular rhythm on his armrest. Drager entered the bridge and wordlessly took a seat next to his brother, not wanting to break the air of concentration in the room.

"Now here's something," Ronnie said finally. He began to sketch out a new diagram on the console. "If we were to swap out the lifter infusers with the good ones from the thrusters—"

"But you just said that they use a lower-grade mix," Nikky interrupted.

"Too low to do both functions," Ronnie continued. "But they'll have enough power to get this crate off the ground."

Drager checked his own figures. "He's right, Nikky. Even with their locked-in presets, we can tweak their calibration enough to work with the lifters. I did something similar with those old Talons we used back on Rainier once they fell out of production. Got a couple more years out of them."

Nikky was skeptical, but propulsion engineering was really Drager's specialty. And if Drager felt Ronnie's plan had merit, who was he to argue?

"Only one problem," Drager added. "That would leave us without any maneuvering capabilities."

"Well," Ronnie said, examining his diagram. "Once we swapped out the infusers, we could try routing a softer mix from the E-drive to the thrusters."

Nikky scratched his balding head with his right hand. "Has that ever been done?"

Ronnie shook his head. "Not to my knowledge. Drager?"

"I've never done it, but the ratios do match up a lot better."

"Exactly." Ronnie tapped a blinking icon on the console. "It's a lot like your idea, Nikky, but it might just be compatible this time."

"All the same," Drager said, "until we got that rigged—and we don't even know if it would work—all we'd have is a bird that could fly straight up." He moved his hand, palm down, straight up toward the ceiling.

"Hey," Ronnie said. "It's a start, isn't it?"

Drager cycled a display screen to the left of the console. "We'd have to be very careful. That mix could be just off-spec enough to cause a resonance that could upset the dampening field."

"Dampening field?" Nikky asked.

Ronnie directed him toward the display. A thin red waveform line bounced within a narrow green-hued band, its peaks and valleys coming very close to the edges several times. "That's a natural dampening field that keeps this planet invisible to long-range scans—it's why we've been able to stay hidden so long. The problem is, it's also very fragile. You see the band there?" He pointed to the green ribbon. "On ascent and descent, as long as our engines operate within that frequency range, we're okay."

Drager touched one of the points where the red line approached the edge of green border, dragging it just outside of the range. "But break out of it just a little, and the field begins to collapse." As if to accent his point, the simulation showed a sudden gap in the green band, its solid configuration pixelating away in the vicinity of his finger.

"Make a big enough disruption," Ronnie continued, "and the entire field would collapse." He made an adjustment in the simulation. The red line began vibrating wildly, the borders of the green band dissolving until there was nothing left. "So we'll just have to be very careful."

Drager nodded. "Yeah, we'll double-check—"

"—triple-check," Ronnie added.

"Yeah, triple-check our settings. Sim it a couple hundred times," Drager continued.

"And we'll make sure Captain D'Felco is up to speed on the entire plan. This bird doesn't get ten meters off the ground without his approval."

"Agreed," Drager said, a rare smile forming. "Wouldn't it be something," he said, mostly to himself, "to finally see some air between this thing and the ground?"

"I think it's time," Ronnie said, patting Drager's shoulder. "What do you say, Nikky?"

Nikky, had been silently staring at the console since the explanation of the dampening field. He finally looked up. "The plan makes sense. But do you think it's worth the risk?"

Ronnie looked again through the viewport at the Pellan landscape—the only landscape the colonists had known the past two years. The gulls had left, chased off by high winds and dark clouds as one of the coast's frequent storms came rushing toward them.

"Yeah, I do."

Chapter 21

"So, we're looking at a ground op," Hagen said, examining the workstation's slowly rotating holo, its soft glow casting a little illumination on the otherwise dark, empty ready room.

"Exactly." Dex indicated a location on the display. "The survivors are hidden deep. We'll go in with the Raven and a couple of escorts, but we've got no approach beyond this point."

The holo showed a network of dozens of interlocking caves, some of them hundreds of meters below the surface of the planet Hephaestus. The honeycombed tangle of caverns was a confusing mess of intersections, switchbacks, and dead ends. It would be easy to get turned around.

"And there's no way to get word to those folks to just meet us at the entrance, I suppose?" Hagen's voice wasn't hopeful—he already knew the answer.

Dex shook his head. "They sent out their location, but they won't know if anyone's coming. I'm not even sure they're certain their message got out at all." He peered at the display. "No. Someone's going to have to go in and get them."

"With that horror-flick reject stalking around out there the entire time."

"That's the problem," Dex agreed. "And if we land too close—if it scans us—we could lead it right to them."

Hagen grunted. "So, what are you suggesting?"

"A small team—two operators at most—both wearing micropulse vests. We drop here, about five klicks away, and go in small and quiet. Then we locate the survivors and escort them to the Raven. The cabin's going to be tight with eleven passengers."

"We hope." Dex caught Hagen's eye as he traced an amber line along the display. They both knew, given the time that had passed since the initial distress comm, that eleven was optimistic. "Rescue One and Two will work their way to the cave entrance here. Once we're in, the two Hornets will patrol, guarding the Raven and covering the cave entrance for the evac—all while staying on lookout for that M-2."

"That doesn't sound too hard."

Dex frowned. "It could be a lot harder than we think. Everything Baker has shown me so far indicates that the thing likely houses an ODF."

Hagen grunted. An Onboard Dampening Field would render the M-2 virtually invisible to the Hornets' passive scanners. If that were true, any contact would have to be visual only.

"All the more reason to find it," Hagen added. "I'd feel a lot better about this excursion if we knew where the blasted thing was."

"Yeah, we both would. Just make sure it doesn't find you first. Baker has sent extensive specs on those monsters' laser cutters. They're high-grade—powerful enough for a sustained burst to cut right through a Hornet, shields and all. Bottom line, if that M-2 sees your Hornet before you get eyes on it, it could go really badly for you."

Hagen leaned forward. "You keep saying 'me' like I'm going to be in a Hornet. But this is primarily a ground op, and a dangerous one at that. Obviously, me and Adahn—"

"Sorry, Sarge." Dex stopped the burly commander short. "Not this time."

Before Hagen could raise a protest, Dex continued. "I'm the most qualified for this op. I've been face to face with one of those monsters."

"And almost died in the process."

"Doesn't matter," Dex said. "I've seen what these things can do firsthand. I've observed their tactics. And as the guy who barely escaped with his life, as you pointed out, I'm in a unique position to anticipate their moves. Besides," he added, "I'm not sure I want to put anyone else in that position."

"Well, you're going to have to, Dex. You already said this was a two-operator recon mission. That leaves one opening." Hagen leaned back. "And I'm your man."

Dex shook his head. "I need you in a Hornet on this one. We don't know where that thing will be, and there isn't anyone I trust more to cover us when it decides to show up. The Hornets have to patrol close—but not too close. The most critical part of this mission is not tipping off the exfil location to the M-2."

"So, if covert air cover is critical, I still think we might be better off with you in a cockpit and me on the ground," Hagen insisted.

Dex suppressed a smile. "Are you forgetting something? We left my Hornet on that asteroid in the Purborus system."

"And you can't borrow my bird, just this once?"

Dex surveyed his friend's two-meter frame. "Your fighter? Your modified fighter? I'd never reach the pedals."

"Okay, so we pick up your Hornet on the way."

"C'mon, that's half a day in the wrong direction. We just don't have that kind of time."

"Fine, so use someone else's. We can't risk you on the ground. I can't lose you again!"

For the first time in their long friendship, Dex saw a fleeting glimmer of fear in his commander's eyes. It gave him pause. "I know," he said softly in stark contrast to what had been a steadily rising volume in the room. He understood Hagen's concerns. A part of him even acknowledged that he was probably right. But he also knew that he had to be there, in person, when that monster threatened. If anyone was going to face down another one of those mechanical terrors, it was going to be him.

For the mission to succeed, Dex needed someone else on the ground with him, but when the M-2 attacked, he needed someone who would cover the colonists without hesitation and let him handle the M-2 alone. He knew Hagen—he knew how he would react. He would protect the survivors but also, impossibly, try to protect his captain at the same time. And against an M-2, Dex knew they did not have the luxury of that kind of double-mindedness. Hagen's loyalty, noble as it was, could ultimately endanger the rest of the mission. But how could he make Hagen understand that?

He realized that he couldn't. So, he wouldn't even try.

"Hagen," he said, his voice catching in his throat. "I just need you in the air, okay?"

Hagen considered his assignment and his friend's request. Dex rarely pulled rank on his second-in-command because he rarely had to.

"All right, boss," he said finally. "I don't suppose you'd let me send Adahn with you then?"

As relieved as Dex was to have at least the first part of the conversation settled, the next exchange wouldn't be any easier. "I'd like to. I really would. But considering where things are at, I don't think either one of us really thinks that's a good idea, do we?"

"Dex, he's the best grunt we have—I've personally trained the kid."

Dex looked toward the holodisplay, unable to fully return the sincerity in Hagen's eyes. "I know. But right now, we can't be one hundred percent certain where his loyalties stand. I want to trust him. In fact, I do trust him. My gut tells me that he's not our mole."

"So what's the problem?"

"The problem is, my gut has been wrong before. And I can't risk the mission—risk the lives of those people holed up in those caves—over a desire to prove a hunch, not when there are other options."

Hagen leaned back in his chair, clearly not satisfied, but resigned to follow his CO's lead for the second time in as many minutes. "Who are you thinking, then?"

Dex scrolled through the ranks listed in the lower right corner of the display. "The Voors are still out, and Seltrice is on my flack list right now. If you and I are going, we need Lee back here keeping a lid on this thing with Adahn—to make sure Seltrice doesn't go spouting off again. That leaves us with Scot and Jani. I'll take Scot with me in the Raven. Jani will fly cover with you."

"Four total. Lean and mean." Hagen pressed his fingers together in front of his chin. "And Lee can handle Seltrice and Adahn, I'm sure of that. But I'm curious about something."

"What's that?"

Hagen looked over at the list of names. "Given the circumstances, don't you think it might be a good idea to put some space between Seltrice and Adahn? You know, put her on the mission, get some separation, just to cool things off a little?"

"I thought about it, Sarge. I seriously thought about leaving Jani back here—Lee could certainly use another cool head in camp. So yeah, I thought about assigning Seltrice to Hornet Two."

"What stopped you?"

Dex looked up from the display, meeting his oldest friend and second-in-command eye to eye. "I'm not sure I trust her either."

*　　*　　*

The office was dark—darker than usual. Whatever light filtered through the tinted windows was absorbed by the deep-colored Riksenian paneling along the walls. Whether Jenkins had intentionally set a particular mood by increasing each pane's polymer dispersion or if this was only an automated response to the late afternoon position of the sun, Darik didn't know. But the effect on him was the same regardless—dreary and foreboding.

"Sit down, Mr. Mason." Jenkins indicated Darik's least favorite chair—the soft cushion, made from the tanned hide of some off-world animal Darik had probably never heard of, invariably left him several degrees below direct eye-contact with his superior. He eased down into the chair, trying not to settle all his weight at once but sinking in additional centimeters all the same. Jenkins leaned back in his own chair. "I've been waiting for your progress report concerning our intelligence leak."

Darik cleared his throat. "Well, there really isn't much to report at this time." He knew he would be roasted for his response, but he had learned with Jenkins that straight, honest answers, however weak, were better than trying any sort of circumlocution. Jenkins could immediately see through any attempt at evasion.

His boss turned his head slightly to one side. "I'm sorry. I'm not sure I understand."

"Sir?"

"A progress report, Mr. Mason"—Jenkins held him with an icy blue stare—"implies that you will report on your progress. When you tell me that there is nothing to report, I have to infer that you have made no progress."

Darik shook his head. "No. That's not true. We…I've—"

Jenkins stayed silent, his gaze never shifting.

"That is, well, I've managed to isolate several points of intrusion, all with the same signature pattern." Darik paused, suddenly not sure how much he should tell his boss. But why? Jenkins was demanding a report. Didn't it make sense to fill him in on the help Liana had provided? After all, she was the one who'd first spotted the hacker's signature. It was her subroutine that would catch the spy the next time he attempted to hack into JenKore's system. So why not just give Jenkins those details? Wasn't that the kind of "progress" he wanted to hear about? And shouldn't Liana receive the credit she deserved?

Nevertheless, his instincts were telling him that it would be better if Jenkins wasn't aware of her involvement. Maybe it was the rumors of Jenkins's personal prejudices that held him back—his boss wouldn't exactly be thrilled to learn that a low-level *female* employee had been given access to sensitive corporate information. More likely, he thought, he was concerned for Liana's wellbeing—as it was, she was already too tangled up in this dangerous assignment for his liking.

"You were saying?"

"Uh, only that the next time the mole tries to break in, I'll be ready, sir."

"You'll be ready." Jenkins didn't blink. "And that is all you have to say?"

Darik looked down at his feet, bracing himself. "Yes, don't worry, sir. I've got it covered."

Jenkins made a note on his workstation. "I'm afraid that I do not share your confidence. I am not accustomed to waiting and hoping for solutions. When I assign a task, I do it with the expectation that I will see results and see those results within a reasonable timeframe. But, time and again, all I seem to get in return for the faith I place in you are delays, obstacles, and excuses."

Darik felt his cheeks begin to flush. How many times had he sat in this exact place, hearing this same lecture? How many impossible assignments had he been given? First, he had been tasked with investigating the original M-2 disappearances—a mystery he had solved with absolutely zero support from his boss. In fact, vital information about the M-2 mods had been withheld from him the entire time, needlessly complicating and prolonging his assignment. The only assistance Darik had received on that project he had recruited, himself, under the table. Nikky Weis had proven to be invaluable, and now, in the aftermath, his friend—Darik stopped himself. Did he really think of Nikky as a friend?

Yes—his friend. And now his friend was gone, possibly dead.

When he'd been promoted to head of the entire M-2/A initiative, Darik had foolishly believed that he'd find his work more satisfying and rewarding. Instead, he had been promptly ordered to track down and isolate an inherent glitch in the M-2s' laser cutter compatibility—another thankless task. At least for that project, Jenkins had actually provided him with a little support, introducing him to Benjamin Whitaker. But even that relationship had come with an all-too-familiar feeling of duplicity and withheld information. As with Jenkins, it seemed as though Whitaker was hiding something from him. And even with Whitaker's supposed help, Darik was no closer to discovering the cause of the cutter malfunctions.

And still, the pile kept growing. Somehow, Jenkins also expected Darik to track down—and eliminate, it was implied—a Coalition mole inside of JenKore. It was yet another assignment for which Darik felt completely unqualified. He had never in life felt so overwhelmed and useless. And now, once again in the face of an impossible task, he had been found wanting in Jenkins's estimation. Darik could provide more nuanced explanations for his apparent lack of results, but he knew that nothing at this point would change his boss's opinion of him. A familiar anger began to well up inside him—he hated Jenkins, he hated this job, and he hated himself. For the first time, thanks to Liana's help, he believed he had a chance at accomplishing his current assignment. Why wouldn't he just tell Jenkins about her?

The anger boiled over into a cold blue rage. Yeah, that's exactly what he would do. He would get out of that stupid chair, grab his boss by the lapels, pull that smug, tanned face close, and tell him how, this time, he was going to beat his rigged game. He would tell him through gritted teeth how he had recruited his *secretary* and how, with her help, they were going to catch the spy and dump his head on Jenkins's ivory-inlaid desk.

That is what Darik desperately wanted to do—to prove how capable, how resourceful, he was, to show Jenkins how wrong he'd been about him, about Liana, about so many things. But he couldn't. He couldn't implicate Liana. He was not going to involve her more than he already had.

Instead, he loosened his grip on the arms of the soft chair, sinking lower into the cushion, defeated.

"Come now, Kirrone, let's not be so hard on the boy."

Darik started at the unexpected voice, nearly coming out of the deep chair as he spun around. How could the presence of someone else in the room so completely escape his notice?

"After all," Graves said, stepping out from a shadowed wall, "while he might not be showing progress on this particular assignment, his assistance in the Vidarr initiative was particularly valuable."

"The Vidarr initiative?" Darik was taken aback. "What are you talking about?"

Graves smiled. "The assault you initiated on the Vidarr terrorists, of course. What did you think I was referring to?"

197

Darik's mind raced back to his last meeting with Jenkins. Afterward, he'd run into Graves in the hall just outside the lift. What had Graves said to him—something about proceeding with their plans? At the time, he hadn't allowed himself to fully consider what he may have been implying. In the lift, on the way down, he had decided it was just Graves being his normal arrogant, creepy self. Now, he wasn't so sure.

"But, but there was no attack—not yet." Darik's heart began pounding in his chest, a sense of dread replacing the anger and defeat he had been feeling only moments before. "I didn't authorize an assault. All I did was remove the maintenance lock while we continue to work on the cutter malfunction."

"And you also chose the target." Jenkins's voice was cold, piercing to his soul.

"And you told me we weren't going to proceed until we agreed that the M-2s were ready!" Darik said, his voice rising.

"And who are you," Jenkins said quietly, "to determine when we are *ready*? You did your job. You released the lock, and you chose Vidarr as the target. I determined that, with certain restrictions removed"—Darik sensed Graves stiffen slightly behind him at Jenkins's statement—"the M-2s were more than ready, more than capable of carrying out their mission."

Jenkins's eyes glistened, his attention seemingly focused far beyond the confines of his dark office.

"And it was glorious," he said.

Darik ground his teeth. "That isn't what you said. You said you were going to wait." He tried to chase away an image of a pack of M-2s cutting their way mercilessly through a group of defenseless colonists. He told himself that the Zealots deserved it—that they received exactly what was coming to them. But despite the knowledge that every one of them was a dangerous, hate-filled thought-terrorist without any hope of re-education, he still found himself forcing down a wave of nausea—the bile rising in his throat, threatening to spill out onto Jenkins's expensive carpet.

He swallowed. "I never agreed to that."

"Oh, but you did." Graves stepped forward, placing a cold hand on his shoulder. "You agreed when you took this job, when you chose this career. You agreed when you accepted Kirrone's offer of advancement. You agreed when you lifted the lock and chose Vidarr as the target. Don't lie to yourself. You knew what kind of people those Zealots were, and in your heart, you knew what Kirrone was going to do."

Graves's fingers tightened on his shoulder, the longest one caressing Darik's collar bone. It felt like an ice pick scratching his shirt fabric. "More importantly, you agreed to this, to all of it, the day you first heard about the meaningless, senseless attack on your parents. You didn't know it at the time, but you resolved in yourself, that very day, that given the opportunity to take action, you would not waver from doing what is necessary. All we have done is provide you with that opportunity."

Darik closed his eyes. He felt drained. When he opened them again, he saw that Graves had moved around the desk and was standing next to Jenkins. His boss's expression was now calm, compassionate.

"Perhaps I have been pushing you too hard," Jenkins said. "Leading the M-2 initiative is a sizeable undertaking with many accompanying challenges. The cutter malfunction, the security leak—those won't be the last unforeseen problems that will need to be solved. I can understand the pressure of your position—not everyone is capable of handling this kind of responsibility. Possibly, if I found someone else…"

Someone else. Isn't that precisely what Darik had been secretly hoping for—someone else to be responsible for the M-2 project, someone else to suffer Jenkins's unrelenting demands? Yes, he was ready to get out, but he wanted it to be on his own terms—and he would be damned if his last moment at JenKore was going to be meekly agreeing with Jenkins that he didn't measure up.

Darik sat up as straight as he could in the soft chair. "No. You don't need to do that. I can handle it."

Jenkins smiled thinly. "All the same, perhaps you have earned some time off."

"Yes," Graves stepped in. "Have you considered a vacation? You could take a companion, possibly that young assistant of yours, the one who was with you at the bistro. What is her name, *Liana*?"

An element of Graves's tone, and the particular way he was staring at Darik, set him on edge.

He set his jaw. "Yes. Liana."

"You seem to have excellent taste—in your dinner companionship as well as your working relationships." Graves's ashen eyes narrowed, the menace behind them betraying the smile on his face. "She is a fascinating young lady," he breathed. "Beautiful, certainly. And someone to be reckoned with, from my observations. She has the potential for a long and bright future here, provided she makes the proper choices. I will have to keep a close eye on her."

Graves's eyes never wavered, his sickly smile causing Darik to again feel nauseous.

The anger returned, stronger than ever, but now directed at a new target. No, Graves would not be "keeping an eye on" Liana. Not if Darik could help it. He wouldn't be getting anywhere near her. Darik knew he had made a mistake getting her involved this far, but he wouldn't make it again. He would protect her from Graves and anyone else who might hurt her, even if it cost him everything.

Darik stood, addressing his boss. He knew what he had to do, and from this point on, he needed to do it alone.

"No, I don't need a vacation. Not right now."

He shot a final dark look at Graves before turning to leave, not waiting to be dismissed.

"I'll do my job."

Chapter 22

The surface of Hephaestus was nothing like Baker's intel had indicated. Slogging through knee-deep muck while swatting away clouds of insects so thick they threatened the acuity of his Heads Up Display, Dex wondered if the inaccuracy in the report of ground conditions was an isolated imprecision or an indication of an entire mission about to go snafu. He pulled his right leg up and forward, willing it free from the vise-like grip of the mire. As he planted his foot, something caught his ankle—most likely another tangle of the ubiquitous weedy roots below the surface of the bog. Sliding his left leg forward, Dex recovered his balance just in time to avoid pitching face-first into the slop. After collecting himself with a single deep breath, he turned his foot a few degrees to the right, felt the snag give way, and continued the arduous trek. Their destination—one of the many rock formations jutting out of the swamp—lay ahead, tantalizingly close. Anticipating firmer terrain, they had planned on covering the distance from the LZ to the first waypoint in under ten minutes, but as it was, they had been trudging along for over an hour with no reprieve in sight.

Dex glanced to his right. Peering through a thick swamp in the dead of night, he normally would've had trouble spotting his traveling companion, but Scot Calgaro stood illuminated against the mist and shadows, the fabric of his fatigues emitting a telltale amber glow visible only through Dex's night goggs. Like Dex, Scot was also methodically lifting one leg out of the mire, then the other, forcing himself forward through the sludge. Dex checked his thumper again. The passive sensor—a portable, less powerful version of the life-sign scanners on board the Hornets—showed no heartbeats, indicating that the micropulse vests both men were wearing were functioning properly, effectively hiding any evidence of circulatory and respiratory activity from all but the most focused scans.

He heard Scot curse softly under his breath.

"Easy, Lieutenant," Dex whispered. This leg of their mission depended upon reaching the cave undetected, and any excess noise could invite unwelcome attention.

"Sorry, Captain," Scot whispered back. "I think something bit my leg." He was bent over, one leg pulled high for examination, looking something like an off-balance, grime-encrusted flamingo.

"I'm sure you'll live," Dex replied. "We're almost there. Keep moving."

Scot took a moment to rub his ankle and then dropped his foot back into the mud, pressing forward. The tactical map projection in Dex's goggles showed the cavern entrance a couple dozen meters ahead to the left, its rocky threshold rising steeply out of the swamp.

It took them several more minutes to reach the incline. Dex grasped a solid outcropping and pulled himself up, his boots slurping as they were released from the suction. He paused a moment to catch his breath, drawing a small amount of satisfaction from the fact that he'd kept up with Scot's pace during the kilometer-long slog through the swamp. His legs were sore, his shoulder ached like hell, and his breathing was still more labored than he would've preferred, but for the first time since Bellona, he was beginning to feel like his old self again.

He took a sip from the hydration stem clipped near his right cheek, resisting the urge to continue gulping down the refreshing nutrient-infused water. It was important for them to conserve their resources. The first leg of their mission had already taken far longer than planned, and they had no way to be certain how long it would take them to find the survivors. Surveying the approach to the entrance, though, Dex had to concede that the time-consuming passage through the swamp had been necessary. Parking the Raven just outside the cave would've made the eventual evac simpler, but besides the obvious risk of leading an M-2 directly to the survivors' hiding place, there was no feasible landing zone in sight—the entire area nothing but muck and tangled vines and sharp rocks rising like teeth out of the mire.

Perhaps that was the reason the survivors had chosen this spot—if not to completely prevent an M-2 from reaching the cave, maybe to at least slow it down or discourage it, if such a thing were possible. In any case, once they located the survivors, it was going to be a challenging exfil. Dex imagined trying to lead the group—some likely injured, all undoubtedly weak and fatigued—back through the swamp, nearly a dozen people fighting their way through the muck, each struggling to take another step, an M-2 closing in from behind.

A dozen if they were lucky.

Scot arrived at the outcropping and took a seat next to Dex. Reaching into a side pocket, he produced a tube of topical anti-venom, kicked his boot partially off, and began rubbing the lotion on his ankle. In the darkness, Dex could not see any evidence of an actual wound, but the universal formula would effectively counteract any adverse effects of a bite—real or imagined.

A stagnant breeze blowing off the swamp whistled through the rocky surface above. Scot took advantage of the extra noise, keeping his voice low.

"You thinking what I'm thinking, Cap'n?"

"That there had to be an easier way to do this? Yeah."

"Well, we're here." Scot turned around. Above them, a dark opening in the rocky slope moaned in the foul wind. "We might as well see who's down there." He placed the tube back in his pocket and looked skyward. "Meanwhile, Sarge and Rabbit are up there probably watching holoflicks."

"We'll have to get their recommendations," Dex said, rising to his feet. "Let's go." He knew he didn't need to justify Hagen and Jani's role in the mission. Scot was well aware how much they would need them if and when they made it back to this point.

Dex crept toward the left side of the entrance with Scot matching his movement on the right. Less than a meter wide, the opening was not large enough for both of them to enter at once. A quick tap of Scot's gloved hand to his chest indicated he would enter first and sweep the interior. Dex double-checked the charge on his side arm. It remained full, not that it would make much of a difference if they encountered an M-2. He had experienced firsthand the ineffectiveness of small arms fire against their shielding. On Bellona, a center-mass shot from his rifle had been casually deflected away—and that weapon had been far more powerful than his pistol or the old carbine that Scot was carrying.

Scot turned to the entrance, his Klobb at the ready, the short barrel pointed at the awaiting darkness. He shifted his aim slowly along one side of the cavern before swinging quickly to the other. Seeing no sign of a threat, he gathered his legs under him and slid into the chamber, disappearing so suddenly that Dex had to lurch himself forward to cover him.

Peering over the drop, he located Scot's amber glow a couple meters below him.

"Clear."

Dex acknowledged the signal by sliding into the cavern himself, coming to rest in a crouch next to his partner.

"My thumper's cold," Scot whispered. "Yours?"

"Same," Dex replied. "But there's a lot of cave down here. Let's keep moving." He crawled forward toward the steep slope ahead. The chamber narrowed to a tight tunnel, its ceiling only a meter high with sharp stalactites reaching nearly to the ground. Scot shook his head.

"Oh, this is going to be fun."

*   *   *

Four hours later, dripping with sweat, Dex motioned for a stop. Thankfully, the head-room in the cavern had opened considerably, but the uneven, often slippery surface, with its steep drops and occasional razor-sharp formations, had made for a slow and treacherous journey. At least, Dex noted, the atmosphere had remained breathable. He was thankful for that for two reasons. One, he and Scot would not have to test the limits of their emergency oxygen supply. The other reason was that breathable air meant that, despite their lack of success so far, it was still possible that the survivors could be down there.

Scot didn't seem to share even that limited confidence. "This is hopeless." In the utter isolation of the cave, he was no longer bothering to keep his voice low. "We've covered, what, a dozen kilometers? And not so much as a whisper of life down here."

Glancing at his HUD, Dex rechecked their labyrinthine route through the tunnels before pulling off his goggles and wiping away the sweaty grime beneath his eyes.

Scot continued. "And that's just a small fraction of the area marked on the map—not to mention all the side routes that aren't even listed." He removed his eyewear as well and activated a compact flare, remembering to keep it dialed down to the lowest intensity. In the soft glow, Dex could make out the frustration on his face. "If we can't even cover all the marked passages, how do you propose we begin to explore the ones that aren't?"

"I don't know," Dex said, his tone short. He gazed at the passage ahead. The flare cast a pale light on the cavern walls before a narrow bend once again hid their path. For a moment, his thoughts turned to what would happen if their flares and goggles failed—the two of them trapped deep below the earth, stumbling around in utter darkness. He chased away the image. "But we have to keep trying. We're the only hope they've got."

"If they're even down here—and still breathing." He pulled a semi-clean swatch of fabric from a breast pocket and began to dab at the lenses on his goggles. "I mean, I want to find them as much as you do, but we have to face some facts here. We've been searching for hours, and we haven't seen a trace, not a single clue to indicate that anyone's down here. I know they're in hiding, but how deep would they go? Tactically speaking, they'd still have to stay close enough to the surface to venture out for supplies." Scot scratched at a particularly stubborn bit of grime, trying to flick it off with his fingernail. "If they were here, we would've found something by now."

"And yet, we're going to keep on looking. We'll find them. They're here."

Scot stopped cleaning his goggles long enough to look directly at Dex. "How can you be so sure?"

"Because Baker said they were here."

Scot sniffed, examining his headgear next to the flare. "Baker. Now there's a guy I'd like to meet someday."

Dex smiled. "Yeah. Me too."

Scot pulled the goggles back over his head, adjusting them and fitting the attached earpiece back in place. "I know you put a lot of trust in the guy, Captain, but it seems like something goes wrong on every mission he sends us on. I mean, the Milk Run alone—"

"Do you *really* want to start a discussion of things that went wrong on the Milk Run, Lieutenant?" Dex had grounded Scot for his insubordination on that mission, a sentence only suspended out of the necessity of needing every available pilot for the Bellona assault.

"That's not the point," Scot said, his tone grim. "How many times have we had bad intel? How many times have we been ambushed? And it always happens during Baker's missions. I mean, think about it—even this one! Nothing is lining up. We've got bad surface intel, bad subterranean maps, and yet here we are, as always, chasing our tails just because some guy we don't even know says that we—hold it."

Scot put a hand to his right ear while reaching down with his left to extinguish the flare. He answered Dex's now-unseen questioning expression with a tight whisper.

"We've got a pulse. Human. Single contact. Forty meters left." He quietly pulled his Hagg-Sauer pistol from its holster. "And approaching."

"Easy," Dex whispered, "this is a rescue mission, remember?" All the same, he un-holstered his own side arm.

"Ten meters." Scot's voice was barely audible. "Stopped." Dex stared intently through the night goggs. The source of the heartbeat signature was just beyond the next bend in the cavern, coming to a halt just short of their field of vision. He heard a soft commotion—it sounded like someone rummaging through a pack. Next to him, Scot held his side arm at the ready, aimed at the first opening in the bend. Scot's carbine was to his right, leaned up against the cavern wall within reach, but neither of them were willing to spare the extra seconds to crouch down and pick it up.

Dex decided to risk making audible contact. If the source of the heartbeat were one of the survivors, he didn't want to be mistaken for a threat.

"Hello," he said. Breaking the silence, his normal voice sounded like a cannon.

A surprised shout echoed in the tunnel. There was a sudden rustling, and a small package tumbled around the corner, rolling to a stop between Scot and Dex.

"Demo charge!" Scot shouted. Neither he nor Dex hesitated. Sprinting back up the tunnel, shoulder to shoulder, they dove into the first available side passage. An instant later, a deafening roar shook the cavern, raining dust and small debris down on them from above.

"What the hell?" Scot shouted. It had, thankfully, been only a small blast, not enough to bring the entire cave down on them, but it had rattled their teeth all the same. Dex removed the safety from his side arm—his body poised and ready, responding automatically from his defensive training and energized by a surge of adrenaline.

For a long moment, there was an eerie stillness—no movement, no sound, no follow-up assault. The floating dust had become nearly blinding in Dex's night goggs, appearing like thousands of shimmering orbs floating in the air. He adjusted the settings, and the cavern once again came into sharp focus.

An answering shout from around the bend broke the silence.

"Hey, are you all right?"

Dex and Scot looked at each other.

"Yeah," Dex answered. "What was that all about?"

The voice was hoarse, coughing from the lingering dust. "I was setting charges. One got away from me." A pause. "You startled me."

"No kidding," Scot said.

"What are you doing setting charges down here?" Dex asked.

The voice gained confidence. "Hey, in case you haven't figured it out, you've really stumbled into the wrong place. Who are you, anyway?"

Dex decided to risk it. Removing his night goggs, he activated his flare and stepped into the main passage. "My name is Dex D'Felco."

"From the 714ᵗʰ?" The voice sounded surprised.

Dex stole one more glance at Scot. Even with most of his face obscured by his headgear, Scot's expression said it all. *It's your call, boss.*

"Yeah, that's us," Dex said.

Ahead, he saw a young man step into view. He was covered with reddish dust and grime. Dex could see worn bandages on his right arm and forehead with darkened blood stains showing through, evidence that the boy had already been wounded prior to the blast. Around his waist, he wore a bandolier with a collection of demo charges, each of them as small as the one that had bounced up the tunnel but, together, capable of collapsing the entire area. His face was entirely masked by dirt, but his open eyes reflected the light of the flare. His expression showed mild surprise—surprise and something more.

"Uncle Dex," he said flatly.

Dex nodded. "Hello, Jason."

"*Uncle* Dex?" Scot looked from Dex to the young man and back. "You're the mad bomber's *uncle*?"

Dex chuckled. "Not exactly. I'm an old friend of the family. The boys used to call me that. Jason and—" he stopped himself.

The young man read his expression. "Jake's fine." He tilted his head back down the tunnel. "He's back in the camp with Mom and the others. But Dad didn't..." His voice trailed off.

"I know, son." Dex stepped forward and embraced him, the memory of the horrifying data feed showing Jonathan "Bulldog" Buhl's execution flooding back into his mind. "I know."

The embrace was not returned. Jason Buhl stood stiff, enduring the display of emotion before glancing past Dex's shoulder at Scot.

"And who is this?"

Dex broke off the awkward hug. "Ah. I'm sorry. Lieutenant Scot Calgaro, meet Jason Buhl." He looked at Jason, shaking his head. "I almost didn't recognize you. You've grown."

Jason shrugged it off. "So, Baker sent you, huh? I kinda thought if he got our message, he might send the actual UCN."

"Sorry to disappoint," Scot grumbled. "What's the big idea anyway, trying to blow us up?"

"I wasn't trying to blow *you* up. I didn't even know you were there until you yelled." Jason indicated the tunnel behind him. "I was setting the charges to collapse this part of the cavern."

Scot scratched his head, a sizable piece of rubble dislodging from his hair. "I don't get it. Why would you collapse your only way out?"

"Only way out?" Jason frowned. "What are you talking about? We just want to close this area off to keep that damn thing from sneaking up on us from behind. That's why I was…wait a second." He broke into a sly grin, a sudden thought occurring to him. "You guys didn't come all the way down here *that* way, did you?"

Dex glanced behind him in the direction Jason was indicating, a menacing row of hanging stalactites reminding him of their slow and arduous journey through the winding maze of tunnels.

"Uh, yeah. We did."

Jason shook his head ruefully. "And Dad always said you Angels were sharp." He turned on his heel. "C'mon. Follow me."

*   *   *

For the past hour, negotiating the cavern had become more manageable with each step, Dex and Scot no longer having to stoop or watch their step quite so carefully on the increasingly smooth surface. Dex also noted that the path had been on a steady upward incline, bringing the three of them ever closer to the surface. He had decided not to press Jason with questions until they reached their destination, and Scot had seemed content to tacitly bring up the rear, keeping his thoughts to himself. Part of Dex's reasoning for keeping silent was that quiet movement remained tactically prudent, but, truthfully, he was at a loss as to what to say to the young man leading them up the passage. He had always been able to relate to Jason, kidding around with him, playing backyard games at Jon and Janet's lakeside home. Now, he barely recognized him.

Pausing before a bend in the tunnel, Jason held up a hand, motioning for Dex and Scot to hold up. Dex could see a brighter glow reflecting off the wall to the left. Apparently, they had arrived. Jason cupped a hand near his mouth and broke the silence.

"Proverbs," he said firmly.

After a brief pause, a voice echoed from up the corridor.

"Eighteen-ten."

Jason turned back to Dex and Scot. "Security," he said. "We change it every time one of us has to venture out. The scripture thing was Mom's idea." Dex glanced at Scot, surprised that Janet and the survivors had arrived at using the same countersign protocol as the Angels to identify friend or foe.

"Well, this is it." Jason motioned them forward. "Welcome to paradise."

Dex and Scot followed him up and around the corner. A few meters further, the passage opened to a larger cavern. A few well-placed compact flares provided enough illumination for Dex to take in the entire room. What he saw both relieved and shocked him.

He counted eight people besides Jason, Scot, and himself. Five of them were lying on makeshift bedrolls, a couple of them softly moaning, fighting the pain of their injuries. A few empty dermo-patch canisters lay nearby—the only evidence of medical supplies that Dex could see. His eyes lingered on the wounded, the flares casting a pale light across their faces. His mind was already trying to determine how ambulatory they might be and working out the best plan to evac them to the Raven. One had a bandaged stump just below the right knee, another was missing an arm—victims, no doubt, of the M-2's laser cutter. The remaining three were on their feet and were quickly moving toward them, greeting Jason while eyeing Dex and Scot with understandable curiosity.

In his few seconds of observation, Dex realized that he was looking at the only known survivors, besides himself, of an M-2 attack. He also realized that two more—two people he had been expecting to see—were missing.

"Jason," he said. "Your mother and Jake...you said they were here?"

He was interrupted by a rustling to his right. Squinting, Dex could see a small ante-chamber in the shadows. A figure inside was struggling to gain footing, a slightly shorter figure giving assistance. Rising from a thin tarp before grasping a makeshift crutch handed to her by her son, Janet Buhl hobbled into the light. Her long black hair was half-tied behind her in a ponytail with a few of the escaped strands matted against her forehead. Her eyes were haggard, the darkened space below them evidence of too much strain and too little sleep. Yet they still held the same steely determination that Dex remembered. He had seen that determination many times as Janet had kept her husband—a UCN captain and Dex's best friend—in line and raised two young boys while that same husband was deployed for months at a time.

Her eyes moved down to her right leg. Dex followed her gaze. The bandage was blackened, oozing. Looking back at the other wounded and the empty dermo-patch containers, Dex understood what Janet had done. Facing a limited supply, she had rationed the changes of bandages—for everyone but herself.

She looked back up from the injured leg. "Sorry I wasn't up to greet you, Dex." She smiled, but her expression quickly turned to a wince as she gamely fought to mask the pain. "I'm afraid I'm not moving as fast lately."

Before Dex could find the words to speak, Jacob burst out from behind her. "Uncle Dex!" He ran forward and embraced Dex in a bear hug. "I *knew* it would be you! I *knew* it!"

Dex returned the hug. "Jake! Of course we came." He looked over Jake's shoulder at Janet. "We got the message."

Janet nodded. "And hello, Scot. I see they're still letting you hang around."

"Ms. Buhl." Scot tapped the rim of his helmet in a quick salute.

"Well, Jason." Janet stood to her full height, either forgetting her pain or ignoring it. "When you left this morning to blow that tunnel, I didn't think you'd be bringing back guests. Everyone!" Her raised voice carried authority, stirring the five on their mats, who, to Dex's relief, were at least able to turn toward them. "I'd like you to meet Captain Dex D'Felco and Lieutenant Scot Calgaro—the two men who are going to get us out of here."

She turned back to Dex and Scot. "Right?"

"Yes, ma'am," Scot said.

* * *

"So, we get everyone to the surface, manage to evade that thing, and find our way to your transport?"

Janet sounded skeptical. She and Dex were hunched over a portable holoprojector. Green icons indicated the locations of the Raven and the cave opening he and Scot had entered. An amber icon showed the updated location of the survivors' camp in the cavern.

"Yeah, it's not going to be easy," Dex acknowledged. He looked back at the group of mats in the corner. Two of the wounded, a man and a woman, were now sitting up.

Janet picked up on his expression. "Suzanne and Mick can move well enough—although Suzanne won't be able to help much with hauling."

Dex noted that Suzanne was the one whose arm had been lost to the M-2's cutter. "And the others?"

"We'll have to fashion a couple of gurneys. Jake's strong for his age, and Jason will push through his injuries. And we've still got Tim, Monica, and Daniel who can help. We'll manage."

"And Scot and I can carry as well." Dex pointed back to the holo. "We'll probably have to work in shifts. It's a long way."

Janet looked puzzled. "What are you talking about?"

Dex pointed to the entrance he and Scot had used. "To get back there. It's at least a five-hour hike, and that's with everyone on their feet. We'll make it, but we're going to have to—"

Janet's light laugh interrupted him. It was so pleasant to hear it again, despite the circumstances, that Dex had to smile.

"What?"

"Didn't Jason tell you?" She held back a second laugh, looking him in the eyes. "Dex, you came in the wrong way."

Suddenly feeling foolish, Dex did his best to avoid sounding defensive. "What do you mean?" He pointed to the holo. "It's the only entrance on Baker's map."

"That's the problem with settling these backwater worlds—so little topographical data. Yeah, that's probably what the orbiting survey scans logged back in the thirties, but it's not accurate." She traced a new line on

211

the holo with her fingertip, starting at their location and ending just a few inches up and to the left.

"There it is," she said. "Just about a hundred meters that way, and we're out." She pointed to the back of the room. The cavern narrowed to a tunnel that was blocked by a huge boulder which extended nearly to the ceiling. Dex had noted the obstruction when he'd arrived, but he now saw a detail that had escaped him earlier—displaced gravel lying around the base of the rock with a couple of thick pipes embedded in the floor to its right.

Janet continued. "A couple good shoulders into that boulder, and we can be on the surface in about five minutes." She forced back another smile.

"What?" Dex asked, his cheeks reddening.

Janet shook her head. "One, I still can't believe you came in that way. And two, I can't believe that Jason didn't rub your face in it."

"Well, now that I think about it, he might have hinted in that direction, but we were still getting reacquainted at the time." He looked over at Jason, who was huddled in another corner, deep in conversation with his younger brother. "Jake seems like the same kid I always knew. A little older, sure." He rubbed his right shoulder, wincing slightly as he made contact with the spot where the M-2 had pierced him. Jake's bear hug had irritated the still unhealed wound. "And he's definitely stronger. But Jason...the way he carries himself...he seems to have changed so much."

Janet's expression darkened. "Responsibility will do that to a person. We've all changed, even Jake. With everything we've been through..."

"I know, Janet. No one can go through what you've survived and come out unscathed."

"But you're seeing something in Jason, aren't you? Something more than that?"

Dex nodded.

She lowered her eyes. "I've seen it, too. There's an edge—a hardness that wasn't there before." She waved her hand around the cavern. "And I don't believe it's just a response to all this."

Dex looked back at the two young men. Jake noticed his attention and smiled. Jason followed his brother's look, but his grim expression didn't change.

"So what do you think it is?"

A small amount of moisture formed at the corners of Janet's eyes—an expression of vulnerability that Dex had never before seen from her.

"He watched his own father being murdered. Executed by that monster, before his very eyes."

Dex remained silent, allowing her to continue.

"I mean, we all saw it. Jon did what he had to. We were trapped—there was no way out. Then Jon taunted the thing, got it to come after him. He ran, hoping it would chase him, and it did." She hesitated, choking back a small sob. "A stun bolt slowed him down, but that thing would have caught him anyway. He *wanted* it to catch him. It had already slaughtered so many. Jon knew it was the only chance for the rest of us to escape."

Dex spoke softly. "And Jason saw the end?" He again recalled the horrific data feed, the image of Jonathan's head falling from his lifeless body. The thought of a seventeen-year-old kid having to see that happen—to his own father—was unbearable.

"We all saw it." She became quiet, staring through the holo at nothing in particular. Dex reached out and placed a hand on her shoulder. She continued staring blankly for a moment before pointing at a location. "We had made it to that ridge. We knew about these caverns, and Jon had figured that if we could just make it to this narrow canyon, we'd have a path to safety, at least for a little while. He was right."

She looked over at him, her eyes not quite meeting his. Dex wasn't sure if he should embrace her or step away and give her some space. Instead, he simply lowered his hand from her shoulder and continued to listen. "Jon did well. He ended up leading the thing back into the compound, a good distance from us. Jason had the only working pod, and he accessed the compound's corridor feeds. We were all watching, hoping that, somehow, he would escape. But it caught him. We saw it all. The blood…" Her voice caught. "Everything. We all watched it happen, but Jason was holding the pod right in his hand. He screamed. Then he dropped the pod and started back down the ridge. If he hadn't already been wounded, I don't think all of us combined could have stopped him. But we did."

"So you…"

"We dragged him, kicking and cursing, down the canyon and into this cave. We were all devastated, but it hit Jason the hardest."

Dex closed his eyes, fighting back the emotion he was feeling. "Jon was a hero. He gave his life for his family, his friends."

"That's not the way he sees it."

"What do you mean?"

Janet looked over at her sons, the pain in her eyes showing through the soft tears.

"He never wanted to be here. Yes, Jason knows that his father gave up his life, but as far as he's concerned, it wasn't for his family or his friends."

Dex followed her gaze to the two boys.

"From Jason's point of view," Janet continued, "his father sacrificed his life for his faith—a faith that Jason doesn't share."

Chapter 23

"Lieutenant Valani?"

Seltrice nearly jumped out of her skin. She straightened up, the top of her head banging against the open canopy of Adahn's Hornet. Cursing under her breath, she whirled around, looking down the access ladder at the mousy little man who had startled her.

"What?" She spat out the word.

Nikky Weis cleared his throat. "Uh, I was trying to find a set of infuser calimeters." He turned to the right and to the left, his head swiveling on his scrawny neck, taking in the entire hanger. "Drager, uh, Sergeant St. James, sent me down here. He said that they were in a bin with the other diagnostic tools, but I'm not sure where that is."

"Over there. To the left." Seltrice gave a dismissive wave in the direction of the south wall where an array of storage containers occupied almost all of the usable space.

"Thank you." Nikky began to move, no more confident of his direction than before.

"Hey, Weis."

Nikky stopped. "Uh, yeah?"

"It is 'Weis,' isn't it?"

"'Nikky' is fine, but yes."

"You're a cyber-dink, right?"

Nikky made a distasteful face. "Well, I wouldn't put it that way."

Seltrice put her hands on her hips. "I meant it as a compliment. Drager said you were some kind of savant—that you can analyze any system..." She trailed off as she looked him over, considering something. She then flashed him a smile. "Come up here for a second."

"Lieutenant?"

"Up the ladder, Weis." Seltrice waved a thumb in the direction of the cockpit. "There's something I want you to take a look at."

Nikky hesitated for a moment, took another look around the hanger, and climbed slowly up the ladder, making sure his lone hand had a good grip each time he traversed a rung. The small platform at the top was never intended to accommodate two people. Nikky had to squeeze uncomfortably close to the lieutenant in order to peer into the cockpit. This close, he could smell a confusing mix of aromas—mechanical oils combined with soft bath soaps and subtle perspiration. It made him dizzy.

"So what do you think?"

Nikky stammered. "It's…it's crowded."

"No, Weis. What do you think of that?" She indicated an open panel with a diagnostic scanner attached to it. The scanner displayed a series of test patterns, rapidly oscillating shapes with points intersecting at random intervals.

"It looks like a comm beacon." Nikky leaned in closer, trying and failing to avoid contact with the side of Seltrice's uniform tunic. Distracted by the sensation, he forced himself to concentrate on the task at hand. "It's, uh, dormant right now, but it's definitely a comm protocol."

"Okay," Seltrice said. "So, here's a question—is it a standard comm?"

"I don't understand."

"Look," Seltrice said. "Here's the fighter's comm bus"—her tone was reminiscent of an impatient teacher scolding a faltering student—"and here's this thing. Is this"—she pointed to the pattern on the display—"part of this?" She jabbed a finger back toward the Hornet's main comm. "Or are they separate systems?"

Nikky pulled in a breath between his pursed lips, the sound emitting like a muted coronet. "I don't really know."

"Take a guess."

"Well." Nikky released the breath. "I did get a chance to monitor your communications over Bellona. These patterns, they aren't *exactly* the same."

Seltrice's eyes widened. "So what are you saying?"

"I'm saying that I'm not sure." Nikky stepped back from the cockpit, taking one more look at the figures as he moved. He started to say something, stopped, and began again. "The protocols show some discrepancies, yes, but whether or not they are out of spec, I have no frame of reference for that."

Seltrice stayed under the canopy, peering at the display. "So, you're saying that we don't have anything concrete here?"

"I'm afraid so, Lieutenant—though it would help if I knew what you were looking for."

The force of her glare nearly knocked him off the platform.

"Sorry," he said quickly. "And no—I don't see anything of interest."

"Dammit." Seltrice's voice was soft, almost too low for Nikky to hear. She stood to her full height, being careful, this time, not to contact the canopy. "That will be all, Weis."

"Excuse me?"

"You can go now," she snapped. "Get out of here." She slapped her hand down on the side of the fighter, the sound echoing throughout the cavernous hanger.

Nikky made his way cautiously down the access ladder. Halfway down, his eyes fell on the bright golden letters inscribed on the silver crebonite fuselage.

"Ghazi"

At the bottom of the ladder, he glanced back up. Seltrice was leaning back under the canopy, oblivious to his presence.

"Lieutenant? Isn't this Officer Manasser's fighter?"

Her voice, coming from inside the cockpit, was muted. "Yeah. What of it?"

"Nothing," Nikky murmured. "Nothing at all."

He turned to leave, momentarily forgetting about the calimeters he had been sent to find, geometric figures dancing in his mind's eye. One way or another, he would have to get another look at that fighter.

*   *   *

Any lingering annoyance or embarrassment Dex had felt regarding his and Scot's interminable trek to the survivors' location was assuaged by his relief when he had confirmed that the proper path to the surface was, in fact, much shorter and far easier to negotiate. Even transporting the more critically wounded on a pair of makeshift gurneys hadn't proven that difficult. Jason and Jake had manned one, and a young couple, Tim and Monica Laurent, had insisted on carrying the second, freeing Dex and Scot to recon and lead the group. Meeting no significant obstacles or resistance, the escape party had made the ascent to the mouth of the cavern in less than fifteen minutes.

True to Janet's description, the cave opened into a narrow canyon at least fifteen meters deep and only a meter and a half wide at its tightest points. High above him through the slender fissure, Dex could make out a few twinkling stars, a glimpse of the night sky over Hephaestus. After spending the last several hours beneath the surface in the dark cavern complex, the sliver of sky was a welcome sight. He imagined that the open air was even more refreshing for the survivors. No one, though, could fully enjoy the moment—not with the knowledge that the M-2 was out there somewhere, perhaps stalking them even now.

"What do you think, Captain?" Scot said, crouching next to Dex. Janet and Tim gathered around as well. Dex typically would've insisted on a private conversation with his lieutenant, but in this case, he welcomed the others' inclusion. They had far better knowledge of the terrain and, somehow, had managed to survive against the M-2 for this long. Their insights could mean the difference between success and catastrophe.

Scot continued. "You figure one of us should make a run for the Raven, fly it over, and lift everyone out right here?"

Dex studied the portable holodisplay in front of them. "I don't know. It would take time to get everyone up through that gap." He pointed to the clear space at the top of the map. The surface terrain did not offer much in the way of cover. "And it looks pretty open, topside."

"Yeah," Scot agreed, "we'd be looking at trouble if that M-2 spots us. I don't imagine we could break silence right now and call Sarge and Rabbit in for some cover?"

Dex considered. According to the plan, Hagen and Jani were, unfortunately, still patrolling near the first entrance—the only entrance they knew about. "We could, but we'd be gambling that the thing wouldn't intercept the comm and get to us first." He once again cursed the fouled ground intel they'd received. As he considered the decision, he envisioned the M-2 slaughtering the emerging group in a flurry of red bolts and slices from its laser cutter, with Jani and Hagen arriving only in time to witness the end of a massacre.

Scot seemed to read his mind. "Risky," he conceded.

"There might be another way." Tim Laurent leaned in, tracing his hand along the glowing canyon. In the short time they had spent together, Dex had developed an appreciation for the young man. According to Janet, months earlier, Tim and Monica had found the hidden cavern that sheltered the eleven surviving colonists, a discovery that had saved all of their lives. The couple, both in their early thirties, was childless—a blessing, in their circumstances, considering the pain and horror other parents in the colony had experienced.

Tim continued, his voice revealing a trace of a French accent. "See this path here? We take the branch to the left, then come out in that sheltered opening. Well, it's at least better sheltered than this. There's cover on three sides."

"He's right," Janet added. "That would be a better starting point for someone to make a run for your transport. You should park it right...here."

Dex studied the holo. "It might be our best shot. What do you think, Lieutenant?"

"We'll have to move fast," Scot said. "Even if we're comm silent to that point, the thing's bound to track the Raven. At that point, it becomes a race." He glanced back at the mouth of the cave, the wounded survivors on the gurneys momentarily hidden from sight.

"Come in hot and make sure your dorsal shields are up—we'll do our part," Janet said firmly.

Jason approached the group, returning from a quick headcount in the cave. "Okay, dumb question. You guys have Hornets, right? I'm assuming you were smart enough to bring a few?"

Scot regarded him for a second. "A couple," he said flatly, surprising Dex with his restraint.

"Well, what about them?"

"There's a problem," Dex explained. "If we call in our Hornets and the M-2 is as close as we think it is, it will pick up the transmission, and odds are it would get to us first. We can't risk giving away our position until we have no other choice."

"So, you can only call in your cover once the transport is on its way?"

"Exactly."

Jason scowled. "So why don't you guys just have your birds already hovering around, waiting for us?"

Scot glared at him, his jaw set. "We do. But right now, they're patrolling the *other* entrance—the one we came in."

Jason shook his head. "Brilliant."

"Hey, we're working off your data-burst here, Magellan."

"Okay." Dex held up a hand. "We're going with Janet's plan. We move everyone into position by the canyon entrance. It's less than two klicks to the Raven from there. I make for the transport—"

"You mean *I* make for the transport," Scot interrupted. "No offense, Cap, but I'm faster than you."

"That won't matter. Speed isn't the issue. If it gets the jump, neither of us is going to outrun the thing."

Scot gritted his teeth. "All the more evidence that you're making an arbitrary choice here."

"It's my call, Lieutenant." He gave Scot a look that told him no further debate would be productive—or welcome. "When we get to the entrance, I go for the Raven. You stay with the rest. If anything goes wrong, break silence and call in Hagen and Jani."

"And hope that they get here first," Jason said. "Some plan."

"All right, people," Janet said, ignoring her son's sarcasm as she addressed the remaining survivors. "Everybody up. We're moving out."

The half-hour march through the canyon felt like an eternity. There was a thick air of dread over the group, an awareness that every step one of them took could be their last. Even for Dex, a seasoned combat veteran, the long passage was more nerve-wracking than anything he had experienced before. When he'd infiltrated the testing facility on Bellona, he had carried the pressure of having to drop the station's defenses for the Angels, but at least the immediate danger on the ground had been his alone to bear, and, later, when the M-2 was hunting him, it had only been his own life that he was trying to save.

Now, leading a dozen other people, most of them wounded, through the dark canyon, facing blind turn after blind turn, feeling completely exposed from above, his normally steady nerves were fraying. He was carrying the weight of responsibility for protecting the group, but he had severe doubts about his ability to save even a single person in the event of an attack. His eyes kept anxiously tracking upward to the top of the steep walls ahead, each time anticipating the sight of the M-2's silhouette peering down at them.

Scot brought up the rear, similarly scanning upward and behind. They had already passed at least half a dozen side passages, any one of which the mechanized monster could be hiding in, waiting to emerge from behind.

Janet was tracking their progress on the holo. "Another hundred and twenty meters," she reported softly. "After that, the canyon opens considerably. There's one more fork ahead. Go left."

Jacob Buhl relayed the information back to Scot. "We're almost there," he said. "So far, so good, right?"

"Yeah," Scot said, double-checking the safety on his carbine. "Maybe this isn't going to be so hard."

An explosion rocked the canyon, dropping a shower of rocks and dust on their heads. It took Scot only a moment to recognize the effects of a concussion grenade. Most of the party in front of him had been knocked off their feet, giving Scot a direct view through the dusty haze. He could see Dex, Janet, and Jason behind a rock outcropping, scrambling to get back on their feet. Thirty meters beyond them and to the left, he could see a figure through the cloud, standing still, poised. The shape had the appearance of a man—but not quite. His heart started pounding.

Then, to his horror, Scot saw Tim Laurent in the middle of the path, struggling to get up, unaware that he was lying directly in front of the machine.

"Yeah," Scot grunted, breaking into a sprint toward the front of the group. "It's gonna be hard."

The M-2 began to advance, moving deceptively fast with long, efficient strides. Scot knew that he would not be able to close the distance in time to save the man, but he had to try. He was only halfway through the scattered group when he saw the machine raise its arm, taking aim at Tim.

Without warning, a figure shot out from the left. It was Monica Laurent, catching her husband in a side tackle, bringing him back to the ground just before the monster's next concussion grenade detonated near the space he had been occupying. The blast showered more debris on the group, most of whom had not yet regained their feet. In the meantime, Tim and Monica, bloodied but not mortally injured, had scrambled on hands and knees to relative, if only temporary, safety behind the outcropping with Dex, Janet, and Jason.

This was unraveling fast. Scot managed to stay on his feet through the blast and continued to stumble forward, determined to do something— what, precisely, he had no idea. The only thing on his mind was to reach the machine before it could reach any of the others. He had covered another handful of meters when Dex inexplicably stepped out from behind the protection of the outcropping, standing squarely in front of the M-2, right where Tim had been.

"Dex! What the hell are you doing?" Scot hit the back of the outcropping in a slide, coming quickly to one knee beside Janet and Jason, shouldering his weapon and positioning himself to cover his captain.

The M-2 came to a stop, its left leg forward, balancing lightly on the micro-feelers beneath its feet—the predator in complete command of its body. There was a brief pause. The machine's single black eye could see in all directions at once, but its body language suggested that it was focused on Dex. Scot lifted his finger from the trigger, realizing that firing on the thing would serve no purpose other than directing its attention back at the vulnerable civilians behind him.

The M-2's slight hesitation seemed to be the cue Dex was looking for. He moved to his right, sprinting down the right fork in the canyon. The M-2 instantly responded, springing into action. A small object shot out from its left appendage, not toward Dex but in the direction of Scot and the survivors.

"Gren—" Scot didn't have time to get the word out of his mouth before the projectile detonated on the canyon wall head-high to his left. If it had been another concussion grenade, he would've been killed instantly. Instead, he was blinded by a bright flash while his lungs filled with noxious gas. He involuntarily dropped to the canyon floor, his ears ringing and his muscles contracting in sharp pain, suffering the debilitating effects of the stun grenade. Through the high-pitched hum, he could hear the moans of the other survivors, similarly immobilized. Turning his head back in the direction of the machine, his blurred vision caught a glimpse of the M-2 before it disappeared down the right fork in the canyon.

Running for his life from an M-2 for the second time in as many months, Dex noted that his plan had worked all too well. He'd had a hunch that he might be a high-priority target for the machines—especially since they had already failed to finish the job once before. He dove around a corner to his right, hearing the scream of the M-2's laser cutter and feeling the heat of the beam, which sheared the rock face just behind him. Dex was hoping that this machine operated under the same rules of engagement as the previous M-2 he had faced—a directive to capture and interrogate its victims prior to execution as opposed to simply killing them as efficiently as possible. Still, if the cutter beam had been any indication, the machine apparently didn't have any restrictions against interrogating an amputee. He completed the dive in a somersault, landing on his feet and continuing his sprint with an even greater sense of urgency.

Without breaking stride, he activated a small homing device on his belt and unlatched a demolition charge. Arming the explosive, he dropped the charge on the path behind him, mentally beginning the countdown to detonation. This was his one chance. If he timed it right, it was possible he could incapacitate the machine.

When the count in his head reached one, he hit the ground, hard. The blast roared, rolling him across the canyon floor, despite his low profile, and smashing him into the rock wall. Shaking his head, he looked back through the falling dust and rock.

Nothing.

Dex rose slowly to his feet, his sharp eyes focused, watching for a sign, anything, that would indicate that the M-2 was still intact and functional.

Nothing. No movement at all.

Dex allowed himself to breathe again. He took a tentative step in the direction of the blast center, anxious to inspect the shattered remains of his pursuer.

Then he heard it—the soft whir of micro-feelers on rocky ground. He didn't wait for visual confirmation. He turned on his heel, sprinting again down the canyon path, the sound of pursuit increasing in pitch as the M-2 accelerated behind him.

Add "demo charge" to the list of weapons that won't stop the damn thing, Dex thought.

He knew he didn't have much time. With each bend in the canyon, the thing closed the gap between them. Once they encountered a longer straight passage, it would be over. Glancing down, he saw that his homing device had been damaged in the blast, effectively ensuring that there would be no one coming to rescue him. The only thing he dared to hope for now was that he could buy enough time for the others.

The path climbed sharply in front of him. Grunting from the exertion, Dex scrambled up the steep incline. And then, suddenly, he was out in the open, a fresh nighttime breeze blowing across his face, thick grass beneath his feet. The view from the plateau was striking—a panorama of stars, bright and clear, all around him, the dark grooves and ridges of the canyon extending out as far as he could see. But his appreciation was fleeting as he realized to his dismay that his immediate surroundings offered nothing in the way of cover. Continuing his sprint, Dex desperately scanned the plateau area for something that could hide him, at least temporarily, from the soulless hunter.

The only notable feature was a short rise about fifty meters ahead, a rocky peninsula surrounded by a sharp drop on three sides. If he could make it to the small cliff and drop himself over the edge, it would be his only opportunity to put some solid rock between him and the M-2— provided he survived the fall. He put his head down and made for the peninsula.

And then he felt the sensation he'd been dreading, a stun bolt striking him, impacting his lower back. The entire right side of his body seized up, causing him to pitch face forward into the ground. Refusing to give in, he reached forward on the grassy surface with his left arm, pulling himself forward, followed by his left leg pushing in alternating lunges. The muscles on the right side of his body were convulsing, screaming in pain. He knew from experience that it would be hours before full mobility would return. He also knew that he had only seconds left to live.

Dex willed himself forward, reaching, crawling, ever sensing the hellish beast moving into position behind him. He had managed to make it out onto the peninsula. Meters ahead and to his right and left, the surface fell away. He couldn't see over the edge and so had no idea whether he could have survived the drop or found any cover. He only knew that he wasn't going to make it.

He reached forward again to pull himself closer to the edge only to be stopped short by a bright thin red line in front of him, the beam so close he could feel its heat on his skin. The M-2's laser cutter cut an arc completely around him, scorching the grass and cutting off any route to escape.

Knowing that it was now directly behind him and that any further movement was futile, Dex pushed himself over with his left hand, turning to face his tormentor this one final time. The thought briefly crossed his mind to reach for his side arm, but he knew that the weapon would have no effect on the machine. He still had fresh scars on his hands from the last time he had attempted a quickdraw on an M-2.

The machine halted twenty meters away. It spoke, its deep, ethereal voice saying one word—a name.

D'Felco.

The M-2 had indeed recognized him. Dex sensed that there would be no interrogation—no, this time the beast's masters were seeking revenge. He had cheated death at the hands of an M-2 once before, and now he was going to pay for making a fool of them. The only question remaining was how slow and painful his death would be.

The machine began to move, a slight hitch in its gait, which Dex attributed to the demo charge. A moral victory, however small. A familiar blue blade extended silently from the machine's right appendage, the appearance of the weapon causing the scars on his neck and shoulder to violently throb, sending an intense burning sensation coursing through his body. He closed his eyes, grimacing from the pain. The chase was at an end. He only hoped it had been enough to allow the others to escape.

He felt the grass move first. It quivered, shifting directions suddenly as a massive air displacement pushed the thick stocks into him from both sides at once. This was followed by a rushing wind from his right and left, accompanied by the distinctive high-pitched whine of twin AI-530 engines.

Dex forced his eyes open, not an easy task in the midst of the sandstorm created by the two S/A-81 Hornet fighters rising over either side of the peninsula. The delightfully lethal-looking birds faced each other, noses pointed slightly down, with Dex and the M-2 directly between them.

The M-2 pivoted its body, facing one then the other, seeming to be momentarily confused. After its split-second indecision, it lifted its laser cutter in the direction of the Hornet to its right, but it was too late. Dex covered his head just in time to hear the deafening discharge of four laser cannons. The bright cannon fire seeped through his tightly closed eyelids, filling his vision with a telltale yellow glow.

When the barrage ceased, the M-2 was no more.

Rocked by the blast, Dex lay with his face pressed into the soft grass, unable to move. The Hornets landed nearby on the plateau. A concerned Jani McLeod fairly leapt from the cockpit, sliding down a hastily deployed ladder in one quick move. To the right, Hagen Lebrian followed suit, a little slower but no less concerned.

"Captain! Dex!" Jani leaned over Dex's inert form. "Are you all right? Dex?"

Hagen arrived at her side, reaching down and gently turning Dex over onto his back.

"Deadeye? C'mon, show us a sign here, Captain."

Dex opened his eyes. He shook his head slowly, working his jaw back and forth before speaking.

"What took you guys so long?"

*   *   *

"Of course I called Sarge and Rabbit in as soon as I was able." Scot Calgaro sat in the Raven's pilot seat, entering the next waypoint into the nav system. Next to him, Dex stared out the cockpit's viewport, the white expanse of nothingness that made up etherspace concealing the fact that Jani and Hagen were out there on their wing, riding out the jump in their Hornets. No human eye or manmade instrument could ever detect them in the oblivion. Despite his knowledge to the contrary, Dex felt like his squadron mates—his friends and rescuers—were no longer there. In the ether, it was like nothing, other than his immediate surroundings, existed now, or ever had.

Feeling foolish, Dex tried to shake away the troubling thoughts that often plagued him during a jump. Instead, he turned in the copilot's seat to survey the eleven survivors of Hephaestus—no easy task, as the effects of the stun bolt still kept his right side stiff and uncooperative. Looking at Janet, Jason, and Jake—crammed into the troop seats in the Raven's small cabin with the Laurents and the remainder of the colonists—he was thankful, and amazed, that they had all made it.

"But you didn't call them in to cover me, did you? As I recall, those weren't my orders."

"In my defense, Captain, you just said to bring them in the moment something went wrong. You didn't say who they were supposed to cover. When Sarge and Rabbit picked up your homing signal, they took off in your direction right away—Sarge's call, boss, not mine." Scot gave a hint of a smile. "Gonna ground *him* this time?"

Dex tried to hide the amusement in his eyes. "I'm thinking about it," he said, turning again to look at the survivors. Janet was assisting one of the wounded with a hydration pack. Though weary and disheveled, she still radiated an air of competence and control—a calming presence that had undoubtedly served those under her care well.

No, he decided—he would not be scrutinizing anyone's decisions this time. The mission, against all odds, had ended up being a complete success. He was thankful that all the survivors had made it out alive and that he had managed to escape yet another encounter with an M-2. He prayed there would not be a third.

"Here. Put this on." Janet appeared behind him, opening a dermo-patch and pressing it to his still bleeding forehead. "Just how close were those pilots of yours when they blasted that thing, anyway?"

Dex had to force himself from recoiling at the fresh pressure on the wound. "Too close. But they didn't have time to wait. Even with their shields up, all it would've taken was a concentrated burst from that thing's laser cutter and it could have gone the other way."

Scot grunted. "Not to mention the fact that it already had you in its sights. Yeah, twenty meters from a cannon blast isn't the way I would have drawn it up, but that's the way it played out."

Dex settled back in his seat, letting the cooling anesthetic sensation of the dermo-patch have its effect. Glancing down at his belt, he examined the mangled remains of the homing device, smashed and silenced when the blast from the demo charge had thrown him against the canyon wall. He had initially activated the device with the intent that Hagen and Jani would come for him only after they had first secured all the colonists on board the Raven. He should have known better. Still, he was impressed with Hagen's ability to take the last signal and quickly extrapolate his direction, calculating the best possible intercept point. The decision to have Jani and Hagen in the Hornets had been a good one, and their skill and quick thinking had saved his life.

"All the same, your body has taken a beating," Janet said, scanning a bio display in front of him. She lowered her voice. "I don't like these readings. I've never seen anything like them before."

Dex followed her prompt, recognizing dangerous spikes in the indicators near his neck and shoulder.

"Old wounds," he said. He opted not to inform Janet that his scars had already been screaming in agony at the appearance of the M-2's blade—he wasn't sure what to make of it himself, much less try to explain it to someone else.

"That settles it." Janet opened a pouch, retrieving a small hypo. "You need rest. You, Captain, are out for the rest of the journey."

Dex was too worn out to protest. He sunk deeper into the seat and closed his eyes, a pleasant weariness settling over him. Sleep, so often fitful and scarce, began to creep in, overtaking his remaining conscious thoughts. The mission had been a success. The surviving colonists were safe. And Janet, Jason, and Jake Buhl, the surviving family of his best friend, were coming home—to their new home, at least.

For you, Bulldog. Rest in peace.

Dex drifted into sleep. His last conscious sensation was Janet's hand, after applying the hypo, remaining on his shoulder and how pleasant and reassuring it had felt.

Chapter 24

The squadron mess had become a lonely place, at least for Seltrice Valani. There had been a brief flurry of activity when the rescue party had returned—everyone excited to congratulate them and see the survivors they'd brought back. Seltrice, for her part, had been more anxious for the Raven to land so that she could have an opportunity to report directly to the captain, to fill him in on her discovery about Adahn's fighter. Yeah, that pipsqueak, Weis, had said that the discrepancy in the comm pattern was inconclusive, but Seltrice felt that it was yet another piece of evidence piled on top of everything else. When all of it was put together, the case against Adahn was overwhelming—she just needed someone to listen to her, and who better than the captain?

However, immediately after landing, they'd rushed him out on a stretcher. An unfamiliar dark-haired woman, holding a med kit under one arm and sporting a crutch under the other, had brushed by her like she owned the place. "He needs to rest," she'd said, and just like that, her window of opportunity with the captain had closed. Seltrice had considered reporting what she knew to Commander Lebrian the moment he'd landed his Hornet, but a stern look from him told her it would have to wait. Besides, she had been down that road before, Lebrian just brushing aside her concerns the last time. She had decided she would have to find a way to inform D'Felco—no one else. The others in the squadron either didn't believe her or didn't have the power to do anything about it. And so, the squadron, the colony, depended on her finding a way to convince the captain that she'd uncovered the traitor.

As far as she knew, though, Dex was still laid up in sickbay, kept in a hypo-induced rest until that makeshift medic lady said it was okay to revive him. Jani, no doubt, was probably right there at his side as well.

Seltrice hadn't seen her since she had landed her own Hornet and rushed, like a puppy dog, to Dex's side.

And now, everything had settled back into the same dull routine, lulling everyone else into a false sense of security. Lebrian and Onigen were preoccupied with setting up the survivors with accommodations in the colony while the Voor twins were still recovering and keeping to themselves in their quarters. Yes, people were busy, distracted—but she had also gotten the sense, particularly around meal times, that they were deliberately avoiding her. At least Scot had returned. While he was a little too full of himself for Seltrice's liking, he at least made for interesting company.

Most of the time. Tonight, however, had been a different story. Scot, at the moment, was absently picking at a limp piece of kale that was floating on a thin slick of olive oil while, across from them, Drager St. James and Job Hansen were eating at a workmanlike pace. They were the only four in the room, and their meal had passed in silence, broken only by an occasional scrape of a chair on the floor, a monotone "excuse me" or "thanks," and a relentless collage of chewing noises.

Seltrice fidgeted in her chair. "Guys, we have to find *something* to do tonight," she fumed. "If I spend one more night just sitting around, I'll go completely nuts." She looked across the table at the exec and flight sergeant. "Hey, what about you two? With Flash and myself, we'd have enough for a game or two of whist."

Drager's eyes brightened just a little, but Job shook his head.

"Sorry, I can't. I've got an ag-rep due for Commander Lebrian tomorrow, and I'm only about halfway through it. Another time, perhaps."

"I'd play if we could still find a fourth." Drager scratched his chin. "Butch or Lorry could probably use a break from reconfiguring the ghillie, but they've never shown interest when I've asked them before. Who else is around?"

The sound of rapid footsteps echoed in the corridor. They looked in time to see Adahn pass by the doorway, his eyes locked straight ahead. It appeared that he wouldn't have even glanced into the mess if Scot hadn't yelled out.

"Hey! Ghazi. Get in here for a second, will you?"

Seltrice made a disgusted hissing noise, but Scot ignored her. Adahn returned to the entrance, hesitated for a moment, and then stepped into the room.

Scot continued. "Adahn. Seltrice, here, has something she wants to ask you."

She gave Scot a venomous look before turning to Adahn. She started to say something, then stopped, a light crimson appearing on her cheeks. Finally, she blurted out, "So, where were you headed in such a hurry?"

Adahn looked puzzled. "What?"

Scot leaned back in his chair. That wasn't the question he had expected, but this was already shaping up to be much more entertaining than a hand of cards.

Seltrice was standing now, her tone blatantly accusatory. "You seemed to be in a hurry. You skipped dinner and were obviously heading somewhere just now. What's going on?"

Adahn shrugged. "I have things to do." He paused. "I'm not really sure that's any of your—"

"What Lieutenant Valani was trying to say," Drager interjected, "was that if you weren't too busy, we're looking for a fourth for a game of whist."

"Yeah," Scot grinned, "that's what she was *trying* to say."

Adahn looked from Scot back to Seltrice, his expression passive, waiting.

"Yeah, well, like you said"—she held his gaze, her dark eyes refusing to blink—"you've got other things to do, right?"

Adahn nodded. "Yes. That's right."

"Plans?"

"You could say that."

Seltrice's eyes narrowed. "Plans that you have no intention of sharing with us."

There was a hint of discomfort in Adahn's expression, but overall, Scot had to admit that his former wingman was playing it very cool.

"As I said, I'm not sure it's any of your concern, but if it matters, I have some reading to catch up on in my quarters." Adahn turned to Drager and Job. "But thank you for the offer. It was very kind. Good night."

He left the room. Scot could hear his measured footsteps receding in the hall. From the pace, it seemed to Scot that Adahn was trying to avoid giving the impression that he was in a hurry.

Scot waited another beat to make sure Adahn was out of earshot. Then he turned to Seltrice, his hands clasped behind his head and a sly smile on his face. "Well, that went well, Viper. You really know how to turn on the charm, don't you?"

"Shut up, Scot! Why do you always have to be such an ass?"

"Hey, I'm not the one treating one of our own pilots like he's a leper. You had a chance to reach out to the guy—to be nice for a change—and you blew it."

She glared at him. "Oh, is that what you were trying to do? Get me and Ghazi around a table, play a few hands of cards, and then everything will be all right? Or were you just stirring things up, as usual, for your own perverse enjoyment?"

Scot set the front legs of his chair pointedly back on the floor, the motion taking him face to face with Seltrice. His smile had vanished. "Look, I don't like the guy any more than you do. I probably don't trust him any more than you do. But it wouldn't hurt to loosen up a little— loosen *him* up a little. But, no. You're wound up way too tight yourself to do that."

"It's not that simple," she said.

"Maybe it is."

Scot and Seltrice both started when Drager cleared his throat. In the heat of their discussion, they had seemed to have forgotten that there were two others still in the room. Seltrice turned on him. "You've got something to add, Sergeant?"

Drager was looking down, drawing patterns on his plate with a fork, his demeaner uncharacteristically deferent. The gruff flight sergeant typically wasn't one to shy away from confrontation—even with superior officers. "Well, sirs, I'm not entirely sure what you have against Officer Manasser, or why you treat him the way you do, but I'm sure you have your reasons—*both* of you." He regarded Scot with a calm expression. Scot hadn't expected to be lumped in with Seltrice, but Drager wasn't off the mark—he had never made much of an effort to hide his distaste for Adahn. He forced himself to maintain eye contact with the stocky mechanic.

"But all the same," Drager continued, "even if Officer Manasser has given you some reason to dislike him, some reason to question his motives, I'm reminded of the proverb: *If your enemy is hungry, give him food to eat. If he is thirsty, give him water to drink.*" He turned his eyes back to Seltrice. "I'm not ready to call Adahn my enemy, but if you're going to, remember that Jesus himself showed compassion to his enemies. And he forgave them. Shouldn't we all do the same?"

There was an uncomfortable pause.

"Well, thank you for that, Brother St. James. I, for one, just love being preached at."

Sarcasm was second-nature for Seltrice, but this time there was a bitter edge in her voice that Scot had never before detected. He looked at the two men across the table. Job looked shocked. Drager just looked sad. A little ashamed that he had set Seltrice up in the first place, baiting her into that confrontation with Adahn, all Scot wanted to do now was defuse the situation.

"Hey, come on now…" Scot tried to put a hand on her shoulder, but she shook it off.

"No." She stared back at Drager. "I suppose I should say I'm sorry, but I'm not."

She looked each man, one by one, in the eye, waiting for a response. When none came, she continued, her exasperation causing her voice to rise, her tone becoming shrill. "None of you seem to understand what's at stake here. Everyone seems so worried about hurting poor Adahn's feelings. Well, I don't care. We are in danger here! This entire colony is at risk! And I'm getting fed up with being the only one who seems to care." She locked eyes again on Drager, her words clipped. "There are more important issues here than faith."

At that, Drager raised his eyebrows but said nothing. For several more awkward seconds, the room was silent. Finally, Scot pushed out his chair, stretching as he stood.

"Well, I tried," he said. "This has been the usual amount of fun, Viper. Maybe try whist again tomorrow?"

Seltrice didn't acknowledge him.

Scot threw an arm around Drager's shoulders. "Come on, preacher. You can tell me more about that proverb." He guided Drager out the door in the direction of the barracks. "Aren't we supposed to shovel hot coals or something on his head after that?"

Seltrice still hadn't moved. Job slowly rose from his chair. "If you will excuse me, as I said, I have that report to complete, so I'd better get to it." He paused at the door. "And Lieutenant?"

Seltrice finally moved, looking up at him, a hint of moisture forming at the edges of her eyes.

"There isn't anything more important than our faith. Please try to remember that."

Seltrice nodded dumbly. "Sure. Get the light on the way out, would you?"

Job slowly passed his hand over the wall sensor, waiting as the lighting panels gradually dimmed. He considered saying something else, then thought better of it and turned to go, leaving Seltrice alone in the darkening room.

Chapter 25

It was a long commute from the Unity Tower to his apartment, but tonight Darik was in no hurry to get home. With Liana gone again for the weekend, all he had to look forward to was a stale leftover meal from the IR oven and then yet another evening of agonizing over his impossible assignment.

Activating the autopilot on his Perseus shuttle, he reclined in the faux-leather driver's seat and closed his eyes to take a moment's rest. His mind, though, would not allow him to fully relax, turning, as it always did of late, to the problem of uncovering the JenKore mole. He had no new information to work from, and so his thoughts settled into their normal groove, working through the next steps he could take, none of which seemed particularly promising. He felt as though a mental fog had settled over him—that there was a creative solution out there somewhere, but he was left stumbling around in a dark haze, grasping aimlessly. What else could he be doing? Was he missing something obvious? So consuming was the problem that he had even begun to dream about it—most recently, chasing a specter through the halls of JenKore, the shadowy figure always just beyond his reach.

It wasn't so long ago that catching the hacker had seemed like a forgone conclusion. After Liana had shared her detection pack with him, he had possessed the means of spotting the hacker's next intrusion, and, just as importantly, he knew what the hacker was after—files pertaining to the M-2/A initiative. Setting the trap, however, had proven to be much more complicated than he'd anticipated. The problem was that even after his promotion, his access to the most secure areas of the JenKore system was restricted, every deep excursion he attempted to make into the M-2/A files resulting in a dead end. The data chip that Nikky had provided him undoubtedly contained the information the mole was searching for, yet it had yielded absolutely no clue as to where Nikky had uncovered those files in the first place. And any attempt to trace their origin had resulted in a maddeningly simple message—*Section Seven: Access Denied.* He had tried using his Access Code Generator, but he didn't have the necessary permissions at that level. Frustrated, he had returned the data chip to the lockbox in his apartment, feeling as though he was completely out of options.

To compound the problem, there had been no detected intrusions since Darik had set about preparing his trap. Either the hacker had been spooked off or, far worse, was somehow getting in and out of the JenKore system completely undetected.

In his desperation, Darik had briefly considered bringing Liana further into the loop—to show her the data chip and everything on it. She had already proven to be incredibly helpful on the case—without her expertise, he would still have no way of isolating the hacker's signature. If she knew what information the mole was after, he'd reasoned, maybe she could devise a clever way to catch him. But he had quickly dismissed the thought, resolving that he would never endanger her by bringing her further into Jenkins's and Graves's world. Despite the help she'd provided, he already regretted involving her at all, at any level. He cared about her too much to put her at risk like that. He loved her, in fact—an admission Darik had made to himself even though he hadn't yet found the courage to say the words to her.

He was struck with a sudden pang of loneliness. At that moment, the thought of returning alone to his empty apartment put a knot in his equally empty stomach. The last thing Darik wanted tonight was to be alone— alone and hungry.

He was reaching for the autopilot, intending to reroute to Alphonse and Josephine's, when an unfamiliar tone from his handpod demanded his attention. Glancing down, he recognized the alarm icon from the lockbox in his apartment. Frowning, Darik waved his right thumb through the icon. A string of text instantly appeared above it, informing him that the box's locking mechanism was being tampered with.

Darik scowled. It had to be a malfunction. He increased the shuttle's speed and tried to recall if the lockbox's instructions had mentioned any possible false alarm errors.

The alarm changed frequencies, a shrill oscillating sequence replacing the previous steady tone. The line of text dissolved to reveal new information. According to his handpod, the lockbox was now open.

Looking up, Darik could see that he was still deep within the downtown mandatory autopilot zone. He ran his index finger to the top of the velocity display, selecting the maximum governed speed. The shuttle lurched forward with a sudden surge of power—a sensation Darik would have quite enjoyed if not for the powerful churning in his gut.

He considered taking the shuttle off autopilot, thereby freeing the vehicle from the velocity governor, but decided against it. Switching to manual control in Compton's financial district would bring a group of enforcement officers around him within moments of flipping the switch.

The shuttle, at least, was making decent progress. Darik felt a light weightless sensation as it dipped quickly into a lower lane, roaring beneath a slower-moving freight transport before popping back up into the main transit lane.

The image of enforcement officers descending upon him gave Darik an idea. How risky would it be to contact the authorities about the break-in at his apartment? He glanced down at his ETA. At this speed, he would never make it in time. If the box was already open, the intruder would be long gone before Darik arrived. Enforcement officers near his building could respond in under half the time it would take him. But if he called in the authorities, what questions would they ask? If the intruder was after the data chip, would it be held and examined as evidence?

No, official enforcement was out of the question. What if, though, he were to contact building security? One selling point of his building was that the staff took their tenants' privacy very seriously. Coupling that with the fact that they would be none-too-pleased that they had allowed an unauthorized entry, the security staff would be anxious to apprehend the burglar and, afterward, far less likely to ask any probing questions about what the perpetrator had been after.

The ETA read five minutes. It was worth the risk. Darik reached for the handpod, silencing the alarm and keying up building security. An incoming call interrupted him.

Kirrone Jenkins.

I don't have time for this right now!

He opened the call. "Darik Mason."

"Mason! What the hell is happening? I've been informed that there is critical information—*classified* data about your M-2/A initiative—being uploaded right at this moment. to a secure government server. Do you understand me?"

"Uh," Darik stammered, "I, uh, don't see how that could be possible, sir." Darik checked his ETA—four and a half minutes. "I mean, our systems are secure. No one could send data externally from our servers." Darik's hand hovered over the autopilot, a sinking revelation forming in his mind. "That's why the spy we're after hasn't been able to move on the information yet. He can't extract it from the JenKore complex, right?"

Jenkins's bile seemed to be transported directly through the ambient sound of Darik's handpod. "My contact tells me that the data is not transmitting from inside JenKore. It's coming from the workstation in your apartment. Explain yourself!"

"Dammit!" Darik hung up, slamming his hand down on the autopilot switch. The shuttle veered violently to the left, knocking Darik's head against the canopy. He reached for the control column, recovering from the swerve just in time to avoid clipping a long-haired airbike operator two lanes over. The airbike driver laid on his horn and raised his right arm in an obscene gesture that Darik fully realized he deserved.

He pressed the velocity to maximum, canceling all traffic fail-safes at the same time. Swerving back to the right, Darik pulled the shuttle up into the next lane, slicing between a mass transit vehicle and an Adonis shuttle, into a clearer space beyond.

There would be no contacting building security now. Even if they could catch the intruder, with the breach being sent to a Coalition government server, the private security firm would have no choice but to obediently release all relevant information on the break-in, including the data that had been transmitted.

He was passing shuttles at a breakneck speed. Stunned that he hadn't seen a trace of traffic enforcement, Darik continued to scan in all directions, fully expecting to see the telltale flashing beacons at any moment.

His handpod sounded again. Stealing a look down, he could see it was Jenkins, trying again to make contact. Even the call tone sounded apoplectic.

A shadow enveloped the entire shuttle's canopy. Looking up, Darik screamed. The largest freight transport he had ever seen was directly ahead, apparently stopped mid-lane.

Both hands slammed the control yoke forward, the shuttle diving toward the underside of the freighter. The rear structure of the behemoth rushed toward his canopy. Darik flinched, instinctively bracing for what he was certain would be an instant decapitation.

The canopy impacted the lower rear of the freighter with a sickening crash. Clear shards rained down on Darik, the glinting fragments covering the interior of the shuttle. The underside of the freighter rushed past in an instant, and Darik emerged—shaken, bloodied, but alive—on the other side.

Noise, wind, and the foul smell of traffic rushed through the now-open canopy. Darik reached forward and knocked some of the loose fragments away, squinting against the overwhelming onrush of vehicles and buildings and lights. His exit from the autopilot zone was just ahead. The ETA, adjusting for his increased speed, showed only a minute to his apartment.

One minute. Then what? Take on the intruder himself? Darik opened the console to his right and retrieved the stun pistol he had taken to carrying in his vehicle ever since he and Nikky had ventured deep beneath JenKore's research facility. He jammed it in his jacket pocket, the pistol resting at an awkward angle. While he had fired the weapon a number of times before, including stunning a couple of guards during his escape from the research facility, he had never before been in a situation in which someone was shooting back. He hoped that the intruder wasn't armed more lethally.

That was, if the intruder was still even in his apartment. With traffic lightening the farther he distanced himself from downtown Compton, Darik used the Perseus's speed to its full advantage, racing toward his building while simultaneously attempting to calculate just how long it would take the burglar to upload the data chip from his admittedly slow workstation. How much data had been transmitted already? Who would it incriminate? Maybe this was his moment to finally leave—to turn the shuttle around and leave Compton, leave Earth. He and Liana could go on the run. There were still frontier planets where one could effectively hide and start a new life.

The parking garage entrance now loomed directly ahead, and Darik faced the sobering reality that there would be no running from this. He had to see this thing through, one way or the other. Steeling his resolve, he hit the entrance at full speed.

A dull thud reverberated throughout the shuttle, a warm, sticky liquid splattering across his face. He slammed on the reverse thrusters, bringing the shuttle to an abrupt sideways stop. Wiping a bit of sour red gore from his mouth, Darik realized what had happened. He had hit something—hard.

Panicking, he jumped out of the shuttle and ran directly to its dented front. Whatever he had hit, it hadn't been large. He desperately hoped that it wasn't a child. Examining the damage, he breathed a short sigh of relief. It was only a small house pet, let out, no doubt, to make its way to the designated relief area. Darik spared only a brief glance at the orange-furred remnant of its mangled body still intertwined in the twisted intake manifold. He was sorry, but there were far more pressing matters at hand.

Ignoring the M-2 attendant bounding toward the shuttle, he raced to the lift, bursting through the open doors and depressing the touch pad, which scanned his prints and routed the lift directly to his apartment. During the ride, Darik keyed a sequence into his handpod, alerting his HCU to silence the lift's arrival chime and bypass the illumination sequence that would normally have lit up the apartment upon his arrival.

When the lift doors opened, it took Darik's eyes a moment to adjust to the darkness. His vision was somewhat aided by the soft glow of periodicals floating over his coffee table's holoprojector. The only other light in the apartment came from down the hall. A soft chirping sound coming from the same direction told him that the small workstation in his bedroom was still uploading data. Whoever the intruder was, he hadn't yet completed his task.

Darik crept forward, nearly stumbling over an ottoman in the center of the living room. Cursing to himself, he drew the stun pistol from his jacket pocket and made his way as quietly as he could down the hallway. He paused at the open closet door. The lockbox was sitting on the stack of poly containers, open. Looking inside, he saw only the ancient knife—the data chip was missing. Well, not missing. Not really. He knew exactly where it was—in his bedroom, plugged into his workstation, dutifully uploading all of its data and destroying his life in the process.

A cold rage crept over him. Inside the box, the blade glowed its pale blue. He reached in and grabbed the knife, sensing the same rush of adrenaline he felt every time he held the carved handle in his hand. Lacking a clear reason for doing so, he placed the stun pistol back into his pocket and continued toward his bedroom, the tip of the knife swaying in front of him. A single thought had come to supersede all others—whoever had broken in had made a huge mistake, and he was going to pay.

The thief was bent over the workstation, intently reviewing open files as a green bar tracked the progress of the data burst. Dressed completely in black, his thin frame was silhouetted in the glow of the screen. His back to the door, he was oblivious to Darik's approach. Darik raised the knife. He knew he wouldn't get a better chance.

Darik moved quickly, too quickly, in fact. He hadn't noticed the bathrobe that had been discarded on the floor at the foot of the unmade bed. Tangling his foot in the sash, he stumbled, just enough for the burglar to hear. Startled, the thief stiffened before he spun around.

He wasn't a "he."

Darik was stunned. It took him a moment to find his voice.

"Liana."

She looked at the glowing knife in Darik's upraised hand. "So, are you planning on using that thing?"

Darik lowered the knife, but just a little. "What?" Darik's head was spinning. He wanted to be relieved that it was Liana standing before him, but *why* was she there? He kept the knife tip pointed in her direction. "What are you doing?"

"Hey," Liana said in a disarming tone as she started forward, but a menacing wave of the knife stopped her.

"I asked you a question. What are you doing?"

Liana hesitated, as if she were considering several responses. Finally, she just asked, "What does it look like I'm doing?"

He couldn't deny what his eyes were taking in. Liana, supposedly away for the weekend, standing there, looking like some kind of cat burglar, his own data chip plugged into the workstation, the glowing screen showing that a majority, if not all, of its incriminating contents had already escaped. The knife tip dropped as his shoulders slumped.

"You. You're the spy. The UC agent."

Liana said nothing. Her resigned expression told Darik all he needed.

"How long?" he rasped.

Liana looked down and sighed. "Before JenKore. I've been with UC Intel since I left university."

Darik felt like the walls of the apartment were going to collapse on him. "Why me?"

Liana's expression was sympathetic. "We had vague information of something going on—something wrong in the M-2 division at JenKore. At first, you were just close enough to the project for me to get in but not so close as to…" Her voice trailed off.

"But not *important* enough to arouse any suspicion." Darik completed her thought. "Then I got promoted, and you got so much closer."

Liana shrugged. "Bellona was an added bonus."

Darik's stomach turned at the memory of the Bellona trip, especially the time they had shared on the way back. "So, everything we've been through, everything we've been to each other"—he indicated the disheveled bed with a sideways nod—"all of that has been a lie?"

"No," she said with conviction. "Not all of it."

Darik felt a fresh sense of anger, a sharp hatred, welling up inside of him. "You used me! You played me the whole time! And for what?"

"Don't be naive." Liana leveled her eyes at him. "You know what's on that chip. You know what's going on here. These people have to be stopped. That's my job, Darik. That's what I do."

"Even if you take me down in the process."

She bit her lip, looking down for just a moment. "It's not like that. It's not what you think."

"Spare me!" Darik sneered. The knife was back up in an instant. He took another step toward her.

"No, listen to me!" Liana's attention was immediately back on him. "I know you. I *care* about you. You can't possibly believe the way these people do. You can't agree with what they're doing!"

Darik fought back a lump rising in his throat. When he spoke, his voice was hoarse.

"You don't know anything about me."

"I know that it's not too late for you. I've seen the files. What JenKore is doing is horrifying, evil. But I haven't implicated you, specifically, in anything. Not yet. If you help me—if you turn yourself in as a witness— you can still get through this."

"Turn myself in?" Darik shook his head, a cold rage again rising to the surface. "Do you have any idea what I've done already? Do you think your friends in the UC are just going to look the other way?"

The workstation chimed once, the unmistakable signal that it had completed its task.

Liana looked pleadingly at Darik, a hint of moisture welling beneath her eyes.

"I'm trying to *help* you."

"No." Darik gripped the knife harder, the vibration of the blade sending shockwaves up his arm and into his chest. "You've destroyed me." He took another step closer.

Liana's voice grew cold. "I'm sorry."

There was only a meter separating them.

"How can you be sorry? You've been planning this all along."

She stared at him. "That's not what I meant."

It took Darik just a moment too long to understand. He didn't even see the pistol, so quickly did Liana pull it from a small shoulder holster. He only felt the powerful bolt slamming into his chest.

He lay flat on his back on the luxuriously plush bedroom carpet, completely conscious but unable to move. Liana walked over to him, knelt beside him, and placed the data chip on his chest.

"You may still need this. It will give you leverage if you choose to cooperate. I'm sorry, but I can't keep you out of this indefinitely. You have twenty-four hours to decide. I'll be in touch."

She leaned down and kissed his forehead gently. With the effects of the stun blast numbing his every sensation, he barely felt the falling tear splash against his face. His eyes, red from strain, welled up as well, for other reasons. If he could have moved, Darik would have driven the knife through her heart.

Chapter 26

Jani McLeod was tired, dead tired, but she wasn't about to let anyone else know that. At the sound of footsteps in the corridor, she perked up in her chair just in time to see Janet Buhl come limping into the infirmary, pausing barely long enough to lean her crutch against the wall.

"So how is he doing?" Janet didn't really wait for an answer, edging past Jani to study a display next to Dex's cot.

Jani shifted positions in the collapsible field chair, stifling back a yawn. "Still out, if that means anything. What do the numbers say?"

"They say that it's a good thing he's still under. I don't like these readings at all. They're like nothing I've ever—" She stopped. "He'll be all right. He just needs time to recover." She picked up a hypo, considered it, and set it back on the tray beside the cot. Checking the display again, she added, "It's too soon for another eszopic course, but the longer he's down the better."

"So, you want to keep him like this?" Jani turned to fully face Janet. "In a drugged-out coma?"

"Yes."

"And you think that's what Dex would want?"

Janet tapped the display, bringing up a subset of readings. "At this point, it doesn't matter what he would want. What's best is to keep him sedated. If he were to come out of it right now, the pain would be unbearable."

Jani turned back toward the cot. She had never seen Dex look so vulnerable. "He can handle it."

"That's not the point. Whatever it was that thing did to him, it's still coursing around inside, throwing off every neurological system in his body. We can't wake him up yet, not until we know what's going on." She settled into another field chair next to the cot. "But it's okay. I can stay with him for a while. You need to get some rest."

"No!" Jani was surprised by the forcefulness in her voice. "I'll stay. I can let you know if he starts to wake up."

"You don't have to do that." Janet looked around the infirmary. "You haven't left his side since we got back. It's all right. I can take a shift."

"You've got other people to worry about," Jani said. "I can do this. I want to be here."

"Uh huh. And when was the last time you slept?"

"Does it matter?"

"Yes, it matters. What if they need you in a fighter all of a sudden? Would you be at your peak?"

"I'll be fine."

"No, you won't." Janet's voice softened. "Look, I know you and Dex are close. I know you feel a sense of responsibility for him. You're his wing—I know how that works. But you know you're not his only friend, right?"

"What's that supposed to mean?"

"It means that as noble as it looks for you to sit here by his side, without eating, without sleeping, you're not doing him, or yourself, any good. There are plenty of us—some who have known Dex a long time— who can take a shift or two."

Jani didn't answer. She simply refolded her hands, leaning forward and watching over her captain.

"Jani…"

She waved her off.

"I know I can't order you to take a break—"

"That's right." Jani turned back to her. "You can't. So, check his numbers, shoot him up again if you have to, but don't try to tell me I can't stay."

"True, I can't order you," Janet continued, "but I know someone who can." She lifted her voice. "Hagen, would you come in here please?"

Hagen's large form filled the doorway. "Is everything all right in here?"

"It will be. Once someone convinces a certain flight lieutenant to get some rest."

Jani sighed. "I'm fine. Florence Nightingale here is way out of line."

Hagen frowned. "Janet, can you give us a moment?"

Janet checked her chrono. "Sure. I have to check on Tim anyway." She looked back at Dex, then at Jani. "I'll be back in five."

Hagen watched her leave before turning to face Jani.

"So, how is he?"

"I don't know, Sarge." Jani's voice cracked a little. "How can I know? He hasn't woken up—he hasn't even stirred. And she just comes in here and thinks she can take over. She's got him so drugged up, I don't even know if he—"

"Jani," Hagen said softly, "she knows what she's doing."

"Does she?" Her eyes flashed. "Has she ever even seen injuries like this before? It sure doesn't sound like it. What qualifies her to decide what's best for Dex—for any of us?"

"Graduating with honors from the academy, twelve years with UCN Medical—you know, stuff like that."

Jani slumped back in her chair. "Not good enough."

"It's going to have to be." With a sweep of his large hand, Hagen indicated the bio display. "We're out of our league here, Lieutenant. We don't know what's going on with Deadeye, what that thing did to him. Janet Buhl, with her experience, is a godsend. We need her."

"Okay, fine, fine. You win. She's qualified. That doesn't mean she gets to tell me what to do."

"Actually…"

"Seriously? You're going to take her side on that, too?" She paused. "Oh, that's right, I forget. You guys are all such old friends."

"Jani."

"What?"

Hagen sat down in the field chair Janet had vacated. "Listen to yourself. This isn't you."

"Caring about the captain? That's not like me?"

"Stop that," Hagen growled. "Now listen to me. You've been off since Bellona. I don't know what happened down there on the surface, but you haven't been the same. I mean, between your attitude and Dex's cowboy tactics…" He trailed off.

"Dex's what? What are you talking about?"

"Come on, Rabbit." Hagen's expression was pained. "You can't tell me you haven't seen it."

"No," Jani said flatly. "I haven't seen anything. Perhaps you should enlighten me."

"All right. Fine." Hagen swallowed. "You know that there's no one more loyal to Dex than I am. I would follow him anywhere. Hell, I *have* followed him anywhere—into some pretty tight spots. And no matter how crazy the mission, no matter how reckless the risks might have seemed from the outside, there was always a plan, a logic, a *reason* for our actions. But this M-2 thing, it's gone beyond reckless for Dex. Normally, when he has to make a difficult decision, I may not always fully agree, but I trust that he's doing what's best. But this…"

He paused, looking down at his friend.

"It's become personal. Think about Bellona—for Dex, that was a suicide mission. He knew that, and he went off anyway with no discussion, no accountability. And then on Hephaestus, it was the same thing. He decided, unilaterally, to take on that thing alone. It's like he's drawn to them—like he thinks he's the only one who can face them." He gestured toward the bio display. "And look where it's gotten him—shot up all to hell, lying there in a coma, with who knows what still coursing through him, poisoning his body."

Jani gave him a hard look. "So what are you saying—that you don't trust him?"

Hagen held her gaze. "I'm saying that when it becomes personal, people make bad decisions—even Dex." He drew a deep breath. "I've seen it before. You know that Dex is a blood ace, right?"

Jani looked down at the cot. "Yeah, who doesn't? The only one since the Frontier War."

"And do you know how it happened?"

She shook her head. "No. He never talks about it."

"And why do you suppose that is?"

"Well, why should he? He's got nothing to prove."

Hagen shifted his eyes to the far wall. "To us, anyway."

Jani considered what Hagen was saying, trying to envision the scenario Dex may have faced the day he recorded his fifth confirmed kill. "It doesn't matter to me. I'm sure he did what he had to do. And who are you to judge, anyway? We've all had missions go south in a hurry. We make split-second decisions and live with the consequences. That's the job."

Hagen remained silent, a faraway look in his eyes.

"So, what are you suggesting," Jani continued, raising an eyebrow. "Some kind of mutiny?"

That snapped Hagen out of it. "What? No. Of course not. Don't be ridiculous. I shouldn't have brought it up."

"But you did. So now I have to know—what are you planning to do?"

"Same thing I always do," Hagen grunted. "When he wakes up, I'm going to set him straight."

"And if he doesn't listen?"

"Then I'll kick his rear end until he remembers who he is and what he stands for. After all," he said, allowing himself a smile, "what are friends for?" He glanced toward the door. "Speaking of which, you've got a friend looking out for you, and you don't even know it. Janet is one of the good ones, Rabbit. And yeah, she does know what she's talking about. If she says that you need some bunk time, then you need to take it. Or do I have to make it an order?"

Jani rubbed the dark sunken flesh below her eyes. "No, Sarge. You win." She looked back at Dex again. "Just give me a few more minutes, okay?"

"You've got two." Hagen stood. "I'll go get Janet. When she gets back here, you are off the clock, understood?"

"Yes, sir. Understood."

She watched Hagen depart, stretched again, and forced herself to get up out of the field chair. Aware that both of her lower legs had fallen asleep, the metal edge at the front of the chair having cut off her circulation over the past four hours, she walked gingerly over to the water container in the corner.

"He's right, you know."

The voice, while weak, was so unexpected, she jumped, almost losing her balance as she spun around.

"What?"

Dex coughed, tried to raise himself up on an elbow, failed, and settled back on the cot again before continuing.

"Hagen. He's right."

"About me?"

"About both of us."

Dex grimaced. Out of the corner of her eye, Jani noticed several indicators on the bio rising at a rapid rate. A soft chime rhythmically sounded, stating that something was not right.

"Lie back. I'll go get the doc."

"No. Wait." Dex reached out, grasping Jani's arm. "I want to say this, now, when it's just the two of us."

Jani glanced at the doorway. With the alarm going off, Janet would undoubtedly be returning at any moment.

"Okay. Shoot. I'm listening."

Dex took in a breath, his face betraying the pain he had to be feeling. "Hagen is right. About everything. I haven't been the same—I haven't been right—not since I first saw that knife."

"Knife? What knife?" Jani stole a quick look at the bio again, wishing that she could fully understand the readings. Was the pain affecting his mind? Was he hallucinating?

"It's not just the knife," Dex rasped. "It's what that thing did to me. I tried to tell you on Bellona, to warn you, but I couldn't. And now you're paying for it."

"Me?" Jani looked toward the door again, not sure if she wanted Janet to burst in or not. "There's nothing wrong with me. Dex, you're the one who was attacked by one of those monsters, not me."

His grip on her arm tightened, surprising her and hurting just a little. "They didn't have to touch you. *They* were there, on the hilltop. They were there with Graves, all around us. I could see their shadows in the dust. I know the effect they had on you. On Nikky. On all of us."

"I don't know what you're talking about. I haven't changed. And neither have you."

"Jani!" Dex's eyes were wild. "Don't lie to me. And don't lie to yourself. Hagen is right. There's something off with me. Something wrong inside. I can feel it." He grasped her even tighter. "Don't let it happen to you."

He gagged, his body convulsing from fresh spasms of pain.

"Dex. Dex! Tell me what you need. What can I do?"

The shaking subsided slightly, allowing Dex to roll on to his side. Still holding her arm, he looked into Jani's eyes.

"Fight it. You have to fight it."

He collapsed onto his back, his eyes closing, just as Janet and Hagen burst back into the infirmary. Only Jani heard his next words before he passed back into unconsciousness.

"And…pray for me."

Chapter 27

Scot didn't see Seltrice until he practically bowled her over. She was wearing black, as usual, and had been standing dead still up against a wall in the darkest section of the corridor, halfway between a pair of dull orange emergency lights.

"Watch it, Flash!" She pushed him aside with a sharp elbow. "What are you doing out here?"

Scot consciously avoided rubbing his side where she had hit him. "I might ask you the same thing."

"What do you think I'm doing? I'm checking up on my favorite squad mate."

Scot leaned against the wall, grinning. "Well, it looks like you found me."

She ignored him, turning her attention back down the corridor. "Didn't you think Adahn was acting odd earlier?"

"You mean more than usual?"

"Come on. You know what I'm saying. He was evasive. Nervous."

"I can't imagine why he'd be nervous around you. Just a wild guess, but do you think it might have something to do with the fact that you've been actively trying to destroy his life?"

She stiffened, then shot back. "Right. Because you've always treated him so kindly."

That elicited a short laugh. "Hey," Scot said, "I've been reforming my ways. If you recall, I was the one who invited him in to play cards."

Seltrice turned to look at him, her dark eyes nearly indistinguishable in the shadows. "Yes. And do you remember why he declined?"

"Uh, he said he was going to his quarters to read."

"Well," she said, nodding down the corridor, "I just came from his quarters, and guess what—your former wingman isn't there."

"What? It's after lockdown."

"No kidding. That's what I've been saying."

Scot glanced back over his shoulder at a phantom noise. "You're overreacting. Look, we're out, too. He's probably in the lav or grabbing coffee or something." Scot tried to move past Seltrice, but she blocked his way.

"Don't bother. I've checked everywhere. He's nowhere on base."

Scot digested this new information. "Well, where do you think he is?"

Seltrice snorted. "Who knows? Down in the colony? Meeting a contact?" Scot could see her eyes more clearly now—they were wide, fierce. "I don't know," she continued, "but for the sake of this squadron, I'm going to find out."

*　　*　　*

While Pella's natural dampening field kept the planet invisible to long-range scans, it did nothing to disguise light emanating from the surface. Despite the long odds of visible detection, colony policy was clear—after 1900, no exterior lights were permitted, and interior lights could operate at no greater than forty percent illumination. On evenings when the largest of Pella's moons was shining bright and full, the light restrictions weren't much of an issue, but on nights when it was in its slim crescent phases, visibility in and around the colony was a challenge. Once every three months, it so happened that the largest moon was new while the smaller satellites stayed hidden below the horizon. On those nights, the darkness was almost oppressive. Such were the conditions this evening, which suited Adahn just fine. Leaving a housing flat on the far-eastern end of the colony, he wasn't anxious to be seen. He crept quietly along a side street, keeping his distance from any illuminated windows. There weren't many to avoid this night.

The same cover of darkness had also concealed the others. Stepping out of the shadows, four men surrounded him, the largest one standing directly in his path, thumbs in his pockets. Adahn took a step to his left, but the man matched his move, blocking his way while the other three closed in on each side.

"Excuse me." Adahn brushed against the burly man's side. A strong, calloused hand grabbed his shoulder, turning him back to the center of the group.

"Sir, you do not want to touch me." Adahn tried once more to ease past the human barricade, but the man placed both hands on his chest, holding him back.

"Now hold on there. Not so fast. We just want to ask you a few questions." The man leaned in close, studying Adahn's face in the dim light. Adahn turned his face to the side, not so much to avoid the scrutiny but to get away from the strong whisky smell permeating the man's stale breath. It was obvious that he was a little drunk. Judging from the way his companions swayed menacingly around him, they probably all were.

The man pulled away. "Yeah, just as we thought, fellas. This here is that Arab pilot."

Adahn felt a rush of heat rise in his chest, but he maintained his composure. "If you'll excuse me," he said curtly as he tried again to push clear.

"What's your hurry?" The man behind him spoke up. "Late for something?"

"Gentlemen, with respect, that's not your business."

"Oh, but it is our business." The heavy man in front stepped in again. "We have a responsibility to keep our colony safe after hours."

Adahn kept his voice steady. "I wasn't aware that Pastor Graham had started a neighborhood watch."

"Pastor Graham," the man to his left scoffed. "If we waited around for him, or that captain of yours, to take action, nothing would ever get done."

"But you'd like that, wouldn't you, kid?" The ringleader with the whisky breath started in again. "From what we hear, you wouldn't mind staying nice and hidden. We've been listening, you see."

"Listening and watching," another said.

"You've been sneaking around down here a lot the last couple of months, haven't you?"

"Yeah, that's right. We know all about you."

"We've got wives, kids."

"And we're not going to just lie down and let you hand this colony over to those metal monsters. We know what you are. And your time's up."

Adahn's fists clenched, but he forced himself to relax them. "You don't know anything about me. Now please—step aside."

He felt a sharp shove to his back. The force carried him forward directly into the large man in front, who shoved him back—hard. "Watch

252

it!" the ringleader shouted, his voice carrying through the night air. "You starting a fight?"

Adahn's mind raced. His body was poised, ready to strike, but he knew that a physical confrontation with men in their condition, their fear and paranoia fueled by whatever home-brewed concoction they had been imbibing, would not end well—for either side. He could feel the unseen eyes of other colonists peeking out of their windows, observing the commotion. If the situation turned ugly, he had little confidence that any of them would come to his aid. If anything, some of them might join in. No, he had to somehow find a way to avoid this engagement.

He held up his hands. "No. I just want to be on my way. That's all." Again, he tried to slide past the man blocking his way.

"And like I said, kid, we still need some answers from you."

Adahn took a breath with an air of resignation. "We both know it won't matter what I say. You're going to believe what you want to believe." He attempted to forcefully push himself through, but the man grabbed his shoulder again, squeezing much harder this time, his fingers digging like talons into the flesh near his collarbone. Adahn instinctively jerked his arm up to shrug off the man's grip. At the same time, the man moved in closer, his chin directly in the path of Adahn's elbow. They connected with a sharp crack.

The guy to his right reacted instantly, pushing Adahn away from his companion. "Hey! What was that?" he demanded, his speech slurred and angry.

Adahn was about to apologize, but he didn't get the chance. The other men moved in quickly. Someone grabbed his arms from behind while another to his left landed a punch just below his rib cage. He doubled over, just in time to receive a sharp knee to his chin from the ringleader.

His adrenaline surging, Adahn jerked deftly to his left, flinging the man behind him to the right. Free from his grasp, Adahn straightened up, elbows bent, fists in front of him. Seeing their foe in a defensive posture, the men hesitated for just a moment before moving in from all sides. Adahn could have struck at any time, discouraging his attackers with a few incapacitating blows, but he had no desire to deliver a beating. He focused, instead, on avoiding one himself. He easily eluded the first two men trying to grab him. Stepping away from the third, however, backed him straight into the arms of the one he had thrown aside. This time, as the man held him tightly, the others didn't hold back. They moved in mercilessly. Blow after blow struck, driving him to the ground. As the barrage continued, epithets and threats accompanied each punch, every kick. A hard shot to the side of his head knocked him dizzy. Stunned, Adahn could feel consciousness starting to slip away. He was surprised, through the invading haze, to find himself not focused on the pain but instead wondering how such ignorance and hatred could possibly exist in a Christian colony.

Then suddenly the assault stopped as quickly as it had started. Adahn was faintly aware of another presence in the fight, pulling one man off him before turning and landing a punch to the jaw of another. The two remaining men tried to double-team the newcomer, but a quick over-the-shoulder throw sent the smaller man hard to the ground on his back. Seeing this, the ringleader, rethinking the odds, turned and stumbled off into the darkness, his three companions scrambling to their feet and disappearing behind him.

Breathing heavily, Adahn's rescuer walked over to him. Scot Calgaro glared down at his squadron mate. "What the hell was that all about?"

*   *   *

Adahn sat on the edge of his bunk, dabbing at his chin with a dermo-patch. Across from him, Scot sat on a footlocker with his hands folded on his lap, leaning forward as he watched his former wingman tend to his bruises.

"This isn't good, Ghazi. You were out of the barracks after lockdown—and down in the colony, no less. You have to tell me what's going on."

Adahn looked past him. "You really don't want to know."

"With everything that's been happening around here, I think I *have* to know."

Adahn looked up over the dermo-patch. "I can tell you this much. It's not what you think."

"And just what am I thinking?"

Adahn sighed. "You're thinking what everyone else is thinking—that I'm the traitor. That I've been selling out the Angels. That I have a contact somewhere, possibly down there in the colony, and that I've been leaking intel about our missions. You figure that if I had the actual coordinates of this planet, I would have spilled it by now, and everyone would be dead."

254

Scot cocked his head to one side, not bothering to deny it. "And?"

"And, like I said, it's not what you think."

"Not good enough. If it's not what I think, then tell me the truth. Give me one good reason why I shouldn't take this straight to Commander Lebrian. I mean, if you weren't out leaking info, then what the hell were you doing out there? Did you know that I actually tried to defend you to Viper tonight? She was sure that you were out there meeting someone. I tried to come up with some other explanation. But no—that's exactly what was going on, wasn't it? You had to be meeting someone. Nobody just—"

A change in Adahn's expression made Scot stop.

"Oh, no. No. It can't be that simple."

Adahn had a trace of a sheepish smile on his lips.

Scot shook his head slowly, looking down at the floor. "Tell me this isn't about a girl."

Adahn looked down, the remnant of a smile still present.

"You. A girl. You've been sneaking off base after hours to see a girl. That's your story?"

Adahn tilted his head to one side, raising his eyebrows, but still saying nothing.

"Okay, okay." Scot considered his former wingman. "You know what? I'm going to need a name. Because without it, no one's going to believe you." He snorted. "Hell, I don't think *I* even believe you. She's going to have to corroborate your story."

Adahn's expression was firm. "I'm sorry, but I can't tell you who she is."

Scot's expression hardened. "What do you mean you *can't*?"

"Our relationship is confidential. I can't tell you her name."

"And why not? What am I supposed to think here, Adahn? Can't you see how this is going to play out? How this looks for you?"

"It's not that simple. Her family—her father, actually—would definitely not approve of our relationship. He wouldn't approve of me."

"Why, because you're Jordanian? What kind of—"

"No," Adahn interrupted him. "It's because I'm a *pilot*."

"What?"

"You may not believe it, Scot, but not everyone in the colony is a fan of the Angels. Not everyone appreciates what we do for them. Some are absolute pacifists and can't stand the thought of being reliant on a military squadron. They're a small minority, but her father is one of them."

255

"So you're telling me that rather than risk her dad getting mad at you, getting mad at her, you're willing to risk being accused a traitor? No girl is worth getting thrown in the brig. Trust me, I know."

Adahn set down the dermo-patch. He met Scot's gaze evenly. "And yet, that is my decision. If I'm not guilty, I have nothing to worry about."

Scot stood up. "You can't be that stupid. This looks bad for you. Really bad. Your only alibi just happens to be an imaginary person that you can't tell us about. It's just a little too convenient."

"You don't believe me." There was no offense in his tone—just a statement of fact.

"No. You know what? I don't. I wanted to believe you, Adahn. I really did. I was willing to fight for you. But this…" he pursed his lips, trailing off.

Adahn was maintaining his usual impassive expression, which Scot was finding particularly annoying at the moment. "So what are you going to do?" Adahn asked.

"What I should have done already. I'm going to turn this whole thing over to Commander Lebrian and let him deal with it. You want to know what the worst part of it is?" He caught Adahn's eye. "It's that, dammit, Seltrice was right. I'll never hear the end of it."

That brought a slight smile to Adahn, but it left just as quickly. "You do what you have to," he said.

Scot stepped toward the door.

"I do have one question."

Scot turned around and leaned on the doorway, arms crossed.

"You've never really liked me." Adahn caught Scot's feigned surprise. "No, don't deny it—we both know it's true. If you're that sure I'm guilty, why did you help me tonight?"

"You're still an Angel," Scot said, his expression dark. "You're right, Ghazi, I don't like you. And I don't believe your bullshit story. I want to see you answer for whatever it is you've been pulling these past few months." He turned again to leave. "But those guys crossed the line tonight. We're Angels. We take care of our own."

He paused outside the door, long enough to shoot a final knowing look at Adahn. "And one way or another, I'm going to take care of you."

*   *   *

Sidnir leaned back in his chair. The Section Seven nerve center was dark and, except for him, deserted. He raised his eyebrows as the message on the terminal completed its decryption. To avoid detection, most transmissions from Blackfriar were short and simple—a planet name, a set of coordinates with a time stamp, brief mission details.

This message was different, both in in its length and content. Sidnir read it carefully, digesting it and trying to determine how best to relay the information to his irritable boss.

Situation untenable. Close to discovery. Demand immediate evac. Prepared to destroy colony in order to reveal location. Scan for level 5 antimatter explosion. Any survivors can be captured upon my evac.

It was clear that Blackfriar was panicking. He had seen it before—a deeply embedded mole, living far too long in midst of the Christian zealots, growing increasingly paranoid until finally snapping under the pressure. And, sitting in the secure confines of the comm center, able to assess the situation more rationally, Sidnir could see that the asset's hastily crafted exit plan, as was invariably the case, was seriously flawed. If Blackfriar had been able to discover the colony's location, he would have revealed it by now. He had long ago reported on the natural dampening field that kept the planet hidden from scans, and the actual coordinates were apparently known only to D'Felco and his second-in-command. Sidnir had little doubt that a level-five antimatter explosion could disrupt the dampening field enough to reveal the planet—that part of the plan made sense. But if Blackfriar had discovered a means to create such an explosion, why was he threatening to destroy the colony in the process? A move like that would undermine the very purpose of his mission. He could only conclude that Blackfriar had lost his mind.

Sidnir was confident of one thing—his boss wanted the location of the hidden colony, but he did not want to swoop in just to inspect a couple thousand charred corpses and rescue their mole, especially a mole who had lost his nerve. His boss wanted the Angels and the colonists alive. Sidnir knew how, precisely, he planned to deal with them, and he also knew how displeased he would be if they all ended up prematurely dead. The promise of a few survivors was an empty one. If Blackfriar pulled off his plan, setting off some kind of explosion that destroyed the colony and killed nearly everyone in the process, then Blackfriar himself would never leave the planet alive—his boss would make certain of that.

Sidnir activated his handpod. Checking a chrono, he cringed at the late hour. He was surprised when Graves picked up immediately, not sounding the least bit groggy despite the late hour. Sidnir cleared his throat.

"Sir, you, uh, might want to come down here. There's something you need to see."

Chapter 28

Darik had considered, and rejected, a dozen different plans for avoiding this meeting with Jenkins. His first thought had been to walk out on his lease, cash out everything he had in savings, and grab a ticket to the most remote planet he could find. Looking at his current account balances, however, he had realized that his plan wouldn't get him any farther than one of the First Six planets, each with a strong JenKore presence of its own. All of his success, his promotions, and he was as place-bound as any ordinary Coalition citizen—probably more so since his mountain of debt was higher than most.

He had also played around with the idea of stealing the *Golden Crow*, taking out the *Midas*-class luxury transport under the guise of pressing business and never looking back. Maybe he would return to Bellona and try to track down Nikky—to find out whether or not he was still alive. If Nikky had somehow survived, the two of them could go on the run together. He imagined it would be helpful to have someone watching his back, especially someone with Nikky's unique skillset. But he had quickly dismissed that line of thinking as well, alarmed by just how desperate he'd become to consider such a foolhardy plan. The moment JenKore discovered that he had gone AWOL, they would remotely shut down the *Crow*'s control functions, likely leaving Darik stranded out in space, either to die of starvation or to be picked up and hauled back in by Graves. He wasn't sure which was worse. And besides, even if Nikky was still alive and he managed to locate him, why would the former JenKore systems analyst ever consider helping him? They hadn't exactly parted on the best of terms.

Darker alternatives had also crossed his mind, but, moral considerations aside, none of those options were practical. Even a JenKore vice president would have difficulty sneaking a weapon past the security checkpoints in the Tower.

In the end, Darik realized that he had no choice but to face Jenkins. He had been had, pure and simple. The spy had been right under his nose the entire time, sitting at her desk outside his office, spending time between his sheets at home. And, as they'd worked together to catch the "hacker," he had unwittingly led the real spy directly to the information she had been searching for, all the while never suspecting a thing. Liana was good at what she did—he had to give her that.

Darik had no idea what his boss was going to do to him, but standing outside Jenkins's office, with the ever-present Clara looking on almost sympathetically, it suddenly occurred to him that none of it mattered. Jenkins could yell at him, discipline him, fire him, even kill him. He had ceased to care—about his job, about anything. When Liana had ripped his heart out, he had been overwhelmed by a surge of emotions—pain, loss, betrayal, rage. But now he only felt empty. Empty and cold.

The door slid open. Darik instinctively squared his shoulders, still aware of the tightness in his chest, the aftereffects of the stun bolt still taking a toll on his body. He ignored the pain and walked inside.

"Mr. Mason. We have much to discuss. Have a seat." Jenkins's tone was neutral, but Darik knew better than to read anything into that.

He experienced a strong sense of déjà vu as he slid into the soft leather chair in front of Jenkins's desk, the slow, sinking effect deliberately designed, he was certain, to put him in a position of subordination and vulnerability. On his right, he took note of the bluish-metal Travarian artifact sitting in its customary spot next to Jenkins's desk. Unlike Darik's past experience, there was no apparent movement, no subtle sounds emanating at the base of his hearing threshold. The incongruous array of razor-sharp tines seemed to be dormant, engendering in him a confusing mixture of relief and disappointment.

Darik felt as though he had only glanced at the idol, but it may have been longer than that. The sound of a clearing throat brought his eyes back forward, where Jenkins was still seated behind his desk, a blank, impassive expression on his face.

"So, are you prepared to explain the events of last night?"

"Well, sir, you know most of it already." His faced burned at the memory, at the embarrassment. "An intruder broke into my apartment, stole sensitive data, and uploaded the contents before I could stop him."

"Him?" Why did I just refer to Liana as a "him?"

"Yes, I am aware of that. What I don't understand is what that information was doing in your apartment, outside the protection of these walls, in the first place."

Darik braced himself. "It was a mistake, sir. In my assignment to track down the spy, I gathered as much information on the M-2/A initiative as I could. I was close to catching him in the system. I thought if I could anticipate his next move, I could set an ID trap and we'd have him. So I dug up as much as I could, trying to get ahead of him."

Jenkins looked at him quizzically. "Dug up?"

"Yeah, I went into the files, searched around…"

Darik stopped. Who was he kidding? His excursions into the system had been thwarted at every turn. Jenkins knew he didn't have that kind of access. Hell, he was obviously the one restricting it in the first place, holding Darik back from the exact intel he needed to do his job. As always, the chasm between what his boss expected him to accomplish and the resources available to him was maddeningly vast. Regardless, Jenkins's expression told him it was time to cut the crap. He looked down.

"It was a copy," he said quietly.

"A copy." Jenkins's voice grew cold. To his right, Darik thought he could just make out the faintest of sounds—a guttural emanation underscored by a low-pitched metallic hum. He felt a sense of dread and resolve, more pleasing than disagreeable. He looked up and met his employer's eyes.

"Yes. A copy. It was a copy of everything Nikky Weis and I discovered that night we were down in the R&D facility."

There. His life was forfeit. And yet, there was something cathartic in finally confessing to Jenkins, in laying it all bare. Well, not all of it—he still hadn't told him about Liana. Maybe he would now. Jenkins had already known of his and Nikky's subterranean excursion, of course. Darik had spilled that information the night of his promotion. But now, he had confessed to keeping that intel on a data chip in his own apartment, outside of the fortress-like confines of JenKore's secure headquarters. It was such an egregious violation—his one catastrophic mistake could potentially bring down the entire company—that he had no doubt Jenkins was going to kill him, or have him killed.

That revelation sent an odd thrilling sensation tingling throughout his body. The deadness he had felt as he'd entered Jenkins's office had slowly been replaced, he'd realized, by a familiar energy, physically uncomfortable but not unwelcome. To his right, there was a rise in pitch, accompanied now by a mesmerizing blue glow. He had felt these effects before—the idol compelling him to action. His mind resisted, but his body was already responding to the idol's call. He found himself gripping the armrests of the chair, preparing to spring out of it, grab Jenkins, and throw him onto the sharp pulsating tines.

Jenkins, however, simply sat there, unmoving, digesting Darik's confession.

Finally he spoke. "That was stupid."

The calmness in Jenkins's voice unnerved Darik, breaking down a substantial portion of the resolve he had felt only moments before.

"Yes," he stammered. "Yes, it was. I…I don't know what I was thinking."

"Oh, I know what you were thinking. In your zeal to perfect the M-2/As, to excel in your assignment, you wanted every bit of information at your disposal. So you kept a copy. Naturally, your own security clearance didn't allow you to rediscover the data you and Mr. Weis had uncovered."

Darik wanted to say a few words about the abject organizational stupidity of restricting a division leader's access to the very information necessary to successfully operate the division, but he remained silent as Jenkins continued.

"Then, when I gave you the assignment of tracking down the Coalition infiltrator, you turned back to your stolen data as a means of accomplishing your task."

Darik didn't like the inflection in Jenkins's voice when he said *stolen*, but he simply nodded. "Yes, that's pretty much it." He was still waiting for the explosion. It didn't come.

Jenkins sighed. "In a way, I should blame myself, I suppose."

Darik was stunned. He couldn't imagine a less likely phrase coming from his boss's mouth. "Well, sure, if I'd had the access, I could have—"

"That's not what I meant." Jenkins's expression remained calm, but his pale blue eyes bored into Darik, reflecting the intensity of the Travarian idol. "I blame myself for failing to ensure that no copies of the stolen data existed. In retrospect, I really should have interrogated you on the matter and terminated your staff as a precaution. Mr. Weis escaped, of course— a detail I still hope to rectify in the future."

Darik couldn't be sure what Jenkins meant precisely by *terminating* his staff, but the placid tone he used in saying it, coupled with more violent sensations coming from the idol, gave him a queasy feeling. And had Jenkins just confirmed that Nikky was still alive? His head spinning, Darik gripped the armrests more firmly, more for balance now than for action.

"All the same," Jenkins continued, "I cannot undo the mistakes of the past. We can only look to the future."

We?

Darik had never felt so disoriented. For the second time in months, he was sitting in Jenkins's office, expecting to be fired, or worse—depending on what *terminated* actually meant—before coming to the realization that his inscrutable boss still had work for him to do. He finally dared a response, finding his voice.

"So, I'm sorry, but, uh, what do we do about this now?"

Jenkins smiled with genuine amusement in his eyes. "Someday, you'll learn to relax and trust me. I know you think I hate you—that I'm trying to make your life miserable, to destroy your career. Nothing could be further from the truth. I'm trying to help you, to protect you. And once you realize that, you'll stop worrying about all these little details that are none of your concern. Rest assured, the information that was leaked from your apartment will go no further, and steps are being taken right now to ensure it will have no lasting effect on our efforts."

Darik didn't understand how that could be possible. The reach of Jenkins's influence apparently had no limits. He tried to guess which lofty Coalition official might be secretly sympathetic to JenKore's hidden cause or what kind of leverage Jenkins might have held over someone, or someones, that could make the contents of that data chip go away. He wanted to know so much more, but he kept his mouth shut, considering that Jenkins had just reprimanded him about asking for details. Breathing an audible sigh, he slumped down further in the chair, his shoulders sagging as he released his grip on the armrests.

Jenkins noted Darik's visible relief. "But it would be a mistake, Mr. Mason, to confuse my confidence in this matter with passive acceptance of the seriousness of this breach, of your failure."

The sense of dread crept back into Darik's stomach. Next to him, he heard the idol emitting a high lilting sound. Was it possible that it was mocking him? Jenkins leaned across his desk.

"We still have the matter of the infiltrator to deal with." He paused, his cold blue eyes piercing Darik's. "Who was it?"

An image of Liana in his apartment, turning to face him and shooting him pointblank in the chest, flashed in Darik's mind. Every ounce of betrayal, shame, and hatred he had felt at that moment came flooding back.

Give her up.

His own inner voice was joined by other murmuring voices—all saying the same thing.

Give her up!

Jenkins's audible voice rose above the whispers. "Identify the intruder. He will be found, and the last link in this unfortunate chain of events will be severed, never to trouble us again." Jenkins leaned closer, his stale breath burning on Darik's cheek. "Help us find this traitor, and your position will be secured. Make this right, and all will be *forgiven.*"

The words began to form in Darik's mind. He believed, he *knew*, that he needed only to say it out loud, to breathe her name to Jenkins, and everything would be set right. Darik would rise from this mess, and Liana would get what she deserved for betraying him. The idol moaned in his inner ear, a dark groaning of unfulfilled vengeance.

"It was…" The name caught in his throat. He couldn't speak. He felt like he was choking on the cheesecake crust back at Bistro Riservata. For a fleeting instant, the memory of that night, and the love he had felt and tried to express, replaced the image of Liana firing the stun bolt into his chest.

"It was," he continued, "too dark to see. He stunned me before I could get a good look." Darik looked down at the expensive carpet, unable to meet Jenkins's eyes.

If Jenkins was disappointed, his expression didn't show it, nor did it reveal whether or not he believed Darik's lie. He sat back in his chair. "Indeed. I read the report from the para-meds that were summoned to your apartment."

Darik already regretted his decision. The voices wailing in his head attacked him, bringing doubt and confusion. Why had he covered for her? What did he possibly owe her?

"And I presume the intruder made off with your data chip after the upload?"

Darik flexed his shoulder, more for show—a visible reminder of the stun blast—than from actual lingering pain. Now that he had lied to

Jenkins, again, there could be no back-tracking. The fact that he still possessed the physical data chip was his last bit of leverage. If he confessed to still owning it, Jenkins would demand its return. "He must have. The chip was gone when the para-meds revived me."

"A pity," Jenkins said. "That is one more loose end we will have to resolve. As I said, do not mistake the fact that I am cleaning up your mess to mean that your failure is in any way acceptable. Your incompetence has seriously compromised this organization—*my* organization—as well as our ability to continue our sacred work against the Zealots. The upload has been neutralized, but your possession and subsequent loss of that data chip, compounded with your inability to identify your assailant, reveals an incompetence and duplicity that I can no longer trust in your position."

None of that came as a surprise to Darik, who was still trying to make sense of his instantly regrettable decision to protect Liana. It had been a foolish, spontaneous lapse in judgment and all because he'd let his guard down, allowing himself to feel a momentary twinge of attachment, an irrational sentimentality for a relationship that had never been real in the first place. It was likely that his grievous misstep with the data chip would have cost him his job regardless, but his apparent ineptitude in failing to identify the thief who had been standing right in front of him had no doubt solidified the decision.

Jenkins made a notation on a recessed workstation. "You are off the M-2/A project. All vice-presidential privileges are immediately revoked. You will be starting from scratch, Mr. Mason, and you will somehow have to find a means of regaining my trust."

Darik was shocked, not by the demotion but by the fact that he still had a job. Still, it was a blow. His mind went immediately to his Perseus shuttle, his midtown apartment, all the trappings he had allowed himself to indulge in. Knowing he should just be grateful that he was going to walk out of the office with his life, he still found himself worrying about how he would pay for it all. Maybe he should have just absconded with the *Golden Crow* after all. Now he wouldn't even have that option at his disposal.

The thought of the *Crow* once again evoked memories of the time he and Liana had spent together. He pushed the images from his mind, upset by his weakness. She was the *cause* of all of this, he reminded himself.

"I understand," Darik said. "What about my staff?"

Jenkins raised a single eyebrow. "Naturally, they will have to be terminated."

Darik's eyes widened. "Killed? Why?"

"Don't be an idiot. They will be discharged immediately. Your failure has cost every one of them their livelihood. You are going to have to live with that." He looked at Darik closely. "That includes your personal assistant, Ms. Reyes. I know you were close to her, but your department will be completely purged—no exceptions."

Darik sensed that Jenkins meant for Liana's firing to be an additional, personal punishment for him, but it suited him just fine. She wouldn't be showing up again after last night, anyway, so her preemptive termination made things far less complicated for him. He hoped he never saw her again.

Darik stood. "I understand, sir." He cleared the lump in his throat. "Thank you for giving me a second chance."

Jenkins remained seated. "On the subject of your *final* chance, I do have an assignment for you in your new, diminished position. In fact, you may find this new task to be more fulfilling, from a personal point of view."

Darik tilted his head. The idol had been quiet for some time. Now, he felt its presence again, a new thrill rising up from his abdomen to his head. "I'm listening."

Jenkins adopted a somber expression. "I know what happened to your parents. It was a tragic day—the mayhem, the senseless violence. Until recently, I didn't know of your personal connection." He caught Darik's eye. "So many innocent people killed by those thugs."

Darik held Jenkins's gaze. "Christian terrorists."

Even as the word *Christian* came out of his mouth, Darik felt a renewed sense of purpose filling him, strengthening him, hardening him.

Jenkins's expression was sympathetic. "You were young. I can't imagine how hard it was for you, to lose them both so suddenly and in such vicious fashion. You never were able to discover the identities or the whereabouts of your parents' murderers, were you?"

Darik shook his head. "No. There was surveillance, forensics, other clues, but nothing ever came of it. My brother and I assumed that they fled off-world."

"And what would you do if you had their identities?"

Darik already knew the answer. "I would do whatever I had to in order to bring them to justice."

"And what do you mean by *justice*?"

Darik set his jaw, this time fighting back emotions of a different sort. "I would see that they were terminated, sir. And I don't mean fired."

Jenkins's satisfied silence allowed Darik to continue. "I know that I'm not in charge of the M-2/A initiative any longer, but I know their capabilities. I know what they can do. And if I ever found the terrorists who killed my parents, it would be my privilege, if you permit me the opportunity, to lead a deployment of M-2s for you and make sure those bastards got what they deserved."

Jenkins smiled broadly. "Please sit back down, Darik. As I said earlier, we have much to discuss."

Chapter 29

"A girlfriend, huh?" Seltrice Valani reclined in a battered lounge chair, one arm draped casually over the back rest, the other hand holding a cup of dark coffee.

Scot stared down at his own cup. "That's what he said."

"And he wouldn't give you a name?"

"No. He said that they needed to keep their relationship confidential—that her father wouldn't approve."

Seltrice absently picked at a piece of loose thread on the backrest. "And do you believe him?"

"Would you?"

She placed her cup on a small table to the right, straightening her posture as she spoke. "Well, Calgaro, I don't want to say I told you so—"

"But you're going to anyway."

Seltrice smiled sardonically. "I'll save it for later. It's enough to know that I was right."

Scot held up his hands. "Hey, we still don't know that. Right now, I'm not sure about anything. He might be telling the truth, or he might be the traitor. The problem is, we still don't have any proof."

Seltrice cocked her head to one side. "Well? What are we waiting for?"

*   *   *

Scot hustled to keep pace with Seltrice, having to break into a light jog to match her long strides.

"I don't like this." He forced himself to keep his voice low. "Shouldn't we just take the whole thing to Lebrian and be done with it?"

"Take what to Lebrian?" Seltrice didn't seem to care as much about volume control as Scot. "Exactly what do we know, concretely, that I haven't told him already? I'm in enough trouble with him as it is for making *baseless accusations*. We need something new, something solid, or no one's going to take us seriously."

"Keep your voice down, would you?" Scot hissed as caught up to her. "So your idea of being taken seriously is to break into Ghazi's quarters without cause? I guarantee Dex won't like it."

"If we find proof, he'll have to consider it, even if he doesn't approve of our methods." Scot didn't like the sound of *our methods*. He glanced over his shoulder, convinced that her voice was carrying at least two halls away. "And if we don't find anything here, I'll check his Hornet again."

"Yeah, about that," Scot whispered. "You told me Adahn's Hornet was a dead end."

"I told you that I'd run into a dead end. That cyber-dink, Nikky what's-his-name, couldn't give me anything solid when I had him look at it."

"So it was a dead end."

"No," Seltrice insisted. "There was something there, in his comm bus. I just couldn't make out what it was." She paused, looking Scot in the eye. "But between that and his sneaking off base in the night—"

"Which he has an explanation for."

"A bullshit explanation and you know it. No, I've almost got him—I can feel it. But I need more if I'm going to put myself out there again and take it to Commander Lebrian. I need to be sure that it's going to stick this time."

Scot looked at Adahn's door. The built-in ID holo glowed back at him: *Flying Officer Adahn "Ghazi" Manasser.*

One of our own, he thought as he looked back at Seltrice. "You're sure he's gone?"

Seltrice was studying the door's locking mechanism. "He's in the gym right now," she said absently, "working out his bumps and bruises from last night's little escapade. This is our chance."

"And just how do you propose we get in there? I can't imagine he's shared his code with you."

"We break the lock if we have to. Or..." Seltrice glanced down the corridor. "Hey! Wilco! Come over here. I want to ask you something."

Ronnie Wilco had been heading in the opposite direction. At Seltrice's command, he stopped in his tracks and turned to face the two lieutenants.

"You've got access to all the room codes, right Ronnie?" Scot detected a lilt in Seltrice's voice that hadn't been there before.

Ronnie looked puzzled. "Well, yeah, I program them, so I have a master override. Why?"

"Well, I was wondering if I could ask you a huge favor?" Scot inwardly cringed at Seltrice's affected helpless tone. She was about as helpless as a Mormosi badger.

Ronnie shuffled his feet, his complexion beginning to take on a reddish hue. "Sure, Lieutenant. What do you need?"

"We need to stop by Officer Manasser's quarters, but he can't know we let ourselves in." Seltrice was smiling sweetly, but Scot could see her evaluating Ronnie's hesitation. "It's a surprise," she added.

Ronnie squinted. "A surprise?" He didn't sound convinced.

"Yeah," Scot chimed in. "You know his birthday's coming up, right?" Scot wouldn't have been able to pinpoint Adahn's birthday if his life depended on it, but he was counting on the fact that Ronnie didn't know either.

Seltrice picked it up. "And the way things have been going lately, we just wanted to do something really special, but we need a holo of his family from his workstation to pull it off. Of course," she said, pouting her lips, "we could always get along without it, or ruin the surprise…"

"No, no, Lieutenant. That's all right. I can let you in, just for a second."

"You're sure?" she asked while lightly touching his arm.

Ronnie straightened up. "Absolutely. I know Officer Manasser's been having a rough time. And I think it's great that you want to do something nice for him. Anything I can do to help."

Seltrice hugged him. "Oh, thanks, Ronnie. You're the best!"

Ronnie moved a few paces down the hall to Adahn's door. His fingers danced over the proximity detector, and the door slid silently to one side.

Seltrice stepped inside while Scot turned to Ronnie. "Thanks. We'll take it from here."

"But…"

"Seriously, we owe you one." Scot slid the door shut behind him.

Seltrice was already on her knees, quickly but carefully sorting through the items in Adahn's footlocker.

"So what exactly are we looking for?" Scot stood over her, casting furtive glances behind him, fully expecting Adahn to walk in at any moment.

Seltrice didn't look up. "Something. Anything. You know. Something suspicious."

"Like a dirty sock?"

Seltrice recoiled at the fabric tube in her hand and tossed it over her shoulder. It hit Scot squarely in face, sticking for a moment before sliding to the floor.

"Nice," he said. "Hurry up. Ghazi could come back any time."

Seltrice moved from the footlocker to peer under Adahn's cot. "You could be helping, you know. Check his workstation." She indicated the terminal with a nod of her head.

"We don't have time to dig through all his files," he said as he moved toward the workstation, "and I don't know how to copy them without being detected. I highly doubt that he left anything suspicious in plain sight." He waved his hand over the sensor, activating the terminal. "*Now let's see—where should I put all of my incriminating evidence. I know! The alpha screen on my workstation! No one will find it there!*"

Seltrice shot Scot a poisonous look over her shoulder but didn't say anything, knowing it would only encourage him. The workstation came out of standby without requiring a passcode. "*Yep, I won't even lock my terminal because not only am I a traitor, but I'm also the biggest moron who ever*—hey, what's that? That shouldn't be there."

Seltrice pushed herself to her feet, sidling up behind him. "What shouldn't be where?"

"That. There." Scot pointed at a small cursor flashing in the lower right corner. "What does that look like to you?"

"A comm protocol," Seltrice said, her eyes widening.

"I think we may have found what you were looking for," Scot said, tapping the cursor. "Let's find out what he's been sending."

The screen resolved to a standard message box. There was nothing in it.

"Blank." Seltrice huffed. "Of course."

Scot swiped at the screen, as if willing the missing text to return. "Well, he was at least smart enough to delete the contents."

"Do you think it was an external comm?" Seltrice asked. Scot couldn't decide whether she sounded more worried or hopeful.

"Have you ever seen anyone on Pella use this particular interface? Looks to me like the sort of protocol someone would have to use if they wanted to get a message off-planet." Scot was surprised to find that his voice was shaking.

"But that's impossible—all our workstations are restricted."

"And yet, there it is."

Seltrice sucked in a breath. "Now I wish I'd brought a scanner. I bet it follows the same pattern I found on his Hornet."

Scot stole a quick glance at the door. "We don't have the time."

Seltrice stepped in, bumping him to the side. "Well, maybe we can at least find out where the message was going."

"And how exactly are you going to…"

He trailed off. Seltrice had pulled up a log file. "The Hornet signal was beyond me, but a basic workstation comm pack isn't. I grew up with two very devious sisters. Information on each other was power." She scrolled to the top of the log. "*This* part, I know how to do."

Scot stared at the screen. The most recent entry had a time stamp within the hour. Seltrice flicked it with an index finger and exhaled slowly at what she saw.

"Earth," Scot said. "He sent a message to Earth."

Seltrice expanded the entry, revealing one additional line of data. "What the hell is a *Blackfriar*?"

*   *   *

"You broke into his quarters?"

Hagen stood up behind the conference table. His two-meter frame towered over Scot and Seltrice.

"Uh, kind of missing the point here, Sarge." Scot looked at Seltrice for support.

"Commander, he had an off-planet transmission logged on his workstation!" Seltrice slid her handpod across the table. "I copied the log. Look at it!"

"Watch your tone, Lieutenant." Hagen picked up the handpod. "We will deal with this, but we are going to proceed properly." He keyed a sequence, and the contents of the copied log appeared over the table.

"There! You see—" Seltrice pointed, but a withering look from Hagen silenced her outburst.

"Yes, I can read it, Lieutenant. And this came from Officer Manasser's workstation?"

Seltrice nodded.

"And you and Lieutenant Calgaro obtained this by breaking into his quarters."

They glanced at one another. "Yes, sir," Scot said.

"All right." Hagen sat back down. "I don't like it. I don't like the way you went about it. But we *are* going to get to the bottom of it. I sent for Officer Manasser as soon as you contacted me. Commander Onigen should be here with him in a moment. We'll get this sorted first, and then I'll deal with the two of you."

"By thanking us for saving the squadron?" Scot's muttering was barely audible.

"What was that, mister?"

"I said I'm looking forward to clearing this up, sir."

Scot braced himself for Hagen's response. He was relieved when, instead, they were interrupted by the door sliding open. Lee Onigen entered with a resigned-looking Adahn in tow.

"Have a seat, Officer." Hagen's voice was calm, but his expression was deadly serious. "Do you know what this is about?"

Adahn slid into a chair next to Seltrice's. She kept her eyes straight ahead, shifting her weight to the left, imperceptibly increasing the distance between them. Onigen circled the table and sat next to Hagen, his hands folded on the table.

"Yes, sir." Adahn shot a sideways look in Seltrice and Scot's direction. "I imagine that it concerns my breaking curfew."

"And would you like to explain that?"

"It's true, sir. I have been leaving the base after lockdown and visiting the colony."

"Yes, Officer," Hagen said, tapping the conference table with his index finger. "We know that it's true. What I am expecting here is for you to explain what you were doing and why."

Out of the corner of his eye, Scot could see Adahn's olive-hued complexion take on a crimson shade, apparently feigning embarrassment at having to confess about his "girlfriend." Scot was coming to the realization that he had been severely underestimating Adahn this entire time. Even now, on the verge of being caught, his act remained entirely convincing. Just straight-laced Adahn—simple, uncomplicated, at times, a bit of a screwup. Only now was Scot beginning to see his true side— cunning, savvy, manipulative. He'd had them all completely fooled for years. Scot could only hope that they'd caught him in time—that he hadn't yet found a way to reveal the colony's true location to his handlers.

"Again, sir, I'm sure that you have been *informed*"—Adahn let the word carry a note of sarcasm—"that there is a young lady in the colony with whom I have had a, um, relationship these past few months."

"A relationship."

"Yes, sir."

"What kind of relationship?"

"Sir?"

Hagen's voice rose significantly. "You heard me. You just admitted that you've been sneaking off this base and having clandestine meetings with a civilian. We need to know who this person is and what precisely you've been meeting about." He paused briefly, studying Adahn's face. The two of them had spent countless hours together putting in extra training, pushing each other in the gym and at the firing range. But, despite all their time together, Hagen had never really gotten to know Adahn on a close, personal level—Adahn wasn't one to naturally open up, and besides, they were meeting to train, not talk. Still, he considered Adahn a friend. "I'm trying to help you here," he said, his voice returning to its normal volume, "but you need to start being straight with us."

"Sir, with all respect, I'd prefer not to drag her into all this."

Lee Onigen had been silent since entering the room. When he spoke, his tone was kind, but even. "Whether you prefer it or not, Adahn, you've already dragged her into this. Now, talking to her is the only way to clear this up."

"You mean *investigating* her, don't you?" Adahn met Onigen's gaze.

Onigen was unruffled. "If that's the term you prefer, yes. I'm not sure you understand how serious this is. We have a security breach in this squadron, and right now, Officer Manasser, your behavior has made you the number one suspect."

Adahn's sideways glance again found Scot and Seltrice. "I'm not surprised."

"Oh, get off it, Ghazi!" Scot had had enough. "Just give them the damn name already!"

"That's enough, Lieutenant." Hagen held up a hand toward Scot and then turned back to Adahn. "Commander Onigen is correct. There is only one way to get to the truth. Who is this young lady?"

Adahn shook his head. "I'm sorry, sir. As I already explained to Lieutenant Calgaro, I can't do that." He sat up straighter. "I am prepared to accept the consequences of my actions, but I cannot reveal her name." He looked down at the table, his voice dropping. "I promised her."

Hagen's voice softened. "Don't you think she would understand, given the circumstances?"

Adahn looked back up. "She might. Her father would not."

"You understand, of course, that we are going to investigate this anyway," Hagen said. "We will find out who this young lady is, and we will find out what exactly has been going on." He paused, stealing a glance at Onigen. "Is there anything else you want to tell us before it gets to that point?"

Adahn's voice was firm. "No. Nothing."

Rather than reply, Hagen swept his hand over the table. The display sprang to life between them.

"Do you recognize this?"

It took Adahn a moment to take in the contents of the screen. "Yes, sir. It appears to be an activity log."

"That's correct. It's the log from your workstation."

Adahn turned his head fully to face Scot and Seltrice. Seltrice returned his glare, a hint of a smirk on her lips.

Hagen continued. "Do you see anything unusual, Officer Manasser?"

Adahn looked back at the screen. "Not really." He spoke slowly, his eyes taking in each line. "Studies, duty rosters, intra-squad comms—"

"Look at the most recent entry."

Adahn scanned upward. His eyes suddenly widened while his mouth stayed silently open. Knowing this moment was coming, Scot made sure to closely study his reaction. Adahn, to him, looked genuinely shocked, to the point that Scot found himself once again questioning his assumptions. No one was that good of an actor.

"But, but that's impossible!" Adahn said, turning to Hagen, his expression pleading. "Sir, my workstation doesn't even *have* external access! I don't know how that entry got there! You have to believe me!"

Seltrice laughed derisively. "Sure, we believe you, *Blackfriar*. You lying son of—"

"Stand down, Lieutenant." Hagen glared at her. "You and Lieutenant Calgaro are dismissed."

"What?"

"You heard me. I'll deal with you later."

"But sir…"

"Do I need to repeat myself?"

"No, sir!" Seltrice and Scot both stood. Seltrice turned toward the door, stopped, and faced Hagen again.

"Sir, check his fighter. I think you'll find the same—"

"Thank you, Lieutenant." Lee Onigen indicated the door. "I believe the commander has dismissed you."

Seltrice and Scot exited the room without another word.

Inside, Hagen turned back to Adahn. "You have no explanation for this entry?"

Adahn still appeared stunned. "No, sir. No explanation."

Hagen and Onigen both stood. "Then you understand," Hagen said softly, "that we have no choice but to place you in confinement for the duration of this investigation."

Adahn stood as well. "I understand, sirs. Under the circumstances, I would do the same."

Hagen cleared his throat. "Officer Adahn Manasser, you are hereby relieved of active duty. You will be escorted to the brig where you will remain, pending investigation and possible court-martial on the charges of conspiracy, espionage, and aiding the enemy."

Outside, in the corridor, Scot and Seltrice moved away from the door.

"And you're welcome, sirs," Seltrice muttered.

Scot looked up to see Nikky Weis scurrying in their direction.

"Lieutenants," he panted, clearly out of breath. "What's going on? I saw them escorting Officer Manasser down here."

Scot hesitated, finding himself at a loss for words. He wanted to dismiss the churning in his gut as a natural response to coming face to face with the squadron mate who'd betrayed them, but he couldn't—that wasn't quite it. Finally, he waved the back of his hand at the conference door. "They're going to take him to the brig," he explained. "Charges of treason, or whatever we're going to call it."

"With no thanks to you," Seltrice added. "We found evidence on his workstation, the same type of evidence that you wouldn't help me pull out of his fighter."

"But that's not—" Nikky stopped himself, his face turning pale. He looked at the closed conference room door, took a step toward it, then seemed to reconsider, turning in the opposite direction and hurrying away.

"Wait, what are you saying?" Scot called after him, but Nikky didn't answer. Scot could hear him mumbling to himself, something about it not being right.

Scot watched him depart. He hardly knew Nikky Weis and had no real reason to trust him. But the guy's reaction to the news about Adahn rattled him, if only because it mirrored a feeling he was fighting within himself.

"What a weird little man." Seltrice shook her head. "But," she brightened, "even without his help, we finally nailed Ghazi."

"Shut up, Viper," Scot said. "Just, shut up."

"What's your problem?"

Scot didn't answer. He strode off in the direction of his quarters. Facts, evidence, and common sense swirled in his head, competing for attention with a growing nagging suspicion.

Nikky Weis was right. Something just didn't feel right.

Chapter 30

"What do you mean? We're just going to sit on this?" Liana couldn't believe what she was hearing.

"Calm down, Agent Reyes. There is more going on here than you realize." Coalition Intelligence Senior Supervisor Donnel Mastersen leaned back in his chair, his hands folded in his lap. "Now why don't you have a seat, and we can discuss this rationally."

"Rationally?" Liana continued to pace back and forth in her superior's office, tracing the same pattern on the floor that she had made countless times before. It was a wonder the carpet hadn't worn through. "There is *nothing* rational about what you're saying. I spend three years—*three years*—undercover at JenKore, I finally get out with all the evidence we could ever need, and now you tell me we're going to do nothing?"

"Yes," he said, "that is precisely what I am telling you."

Liana turned to face her boss. Leaning forward, she gripped the edge of his desk. She could feel her accelerated pulse throbbing through her fingertips. "That, sir, is completely unacceptable."

"All the same, that is how it is going to be," Mastersen said flatly, "for now."

"But why?" Liana resumed her pacing. "We got it all—the modifications, the hit lists, even the POV executions. What more could you possibly be waiting for? Look, they know we have this stuff. They're going to be taking steps—they're taking steps *right now*, I'm sure—to cover themselves. If we're going to move on them, we have to move now! This is your call, Don. In all the years we've worked together, I've never known you to..."

A hint in Mastersen's expression caused Liana to stop.

"Wait a minute. This isn't your call, is it?"

Mastersen's hands dropped slowly to his desk. He began rearranging some data chips, his handpod, and other paraphernalia on the surface.

"That will be all, Agent Reyes," he said distractedly. "We're done here."

"Oh, no—you're not getting off that easily." Liana cocked her head to one side. "I'm fighting for you, too, remember? You've put way too much time into this operation to just drop it at the finish line. You want these guys as badly as I do."

Mastersen said nothing. He stared at Liana, his face a mask of non-commitment.

She met his gaze while nodding to herself. "Uh huh. So that's it. You're under orders."

He raised his eyebrows, saying volumes with his silence.

"But why?" Liana insisted. "We can't possibly be going after a bigger fish. These guys *are* the big fish. The whole purpose of the Asimov Accords was to prevent something like this from happening. They are murdering Coalition citizens! If we won't stop them, who will?" Liana slapped the front of the desk, sending a stray data chip bouncing to the floor. "I know, I know, they're *only Christians*, but there still needs to be due process. JenKore can't just decide to go off and wage their own private war against these people."

Mastersen shook his head. "It is wrong. That's for sure."

Again, the hint in his eyes. A horrifying thought began to form in Liana's mind.

"It's not just a private war, is it?"

Mastersen said nothing.

"Please tell me the Council isn't supporting this."

Mastersen absently leaned over and picked the stray data chip off the carpet. He held it between his finger and thumb, casually examining it. "We received your data upload. It contained everything we've been looking for and more. That was outstanding deep-cover work. Congratulations on a job well done."

"Thanks." Liana couldn't meet his eyes.

Mastersen continued to stare at the object in his hand. "And what did you say happened to the original data chip?"

Liana frowned. "I covered that in my report. I was discovered during the upload. I had to get out in a hurry."

"And you left the original chip there, at a JenKore executive's apartment."

"That's right."

Mastersen's eyes narrowed. "Mason's apartment."

Liana kept her own face a mask. "That's right, sir. It's all there in my report."

Mastersen dropped the chip to his desk. It clattered to a stop next to a sweating glass of water. "Careless of you, wouldn't you say?"

Liana bristled. "Are you questioning my competence, sir?"

"No, no, of course not." He held up a hand, waving off her concern. His voice lowered as he looked directly at her. "Your judgment, perhaps."

Liana was taken aback. "What are you saying?"

Mastersen stood. "Only what I said at the beginning of this conversation. There is more going on here than you realize, powerful forces working behind the scenes, forces that you, that I, cannot control. My advice to you, Agent Reyes"—he paused, some warmth coming to his eyes—"my advice to you, Liana, is to back off. Take a well-earned vacation. Go to Virgilia or somewhere. You've done your job, and you've done it well. Now it's time to leave it alone."

Liana stiffened. "Is that an order, sir?"

"It can be."

"You know I can't let this go." Liana turned and stepped toward the door, pausing as it opened. "This isn't over."

"Are you resigning?"

Liana laughed without humor. "No. Don't be stupid."

"I might give the same advice to you. Be careful, Liana. You know how these people operate, what they do to their enemies. If you keep pressing this, I can't help you."

"I know. And if you're somehow tangled up in all this, Don, I can't help you."

The door slid shut behind her.

Several blocks away, Liana stopped in an alley, satisfied that she had not been followed. A sliver attachment to her handpod informed her that her conversation with Mastersen had not been recorded and that she was currently not under surveillance.

She pulled a second handpod from her pocket. Unlocking it, she saw that her last comm had been to Darik. Her finger hovered over his name. She'd told him, back in his apartment, that she would be contacting him soon to give him one last opportunity to turn on JenKore. But that had been before her meeting with Mastersen. Now, even if Darik cooperated, she wasn't sure she could protect him from her own agency. For all she knew, she was the only person in UCI who hadn't been compromised by Jenkins.

She could call to warn him then. But what exactly would she say? That his life was in danger if he stayed at JenKore? Darik wasn't stupid—he knew that already.

No, Liana knew the real reason she'd lingered on his screen—she wanted to find a way to explain herself to him, to convince him that, while their relationship had begun under false pretenses, the feelings they'd shared, at least for her part, had been genuine.

She flicked away from his name. It was too soon. There was no way, right now, that he would want to hear a single word she had to say. In time, maybe, but not yet. She activated a different contact and resumed walking down the alley. The best thing she could do for Darik, for anyone she cared about, was to continue working to take down JenKore.

"Hello. Liana Reyes here. Yes, I'd like to speak to Admiral Pickett please."

*　　*　　*

"Darik, you shouldn't be here!"

In all the time he had known Josephine, Darik had never heard her sound so insistent, or so frightened.

"I just don't understand. Help me understand." Darik frantically tried to keep up with her, stepping around a cluster of packing crates on Bistro Riservata's dining room floor. "How can you just up and leave like this?"

Josephine stopped, turned, and faced Darik, her expression a mixture of pain and anger.

"You should, perhaps, discuss that with your friend, Mr. Graves." She turned back to the crate in front of her, hurriedly stuffing a pile of table centerpieces into it.

"He's not my...I mean, what did he say to you? What did he do?" Darik looked from Josephine to Alphonse and back again. Alphonse, on the other side of the room, was slowly emptying a wall shelf of ceramic knick-knacks into a similar crate.

Josephine didn't turn around. "It doesn't matter. If you don't already know, it might be better if you didn't."

Darik walked around the crate to face her again. "What do you mean, *if I don't already know*? Do you think that I'm somehow involved in whatever this is?" He grabbed her fleshy shoulders, stopping her momentarily. "I'm not, Josie. I'm not!"

She allowed her shoulders to droop just enough for Darik's hands to slide off and then brushed past him to pick up another crate. Darik closed his eyes and took a breath, wishing he could undo whatever event had driven his friends to the rash decision to abruptly close the bistro and flee Compton.

"Whatever Graves told you—he's lying."

He heard Alphonse speak from across the room. "You haven't been persecuting Christians?" There was no accusatory edge in his tone—rather, his somber voice carried a note of hope. Darik turned to see that his old friend had ceased his packing and was looking directly at him. He hesitated at the question, which seemed to tell Alphonse what he needed to know. His friend's eyes began to well up, and he hid his face from Darik, returning to the empty shelf.

Darik felt a familiar sensation building up inside of him, an anger that he did not want to direct at his friends. He took a deep, ragged breath, trying to steady himself.

"You don't understand," he said.

"You don't deny it then?" Josephine demanded. Unlike Alphonse, she made no effort to hide her emotions.

"It's complicated," Darik replied weakly.

Josephine activated a seal on the packing crate. The logo of a storage company appeared over the lock, a company that would arrive soon to transport the entire contents of the bistro—their life—to a cold holding facility. "Well, for us it's simple. We have to leave, now."

"But why?" Darik stammered. "There must be something I can do."

Alphonse crossed the room toward him. At first, Darik thought he was coming to confront him, then realized he was simply on his way to the back room. Darik stepped to the side in order to let the large man pass. "You've done enough, Darik," he said, not quite looking him in the eye.

Darik followed Alphonse into the back room—the same room where he and Liana had enjoyed their idyllic dinner together. It was nearly empty now, darkened except for the glowing holo of Pope Stephen XII still illuminating the wall around its frame. The changed effect of the room intensified the feeling in Darik that his date with Liana had taken place in another time, in another life.

"Now wait a minute," he said, turning from the wall. "You have no right to judge me." Out of the corner of his eye, he saw that Josephine had followed them into the room. She walked over, joining her husband. Darik addressed them both, two people he had grown attached to over the years, but he would be a fool to think that they had ever been close friends.

"You have no idea what I've been through. How could you? You've been nice, sure, but you never really knew anything about me, did you? And yet, you have the gall to imply that this is somehow my fault?" He noticed Josephine's shoulders starting to tremble, tears forming at the edges of her eyes.

Rather than engendering sympathy, the show of emotion only increased the disdain Darik was feeling at the moment. With a sweep of his hand, he indicated the wall holo, his voice rising as he continued. "And what did you expect? You flaunt your religion—a dangerous one at that—right out here in front of everyone, and you don't expect that there would be consequences?"

"Dangerous, you say." Alphonse shook his head.

"Yes, dangerous. I tried to warn you, but you wouldn't have listened, would you?"

Alphonse stepped forward, his eyes red, moist. Suddenly, before Darik could avoid it, he spread his arms, enveloping both Darik and Josephine in a massive bear hug.

"No, Darik, we wouldn't have listened. And neither should you." He spoke directly into Darik's ear, his warm breath coming out in a husky whisper. "There are things in this world and beyond that are more important than our little restaurant, our livelihood, even our very lives. Our faith is worth protecting, and not just protecting, but celebrating—openly." He glanced toward the holo. "It brings us life, and it's worth dying for."

Darik felt his heart grow cold—as cold as blue steel. He pushed the couple away.

"Worth dying for," he repeated. He thought of his parents, his brother's grief, and the terrorists responsible for all of it. The steel in his heart brightened at the thought of Jenkins's promise that he would personally be bringing them the justice they deserved. "That's the part that worries me. That's why I do what I do. I don't expect you to understand."

Alphonse slowly blinked back his tears, a single stream running down one of his cheeks. He pulled a small storage device from his pocket and pointed it at the framed holo. With a flick of his thumb, Pope Stephen's image vanished from the wall. Alphonse placed the unit back in his pocket, his eyes barely visible, the only light remaining coming from the doorway behind them.

"I understand that you've been blind. But I pray..." He paused, placing a hand on Darik's shoulder. "No. I *know* that one day your eyes will be opened. And sooner than you think."

He turned and walked out the door. Josephine stood before Darik, the light behind her obscuring her expression. Darik thought that she wanted to say something, but finally she bowed her head, pivoted slowly around, and left the room to return to her packing.

Darik didn't see the point of following them back into the bistro's main dining room. The thought of enduring their sad but accusing expressions one more time, even to say goodbye, just wasn't worth the effort. He felt his way around the now darkened room to the emergency exit. Hoping that they had already shut down the alarm with the rest of the bistro's systems, he hit the panic bar and felt the door give way without the customary siren.

The alleyway suffered from the same lack of maintenance and lighting panels that plagued most of the surrounding district. He would have to watch his step. Edging his way around an overturned trash bin, he felt his boot step on something soft, an oozing, squirting sound emitting from the object under his weight. A foul smell, overriding the rest of the refuse and rot in the alley, wafted up, invading his nostrils.

Darik bent over, squinting to see what he had squashed. It was a dead rat, one of the millions infesting the seamier sections of the city, and one of the largest Darik had ever seen. The pressure from his foot had burst the creature's bloated belly, spewing its already decomposing contents across the dirty pavement and all over his boot and pant leg.

Disgusted, Darik kicked the thing across the alley. He tried, unsuccessfully, to wipe his foot off on a piece of fiber packaging before giving up, shoving his hands in his pockets, and striding off into the night.

Chapter 31

The east passage marked the farthest Ravi and Purnima had ventured on their now daily rehab walks. The pair was feeling the effects of their extra effort, their gait becoming increasingly unsteady with each additional step.

Ravi stopped, leaning on a wall, hands on his knees, his breath coming in short gasps. "Maybe...it would be a good idea...to head back?"

Purnima supported herself against the opposite wall. "Just a little more," she said. "We're getting stronger every time. I can feel it."

"All the same," Ravi said, straightening slowly, "if we go any farther, we might not make it back. How embarrassing would it be if Commander Lebrian or someone had to pick us off the floor a few meters from our quarters?"

Purnima drew a deep breath. "Not as embarrassing as continuing to languish in bed while the rest of the squadron is on active duty."

Despite his weariness, Ravi regarded his twin with amusement.

"What?"

Ravi smiled. "Nothing."

It was clear from Purnima's insistent expression that she wasn't going to let the moment pass. Ravi continued. "It's just that lately you seem to be coming to grips with our place on this team."

Purnima blinked slowly. "Well, you said yourself that the squadron is going to need us."

"So, does that mean you're ready to trust them?"

She shook her head. "I'm not saying that." She considered a moment. "It's not that I'm not ready to trust the squadron. It's more like I'm not sure that they are ready to trust *us*."

"Sounds like the same thing to me."

Purnima set her jaw. "You know what I mean."

"You're worried what will happen if they find out about us. If they find out *everything*."

She caught his eye and nodded silently.

He looked back down the long corridor, observing the progress they'd made. "Well, baby steps, right? We haven't even told anyone about the experience we had with Officer Manasser. Now that he's been detained, don't you think we should at least report what happened?"

"To who?" Purnima asked. "Captain D'Felco is still laid up in the infirmary."

"Don't you think Commander Lebrian would want to know? If they have enough suspicion of Officer Manasser to arrest him, he will want to have every fact at his disposal."

Purnima huffed out a breath. "What facts? We still don't know if what we experienced was real. And it hasn't happened again, at least not to me. What about you?"

He gave her a look. Neither of them could envision a scenario in which one of them would experience something like that without the other knowing.

"So you think we imagined it?"

Purnima looked down. "No. Of course not."

Ravi pushed himself away from the wall, nearly falling forward in the process. He caught himself and squared his shoulders. "Then I think it's time we shared what we know. Adahn was breaking curfew, and we know, we *know*, that he lied to us about it. We have to report the incident to Commander Lebrian. How he reacts, what sorts of questions it leads to— we have to be okay with it. We have to start trusting our friends." He grasped her hand, pulling her back in the direction they had come. "It's our duty."

Purnima's reply was cut short by the sound of a supply room door to their right sliding open. Startled, both twins turned to see Ronnie Wilco stepping into the hall, a satchel slung over his shoulder and his arms loaded with a container overflowing with fibroc cables and matter inducers. "Oh! Sorry, Officers," he said. "I didn't see you out here."

"It's all right," Ravi replied. "You're in a hurry. Another project?"

Ronnie smiled, looking down at the box. "Yeah. I'm on my way to the *Forerunner*. I might have finally cracked the E-drive problem."

Ravi felt Purnima grip his arm tightly. A cold sensation ran up his shoulder and down his spine. He shook the feeling off, trying to keep his concentration on the ops tech standing before him.

"Solved the E-drive?" he said evenly.

"Yes," Ronnie continued. "Nikky, Drager, and I have been trying to get the thing functional again. Been working pretty much non-stop without a lot of luck." He jiggled the box of parts. "But I think I have the last piece of the puzzle right here."

Purnima squeezed Ravi's arm again. This time, the chill shot straight to his head. Behind his eyes, he saw Ronnie on his back, beneath a control console, affixing a glowing cable to a power conduit. He leaned on Purnima's arm to steady himself. Ronnie was still standing directly in front of him.

"Mr. Weis and Sergeant St. James must be very excited," Purnima said. She continued to dig her fingers into Ravi's arm.

"Uh, yeah, they are," Ronnie said, eying them uncertainly. "As a matter of fact, they're waiting for me now. I really should get going."

"He's lying!"

Ravi turned to his sister in shock. He had distinctly heard her voice in his ear, but her lips had not moved. When she did speak, it was to Ronnie, her voice calm and measured.

"I will be happy to see the *Forerunner* in the air again."

Ronnie turned to leave. "Yes. I think everyone will be."

Ravi had to brace himself against the wall to keep from falling. At Ronnie's words, another vision appeared, unbidden, as clear as if it were happening directly in front of him. He saw the *Forerunner* hovering several hundred meters over its current resting place, just east of the colony. Suddenly, the massive craft listed to one side, plummeting along an angled plane directly into the heart of the colony. It struck the phirmium buildings with a sickening crash, leveling them in a huge cloud of gray dust. Ravi's entire field of vision was obscured by an unbearably bright flash as the *Forerunner*'s ether-drive engines detonated upon impact. Nothing, no one, could have survived the explosion.

"Officer Voor, are you all right?"

Ravi blinked. Ronnie was still there, holding his box of spare parts and regarding him with a quizzical expression.

"Yes. Yes, I'm fine," Ravi stammered. "Still getting my strength back, I guess."

"We've probably overdone it," Purnima jumped in. "In fact, we really should be getting back to our quarters."

"Sure," Ronnie said. "I should probably get to the ship. Are you sure you two will be all right?"

"We'll be fine," Purnima assured him. "Good luck with your repairs."

Ronnie gave a quick nod and made his way down the corridor. Ravi continued to lean on the wall with Purnima supporting him. The twins waited until Ronnie was out of earshot.

"It happened again, didn't it?" Ravi breathed.

"But so much stronger this time." Purnima's voice was shaking. "With Officer Manasser, it was just an impression. But this time, I could *see* it! While he was talking, I could see what was actually going to happen!"

"Yeah, I saw it, too. The crash. The explosion. Do you think it's an accident or…"

Purnima's eyes turned cold. "He was lying to us. He's been lying to everyone." She stepped away from the wall. "We have to tell someone. We have to stop it!"

Ravi held his hands up. "Are you sure we can trust what we saw? We can't be wrong about this. It would be bad for Ronnie"—he leveled his gaze at her—"and it would be bad for us." Ravi read Purnima's expression. Through the signs of exhaustion and physical discomfort, there was a steely determination in her eyes. Gone was any fear about being discovered.

"All right," he said, reaching into his tunic, "first, we need to find out if what we saw is possible." Pulling out his handpod, he selected a contact. Nikky Weis answered promptly.

"Mr. Weis, this is Officer Voor. May I ask where you are right now?"

"I'm in the detention area." With the pod on its ambient setting, both of them could hear the hesitation in Nikky's voice. "I'm visiting with Officer Manasser," he added.

"We're not far from you." Ravi looked at his sister, who nodded. "Could we ask that you stay there? We have something we need to ask you."

*   *   *

Ravi and Purnima staggered into the detention area. Even the short walk had all but drained their remaining strength. Adahn was standing

288

behind the crebonite bars, engaged in a quiet conversation with Nikky Weis.

"Mr. Weis," Ravi said, struggling to catch his breath. "Can we talk?"

Nikky turned and tilted his head, a wary look in his eyes. "Of course. What do you need?"

Purnima looked past him at Adahn. "Perhaps it would be better is we spoke in private? It concerns your work on the *Forerunner*. The colony may be in danger."

Nikky followed her glance back over his shoulder. "If you're worried about Officer Manasser, you don't need to be. He's innocent."

Ravi shook his head. "Not everything is as it appears to be."

"That's true," Nikky said flatly. "In fact, unauthorized comm beacons on a fighter might look like they were transmitted just before a jump to Bellona, when they were, in fact, inserted and time stamped well after the fact."

"What?" Ravi was puzzled. "What are you talking about?"

"The evidence found on Officer Manasser's fighter. It's been falsified. It was planted there, in his comm system, back here on Pella. All I had to do was trace back the latent chrono—" Nikky held up his only hand. "You know what? It's not important right now. Just know that Officer Manasser is not the traitor you are looking for. So if you have something to say, this is as good a place as any."

Ravi considered the information. "You may be correct, Mr. Weis."

Nikky raised an eyebrow. "I *may* be?"

"Yes," Ravi said. "We just had the strangest conversation."

"The real traitor could still be out there, but we're not sure," Purnima added. She turned her back to the cell and lowered her voice as she continued speaking to Nikky. "We need to ask you—"

"If this has anything to do with the traitor, I want to hear it," Adahn interjected, grasping the bars of his cell.

Ravi and Purnima exchanged glances.

"You said the colony may be in danger." Adahn's knuckles had turned white. "Please."

Ravi cleared his throat. He looked at Adahn, back at his sister, and finally at Nikky. "Mr. Weis, the work you and Sergeant St. James are doing on the *Forerunner*—did Mr. Wilco speak with you about a new breakthrough?"

Nikky rubbed the stub of his left wrist. "No, we were close, very close, but now we've reached an impasse. The ship will hover, but it can't maneuver. There's no way to even test it right now. It's too unstable. If it lost power, it could keel over right into the colony."

"But you're not meeting Mr. Wilco right now to work on it?" Purnima asked.

Nikky frowned. "No. Of course not." He looked back at Adahn. "I'm right here, and I'm still working things out with Officer Manasser. Why?"

Ravi caught Purnima's eye. "Ronnie said that you and Sergeant St. James were waiting for him at the *Forerunner*—that you were excited about him solving the problem with the E-drive."

"The E-drive?" Nikky almost laughed. "The E-drive isn't going anywhere. It's fried—pure and simple."

"He told us that he had the last piece to the puzzle. He was holding a box of matter inducers."

"And even if we got it going," Nikky continued, "without maneuverability, there's no way we could—wait. What did you say?"

"He was holding a box of matter inducers."

"Matter inducers." Nikky scratched the sparse stubble on his chin. "Why would he need matter inducers? Those are about the only components in the ether system that *are* working."

"We believe he is going to install them in a control console," Purnima volunteered, glancing at Ravi.

Nikky looked at them both. "What makes you think that?"

She swallowed. "It's difficult to explain. We, we—"

"We saw it," Ravi interrupted.

"What do you mean?" Adahn stared at the twins. "You said he's *going* to install them. How did you see him if he hasn't done it yet?"

Purnima turned to face him. "As we said, it's difficult to explain. But as we were talking with him, we both could see Ops Tech Wilco beneath a console, fastening a power cable to a matter inducer."

"Wait a minute!" Nikky grabbed Purnima's shoulders. "The matter inducer! You said he was installing it under a console?

"Yes."

"Under a console, on the bridge?"

Ravi pursed his lips. "I...I think so. It looked like it, at least."

"Was he mounting it in a casing?"

Purnima closed her eyes, concentrating.

"Yes, he was," she said.

"Okay, this is important. Think hard. What color was the casing?"

Ravi felt Purnima grasp his hand. "Blue," they said in unison. "It was blue."

Nikky let go of Purnima's shoulders, turning to Adahn. His voice was flat. "He's going to blow up the ship."

"What?"

Nikky braced himself against the holding cell bars. "There is nothing wrong with the *Forerunner*'s inducers. There is only one reason to install extras, right there, at *that* junction. It's to place them in series."

Adahn frowned. "Doubling their power."

"No," Nikky said. "Not doubling. Not quadrupling. Placing them in series will *exponentially* increase their power."

"Overloading the engines," Adahn breathed.

"Inducing a level-five antimatter explosion," Nikky finished.

"Mr. Weis," Ravi said, grasping Nikky's arm and turning him back around. "That is exactly what we saw."

Adahn shook the cell bars. "Get me out of here! Now!"

All three turned to face him.

"We'll call the captain." Ravi spoke quickly. "He needs to know."

"There's no time!" Adahn shouted. "You said that Ronnie was on his way to the *Forerunner*. The captain and everyone else are either in barracks or on the other side of the base. We're the closest. By the time we alert them, it will be too late."

"He's right," Purnima said. "It has to be us." She turned toward the door but staggered, barely able to retain her footing. Ravi reached out to steady her, nearly falling himself.

"They're in no condition to do this, Nikky!" Adahn's eyes were wild. "It has to be me."

"I'll go," Nikky said. "I know how to safely disconnect the inducers."

"And if he confronts you?" Adahn indicated Nikky's missing hand with a glance.

"Good point." Nikky deliberated only a moment before moving to the access panel, his fingers dancing over the proximity sensors in a complex pattern. With a satisfied click of his tongue, he pressed a final command. The cell bars slid to one side, freeing Adahn. He moved directly to a bin that held his personal belongings, grabbing his handpod without breaking stride and exiting the brig at a full sprint.

"Uh, right behind you," Nikky murmured, following Adahn at his best, albeit much slower, pace.

"Call it in," Adahn shouted over his shoulder, "and get everyone out of the colony!"

*   *   *

Adahn approached the forward hatch of the *Forerunner* quickly but silently—his training having kicked in the moment he left his cell. The hulking cruiser lay right where it had rested the last two years, dug in to the soft loam where she had crash-landed, listing slightly to one side. Fresh soil splayed out from beneath the ship in all directions, evidence of the test firings Wilco, Weis, and St. James had performed in an attempt to get her off the ground. Fresh prints in the scattered dirt told him that his quarry had entered the forward hatch just moments before.

He considered bursting in right there but thought better of it. He was unarmed, and until proven otherwise, he had to operate under the assumption that Wilco was carrying a weapon. The forward hatch led directly to the bridge, and Ronnie was almost certainly just inside. It would be impossible for Adahn to enter the bridge from the forward hatch without his notice, and Wilco, if armed, would have the advantage. Adahn fought back against the urging of his internal clock, forcing himself to re-evaluate. Getting himself shot the moment he entered the ship wouldn't do the colony any good.

Looking up, he noted the location of the *Forerunner*'s external sensor nodes. He had no idea whether they were working or not. For all he knew, Wilco had already observed his approach and was waiting in ambush. A sense of hopelessness began creeping in, but he chased the feeling away. Even at a severe disadvantage, he had to keep trying. He was the only one who had any chance, however slim, of stopping Ronnie.

Ducking beneath the curvature of the outer hull, Adahn skirted aft along the ventral surface until he came to another hatch at midship. Grasping the manual release, he pulled, hoping it hadn't been secured from the inside. The release turned easily in his hand, unlocking the hatch and allowing Adahn to push with his shoulder, digging his feet into the ground for leverage.

The hatch gave, creaking open with a groan that, while not all that loud, sounded like an explosion to Adahn's nervous ears. He hoisted himself up into a pitch-black enclosure. Pausing, he closed his eyes for a few seconds, allowing himself time to get acclimated to the darkness. After a couple deep breaths, he opened his eyes and moved confidently across the airlock to the inner access port. It opened without nearly as much noise, a favor for which Adahn breathed a prayer of thankfulness. He was also pleased to see that the inner passageway was just as dark as the airlock— now that his eyes had adjusted, the darkness worked to his advantage, providing cover. Mindful of the noise of his boots on the duranium deck plates, he moved forward in the direction of the bridge.

Adahn hadn't gone three steps when he heard a low hum accompanied by a steady vibration of the deck. A moment later, the entire passageway lit up with the orange glow of service lighting. He didn't hesitate. Ronnie Wilco was on the bridge, powering up the *Forerunner*. There was no longer time for subtlety. Adahn broke into a sprint.

He entered the bridge in a dead run. Ronnie was rising from beneath a control console, his back to Adahn, focusing his attention on a panel of indicators, half of which had turned from green to red. Without breaking stride, Adahn threw his full weight into Wilco's back in a flying tackle, both men bouncing off the console to the floor.

Adahn was surprised when Ronnie managed to scramble to his feet first, backing away from Adahn in an unmistakably defensive posture.

"What the hell are you doing, Manasser?" Ronnie shouted. He cocked his head to one side, his expression turning from startled to questioning. "And what are you doing out of the brig?"

Adahn recognized Ronnie's stance. Despite his confused facial expression, Wilco's posture revealed that he was anything but unprepared. The ops tech crouched in a classic left-dominant *Nuba-Jistsu* stance. Adahn reflexively adopted a counter-stance, his weight low, back straight, head up. Adahn slowly brought his arms up, his right extended, his left hand back with the thumb just brushing his cheek.

"I might ask you the same thing." Adahn sidestepped smoothly to his right. "What are you doing?"

"I'm doing my job." Ronnie indicated the control panel with a sideways nod, his hands never straying from their defensive position. "I'm trying to get this crate operational again."

Adahn followed his eyes to the panel. Several more of the indicators had changed from green to red.

"By blowing it up?"

Ronnie scoffed, dropping his hands slightly. "What are you talking about?"

"The matter inducers you just installed." Adahn moved toward the panel. "They're set up in series. You're overloading the engines."

Ronnie's incredulous expression vanished instantly. He kept his eyes locked on Adahn, matching him step for step as he moved closer to the control panel. "Weis," he said. "He figured it out."

Adahn closed the distance to the panel, cutting Wilco off. "It's over, Ronnie. I'm shutting it down." Keeping his right arm in a defensive position, he tapped his handpod with his left. "Nikky, I'm going to need some instructions here."

He was surprised by the ferocity of the attack when it came. The wiry ops tech stunned him with a lightning fast blow to his jaw before driving him into the deck with a double leg takedown. Adahn landed hard on his shoulder but managed to use the momentum of the fall to push Ronnie off him, throwing him into a bulkhead.

Rolling over, Adahn barely had time to regain his footing before Ronnie was on him again. This time, the two men grasped each other high. Adahn grappled for leverage on the side of Ronnie's head while Ronnie employed a *jujime* collar choke, gripping both of Adahn's collar bones and pressing his windpipe with his wrists.

In all of his hand-to-hand training—at the academy and even in his grueling sessions with Commander Lebrian—Adahn had never felt so overmatched. Along with his apparent technical skill, Ronnie was faster than anyone he had ever gone up against and deceptively strong. Knowing that he had to break the collar choke as quickly as possible, he braced his rear leg enough to execute a sweep with his front, using his weight advantage to temporarily knock Wilco off his base. Ronnie's grip weakened as he fought to regain his balance, enabling Adahn to shoot both of his arms across his chest, knocking Wilco's hands back. Unfazed, Ronnie countered with a hard strike to Adahn's stomach, sending him stumbling back. Adahn, though, exaggerated the impact of the blow. His first unsteady step backward was genuine—his second was bait. Ronnie, sensing an opening, lunged forward, and Adahn, with an unexpectedly quick move of his own, grasped Ronnie behind the head while swinging his left leg up—his knee impacting Wilco's cheek and nose with a sharp crack.

Ronnie staggered back, blood pouring from a broken nose. Adahn pressed the attack, hoping to take advantage of Wilco's sudden vulnerability. Cocking back his right arm, he swung at Ronnie's head, but Wilco easily ducked under the punch and rolled away, rising to his feet next to the control console.

Nikky's voice sounded through the ambient setting on Adahn's handpod. "Adahn, I'm almost there. Do you need assistance disconnecting the inducers?"

A smile formed on Ronnie's bleeding lip. "It's too late." He raised his voice enough for Adahn's handpod to pick it up. "You hear me, Weis? It's too late." Ronnie reached behind himself, keying a sequence into a control panel. "Oh, and by the way, so are you."

Adahn recognized the low hum of the ship's shields powering up. Outside, soil and rocks exploded outward from the hull as the repelling forces activated. Adahn shouted at his handpod. "Nikky! Stop! The ship is shielded!"

Ronnie maintained a defensive stance, daring Adahn to make a move for the controls. "Oh, I imagine that even someone with Weis's limited abilities could find a way to override them." He raised his voice again. "But I think we both know he's not going to have the time, right, Nikky?"

As he spoke, the remainder of the indicators switched from green to red. The crimson glow pulsated in time with a low hum emanating from deep within the *Forerunner*'s hull.

"Nikky. Is he right? The whole panel is red. Nikky! Is he right?"

Nikky's voice was soft, resigned. "He's right. The ship's going to blow. There's nothing we can do to stop it. Even if I could get in, it's too late."

Adahn's attention hadn't strayed from Ronnie as he'd spoken with Nikky. He looked the ops tech in the eye, searching for any sort of reason for this madness. "Why?" he asked quietly.

Ronnie's mouth was still bleeding, and his nose had begun to swell shut. As he spoke, another drop of blood fell, splattering on the deck. "Because it was time for me to leave. I never signed on for all this."

"But to blow up the ship? This close to the colony? You know that's going to kill everyone."

"How else was I supposed to get off this rock? None of us even know where we *are*, thanks to your captain and his paranoia. The only way to get a ride off this planet is to upset the dampening field and reveal your location to my superiors."

"Your superiors?"

Ronnie's voice was becoming clipped and raspy as his nose continued to swell. "Wake up, Manasser! Isn't it all obvious by now?"

Adahn forced himself to keep looking at Ronnie, not daring to steal a glance at the flight controls as he slowly slid to his left. "It's obvious that you've been the one leaking intel, sabotaging our missions. What I don't know is how you did it."

Ronnie smirked, a gruesome sight through the blood. "Well, your fighter came in very handy. I'll admit that part was fun—watching poor St. James muddling around, trying to pin down that subroutine I had running through your Hornet's comm bus. He even asked me for help! Together, we found the 'problem' and removed the bug. After Bellona, I just put it back in, a little more conspicuously this time so your friend, Valani, could find it. Same thing with your workstation—a simple hack of your comm program and a smother-proxy to cover it up. It was getting a little annoying, how I had to keep making the clues easier to find. Your friends are kind of dull."

"But why me? Why did you frame me specifically?"

That elicited a short, exasperated laugh from Ronnie. "You still don't get it. You blindly follow your pastor, your captain, anyone else who's fed you this bullshit your entire life. But then, the moment something goes wrong, who do they turn on? Who do they blame? Was Jani ever under suspicion? How many times did Scot directly defy orders—and has anyone ever accused him of being the traitor? No, Adahn, they blame the dark-skinned guy from the Middle East whose ancient religious heritage differs ever so slightly from their own. Can't you see how screwed up that is? You all turned on yourselves because that's what religion does—it divides. It divides and controls and punishes anyone who dares to think for themselves."

Adahn swallowed. "You didn't betray us—you were against us from the start."

"I've just been doing my part to stop your religious disease from spreading. I was assigned to the colony on Aphea—my job was to filter intel out to my handlers. But when the time came for our attack, the colony had just enough warning to herd everyone on this ship, including me. And then, of course, your squadron showed up and really made a mess of things." He paused. "So I improvised."

Adahn took another sliding step to his left. "So you held the ship together and managed to crash land it here, saving everyone and setting yourself up as a hero."

"It was the only option. My superiors don't really want you dead, at least not right away. They want you to have chance to learn, to open your minds—a chance to renounce the beliefs you cling to."

"By torturing us with M-2s."

Ronnie smiled. "Exactly. Then, they want you to die." He leaned back on the bulkhead next to the forward escape hatch. "So you see, since you were all going to die anyway, I'm actually doing you a favor. When this ship blows, it's going to be much faster for everyone. Oh, don't bother thanking me. If we could have restored maneuvering and landing control to this heap, I would have moved her to the other side of the planet before setting her off. That would have revealed your location while also allowing the M-2s to come and complete their work. But, since it won't maneuver, everyone here gets the benefit of a quick death." He reached down, keying a sequence into the pad. The hatch door clicked with the distinctive sound of all bolts withdrawing into their sockets. At the same time, the humming ceased as the external shields dropped. "Like I said, all I really want is to finally get off this rock, so, if you'll excuse me, I need to put some distance between us in the next few minutes."

"Nikky's out there," Adahn said, his tone lacking conviction. "The captain and the others can't be far behind. They'll stop you."

Ronnie snorted—a mistake as a fresh gushing of blood poured down his face. "The captain? You think I didn't consider that? You think I haven't been planning this down to the last detail? I've locked down the hanger and scrambled all launch codes. I'm sure Weis would be able to re-crack all the codes eventually, but he'll be long dead before then." He wiped the blood from his mouth as he looked back toward the hatch. "And sooner if he tries to stop me."

Adahn lunged to his left. "I don't think so." He grabbed the lifter control handle while simultaneously slamming the ventral thrusters to full power. The *Forerunner* groaned as hull plating, long settled, shifted from the sudden surge of power. The hulking cruiser lifted from the depression in the soil, slowly at first and then with increasing speed at it cleared the grasp of Pella's surface.

"What are you doing?" Ronnie yelled.

"I'm taking her up. She still goes up, right?" Adahn hollered back.

"What good will that do?" Ronnie took a step toward Adahn, but a warning look in Adahn's eye held him back. "We're still over the colony!" Ronnie shouted. "You're not helping anyone."

Adahn turned to his handpod in response. "Nikky. A level-five antimatter explosion. What will that do to the *Forerunner*?"

Nikky's voice sounded even more nervous than usual. "It would disintegrate it. There wouldn't be anything left much larger than a data chip. Adahn, what are you doing? You're not going to—"

Adahn reached down and ended the transmission. An altitude display indicated that the *Forerunner* had already lifted to a thousand meters. "You heard him, Ronnie. We get high enough, I think the colony might just survive this. What do you think?"

"I think you better step away from the console."

Adahn turned his shoulders while continuing to hold the lifter control with his left hand. A satchel next to Ronnie's feet lay open. He was holding a Hagg-Sauer pistol, aiming it directly at Adahn's head.

"I don't think you want to shoot me."

"Why not? I can still put the ship down and be safely away before it blows."

Adahn cocked his head toward the console. "As far as I can see, the landing sequencer is still fried. Too bad you didn't get around to fixing that. If I let go of this handle, she'll drop like a stone."

Ronnie smiled thinly. "I'll take that chance."

"Yeah. I thought you might."

Adahn let go of the lifter control. The *Forerunner* instantly lost altitude, throwing both men up off their feet—Adahn landing on top of the control console, Ronnie up against the escape hatch.

His stomach in his throat, Adahn reached down, grabbing the edge of the console. With his other hand, he grasped the lifter control, pulling it fully back. He was instantly thrown to the floor, barely managing to keep a grip on the handle as his body slammed into the deck. His ears popped from rapidly dropping pressure while, to his right, he heard a violent clanging sound and a clipped scream. A torrent of air was rushing past, warping his skin. Tightening his grip on the control handle, he strained to look behind him. The escape hatch was open, but Ronnie Wilco was gone. He had fallen, headlong, to the earth below.

The altitude display continued to climb, rising past three thousand meters. Using his free hand, Adahn engaged the hatch control. He was rewarded with the sound of groaning servos, followed by the hatch swinging shut and locking in place. As the cabin pressure began to equalize, the comm system sounded an alert. Adahn opened the transmission.

"Ghazi, this is Deadeye. What exactly do you think you are doing, mister?"

"I'm sorry, Captain. This is the only way."

Down in the comm center, tucked away in the northeast corner of the squadron hanger, Dex D'Felco looked at the group assembled around him. The moment he had received word from Nikky about the *Forerunner*, he had given a scramble order before yanking out his IVs and breaking into a staggered run toward the hanger. Scot, Seltrice, and Jani had been the first to reach their fighters, climbing into their cockpits only to realize that the launch codes had been changed, leaving the squadron grounded. Hagen, Onigen, and Drager had arrived shortly after, while Dex had brought up the rear, every muscle in his body protesting from the effort of his tortured sprint.

With the anxious eyes of his friends fixed on him, Dex replied, his tone softening. "Adahn, put the ship down. We still have a little time. We'll think of something."

There was a brief silence before Adahn's voice sounded again over the comm. "I can't do that, sir. If I let go, she'll fall. I tried it once already. That's how Wilco ended up outside."

"Yeah, we saw it," Dex said grimly. He turned to Drager. "How long?" he mouthed.

Drager raised two fingers and then, hesitantly, a third.

"What about the Raven?" Hagen asked. "We could evac him if..." A quick look at Scot caused him to trail off. The lieutenant shook his head.

"No good, Sarge. Wilco scrambled the Raven's codes, too. Nothing's taking off."

Adahn's voice echoed through the hanger. "Captain, don't worry. It's okay. I've got this."

"No!" Dex shouted. "It's not okay." He raised his handpod. "Nikky, can you hear me?"

"Yes, I'm here."

"Patch yourself in to this comm. I want all of us on the same signal."

A moment later, they all heard Nikky's voice. "Done."

"Nikky, can Adahn remove those inducers?"

"Well...uh..."

"Think! What would happen if he removed the inducers?"

Hagen grasped Dex's shoulder. "Dex," he whispered, "those engines are already on override."

Dex shook him off. "You heard me, Nikky. What would happen?"

There was a long pause. When he spoke, Nikky's voice was uncertain. "I...I don't know. Nothing, perhaps, or a detonation right there in the bridge. It's too far along. There's no telling what it would do."

Dex shot a look at Drager. The flight sergeant's brow was furrowed. "We really don't know, Captain. But there is a chance—"

Dex turned back to the comm. "Nikky, Adahn. Listen up. Nikky, how does Adahn remove those inducers?"

Onigen was monitoring a sensor array. "One minute," he reported. "If we're going to do this, it has to be now."

Nikky's voice was wavering. "At this point, there's really no safe way to do it," he said. "Basically, all you can do now is just grab one and pull. But we still don't know what will—"

"Adahn," Dex said firmly, "pull the inducers, now."

"I can't reach." Adahn voice was strained. "It's too far. I'd have to let go of the lifter."

"Can he brace it with something?" Hagen asked, but Drager again shook his head.

"It's touch sensitive," he said. "When he lets go, the ship will drop."

"I gave you an order, Ghazi." Dex gripped the edges of the comm console. "Pull those inducers. Now!"

On the *Forerunner*'s bridge, Adahn stretched out as far as he could. Keeping his left hand on the lifter control, he reached out with his right. The inducers on the underside of the control console were tantalizingly close, just beyond the grasp of his fingers.

"Do it!" He heard the voice of his captain through the comm.

Adahn's fingertips brushed the inducer casings, but the extra effort caused his hand to slip from the control handle. The ship violently dropped and listed to the right, throwing Adahn against the upper left bulkhead, his head spinning from the impact.

In the squadron hanger, every skylight darkened as the *Forerunner* temporarily eclipsed the sun, the ship falling like a meteor.

Adahn shoved himself away from the bulkhead, sprawling toward the lifter control. His first lunge came up empty, failing to slow the *Forerunner*'s rapid descent toward the colony. Gathering his legs beneath him, Adahn pushed forward again, his hand this time firmly grasping the handle. The ship groaned as the thrusters roared back to life, fighting the downward momentum. After an eternity, the skewed deck leveled, and Adahn could feel the cruiser finally beginning to regain altitude. He checked the altimeter. He had lost a couple thousand meters in the attempt.

"Officer Manasser, report." It was Dex again over the comm. "Were you successful?"

"Negative, Captain. I couldn't get to them."

"Okay, Adahn. Okay. Get ready to try again."

A warning klaxon pealed. Beneath it, a placid female voice began cooing, "Warning. Engine detonation imminent." Adahn silenced both with a flick.

"Sorry, sir. We're out of time." He looked up through the forward viewport, gazing out across the sky. It was an uncommonly clear day, the sun glimmering off the few patches of clouds below. "I appreciate it, Dex. I really do. But now I just need to put as much distance between us as possible."

"Adahn, no! You can't do this!"

The voice didn't belong to Dex. It was a female voice, strained, but immediately recognizable. It was a voice Adahn had heard all too often in the past few weeks, filled with scorn, suspicion, and contempt. But now, there was something in that voice that Adahn had never heard before—tenderness.

"It's okay, Seltrice," he said. "It has to be this way."

Adahn felt a dull roar beginning behind him, deep within the bowels of the ship. Every control panel on the bridge increased in brightness, responding to the sudden power surge. The cabin lighting panels grew painfully bright, nearly blinding him.

"Adahn!" Seltrice sobbed over the comm. "Adahn, I'm so sorry."

The light throughout the cabin was overwhelming, shutting out every other sensation. Adahn was suddenly aware that it no longer seemed to be coming from the lighting panels. And it was no longer painful. The light surrounded him, enveloped him, comforted him.

Still gripping the lifter control, he closed his eyes and spoke, his voice calm, mirroring the peace he felt within.

"I know you are, Seltrice, I know. I forgive you."

"Adahn, I was wrong. So wrong."

The deck plates shook violently. Adahn felt the sensation that he was floating just above them. The light continued to envelop him, filling him and breathing unspoken words, words of serenity for him—and urgency for someone else.

"Seltrice!"

"Yes?"

"Whatever you do, don't give up, you hear me?"

"Adahn?"

"Just don't give up! Don't let this tear you apart!"

"What? Adahn, I don't—"

"Promise me!"

Seltrice's voice faltered. "I...I prom—"

A blinding light flashed through the hanger's skylights. Seltrice slumped forward, burying her face in her hands as the *Forerunner* exploded into a billion tiny fragments. It took several minutes for the first remnants to reach the ground, falling harmlessly over an area dozens of kilometers in diameter, a rain that would last for over an hour.

Epilogue

"Nikky!" Drager St. James spotted his brother staggering down the incline toward the squadron hanger. His face was smeared with dirt, and he was holding the stump of his left wrist. A dark red trickle oozing between his fingertips told Drager that his wound had reopened. He knew that Nikky had been close to the *Forerunner* when the shields had engaged, but, until now, he hadn't realized how close.

"Drager," Nikky said, stumbling into his arms. "Why?"

Drager could see the streaks running down Nikky's face, channels of lighter brown where the tears had partially washed away some of the grime covering his cheeks. In all their years growing up, Drager realized, he had never seen his brother cry.

Drager shook his head. "I don't know, Nik, what drives a man to do something like that? To betray his friends, to try to kill so many—"

"No, not Ronnie." Nikky looked up in the direction where the *Forerunner* had blown. The sky was still hazy, the smoke and microscopic debris having not yet completely dissipated on the windless day. "Adahn. He was innocent. Why would he give himself up like that? There had to be a better way."

"I don't think there was." Drager followed Nikky's gaze upward. Pella's sun was penetrating the haze, shooting multi-hued shafts of light toward the surface of the planet. "Adahn did what he needed to. He did what any of us hope we would have the courage to do."

"It's not just that. On the comm, just before the end, he sounded so..." Nikky's voice caught. He swallowed and continued. "He sounded so peaceful, so...sure." He stumbled over a small rock, grabbing hold of Drager for support. "I don't understand."

Drager gently guided Nikky back toward the hanger. It had taken him the better part of the last half-hour to reprogram the locking system.

Together, they stepped through the space between the giant half-open doors. "I don't fully understand it either." Inside, he stopped at a diagnostic display, his eyes narrowing at a peculiar flashing in the upper right corner. "I don't know if you can until the moment comes."

Drager's attention bounced between looking at his brother and glancing at the persistent flashing icon.

"I pray, Nik, that some...hold on." Drager swiped at the display.

"Uh-oh." Nikky was instantly alert. "I was afraid of this."

"Yeah, me too." Drager turned toward the interior of the hanger. "Captain! Commander! You're going to want to see this."

Dex pulled his arm from an open access hatch and joined Drager and Nikky at the display with Hagen following close behind.

"Take a look." Drager pointed to the screen. A simplified rendering of the planet glowed at the center. Around it, the last remnant of a green band slowly pixelated, disappearing from the display.

"There it goes," Nikky breathed.

Drager turned to Dex. "Captain, do you know what this means? That blast disrupted the dampening field."

"I see it, Sergeant." Dex reached toward the display, widening the scanning bandwidth. The green band that represented Pella's natural dampening field had completely vanished. All that remained on the screen was the planet, alone and vulnerable.

"I don't suppose there's any chance the field will reestablish itself?" Hagen asked. Drager shook his head.

"That's it, Hagen," Dex said, looking at his oldest living friend. "We're visible. And with the size of that explosion, we have to assume it was detected."

He looked out across the hanger. Scot was in the cockpit of his Hornet, swearing to himself as each attempt to override Ronnie's launch code sabotage failed. The Voor twins were huddled in a corner with their heads together. Lee Onigen was at a launch monitor, entering code after code while giving a series of instructions to Seltrice, who was sitting motionless in her Hornet, staring blankly ahead. There had been no indication that any of their fighters were close to being operational again. The Angels were grounded.

Dex took a breath and stood tall. Stepping toward the group, he felt himself about to stagger, recovered, and resumed striding confidently forward. "Nikky, Drager!" he barked. "Man that console. We're not going to stop running diagnostics until every single one of these birds is back in the air. Ninja, mount up. Sunfire, Moonlight! That means you, too. Move!" Lee, Ravi, and Purnima all scrambled to join Scot and Seltrice in their cockpits.

"You heard him people!" Hagen bellowed, a trace of a smile on his face. The smile disappeared, though, when he turned and looked at Dex. "Are you okay?" he asked quietly. "You don't look so good."

Dex rubbed at the scar on his neck. "We have to prepare for an all-out assault, Sarge." A familiar electric sensation burned from his neck to his shoulder, a blue haze of pain radiating throughout the rest of his body. He couldn't be sure if it was a psychosomatic reaction—a traumatic stress response that he would live with forever—or if it was something more. And he didn't have time at the moment to sit there and analyze it. Returning Hagen's questioning stare, Dex D'Felco was certain of only one thing.

"They're coming."

Acknowledgments

In the fall of 2012 as we were preparing to release *Flight of the Angels*, we had a couple questions: How would anyone ever hear about this book? And would anyone read it?

This led us to search the words "sci-fi" and "Christian" on the Web, and we were surprised and excited to find that not only were there communities out there who were blending faith and genre enthusiasm, but these groups were diverse, vibrant, and growing! (Good sense might have dictated our doing this modest market research *before* writing the book, but that has never been our strong suit.)

We were soon introduced to so many fantastic people, all of whom helped us get the word out about *Flight of the Angels* and encouraged us throughout the admittedly long task of bringing *Hornet's Nest* to you now:

Ben Avery, of the Strangers and Aliens podcast, a stalwart advocate that Christian sci-fi can and should be of the highest quality, who gave us our very first podcast interview;

E. Stephen Burnett, of Speculative Faith, who allowed us to post a guest column on his website and provided awesome promotion for FOTA during our giveaways;

Tony Breeden, of Tony Breeden Books and The Bookwyrm's Lair, who shared FOTA through reviews and "best of" lists and provided much encouragement all along the way;

David Alderman—founder of The Crossover Alliance, a publishing company that specializes in edgy Christian fiction—who included "Blood

Ace," a short story that fleshes out Dex's history, in Volume 1 of *The Crossover Alliance Anthology*;

Nathan J. Norman, of the Untold Podcast (which has featured "Blood Ace"), Robert Mullin, Ethan Erway, Nissa Annakindt, Adam Collings, Mark Adams, Peter Younghusband, and David G. Johnson, podcasters, fellow authors, or both—all friends who challenged and encouraged us every step of the way.

And finally, the top hit when we searched "sci-fi" and "Christian" seven years ago was a podcast called, appropriately, "The Sci-Fi Christian." We had no idea at the time that a simple Google search would lead us to two guys who would not only be great supporters—inviting us on the podcast, holding a FOTA reading contest, highlighting the book regularly during episodes (to an almost embarrassing degree), narrating and editing the FOTA audiobook, and beta reading *Hornet's Nest*—but who would also become our close friends. It is a friendship we cherish. So, it is in that friendship, Matt Anderson and Ben De Bono, that we dedicate this book to you.

About the Authors

Allan Reini is an enthusiastic sci-fi fan with over thirty years of business and leadership experience. Allan lives in Hibbing, Minnesota, where he and his wife, Becky, are thankful to have three of their adult children and their six grandchildren in close proximity (with missionary son, Michael, available via Skype). He has admittedly raised a family of self-professed nerds, including his eldest son and co-author, Aaron.

Aaron Reini, his wife, Jill, and their four children also live in Hibbing, Minnesota. Aaron taught English for eight years at Hibbing Community College prior to moving into administration (though he still finds any excuse he can to get into the classroom). He has been writing collaboratively with his father since 2008.

Also from Allan and Aaron Reini

Flight of the Angels
Available in paperback and Kindle at Amazon.com
Audiobook available at Audible.com

"Blood Ace"
A *Flight of the Angels* short story
Available in The Crossover Alliance Anthology Vol. 1
and on Kindle at Amazon.com
Audio dramatization available at Untoldpodcast.com

Questions for Allan or Aaron?
Email us at mail@flightoftheangels.com

For more information including a glossary of terms, pilot brevity codes, and the history of the S/A-81 Hornet, visit us at
www.flightoftheangels.com

Join the Angels: Like us on Facebook
http://www.facebook.com/FlightOfTheAngels

Follow Flight of the Angels on Twitter @PellaColony

One Last Note from the Authors: If you have enjoyed *Hornet's Nest* and believe it is worth sharing, would you take a few moments to tell your friends about it? We would also be very grateful if you could rate the book and leave a review on Amazon.com. Your words of support will help us get the next book in the series, *Phantoms of the Void*, out as quickly as possible.

Thank you!

Allan & Aaron